Sex

In The Hood

Sex

In The Hood

White Chocolate

Sex *In The Hood*

White Chocolate

Urban Books
6 Vanderbilt Parkway
Dix Hills, NY 11746

ISBN 0-7394-6054-4

My most gracious gratitude goes to God.

Thank you for blessing me with the passion, power and privilege of writing and sharing this gift with the world. Thank you for honoring me with an amazing family that energizes and encourages me to reach for the stars.

And here's an exuberant THANK YOU to Carl Weber for affirming that there's magic in believing...

SEX IN THE HOOD

WHITE CHOCOLATE

Chapter 1

Duke Johnson towered over a fucking, sucking tangle of bodies at his feet. The wall-to-wall carpet of black, brown and beige asses, titties, legs, arms and dicks extended up the huge staircase and under tall archways on each side. To the left and to the right were huge rooms where hundreds of people were bouncing and banging and blowing to a deafening bass beat and nasty rap lyrics.

Straight ahead, double glass doors reflected Duke's six feet six inches of smooth, dark muscle draped in white linen pants and matching shirt. The dim light cast a crown-like glow around his bald head and made his diamond ring sparkle as he surveyed his enterprise, including the dozens of Barriors, black warriors who flexed like the ninja motherfuckers they were supposed to be if some fool went crazy in the middle of all this pussy. Wearing black from head to toe, the Barriors were double-strapped at the hips, watching to make sure everybody followed the rules in the hot, intoxicating fumes of booty, booze and blunt.

Yeah, it looked and felt like the kind of pussy party that made Babylon the baddest in the business, but something didn't smell right. So, The Duke was about to collect the bank his damn self and remind everybody who was the boss. Not Izz, the host of this Sunday afternoon fuck fest. Not any of these warriors who worked for him and were conspiring with Izz to steal his cash. And not Knight, who was reputedly trying to call the shots from behind bars.

Hell naw. The only one in charge of Babylon and beyond was The Duke—and only The Duke, now and forever. Especially after today, when he would meet the goddess who was going to help him take Babylon coast to coast.

WHITE CHOCOLATE

"We gon' be in an' out in a Motor City minute," Duke told his boy, Beamer, who stood beside him. "I ain't gon' let Izz's bullshit make me late to get my Duchess."

"You trippin'," Beamer said. "You crazy if you think that half-white rich bitch from TV is gon' come down to D-town worse hood an' get wit' yo' gangsta ass."

"Watch me," Duke said, staring each Barrior in the eye. He had no time for anybody's scheme right now, since Knight would be out in two weeks. Duke had to make everything perfect, to show he was handling business himself and building Babylon even bigger and better than what his older brothers started.

The four Barriors at the front door approached, handing Duke a miniature gold treasure chest full of cash.

"Babylon!" They shouted the way Marines would say "Attention!" with the loudest emphasis on the last part of the word. As they bowed to Duke, the tall, muscular men each pounded their right fists over their hearts and said in unison, "Massa Duke rule Babylon!"

"Wha'z up." Duke's nod let them know they could march back to the door.

"A lotta dicks is what's up," Beamer said, taking the heavy money chest and sliding it into his sleek black shoulder bag.

Beamer was usually obedient and reliable, but right now Duke wanted to slap the silly out of his boy's big Bambi eyes. A goofy glow always seemed to jump off Beamer's face, from the cinnamon-hued freckles on his plump, peanut butter brown cheeks to his thin brown lips. His wide, flat nose was pointed down at the tip. His hair, dark brown with a slight red cast, snaked back in cornrows that gathered in a ponytail down his neck as he watched a girl's titties flap while she fucked.

"Stop gawkin' like this the first time you seen pussy," Duke said, biting down to make his jaw muscles flex.

"Yes, Massa Duke." Beamer wrapped his chubby fingers around the BMW medallion hanging over his red, white and blue Detroit Pistons jersey. His fast-talk was even more jovial than usual as he said, "This ain't nothin' compared to what your

3

birthday party gon' be Friday. Check out homegirl. She earnin' her keep today."

At the foot of the stairs, a Slut was working two guys. They were laying on their backs, their heads pointing in opposite directions. She was squatting down, fucking one guy with her ass pointed toward his face, while she bent over to suck the other guy's dick. Both of them wore condoms to protect her mouth and her pussy, according to Babylon rules. She was like a pump; her ass went up when her head went down, and vice versa.

The dude under her pussy was squeezing her ass, with one black hand on each of her big, brown booty bubble cheeks. The guy under her mouth had his redbone fingers all up in her black braids. They were flying all over his belly and hips as she worked it to the rhythm of some rapper chick squealing lyrics about how she loved to "bounce that ass, make it fas', make it last, bounce that ass." That's what hundreds of people were doing on each side of this foyer, where big archways opened onto huge rooms full of sex.

"Damn," Beamer said, scanning the scene that was littered with rubbers and wrappers. "They 'bout to play musical pussies."

Duke looked to the right, where about fifty Sluts stood facing the four walls, pressing their hands to the red paint, bending over and sticking out every size and shape of booty. Some orange Victorian-style lamps, the kind with the fabric shades and hanging beads, cast an orange light on the chicks' asses, which were every color from almost white to blue-black.

In the middle of the room, a Barrior stood with a whistle, surrounded by fifty nude dudes with condom-covered cocks ready to rock. The whistle blew, and every guy found a pussy to drill. Thirty seconds into the act, the whistle blew again, and all the dicks had to swing to the next pussy on the right. All kinds of dicks—from that huge-ass licorice stick covered in cream to that brown pencil prick in the corner to that fat, brown sausage to the left—they all came out, shining like a mug with sex juice, then disappearing under some of the prettiest asses in Motown. They

WHITE CHOCOLATE

did this over and over, until each guy made his way around the room, sticking his dick into all fifty of those hot, wet holes. They were healthy holes, as the Sluts were checked by the doctor every week back at Babylon HQ, and the mandatory jimmy rule made sure all that pussy meat stayed clean.

Duke watched this symphony of sex being played by every kind of human instrument: titties that were pointed, flat, swole, bite-size, natural, silicone, suntanned and freckled, with nipples that looked like pepperonis, pink frosting, licorice discs, copper pennies, or bronze slots at the casinos, all with a little point or a big udder tip on the end.

He watched asses of every shape and size: huge, ripply ones that looked like if somebody put his hand on it, the booty would ripple like a rock in a pond, and tiny butts that were so skinny the whole asshole was exposed when they weren't even bent over. But mostly, perfect booties filled the room—big and round, firm and smooth, muscular and athletic—as if the bitch could buck and ride for hours and never get tired.

There was pussy hair that sprayed out like afros or was shaved into shapes like hearts and stars and lips. Others had just a little strip of hair at the top—a Brazilian wax like Duke's first baby momma, Milan, had—so everything else, including the pussy lips, was bald. Some of the chicks were shaved completely hairless. Other girls had pussy hair that was so nappy it looked like little black ants crawling around the tops of their thighs. Others had silky black fur that made a nigga just want to pet it like a cat while he was lapping up the milk in her steamy bowl.

The Sluts wore the hair on their heads in every imaginable style—braids, twists, dreds, bald, long weaves from platinum blond to vampire black—all of it bouncing and flying around as they fucked like rabbits without getting tired. Lee Lee worked them in the gym as tough as she conditioned Babylon's Secret Service because this was their job, and they had to be in shape . . . and healthy. But if Milan kept acting crazy, Duke was going to have to replace her scheming ass with somebody who could concentrate on keeping the Sex Squad schedules, doctor's appointments and income on time and accounted for. All of it.

Sudden vibration on his waistband made Duke pull the cell phone from his belt. MILAN flashed across the blue screen for the fourth time in an hour. He pressed his thumb to the little silver button to put that wanna-be-who-ain't-gonna-be into voicemail. He'd heard enough of her bitching and whining for today, because this was a day for the history books of Babylon as ruled by The Duke. This was the day the black god that he was would meet the ultimate female partner — in business and in bed — and give her the power and glory that every bitch in the hood would kill to have as The Duchess.

"She trippin'," Beamer said, holding up his red-flashing phone which read: MILAN. Duke shook his head. Beamer reattached the phone to the pocket of his saggy jeans. "Dog, I got a bad feelin'. Just like that night Prince got shot."

"Shut the fuck up," Duke said. "Don't jinx my shit, ma'fucka. Don't never say that to me again. Jus' let me work. An' tell me if Pound call. We gotta be on the spot right when Duchess come."

"Yes, Massa Duke."

"We rollin' strong," Duke said, referring to the back-up he had outside the kitchen windows and door, just in case. "But if you act like a bitch, I'll treat you like one."

A girl to the right screamed. "Fuck ma pussy, punk! Not ma assho'!"

In a flash, the nearest Barrior was on him, saying, "You out."

"Aw, man, I won't do it again." The rule-breaker had a punk look on his face.

The Barrior's big hand on homeboy's shoulder made him sober up. "I said you out," the Barrior repeated, pushing the punk toward the door. "Go to the Black Room. Ain't no rules in there."

The booty-poker stroked his cock as he left. He walked across the foyer to the room that was pitch black except for a few purple lightbulbs, which cast a lavender glow over the twist of

6

shiny bodies. They were grinding and banging and shaking in every inch of the room.

"Look like a bowl of purple chitlins," Beamer said with a laugh. "And if somebody get they period, it's gon' look like they poured hot sauce on the chitlins."

"You a nasty ma'fucka," Duke said, turning back to the musical fucking, where another dude took the booty-poker's place.

"Shit!" another Slut shouted. "My pussy ain't the Windsor Tunnel, an' I ain't lettin' yo' eighteen-wheeler bust through!"

"Ooh," another girl purred. "Send 'im to me."

The Barriors rearranged the guys, blew the whistle, and let the fucking begin again.

Duke loved to look at all this sex. No matter how many times he had seen this, his dick would get cocked as hell. But right now, Timbo wasn't swole for any of these bitches. Timbo was as big and hard as a tree trunk with only one pussy in mind. Her ridiculously fine face on TV this morning was stuck in his head like a hologram, touching every thought, shooting a laser beam down to his dick. Even his fingertips were tingling with the need to give that virgin pussy the Mandingo dick-down of the millennium, which The Duke would do before the night was over.

Even though he'd never met the girl, he just knew he had to have her the first time he saw her beautiful face and heard her brilliant, sultry voice on the news a few weeks ago. "And so it is written," he had said, quoting the Ancient Egyptian pharoah Ramses from *The Ten Commandments*. "And so it is done."

And it would be done in a couple of hours. But for now, Timbo was hard as hell for another reason. Every one of those pussies and every one of those dicks represented big dollar signs in Duke's mind. Big, big dollar signs. Money he learned how to make from Prince. Money he earned by building the Sex Squad to three times what Prince had started. Money he planned to make even more of once he got Duchess in on negotiating and strategizing to make every part of Babylon bigger, better, badder.

SEX IN THE HOOD

With a brilliant business mind, a pretty, light-bright face and the queen's English, that chick was about to become the money-making face and voice of Babylon. And if he had any concern about how her lily white suburban-raised ass would react to this, he knew she would get over it in a Motor City minute. The sex power in her eyes was so strong he had felt a chill when she looked into the TV camera and out the screen, right into his soul.

She'll be all into this. Might like it too much. But I'll be bangin' her fine ass so tough, I'll give her some Timbo ten times a day if she want it. An' she will.

Gold-tipped titties came bouncin' his way. Long fingernails tickled his cheek. Like a brown Barbie with straight black bangs, a bob-style haircut that swayed just below her ears, and thick fake eyelashes, Chanel's face came at him.

"What'cha need, Massa Duke?" she whispered, her sparkly gold pasty crushing into his arm along with her big, ripe, caramel brown titties. She smelled like expensive perfume as she did a pole dance on him. Standing on one gold six-inch stiletto boot that came up over her knee, she rubbed the side of his thigh with the gold lamé crotch of her thong. It was held up by three gold chains that draped over her hips and came down to the crack of her ass, where they disappeared. Her other leg was up in front of him, in the gold boot, and her knee was stroking Timbo.

"I need somethin' ta suck," she whispered through big, swollen lips shining with coral-colored gloss.

"Chanel, baby girl, you fine as hell," Duke said, loving that intoxicated-by-lust look in her big, dark eyes. It was a look that he would soon put into Duchess's eyes and keep there. Forever.

He reached down, squeezed her soft ass and said, "I got bidness ta han'le. Hook up ma boy, Beamer. He hurtin'."

Chanel puckered and squinted those false eyelashes together. She mouthed "I miss you," then she slid to her knees, kicked her spike heels up to her pretty ass, and worked Beamer's jeans with those long, gold fingernails. His big, peanut butter brown dick came flying out like an arrow, making a bulls-eye into Chanel's shiny mouth. Didn't take but a minute to blow his

8

nut. Chanel knew right when to stand up, turn around and bend over, letting Beamer jack his hose as he sprayed a white fountain all over the caramel curves of her ass. His cum dripped down her round, mouth-watering booty like sugar glaze on a golden brown donut.

"Hell yeah," Duke groaned. For a second he was tempted to pull them gold chains to the side of her booty crack and drill himself some relief in a pussy that had never disappointed Timbo. But he had work to do, and he didn't need the mellowing powers of pussy to dull his mind when he was talking with bad-ass niggas about his bank.

Sex transmutation. That was the term in one of Duke's favorite self-help audiotapes based on the book, *Think and Grow Rich* by Napoleon Hill. It said most men didn't earn their fame and fortune until after they turned forty because they were so distracted by chasing pussy. In the hood, forty was the equivalent of ninety in the white world. Duke was damn lucky he was about to celebrate twenty-one, let alone fucking forty. So, on the hood accelerated life plan, he was right on target. And he was going to stay that way, with Duchess's help.

Once in chemistry class in seventh grade, the teacher talked about "shelf life," how a chemical lost its full potential because it would start decomposing or getting weaker after a few days, months or years. All of Duke's friends started talking about "hood life," how they only had a few years to do what they were going to do before they got shot, went to prison or got killed. And it was true. Most of his boys were either dead, locked up, fucked up on drugs or bums with babies they weren't taking care of. No plan, no goal, no vision. Just living down to the sorry-ass expectations the white world had laid out for them since the first slave ship left Africa four hundred and some years ago.

So, when Duke listened to that book—hoping that someday he could actually read it—he decided he needed to focus his sex energy into his work and find just one woman to take care of it for life. That way he wouldn't be squandering his sex power on every ho in D-town. He'd be building his business every time he was fucking his sexy-ass partner in business and in life. His wife. Duchess. Even though all this pussy was his for the taking any time, any way, any day, he knew no pussy could compare to the one he wanted. Now, rather than snack on some always available chicken wings, he would wait for the rare cut of premium filet mignon.

First he had to made dog meat of Izz and any one of these Barrior motherfuckers who were giving each other looks that let Duke know something was up. And wrong.

"Let's roll," Duke said to Beamer, who had zipped up his pants and was on the phone with Pound, checking to see if Duchess had arrived in the hood yet. Beamer tapped his phone to his heart, his signal that everything was cool for now.

Duke stepped toward the hallway leading under the staircase to the back of the house.

Where Izz might be stealin' from me right now.

He walked fast, with purpose, into the kitchen. Izz was at the table counting bricks of Benjamins. Two handguns sat like black eggs in a nest of cash. One of Izz's titty bitches was standing behind him, braiding his hair and shaking her butt-naked ass to the beat of the music. Some orange platform shoes were sticking out from under the table where another of Izz's own hoes must have been sucking his dick.

Dumb-ass ma'fucka cain't concentrate on cash and cummin' at the same time.

His boy, Rake, who was supposed to have Izz's back, was standing at the counter, scarfing down deep dish pizza. And catching bricks. First Rake would take a bite of pizza then look over at Izz, who would toss a brick. Rake would catch it and toss it into a brown leather backpack next to the pizza box on the counter. They did it again, and Rake didn't even look up. He just held out his hand and caught the cash.

My cash. These ridiculous ma'fuckas makin' a game outta tryin' ta get ova on The Duke.

Duke hit that switch in his head marked BAD-ASS NIGGA TURBO-DRIVE. He moved so fast, he was like a cat pouncing a mouse.

10

WHITE CHOCOLATE

Before Izz could blink, Duke was on him, with the silver tip of a gun on each of Izz's ashy ears. Duke's voice was deep and hard. "Ma'fucka, fin' the rest o' ma bank you an' Rake stashed, an' you can keep havin' yo' dick sucked."

Izz froze. Beamer was in front of the table, double-aiming at Rake.

Izz groaned. "I ain't—"

Duke pressed the cold metal into his ears harder, to help him think more clearly.

Izz grunted. "Yo, man. Rake." The brown leather bag came flying. It landed on the table, making money flutter up.

"Put it all in the bag." Duke pressed the barrel tips harder into this empty-skulled motherfucker. "An' listen close, bof y'all.

"One mo' whispa that y'all even *thinkin' 'bout* takin' wha's mine—" Duke loved the power of his deep voice that put the whole room on freeze-frame. "An' you bof gon' get a up close an' personal introduction to ma favorite brotha, Prince."

11

Chapter 2

Babylon Street was jumping as Duke screeched his ivory convertible Porsche between TV trucks, Escalades and hoopties. Folks packed the porches in every direction, dancing, barbecuing and talking about this mixed rich bitch from TV who was moving into their hood. Whether they loved her or hated her, they couldn't touch her. Duke had big, bad Barriors standing guard on every corner, just like they did for school kids and grandmothers and anybody else who hired Babylon's protection services.

Now, all eyes were on Miss Green's crumbling little wood-sided house with faded, peeling blue paint, a sagging porch and dirt for a front yard. A media mob was already camped out on the cracked front sidewalk. A strip of dirt stretched between them and the curb, where Pound Dog sat inside a black Hummer. TV trucks were parked in front and in back of the big vehicle that was holding the hottest spot in the hood right now.

"It's on," Beamer said into his cell phone.

In a flash, the Hummer pulled out and Duke pulled in, just in time to watch his Duchess get dropped by fate right into his lap.

"Tell me I ain't the baddest ma'fucka in the galaxy," Duke said, loving how his voice was vibrating as deep as the funky electric beat of his Bang Squad CD. "Ain't no otha ma'fucka got his own theme song to rock wit'. Jamal finally finish cuttin' 'Duchess' jus' in time." Duke's diamond "D" ring sparkled as his enormous left hand fell from the polished teakwood steering wheel to the tentpole in his white linen pants. "Damn, Timbo ain't neva been this cocked. An' I ain't even seen her in person yet. This bitch gon' rule."

12

WHITE CHOCOLATE

"No joke, Massa Duke," Beamer said, pulling a thin gold box from the dash. "If I didn't know you better, I'd ask what you been smokin'."

"B, why you think TV here?" Duke nodded toward reporters and cameramen who were running around like ants, jockeying for a spot on the three-foot swath of dirt between his gold rims and the sidewalk. "'Cause e'rybody wanna see the mos' wild, whack give-you-a-heart-attack love story ev'a!"

"She gon' look at you an' run!" Beamer laughed then shouted to the media mob. "Yo! We security. Y'all cain't block us."

A white female reporter cut her eyes at him and shook her head, but she got out of the way anyway. So did the big black dude with the camera on his shoulder, and some other reporters with notebooks and tape recorders.

"You definitely on pussy patrol now," Beamer said, nodding across the street where Sha'anté and her hoochie crew were blasting "Move, bitch! Get out da way!" from the porch of their second story flat. They were also smirking down at the news trucks raising their poles to broadcast live from this urban warzone where the *rat-tat-tat* of gunfire was as common as sirens and screaming.

"Media on one side," Beamer said, "and them blew-out hoes across the street at Sha'anté house, plottin' a bitch hunt."

"Hell no." Duke stiffened with the overwhelming need to protect his Duchess. Sweat prickled down his solid muscles that he had pumped tougher in the gym with the Barriors this morning. He glanced up at those jealous, hard-ass hoes then he looked down at the silver metal nestled between his leather bucket seat and the center console. "Let a bitch try."

Above, the rhythmic beat of helicopter blades stirred up frenzied noise and movement amongst the kids on bikes by the weed-clogged lot next door, the dark faces crammimg every inch of porches on crumbling Cape Cod-style cribs, and the brothas and bitches parked in cars up and down the street sparkling with broken glass. Duke cranked the Bang Squad on the stereo and

13

nodded with Beamer to the deep, steady drumbeat, like marching soldiers, and a chorus of Barriors chanting "Babylon!" Their voices vibrated through Duke with the powerful force of the black warrior motherfuckers he created.

Jus' like they boss. Me. Duke flipped down the mirror. His black wrap-around sunglasses were cool as hell against the angular planes of his dark-dark brown, clean-shaven face and his bald head. The shades rested on an exact replica of King Tut's nose as it appeared on all the gold masks Duke had at Babylon HQ. His heart was hammering so tough, he could see it pumping through those thick veins on each side of his wide neck, all the way from the white linen collar of his shirt to the little silver hoop earrings in each ear. They flashed in the late afternoon sun as Duke nodded harder and pointed to the stereo.

"Here go Jamal." The background chant continued as Jamal preached. It was like the ghetto gospel according to rap.

"Babylon rule, wit' D-town cool, urban jewel, win any duel, jack a fool, sexy seductive, serve an' protect, in Babylon, Duke an' Duchess get respect."

The male chorus got louder then faded as the girls rapped over a belly dancer beat. "Babylon men, I'll take ten, rock this ass, oh so fast, they last an' last, like a rocket blast. The Duke, he rule, wit' D-town cool."

Duke smiled into the mirror, watching what all his females called his "sucka lips." So plump and juicy, girls always told him they wanted to suck on his lips at first sight. Even a half-white girl who was being thrown out of her lakeside mansion and dropped in the deepest, darkest spot in the hood.

"Watch," Duke said. "She got a light-bright face, white voice, white brain—wit' black balls big as mine."

A week's worth of TV reports flashed in his mind about the girl who would soon be formerly known as Victoria Winston. She had worked for her millionaire daddy in his business. Got straight A's at private school and was scheduled to start classes this week at the University of Michigan in nearby Ann Arbor. She was star of the debate club and school play.

14

WHITE CHOCOLATE

"B, read 'bout how her daddy let her do deals."

Beamer snatched the newspaper from the back seat and read aloud. "Victoria Winston was apparently so wise and mature beyond her years that her father—who was known for his distrust of others—entrusted her to secure six-figure negotiations."

"Tha's what I call good home trainin'," Duke said. "She perfect for helpin' me manifest my urban destiny, 'specially when we meet wit' the Moreno Triplets and Mr. and Mrs. Marx out west. They an' the rest o' the world betta sit down an' shut up. 'Cause Duke Johnson and his Duchess takin' ova, side by side."

"Who you kiddin'?" Beamer said, laughing. "You know damn well that bigger, badder Knight gon' come back an' snatch Babylon back from baby br'a."

"Hell naw." Duke bit down, making his jaw muscles ripple so they'd stop trembling like the rest of him. "Knight know I be runnin' it as good as him an' Prince was."

Even though I shoulda had all this shit did when Knight firs' got locked up. But it took me this long to figure out what the fuck I was doin', all by my damn self. Now I know, an' I'm gon' make Knight finally give me my props.

"Yeah," Duke said. "Me an' Knight gon' be equals, like him an' Prince was."

"Then why you look scared jus' thinkin' about it?" Beamer asked. "Cain't nothin' or nobody else scare The Duke."

Duke cranked the music louder.

"Except Knight," Beamer said. "An' you should be scared o' your girl, Milan. She gon' go off! If you make some new, light-skinded, long-haired, blue-eyed *bitch* yo' Duchess, it's gon' be baby momma mutiny."

"Milan ain't it." Duke ignored the vibration of his phone flashing her number. "Blowin' up my phone. She all external. Got too damn skinny, tryin' to be like a model, obsessed wit' looks an' clothes. Greedy, powa-hungry bitch who'd stab my back if I didn't have her watched. Talkin' white, perpetratin' like she so smart."

15

"She ain't stupid." Beamer put the newspaper on the floor.

"Yeah, she stupid, thinkin' she can get over on me. I hate how she be perpetratin' like she so bougie. The spa. Her aromatherapy. Tellin' me spaghetti ain't spaghetti, it's vermicelli. Michelle ain't Michelle, she fake-ass Milan."

"No joke, Massa Duke, I'd take Milan in a Motor City minute if you 'bout to put 'er out wit' the trash."

"What bank you think you got to get that gold-diggin' diva?"

Scheme flashed in Beamer's goofy-ass eyes as he slid his Glock between the ivory leather seat and the console. He ran his hand over that gold box on his lap, pulled off the lid and stared at a dozen chocolate truffles.

He inhaled loudly, then said, "I'ma get my treasure. But while we on it, how you think yo' num'a one boy feel gettin' trumped by some snowflake you fell in love wit' through a TV screen?" Beamer popped a chocolate ball into his mouth. "Damn, these good when they half-melted in the sun."

Duke shook his head. "Listen to you, ridiculous ma'fucka. Lookin' at chocolate like it's some good pussy. An' you want The Duke to take you serious about havin' juice at Babylon."

"Why you lookin' at me like I ain't shit?" Beamer turned pale. The chocolate ball bulged in his cheek.

"'Cause you lack vision, ma'fucka."

"I got vision, man." Beamer nodded at a dark blue Caddie turning into Miss Green's driveway. "Here come Lily White."

"The gods 'bout to deliver my Duchess. Delivered into some Timbo temptation she cain't neva resist."

"Mo' like Miss Lily White 'bout to get delivered into Terror Nation," Beamer snickered. "She probably the mos' scary, prissy-ass brat who gon' get here, say 'hell naw', then do jus' like her daddy and take the quickest exit off Planet Black!" Beamer pointed his Glock at the sky and imitated that nursery rhyme, "Pop Goes the Weasel"

"Pop go the white girl!"

WHITE CHOCOLATE

"Omma pop yo' ridiculous P.O.W. ass, like I thought about when I captured you," Duke said. "You ain't said it yet today."

Beamer looked down and bowed his head, just like he did two years ago when Duke decided to let him live. "You gave me life, Massa Duke. You give me life every day, so I serve The Duke in every way."

"Don't forget it, neither." Duke cut his glare away from Beamer and focused on his goddess inside that Caddie about fifteen feet away. All he could see was the back of a white man's head in the driver's seat. The sun glare on the window was blocking her.

His heart hammered so loud, it made static in his ears.

The car door opened. Her long, black hair appeared like a silky, swaying cape as she stood up. "Hell yeah!" Duke groaned with his hand on his dick. Timbo was damn near doing flips. She slammed the door like she was mad at the world. She should be, the way the media was blackwashing her Daddy's scandal all day and night. It was a good thing, too, otherwise Duke never would have seen her on TV, thanks to Henry "Pound Dog" Green, who had pointed to the screen and said that was his cousin who was coming to live on Babylon Street.

Today. Sunday, September 15, at 3:30.

Welcome to my urban empire. Duke was like King Tut and Ramses and Caesar and Alexander the Great, all rolled into one. She would become his Cleopatra, conquering new territories, plundering the treasures and the pleasures of their kingdom together.

All in time for Knight to come home an' see I ain't a stupid, scared ma'fucka. I'm gon' be rulin' coas' ta coas' . . . an' he gon' be proud to join back wit' me. Talk to him e'ryday about e'rythang . . . me an' big br'a, tight as ev'a.

And fate was helping them out, right now, delivering the face, the mouth, the brain and body they needed to represent Babylon.

It wasn't a coincidence that Victoria Winston just happened to come on the news while Pound Dog was up in Duke's office at

17

Babylon. Her cousin was a soldier who understood there was no such thing as coincidence when a great leader was manifesting the destiny of Babylon. When shit was divine, all the loyal folk a man needed to make it happen just came, like magic. Like the Universe just called them up and said "Yo, go see The Duke. He got a job fo' ya."

And now his top diva was appearing before his eyes. Cameras were snapping. Reporters and their video crews were running all up on her. She walked tall, proud and regally down the driveway. Her pink sweater hugged round, ripe titties. Her tight-ass jeans squeezed almost-thick thighs. Her legs were as long and graceful as a giraffe. That hair swinging down to her ass was like a shiny black cape that had to be sexy as hell over them creamy shoulders when she was naked. On red sandals that matched her purse, she stopped at the popped-open trunk, bent over and—

"Ka-pow!" Duke said, his mouth watering at the two ripe cantaloupes pointing his way. "I'ma slurp all ova that juicylicious booty."

"Dang, Duke." Beamer laughed. "Close your mouth, dog. Wit' all the bitches you got, why you—"

"Look at them big chocolate kisses on that ass!" Duke groaned. His dick was marble.

She yanked out a suitcase like it didn't weigh anything, then she turned around.

"Check out my Duchess, man. Got a poker face like a mug. Cain't never tell her daddy blew his brains out last week. Now e'rybody know she black, broke and comin' to live in the hood wit' her grammomma."

Sha'anté and her crew were blasting their music so loud, it was rattling the windows. They sneered down at Duchess and shouted, "Move, bitch! Get out da way!"

"If she scared," Duke said, "she ain't showin' it. Like a true B'Amazon. Look at that sexy-ass mouth, like that ma'fuckin' pucker-fish I seen at the zoo wit' my kids." Duke's mouth watered. Her lips were plump and puckered. And red. Extra red against a face that looked like it came straight out of one of Duke's books on Ancient Egypt.

"Damn, this some scary shit, like this chick just popped straight outta one of my dreams." Duke could not believe how her face looked so much like the golden Cleopatra masks they had back at Babylon. Her skin was golden-bronze, her cheeks were pink, and her nose was just like a Barbie doll. Her big, metallic-blue eyes had to be the answer to Duke's silver-dollar wishes shining back from the Zeus fountain in Vegas.

For New Year's Eve, he had taken his crew to Caesar's Palace. In the Forum Shops, after the fiery, thunderous display of the Greek Gods show, he had stepped to the fountain, tossed a handful of coins, closed his eyes and wished for his Duchess to walk into his life like Momma said she would someday. And he'd just know it was her.

Now I know. Fo' sho'.

His dick was throbbing so hard it hurt. Bangin' it up into that virgin pussy couldn't come soon enough if it had happened yesterday.

"Timbo hard as hell. 'Cause she gon' take one look at this six-foot-six Mandingo warrior ma'fucka, an' she ain't neva gon' think about anotha dick. In life."

"We need ta work on yo' self esteem, br'a," Beamer said playfully. "No joke. Maybe crank up the confidence a rung or two."

The reporters clustered around her like a swarm of bees. They had already stung her dead daddy and her momma. Now they wanted to suck the honey outta her. Like a reflex, Duke grabbed the side of the door, raised his knees to leap out and shield her from those vultures.

"Massa Duke!" Beamer grabbed his arm. "The las' thing you need is yo' face on TV! You cain't be brawlin' wit' the media 'less you want 'em aimin' they cameras down the street at Babylon."

Duke froze.

"An' wit' Knight in jail, Prince dead, and some new territory to handle wit' the gangsta-ass Moreno Triplets—"

19

SEX IN THE HOOD

Prince. He would pimp-slap my ass right now, 'cause I know betta.

This was just like the day, three years ago, when the mayor walked through the hood with a national TV crew talking to folks about urban renewal. Duke wanted to give them and the world a peek at Babylon HQ, from the outside only, to show how he and his brothers had transformed the 100-year-old warehouse into apartments and offices. He wanted them to see how the Barriors were patrolling the streets to keep everybody safe. But as soon as Duke had said it, Prince smacked his bald head and shouted, "Li'l Tut! You wanna audition for a future episode of *America's Most Wanted?* 'Cause I guarantee one ma'fucka watchin' the news gon' say 'Look at that proud nigga. Cain't be doin' nothin' legal to pay fo' dat, so let's bring 'im down.' Then they'll write a script for the perfect crime, frame it wit' yo' face, an' put it all ova TV 'til yo' mortals call in to bus' on they enemy."

Prince's eyes always had that wiser-than-you look, just like Knight's did. His big brothers had the same face as Duke, except Prince was a little lighter, and Knight was a little darker. But both brothers were always looking at Duke and talking to him like he was a knucklehead.

Even as Duke held Prince in his lap as he died, his eyes still looked up like *I'll always be smarter'n you, ma'fucka.* Prince looked at him that way even as his last breath bubbled through his lips with a gush of blood and the worst gurgle sound Duke ever heard. It was a sound Duke didn't ever want to hear pass through his own mouth. The sound of death.

Duke slid down in his seat, hoping no cameras had already caught him in pictures or on video. Damn, Knight would probably kick his ass for this too. That was why he hadn't told his brother about The Duchess yet. Duke needed to transform her into a hood goddess before she could come close to passing Knight's ridiculous standards of excellence.

He gon' love her an' think I'm a genius.

So, right now, Duke could break the rules for a minute because he was here to collect the female treasure being dropped from the sky.

20

WHITE CHOCOLATE

"You are all wicked!" Her strong but satin-smooth voice, deep and sexy, came at him as she faced the TV cameras and reporters. "Everything you printed and broadcast about my dad and my mom was malicious and racist and wrong. Wrong!"

She stomped through the swarm, tossing her head with a slight jerk to her neck, making all that hair fly up, like at the end of a movie when the screen faded to black. It was like she was dismissing all the Motown media with a toss of her pretty head.

"Tol' you baby girl got balls big as mine," Duke said, the corners of his mouth curling up. As he watched her strong, elegant stride on the sidewalk, he whispered, "Damn, her legs like a giraffe."

"Bof y'all crazy," Beamer said, smacking on his chocolate.

"Naw, just watch her," Duke said. The way she carried herself so tall and proud reminded him of his mother—regal, no matter how hard life was. Now, Duke took care of Momma the way she deserved to live, like the Queen that Big Ma named her.

But how would Momma react if Duke brought something that bright home to dinner? When Momma had seen her on the news the other night, she said, "Po' chil'. Don't nobody deserve that. I'd give 'er a hug if I could."

His mother sure couldn't stand to see the dollar signs flashing in Milan's eyes, or the bossy, fake proper way she started talking since she went to that white prep school and renamed herself after the fashion capital of Italy. But something about this chick Victoria Winston, she looked and sounded one hundred percent real.

"She look like she taste like praline ice cream." Duke could almost feel those long legs wrapped around him for her homecoming, letting loose that wild, freaky black pussy that had been kept under lily white wraps in the suburbs. She was in the hood now.

And she mine.

She was all natural, without a lick of makeup. Perfect black eyebrows arched over lashes so long and thick they looked like awnings over windows—windows to his soul mate. She had a

21

long, pretty giraffe neck, too, and a choker-style necklace that made a sunburst shape in the center with turquoise stones surrounded by shiny black stones. It sparkled in the sunshine as she walked closer. With her long, black hair falling straight around her face and that Indian-style necklace, she looked like a Native American princess, a squaw walking toward the chief.

She was about three feet away on the sidewalk when she turned to him. Locked those silver-dollar eyes right on him. Her face wore no expression, but the sex power in her stare hit him like two blue-flamed blow torches. Sucked the air out of him. His mouth, nose and throat burned dry as the desert, air stuck up, down and sideways inside his lungs. It felt like a firestorm inside him, sucking up all the air, singeing his lungs, his stomach, even his asshole.

His heart beat fast and hot, blowing blood up to his brain like a hot air balloon. His head felt light and swirly, like steam was shooting out of his every pore, from his bald head to his toes in his brown leather loafers. His eyes bugged as big as doorknobs behind the sunglasses that steamed up and blurred his focus as she checked him out.

And Timbo, he was flipping around like a giant, caught fish just laid out on the dock under the burning sun, trying to dive back into familiar waters. But it bit that juicy bait worm, so now he was caught. Used to being king of the sea, it was now about to be served up as a feast for a creature who was bigger, better, smarter.

Ma'fuck me! What the fuck kinda crazy feelin's am I settin' off? This bitch gon' kill me wit' one glance!

"Duke?" Beamer knit his thick eyebrows, leaning close. "Look like you havin' a heart attack. What the fuck?"

It was as if Duke's eyes were a magnet and she was a rod of gold. He couldn't separate the two. He was paralyzed on it.

"Dang, she got The Duke kronk'd wit' a right look," Beamer exclaimed. "He out cold!"

The hot spotlight of her stare turned cool as she looked to her left, toward Miss Green's house. Duke sucked in air. She turned her back, walked up the front walk toward the porch. Her ass was bouncing, *Bam! Shazam!* with every step.

His every muscle was trembling, like when he didn't eat for three days after Prince died. His stomach was jumping, and his whole body felt like he was cumming, wracked with delicious spasms. That light-headed feeling was rolling down his whole body, like he was about to float away.

His soul had just found its mate. In fact, it was the same soul, born in two different bodies, in two different worlds. Now it just wanted to run over, dance around with its other half inside her, and come right back here inside Duke.

"Duke, you look possessed. I'm 'bout to call a priest, sprinkle some holy water over yo' Exorcist ass."

"Ridiculous ma'fucka," Duke said coolly despite his jittery insides. "That Mexican food we had fo' lunch crampin' my gut. Stole my breath for a minute."

Duke watched her walk up the steps into the house.

"You the ridiculous one, Duke," Beamer said. "Sayin' 'my' about some chick who might be crazy as hell after what she went through. Black momma got fucked to death. Daddy blew his brains out. Now she gotta move outta a big-ass palace an' move into that ghetto shack." Beamer nodded toward her as she ascended the stairs.

"It ain't a question," Duke said, watching her ass cheeks pop as she stepped up. "She gon' move into Babylon tonight." Duke deepened his voice to imitate bad-ass Yul Brenner playing Ramses in *The Ten Commandments*. "And so it is written, and so it is done."

Chapter 3

I am Alice in Ghettoland.
Victoria Winston wished she could pop a pill to escape back to her white wonderland. Then she could get away from the wicked media, the big black guys in that Porsche and the hostile girls across the street. But right now, she had only one magic trick—rubbing her fingertips over her throbbing clit and cumming so hard that her mind, body and spirit would be transported to another dimension where she felt nothing but raw pleasure.
I'm gonna faint if I don't make myself cum. Now.
Every time her knee rose to step up the stairs, the hard crotch of her jeans rubbed against her hot, wet pussy. Her extreme craving to cum made her sleep-deprived body feel wobbly and off-balance. She concentrated on lifting one red leather sandal after the other up the five porch steps. Lumpy shreds of brown indoor-outdoor carpet were a trip-and-fall waiting to happen.
I want two fingers in the pussy and that special flicker-stroke on the clit. Non-stop. That was Celeste, her sex power voice, dictating exactly how to deal with this nightmare. Celeste was Victoria's best friend and worst enemy, because even though Celeste screamed for attention 24/7, she always responded with intoxicating sensations that defied words. Celeste didn't just make Victoria cum; she gave her power to make dreams and visions come true, especially when Dildo Dick joined the party.
Now, Victoria's sweaty palm gripped the handle of her suitcase, where Dick was nestled between the few jeans, sweaters and shirts she had salvaged as the feds seized Winston Hill this morning. If her pussy weren't making such a hot, creamy mess of her panties, Victoria would feel a horrible ache and emptiness. For a hug. For assurance that everything would be okay. For the kind of loving gaze her parents used to give her and each other.

WHITE CHOCOLATE

Now I have nothing and no one except Celeste as my constant companion. Without that luscious relief, Victoria would have lost her mind the minute she walked into Daddy's blood- and brains-splattered office.

No, she could not let those horrible memories replay in her head. She had to get inside this house and soothe herself the only way she knew how.

I need you to slide your fingers outta your pussy . . . rub your wet fingertips over your hard nipples . . . then cum like your life depends on it.

It did, because orgasms were the ultimate brainstorms for Victoria Winston. In the middle of shivering and gasping, the best ideas always popped into her head. Or, if she already had a goal or a dream, thinking about it while she came would always give it the power to make it come true. Now her goal was getting the hell out of this ghetto, finding some money and starting college forty-five minutes away in Ann Arbor.

After she satisfied herself, she could finally, after half a week with no sleep, slip into a peaceful slumber for a day or two. Now, though, the less she slept, the more irritable and panicky she felt. That made her crave her pussy power all the more. It was her pacifier, her valium, and the closest thing Victoria had to the little pills that Alice popped to grow, shrink or escape from one terrifying experience to the next.

"White bitch!" those girls screamed from across the street. "We gon' stomp yo' ass!"

Would those ogling thugs in the black Porsche parked at the curb—whose stares were burning her backside—stop those chicks from hurting her? What about all the muscular guys and girls in black who were standing on the corners and mid-block like undercover cops? Were they gun-toting drug dealers? Pimps? Friends of her cousin Henry?

A sinister bass beat vibrated from the Porsche, from those girls' upstairs porch, from every car that rattled past, and from inside Gramma Green's house that was smaller than the garage at Winston Hill. Gone forever.

SEX IN THE HOOD

"There is absolutely no money," John Stanley, Daddy's top lawyer, had said when he dropped her off. "Even the insurance policy was seized to pay your dad's debts. Including your college fund. I'm sorry, Victoria. If anything changes, I'll contact you here." And with the slam of a car door, life had booted her into the gutter.

Now, tears blurred the banged-up, dirty aluminum door, its blackened screen ripped and ragged. She coughed on the odor of bacon, dogs and cigarette smoke. If it was this choking on the porch, she would suffocate inside.

I have to escape, but I have nowhere to go. No credit cards to check into a hotel, no car, no cell phone, no friends.

The sadness felt like her insides were melting. The worse she felt, the more ferociously Celeste throbbed for attention. *God, get me to the bathroom!* She'd been indulging this secret pacifier for as long as she could remember, with the orgasms starting around age eleven. Stroking Celeste was just like when her former best friend Tiffany would ease nervousness by smoking cigarettes, or like her sister Melanie, who calmed stress with chocolate chip cookies and milk. Her brother Nicholas was a neat freak, always washing his hands. And her boyfriend, no, ex-boyfriend Brian, did tequila shots to mellow out. But Victoria's tried and true stressbuster was to dance her fingertips over her always hot, quivering clit then shiver away anxiety and angst. Worked every time. The ultimate opium. All-natural. Free. Safe.

She'd even written a poem about it in her journal, which was crammed in a box along with dozens of others—years' worth of her most private thoughts—in her closet at the house she was evicted from today. Victoria tried to remember what she'd written.

I touch Celeste when I'm stressed the best, whether rubbed or pressed . . . like a button, all of a sudden I'm electric, ooh eclectic, feel hectic . . . in my nerves as my hips swerve to get what I deserve, my fingers serve me so well . . . this hot swell, never tell or go to hell, can't let anyone under my spell . . . or I will kill with my skill, my sex power thrill . . . so good that it could make history repeat, like Mom and Dad,

26

so sad to defeat the men that I meet who want to eat my meat, so erotic and exotic but toxic . . . so I gotta keep it virgin, even though it's surgin' with hot cream, lusty steam, and it seems to possess me, ooh caress me, I'm feelin' so sexy . . .

Victoria almost smiled. She'd performed poems in the spoken word style at the cool coffeehouse where she used to hang out with Brian and Tiffany, but never that poem, of course. They were more innocent ones, about life and love and whatever came to mind at the moment. Brian never believed her when she said she'd made it up as she went along, but she did. And she could remember them, too. Only problem was that one she just recited in her mind was making her pussy *burn*. And making her feel a million miles away from the hip coffee house in the rich suburb with her fancy friends. They were fake friends who loved her "exotic" Native American look, until they found out her creamed coffee complexion had some real black coffee in the mix. It was as if she turned to chum before their eyes, because once they sniffed black blood, they bit like sharks and left her with a bleeding heart.

Right now, she was going to counter every bit of sadness and rage with an equally powerful orgasm.

I'm gonna have hot pussy meltdown if I don't get inside and find the bathroom.

The screen door creaked as Victoria pulled it open. A hot gust of thick air—it reeked ten times worse than on the porch— assaulted her nose and mouth.

How in the world am I gonna breathe in here? Much less breathe hard as I cum.

"Com'ere, sweet chil'," Gramma Green wheezed from the plastic-covered yellow couch facing the door. An oxygen tube extended from her nose to a dark green tank beside the couch. Her swollen legs protruded from a quilt over her lap, and a crusty black sore dotted her heel. "Thought you was neva gon' get here."

If Victoria hadn't seen her grandmother at Daddy's funeral the day before, she wouldn't even recognize her. When Mommy died, Gramma Green had a full, nutmeg-brown face with beautiful, flowing black "Indian" hair. But the past ten years had etched a dark, raccoon-like streak around her watery eyes, and an ashen gray pallor accentuated her sunken cheeks. Who knew what was under that ratty auburn wig?

Victoria froze. Dogs were barking in the room at the end of the little hallway that led back from the front door.

"Lawd, if Henry 'nem don't get them animals out ma house—" Gramma Green doubled over, hacking. Her movement exposed the framed pictures on the table next to the couch. Among them was Victoria's first grade school picture, when she was six, the last time she came to visit here with her mother. After Mommy died, Daddy said it wasn't safe or wise for Victoria to come here and be influenced by her cousins.

Gramma Green sat up, blocking the picture. She spit a wad of slime into a tissue then looked back up at Victoria.

How is this sick old woman gonna take care of me? And how did Mommy grow up in this place? She escaped, scooped up by her white knight, who made her princess of his castle. But now some wicked spell was reversing the good fortune.

"Grrrrr!" Victoria glanced to the right, down a dim hallway. A white pit bull with red-rimmed eyes was charging at her. She screamed, dropped her suitcase and raised her arms over her head. Her mind flashed with news reports she had heard about those vicious attack dogs clamping their teeth onto a person's neck, shaking violently, and killing men, women and children.

The dog's sharp white teeth flashed. It leaped up at her.

It's over. Three minutes in the ghetto and I'm killed by a pit bull. Yet another tragic tidbit for the media to sensationalize Daddy's scandal. Maybe the TV stations would even show her chewed-up, bloody body being dragged out of this little hut while all those people on the street cheered "Whitey's dead!"

And I didn't even get to make myself cum one last time.

Male laughter shot into the room along with a high-pitched dog whimper and a rattling chain. Victoria peeked between the pink sleeves of her shirt. The dog was flinging backwards on a leash held by a young black guy who was cracking up.

"Henry!" Victoria shouted. She hit him on the arm playfully, like when they were kids in the backyard or at the family's annual picnic at Belle Isle park. "Don't you remember I'm scared of dogs?"

"Welcome to da hood, baby!" Finally, a familiar, vibrant face. Henry's big, dark eyes sparkled from his oatmeal-colored face. He had a cool goatee and mustache that was so finely groomed it looked painted on. His oversized, super-white teeth flashed as he grinned then leaned down to tighten the dog's leash. His black hair was carved with block letters that spelled POUND across the back of his thick head. The same word scrolled across the wide back of his red football jersey, which hung long over his baggy jeans. He dropped the leash and kept the dog in one spot by pressing a red leather gym shoe onto the chain.

"Henry, you scared me!" Victoria pressed her right hand just below the C-cup curve filling out her soft pink sweater. If only she could caress her nipples and take care of Celeste right now! The terror of that moment intensified her self-sex craving so strong, Victoria was dizzy.

"Girl, you ain't gotta worry 'bout nothin'," Henry said as the dog growled. "You my favorite cousin. An' I got'cha back!"

"Then can you take me to the bathroom—"

"Grandbaby, this Joe," Gramma Green said over a soap opera blasting from the giant-screen TV. It was next to the window facing the street, but the heavy drapes were closed. Bluish light from the screen illuminated a corner where a white-haired man with dark skin sat in work pants, a white wife beater and suspenders. Candy wrappers dotted the worn-to-the-weaving carpet around his La-Z-Boy. He nodded.

Gramma Green held out her arms. "Give me some suga, girl."

Victoria felt Joe's eyes on her body as she bent to kiss Gramma's clammy forehead. She wanted to say, *Thanks for taking me in when everybody turned their back,* but putting it into words would somehow make this feel real, and right now it still felt like a bad dream.

As she inhaled Gramma's perfumed medicine scent, Victoria's mind flashed with the images of Daddy's waxy white face, the eery stillness of his elegant hands crossed over his chest, all those folds of beige satin, and the casket closing on her life, too. None of his family had come to the funeral. In their eyes, Daddy had died when he said "I do" to life with the woman he loved. Those nameless, faceless relatives had never met Mommy, never seen Victoria or her siblings. And they certainly hadn't come forward to take any of them in.

"You gon' stay in Kay-Kay room," Gramma said, pointing with chipped fingernails splotched with the remains of red polish. "Slow that fas' chil' down. But first, Henry, take her to eat in the kitchen. I know you hungry."

"I'm starving," Victoria said. She was starving—for satisfaction from food and her fingers. A heaping plate of chicken, rice and salad would be perfect. "But I need the bathroom!"

Henry led her into that dark hallway ringing with foul language carried on deep male voices, along with the sound of growling dogs and loud, chewing-smacking sounds. He stopped at a door, turned the knob, and pushed it open.

"Eh!" a man yelled.

"Yo, ma bad," Henry answered. "Sorry, Vic, the throne room occupied. C'mon."

Victoria followed him into the kitchen. To her left, on the stove, pots and pans held pork chops in gravy, cornbread, green beans overcooked with chunks of bacon, and super-fattening macaroni and cheese. Yuck. She never ate artery-clogging crap that would make her butt as wide as that old refrigerator, the one being used as a race track for three roaches.

Oh my God.

"Day-um!" exclaimed one of four guys kneeling around four pit bulls that were ripping raw steaks to shreds in the middle of the floor. In the corner, a dog was running on a miniature treadmill.

"This *cain't* be little Victoria," said another guy who was Henry's younger brother, Hank. "Ain't nobody that fine in this family."

"Her momma was," Henry said. "Our momma was, 'til she hit that pipe." Henry glanced back at a table in a sunlit alcove. Beyond three black handguns and a box of bullets, Aunt Harriett sat dazed, her skinny, scarred legs crossed. Bony brown shoulders protruded with grotesque skinniness from a halter top as she smoked a cigarette.

Victoria's stomach burned with disgust. How could *that* be Mommy's sister? Something about the shape of Harriett's dark brown eyes resembled Mommy's so much. A sour heave bubbled up Victoria's throat.

"Git!" Henry shouted at his dog. It scampered to the others to slurp that meaty mess on the floor.

The guys circled Victoria, steamrolling her body with four pairs of eyes. She wished she hadn't worn the pink sweater that always made Brian so hot and bothered, the way it pushed up her C-cups and exposed just a slice of stomach above those black jeans that were too snug for this ghetto family reunion.

Brian. *That bastard said he loved me.* He said they'd be together forever . . . graduate together from The Academy, attend business school at the University of Michigan, then open their own company.

"Pretend we never met," Brian said just days ago, his blue eyes turning to ice as she sobbed her fate. She begged him and his parents to let her live in one of the wings of their mansion across the lake from Winston Hill.

His dad looked up from the Sunday newspaper with Daddy's picture on page one along with a story that revealed Mommy was black. "You deceived us, Victoria," Mr. Martin said. "We knew about your Indian grandmother, not your black mother." Mrs. Martin flinched as her husband continued. "Had you been open and honest with us, perhaps we could be more obliging to your tragic plight right now, but I'm afraid we could never trust you."

Then, after Brian ripped out her heart, he smashed it to bits by reading—with an executioner's accusatory tone—the newspaper's sidebar article about Mommy's mysterious death "An unnamed source tells *The News* that 32-year-old Lynnette Winston's dark beauty—with her caramel brown skin and black satin mane—was so bewitching and seductive, she literally aroused her husband to make love to her with such frequency and force that it killed her."

Brian looked up from the paper. His sandy hair clumped on his sweaty forehead, his angular cheeks reddened, his blue eyes glowed with disgust as he growled, "Your mom was a little freak and you won't even fuck me!" Then he read more. " 'Mrs. Winston's death certificate read: cardiac arrest from an undiagnosed congenital heart defect.' Shoulda said sexual overdose! You little freaky bitch! It's a good thing you're finding this out now, before you let me or anybody else fuck you to death too!" He snatched her arm, yanking her into a little room where his parents would never hear him act on the rape roiling in his eyes.

She kicked him in the dick she had sucked so many times. And she ran, crying, trembling, hating the world. She ran a whole mile to Tiffany's house, where her parents were also reading the Sunday paper.

"Earth to Victoria!" Henry shouted, laughing. "Girl, you trippin' up in the Twilight Zone! You in'a hood now. Betta pay attention, front, back and sideways."

"You gon' live *here*?" asked a guy with cornrows and denim overalls. "Yo, Pound, dis dat chick you was showin' us on da news? Da one who daddy suck down some lead?"

"Shut the fuck up," Henry shouted at him.

"Dog, you sho' she black?" another guy asked.

"Booty don't lie," Henry said, his eyes scanning her jeans. "Girl, I got your back around these fools, too. Kay-Kay, though, she crazy. Keep your legs crossed when you sleep, else she'll try to lick your pussy all night long."

Victoria kept her face a stiff mask, just like Daddy taught her.

"Her girl stay here half the time, so she straight," the guy in overalls said. "I mean she gay, but she straight when her girl—"

The other guys cracked up.

"Let me get you away from these clowns," Henry said, putting his arm around Victoria. "'Fore they scare you half to death."

As he led her down the hallway, Victoria remembered how Henry taunted her in the church dinner hall after Mommy's funeral. "Yo' momma got fucked to death. Yo' daddy loved black pussy so much he banged it up, dead."

Victoria, who was six, had no idea what Henry was talking about. All she knew was that whatever Mommy did to die that way, Victoria was never gonna do when she grew up.

Ever.

Chapter 4

Milan Henderson's insides were a pent-up coil about to spring loose if Dr. Reynolds didn't hurry up. It had been three hours, and ten more Studs and Sluts were still lounging around the plush red couches up here in Sex Squad HQ. Above them, in the tall paned windows set in exposed brick, the late afternoon sun cast an orange haze as they watched TV, flipped through magazines and missed five o'clock sexercise.

"Madame Milan, you fine as hell in them pants," said Johnny "Flame" Watts, flashing those famous smoky gray bedroom eyes. His black-as-leather linebacker body stretched on the couch, facing the TV, barely covered in white cotton bike shorts and a tank top. The shining black head of his legendary dick stuck out of the waistband, resting on his flat abdomen. Against the white fabric of his cotton tank top, it was so swollen that it looked like the triangle-shaped head of a big snake, lying in wait for a treat. He was one of the most requested Studs, who could slither like no other.

"Yo' ass look like two tiny apples," he said. "Madame Milan, if you was my woman—"

"Yo, G, she ain't," Danté Williams snickered. "So, 'less you wanna get Duked, put'cha eyes back in ya head and zip them pretty-ass lips. Let a brotha watch the news in silence."

Sharon "Lollipop" Barnes sucked her teeth. "Niggas."

The way she was sitting, she looked like an indigo wishbone. Her black sundress was raised around her waist, and each long, elegant leg was hoisted over the arms of the chair. She was holding a hand mirror and examining her pussy.

"Madame Milan, that new chick down in the salon jacked my cunt up wit' her no-bikini-wax-havin' self. Shit! When you gon' get Freida back? That girl can work wit' some pussy hair."

WHITE CHOCOLATE

"I need some ointment for the same thing," Danté said, running a hand over his pecs that were bulging through a muscle T-shirt. "Call herself waxin' my chest. Sheee-it! Coulda done a better job wit' a lawnmower. What's takin' Doc so damn long?" Milan crossed her thin arms, closing her eyes, trying to block out Danté's prattle. "Ma clients ain't tryin' ta lay up agains' no nasty-ass rash."

Milan ground her teeth to make the sudden wave of nausea stop. Why did they call it morning sickness when it lasted all day? And what was the name for the extreme horniness she always felt when another baby was growing up in there?

I have to talk to Duke. Now.

It was time for him to make good on his childhood promise to marry her and call her Duchess. No more of this grunt work, overseeing the Sex Squad, their checkups and all their drama. It had been two years since she graduated, thanks to a scholarship at the exclusive prep school. She had come to work for Duke instead of going to college. Now it was time for her ultimate promotion to Duchess. Wife. And mother of two—soon three—of his babies.

Her breasts felt swollen, extra sensitive and too tight inside her lace bra. She had a serious Dolly Parton look in her green silk blouse. She reached under, to the green alligator belt around her slim waist, where she unclipped the cell phone. The metallic jade rectangle flashed 5:03 p.m. on the display.

That bastard hasn't called me back all afternoon. Beamer either. He'd better not be out fuckin'.

Her muscles tensed, as if that coil inside her was tightening even more. Sobbing echoed from the exam room. Milan's green gator pumps tapped the polished hardwood floor as she made a beeline to the orange door marked EXAM ROOM. When the next Squad member came out, Milan was going to talk some sense into that dingy broad, Dr. Reynolds. Was she fucking one of the Studs? Eating some Slut pussy?

"I will fire her rule-breakin' ass if she even thinks about it," Milan mumbled under her breath as her knuckles rapped on the door. "And sic Uncle Sam on her house out in West Bloomfield. Let *him* ask her how she can live so large with her little clinic in the hood."

"A few more minutes," Dr. Reynolds called. Somebody was crying. A woman.

"I don't have time for this drama," Milan said, opening the door. Duke needed to understand that her brainpower, her class and sophistication needed to be put to more challenging and important work, like negotiations with the Moreno Triplets and strategizing the future of Babylon. Not what she was doing now, opening the exam room door to see Janelle Rhodes, a.k.a. Hot Box, slumped like a big heap of butt-naked brown sugar on the table. Janelle's platinum blond braids were all over the place like Medusa's snakes, all the way down to the red heart tattoo over her plump ass.

Milan's nipples hardened. She remembered the feel of Janelle's smooth ass and the taste of her pussy at one of the Duke Joint parties. That was well before Janelle started to look so used up and through.

"You look like hell," Milan said, closing the door and crossing her arms. "You must have this medical exam room confused with a psychologist's couch. And *greet* me when I enter the room!"

Janelle stared through bloodshot brown eyes ringed by plum arcs of fatigue from fucking for a living. No words passed over her chapped, quivering lips.

"I said greet me," Milan ordered. Her every muscle was tensing so hard it hurt. "I don't care how bad you look or feel, Slut. Show your respect."

"I ain't callin' you Madame Milan no mo'. Fake bitch, stuck-up snob, yeah. Walkin' 'round like you da queen when all you really is is a prissy-ass P-I-M-P!"

Milan ground her teeth. *I will not waste my energy going off on this worn-out wretch.*

"Janelle, you've obviously been smoking something or taking a hallucinogen, both of which are grounds for termination from the Squad. Not to mention your appearance has been going from bad to worse by the week."

"Excuse me, Madame Milan," Dr. Reynolds said. "It's time for Janelle to retire."

"What did you catch, Slut?" Milan noticed purple bruises dotting her thigh and upper arms. "And who beat you?"

"My client," she sobbed. "He seen somethin' on my pussy after we fucked."

"I just tested Janelle. She's got genital warts. And HIV."

Milan stared hard into Dr. Reynolds' almond-shaped eyes behind those big, purple glasses. "Why the fuck didn't you see this at her exam last week? Thank goodness I didn't send you to the party on Chicago this afternoon. Stupid bitch."

Dr. Reynolds said, "As you know, HIV can take three months to register on a test. And Janelle's vagina was so swollen and red from a yeast infection last week that the warts were not visible."

"Let me see," Milan said.

"Hell naw!" Janelle drew her knees to her chest.

"Now!"

"Janelle," Dr. Reynolds said softly.

Janelle put her heels in the stirrups at the end of the exam table then dropped her knees to each side. Milan put on a clear Plexiglas face shield, the kind welders wore. Dr. Reynolds, wearing latex gloves, peeled back the base of the labia. She pointed to whitish-gray bumps in the pink folds just inside the vagina.

"You'd have to really be looking to see that," Milan said. "I told you to abstain for a week until the infection—" A wave of nausea rippled through her. All the nasty stuff out there, now that she was pregnant, Duke had better not be drillin' anywhere but her bedroom. "Janelle, did you use condoms like you're supposed to with clients?"

Janelle sobbed into the crinkly paper on the exam bed.

"Stupid bitch," Milan said. Her neck muscles were so tense she was sure that coil was going to spring and she'd just go off. "Who's the john?"

Janelle sobbed louder. "He gon' kill me!"

"Who?"

"Wilbur Landberry. On city council."

"If that perverted mothafucka catches something, he can't pin it on you. He's all up and down 8 Mile."

"He said if he grow warts on his dick, he's gonna come choke me to death with it. And his wife—"

"*Now* he worries about his wife," Dr. Reynolds said. "I recommend that you leave town for a while. Visit your family in Texas."

"Just go," Milan said. "Get dressed. Go to your room. Pack your things. Leave out by six o'clock. You know the drill. If we catch you tryin' to do business on Babylon turf—"

"I ain't got no death wish, bitch," Janelle shrieked. "You always walkin' 'round here like you a drill sergeant. Maybe if you act like a woman, the man you think yo' man would give you the time o' day!" Nausea made Milan want to grip the edge of the exam table, but she stopped. She didn't want to touch Janelle's nasty-ass germs.

"I know Babylon gon' pay for my HIV drugs," Janelle snapped.

"Out," Milan ordered. Janelle darted from the room.

"It'll be a few minutes, everybody," Milan told the Squad members in the lounge. All of them were staring up at the TV.

"That is Duke," Flame said. "Him an' Beamer."

"That's the mixed chick who been on the news all week," Danté exclaimed, sitting up straight.

Milan glared up at the TV. If Duke thought he was gonna jump on that half-white bitch right under her nose . . .

"Hey," Flame said, shooting up like a rocket over to the window. His hard, round ass looked better than any male underwear commercial as he looked through the horizontal

38

blinds, down and to the right. "That's all down at Dog Pound house."

Milan sprang to the window. There was Duke in his Porsche. There was the bitch on the porch, cameras, eyes and probably a few guns all aimed at her fat ass. A hot, burning sensation shot up Milan's throat. She ran to the bathroom, a door beside the exam room. She barely made it to the toilet before she vomited. That coil of tension inside her was sprung, and it was bringing up the seafood salad she ate for lunch, along with all the toxic thoughts and feelings.

Her mind tripped forward over so many scenarios. She could go down there right now, tell Duke off to his face and put him and that bitch on notice that Milan Henderson was Duke Johnson's first and last, his one and only. She could call him real sweet, plan a candlelight dinner, and convince him how much he loved her and only her. Or she could bitch-slap him into submission by treating him the way he needed to be treated until he acted right.

She splashed water on her face, brushed her teeth, gargled then stared at her diamond-shaped face. Her usual color—the same yellow-beige as the lightest part of a walnut—was more gray-green. But one good thing about morning sickness, all this vomiting was making her cheeks look chiseled like those fashion models she saw on the runway during Fashion Week last fall in New York. Duke was so sweet, sending her there to enjoy the glitterati and stay in one of Bang Squad's penthouses. Since then, she had starved her 5-foot 3-inch hourglass from a size eight to a size four. Now, her little triangle of a nose looked more pointed than ever. Her eyes, the same rich light brown color as maple syrup, appeared bigger, more intense. Her relaxed-straight brown hair was thick and shiny, parted at the side and pulled back to show off the raisin-sized rocks in her ears. The earrings were gifts from Duke, of course, on the day one-year-old Hercules was born. The diamond studs were double the size of the ones he gave her in the hospital when their first baby, two-year-old Zeus came into the world.

39

She fingered the necklace at the base of her much-skinnier neck, displayed so rich-looking between the stiff collar of her green silk blouse. *Milan,* it said, scrolled in diamonds. She remembered the love in Duke's eyes five years ago when he gave her that and said, "You in ma blood, baby girl. E'ry time ma blood pump through ma heart, you there."

And I will not let him get a white blood transfusion to flush me out or deprive me of the best dick in Detroit. Duke is mine.

Horny as she was, carrying their child, Duke *was* going to take care of her pussy, her life, their family. The right way. With a ring. A wedding. A proper household. Not that either of them had ever had that, but Milan wanted it, and she always got what she wanted, even if she had to take it.

"And no suburban cream puff is going to steal my spot at Babylon," she whispered. "Never."

Milan walked calmly back into the lounge just as Flame was coming out of the exam room. She took his hand, led him into her office and closed the door. Then she stepped to the window, rested her elbows on the ledge, and stared down at Duke in his Porsche with one hand holding his phone to his ear, the other hand on Timbo, eyes on Miss Thing's ass.

"You like my pants," Milan said lustfully back at Flame. "Pull 'em down and fuck me."

As his huge hands unbuckled her belt and pulled her pants down over her pooted-out ass, her phone fell to the floor and began to ring. DUKE flashed on the screen. She was watching him call her back—finally—but she let it ring. She was busy moaning, grinding her back on the baseball bat and big balls connected to this Stud. No, she couldn't hear Duke ringing her phone now. Not when she cried out as Flame slammed her hot, wet pussy into the outfield.

Chapter 5

"Henry, it's beyond urgent!" Victoria exclaimed outside the bathroom door. She crossed her legs and squatted a little, as if she were holding in pee. She was actually rubbing her clit against her jeans and squeezing the muscles between her legs. The massage sensation teased like a crumb when she was craving the whole cookie.

Henry banged his knuckles on the door. An angry male grunted back. "Yo, let a nigga take a shit."

"Ugh," Victoria groaned, standing up. "If I don't get in there, I'm gonna faint. Seriously."

"Seein' Kay-Kay gon' make you fa'git," Henry said, leading her to another door. He grabbed her suitcase from the living room and said, "Anyway, let them fumes air out befo' you come back. Lonnie stink bombs notorious!" Henry opened the bedroom door. Sweet-scented smoke stole Victoria's breath.

"Girls only!" Kay-Kay shouted from somewhere beyond the cloud.

"Iss ma fav'rite cousin!" Kay-Kay emerged from the smoke. Her skinny brown arms were extended, her raisin-colored nipples were hard, pointing forward, and a silver ring formed an "O" at the center of what looked like a black olive in a dark nest.

Victoria gasped. Kay-Kay's marijuana breath was so strong, Victoria could taste it. She stared hard at Kay-Kay's face. "What happe—"

Her resemblance to herself and Mommy was eery and freakish. They had the same big, round eyes with long, thick lashes, same Indian priestess cheekbones, pillowy, puckered lips, and luxurious hair. A center part divided two thick black plaits extending down her bony shoulders. But her skin was horrible—splotchy, with scaly patches. A dark scar streaked across her stomach and upper thigh like a tire track.

41

"Girl," another female voice cried out from the smoke. "Why you ain't tell me she *that* fine?" She leaped out of the smoke and put her arm around Kay-Kay. She was a little plumper, with skin the color of corn chips, and nipples that looked like the tips of those snack sausages on the counter in party stores. The girl extended a joint pinched between long, blue fingernails with sparkles and stripes. "New girl, I'm LaKwonda."

Victoria held her breath. Her eyes burned. They were wide open, staring. As the smoke thinned, bunkbeds came into focus behind the girls. Threadbare, dirty yellow comforters hung over their edges. Nearby, studded jeans and T-shirts covered a wooden chair. Clothes covered the chipped, faux-wood desk, the dusty green tile floor, and hooks on the closet door.

"Dorothy straight outta Kansas." LaKwonda giggled, sucking on the joint, which glowed red. "Girl," she squinted, "you in the hood now. Look, she even got red shoes."

"I have to open the window," Victoria gasped. To her right, late afternoon sunshine sliced through a rip in the yellowed window blind and dust particles danced in the smoke. No way was she going to jeopardize her health—or the track scholarship she now needed to attend college—by breathing their toxic air.

College, right. She was supposed to be at the University of Michigan *right now*. But the money was gone. So now, as soon as she got settled in this rathole, she would figure out how to apply for a track scholarship and get to the Ann Arbor campus right away. There was no other option; not a community college, or worse, missing out on higher education altogether. No, she had to get up and out. Now. Without breathing all these toxic fumes.

"I can't deal with smoke," Victoria said, squeezing her pussy muscles to calm her nerves with a delicious throb. At the same time, a rhyme came to mind.

Alice in Ghettoland can't stand secondhand smoke . . . or dope. The scope of this nightmare I don't dare stare . . . at reality, brutality. Gotta go, but don't know. I'm snow . . . falling to the gutter, melting like butter, I shudder to wonder . . .

WHITE CHOCOLATE

"Pull that stick out yo' ass, girl." Kay-Kay laughed. "Ain't nobody tryin' to be prissy down here. Show some love fo' yo' kin now that you comin' back to yo' black roots."

Victoria stared. Looking at Kay-Kay was like looking in a carnival mirror that distorted color rather than size. Her face was the darker, drugged-out, unhealthy and haunting version of her own. And her mother's.

This is the freakish and deviant extreme of unleashing our mix-race woman power.

Kay-Kay had it, too, from her mother Harriette, the crack-head x-ray in the kitchen, who got pregnant by a Mexican migrant worker a year after Victoria was born.

All this was silencing Celeste. Numb.

Victoria hated that she could see her mother so strongly in Kay-Kay's face. It was taking her back . . . ten, eleven years, to their big, pretty house, when Mommy took her on her lap on the frilly vanity chair, pointing at the ornate mirror where, in the soft perfumed air of her bedroom, mother and daughter reflected back the identical face—one girl-sized vanilla, the other full-grown caramel brown. Both were framed by flowing ebony hair that shone in the soft light. Both had big, sparkling aquamarine eyes fringed with thick black lashes, naturally ruby lips parting over perfect white teeth, and smiles beaming with mother-daughter love.

"Victoria," Mommy would say, pressing her soft, Indian priestess cheek to the girl's plump one. "You inherited a special power, a force. I call her Celeste. She will always be within you. And when you're older, I'll teach you how to use her to get any and everything you want and need in life."

"Where does it come from?" Victoria asked.

Her mother tapped an elegant fingertip to Victoria's forehead. "She's in here. My grandmother, she was Blackfoot Indian, she taught me that mix-breed women like us possess the power of many races. African plus European plus Native American, all contained in a beautiful female form, is the most potent power in the universe."

Her mother smiled. "Our female essence activates that power, and it makes us magic. And there are ways you can draw in even more power. Back when I had nothing, Celeste made your Daddy fall in love with me and bring me here to live like a princess."

But Mommy died before she could teach Victoria how to summon and use Celeste. That was okay. Little Victoria figured out that any power so strong it made Daddy fall in love with Mommy and ultimately kill her with adult love in a way she didn't understand, Victoria didn't want anything to do with that—neither the race mix that brought it on, nor the sex that brought it out.

So, Victoria vowed to stay a virgin forever. Despite overwhelming adolescent hormones and a pleading boyfriend, Victoria made a deal with herself. As long as she controlled her body and never shared Celeste's power, she would never risk killing herself—or someone else. And she learned to channel this magic power. While masturbating, she would envision a goal: winning the 50-yard dash at the school track meet, getting an A on her chemistry final exam or being a perfect, charming lady in formal gowns at all those black tie events Brian's parents hosted in their ballroom. As she orgasmed, she would hold that image in her mind in perfect detail.

Life imitated eroticism every time. She never failed to win track medals, straight A's, and praise from Brian's parents. Victoria never outright made a mental call to Celeste in the way her mother had described, like an angel or a fairy godmother.

"Vic, what you been smokin'? I don't want nothin' that make me that spaced out." Kay-Kay and LaKwonda giggled then dove onto the bottom bunk.

The stillness and silence snapped Victoria out of her flashback. The girls came into focus. Their limbs were tangled together and they were French kissing.

Victoria dashed from the room. A swath of light shined from the bathroom. She ran in, closed the door. Whether it reeked or not, she'd never know. She pulled the top of her sweater up over

WHITE CHOCOLATE

her nose and inhaled the soft floral scent of the perfume she abandoned at her house. The doorknob jiggled when she turned the lock from horizontal to vertical.

"Oh my God, finally." She unzipped her jeans, pulled them and her pink satin panties off, and hung them on a hook on the back of the door. The filth of the bathroom barely registered as the cool air hit the steaming hot gush between her legs. With her sandals on, Victoria raised her right foot onto the chipped blue tile of the sinktop vanity. She balanced on her left foot, spread-eagled with her right leg bent at the knee to expose her red-hot, throbbing pussy. She washed her hands. There was no soap, but she scrubbed them together hard under hot water. She balanced her right fingertips over her swollen clit—

Why was that music so loud? And those guys's laughter. One of them was saying, "Whoo-wee!" She scanned the wall.

Oh my God! Hank's dark eyes flashed in a hole in the wall between the toilet and the mirror. About the size of a man's fist, chipped plaster ringed a circular peephole into the kitchen.

"Excuse me!" Victoria exclaimed as she bent at the waist to cover herself. If questioned, she would say she was about to insert a tampon. "Never complain, never explain," Daddy used to always say. So no, she wouldn't say anything. Instead, she stepped to the wall, pressed her back against the hole and raised her foot onto the lid of the toilet.

"Yes," she whispered.

Touching her clit was like pressing a button that released tiny purple lightning bolts from a super-charged warehouse between her legs. Each bolt shot with tingling intensity, zig-zagging up to every inch of her skin, making it tickle. And as her fingers made little circles round and round the swollen ball, the lightening bolts danced behind her closed eyelids in streaks of orange, red, yellow. Her pussy was pulsating so hard it was like her heart, pumping, pounding, beating the life through her. And that sweet, salty smell was so intoxicating, she pulled her shirt off her face so she could inhale loudly.

She would use this energy, the most powerful energy available to humans, to conceive an idea, a plan, a vision for how she could escape this inner-city nightmare. Immediately. Without violating her vow of celibacy for Celeste. For a second, she remembered Dildo Dick in Kay-Kay's lesbian lair. He would make this all the more awesome, but no way was she about to go back into that room. She'd have to make do on her own.

Victoria shoved her left middle finger into the hot, tight hole while her right fingers rubbed away angst and anxiety. With all the questions quiet, her brain was a silent workshop where innovative ideas could stand up and shout.

Celeste, Victoria thought as wonderful shivers rippled through her flesh. *I am calling on you right now to give me the power to leave here and live like I'm used to.*

"Your mix-race woman powers," a voice answered. Victoria's fingers stopped mid-stroke, even though she was about to cum.

A voice answered! She moved her finger in and out of her slick hole, rubbed her clit with perfect precision, so that her body was trembling.

"Mix-race woman powers," the voice said, "will get you up and out. But you—"

Victoria's every cell exploded in orgasm. Her arms and legs convulsed. Her nipples poked through her pink sweater. The sensuous intoxication was so strong, such a relief from the horrors of the day, her face twisted into a sob.

The voice screamed in her mind, "But you have to share your sex."

"No!" Victoria cried. Alice found the little pill to pop and escape from Ghettoland, but the bottle was marked with a skull and crossbones! "No!" Victoria was gasping and sobbing and saying with a tone that was erotic and anguished all at once. "No! No! No!"

The bathroom door burst open. Henry's eyes bugged. Silver flashed at his side—a gun. "What the fuck, Vee! Sound like somebody hurtin' you, but you in here havin' a freak party all by ya damn self! Shit!"

Victoria glared at him through tears. Her lips trembled as she shouted, "Get me out of here!"

Chapter 6

As Duke wove the Porsche through the clog of trucks and cars on the Lodge Freeway, Beamer sat in the passenger seat, popping another Godiva chocolate truffle into his mouth. It was like lobbing a cocoa grenade into his gut to blow up and sugarcoat the fucked up feelings he had right now about Duke and that almost-white chick.

But he had to speak. Couldn't hold it in no longer, even though there was no tellin' how Duke would react. "Yo, dude, that's some whack shit about makin' Snow White your partner," Beamer said. "I been yo' devoted servant two years now. Time to make me Lieutenant o' Babylon."

Duke tossed back his head, opened his mouth wide to the sky. A deep laugh busted out. Beamer's heart rattled. Duke's laughter was like poison fangs stabbing every inch of his skin. Rage seeped into his blood. He was dizzy.

"You workin' on a routine for open mic night down at the comedy club?" Duke laughed.

Beamer hated that emotion was making his voice sound shaky. "I'm serious as a heart attack, dude."

As he laughed, Duke's big, white teeth flashed along with his diamond "D" ring on the hand holding his stomach.

Beamer had to state his case. "I know how e'rythang at Babylon work. Top to bottom. The B'Amazons, the Barriors, the Secret Service, the Sex Squad. Now, I'm puttin' you on notice. Beamer up for promotion in the biggest way."

Duke's big hand gripped the steering wheel. Other than that and his foot moving on the gas pedal, he was still as a statue, even when he sped up to squeeze through what looked like the eye of a needle between two cars to get into the fast lane. The speedometer moved from ninety-five to ninety-seven to ninety-nine. Beamer put on his seatbelt.

48

WHITE CHOCOLATE

"Yo, dog," Duke said with that smooth, deep voice that always made everybody in the room shut up. Now he mimicked a game show host. "Mr. Beamer, you're the lucky winner of two choices."

Beamer laughed and popped another chocolate into his mouth.

"Choice number one," Duke said, "you can keep kidding yourself through the helluva magnifying glass you got between yourself and reality. Or you can focus in on the 20/20 now, before the hindsight at your last breath makes you see you were fucking up in grand style."

Beamer sucked the chocolate, laughing loudly, but he spoke in all seriousness. "Ain't squat distorted. I'm speakin' for Milan too."

"Now you really in the comedy zone. Milan look at the world through eyes so greedy and jealous, half the time she don't know a dolla from a dick."

"Dude," Beamer said, "she know Babylon even more 'n me. She—"

"She a professional ho. Two kids and knowin' her my whole life, b'lieve me, Milan ain't nobody friend. She out fo' num'a one. And damn the foo' who think she ain't gon' back, front and side-stab 'im to get her way."

"So, you diss yo' girl but think Miss White Thang gon' want some thug love? Milan'll kill bof y'all." Beamer popped another chocolate into his mouth.

"All that chocolate mus' be helpin' you grow some balls," Duke said. "That's good, but dig this: You ain't my partner. You my assistant. Helper. Servant. You owe me your life. You oughta wake up every morning and kiss my feet before you take your first breath."

Beamer froze. The chocolate melted on his tongue.

"I am God, ma'fucka. I gave you life. I give you life e'ry day. I'm the king. You're the servant. When I get my pretty-ass, half-white Duchess, who prob'ly got more brains and balls than ten o' you put together, you gon' serve her too. So, get that scheme outta your eye."

Duke stared hard, right into Beamer's eyes. "I'll put it on repeat fo' ya. You my servant, not my partner. I'm the king. I need a queen, and she it. And so it is written, and so it is done."

Beamer was already spinning back, remembering vividly the carnage that Duke spared him from, working as second in command for Duke's archrival, whom he dominated and defeated. But when it happened, Beamer had vowed to someday reign over Duke.

"Know why it was so easy for me to bring Pinks down? 'Cause you was holdin' him up. Some people was born to lead, some to follow, some to serve. You serve me. Now, what was the exact words?"

Beamer said, "I promise to protect and serve you with my life forever."

"And what is the punishment for breakin' that promise?"

"Finish what you was about to start."

"Cool. Now that we got that refreshed, shut the fuck up. Speak to me when spoken to, ma'fucka. Speak about me, schemin', we gon' hopscotch back to square one wit' my gat up yo' ass."

What the fuck am I thinkin'? I would be one dead son of a bitch if it wa'n't fo' Duke. Damn sho' wouldn't be sittin' in no Porsche eatin' gourmet chocolate, wit' my own laid apartment back at Babylon.

He glanced at his savior. "Duke, man, lemme call an' set up yo' manicure and pedicure," Beamer said. "Hit you wit' a facial too?"

"Yeah, gotta be soft as black satin when the Duchess rub her face all up in mine," he said raspily, turning onto Babylon Street. "Now, do it quick. We almost there."

Chapter 7

Victoria perched on a ratty lawn chair on the porch, wishing Henry would wait until she was gone before he played biscuit toss with those three pit bulls. He was sitting right beside her, refusing to say who was coming to get her.

"Those are the scariest dogs," Victoria sneered, hating their smell and their chewing and chomping noises. She curled her feet under the chair so that the growling animals couldn't trample her red-painted toenails. "Hardly anybody's best friend."

"Naw, but they tight wit' Benjamin," Henry said playfully. "An' Benjamin keep me rollin' in style." He nodded toward the black Hummer parked at the curb where those thugs had ogled her from that pearlescent Porsche. Thank goodness they and all those reporters were gone. Didn't they have anything better to do than hound an eighteen-year-old girl as she descended into hell? Sitting here, literally, with the hounds.

"Are you a breeder? Is that why they call you Pound?"

"Som'm like that," Henry said, grasping the brown dog's ear to examine a huge, oozing sore. "Damn," he groaned. "Yeah, I'm in the dog business."

"You're almost as vague about what you do as you are about who's coming to pick me up. And why are those girls across the street still staring at me? If looks could kill."

"Vee, you in the best hands," Henry said. "If it's anybody 'round here you can trust, it's me and the boss man."

"Oh, great," she said sarcastically, wrapping her arms around herself to rub away a shiver in spite of the warm weather. Even her still-throbbing sex couldn't stop the terrifying barrage of questions assaulting her brain. "I'm in the middle of Detroit and now *the boss man* is coming to get me. Sounds like a really bad scene from an even worse superhero comic book."

Henry laughed. "Yeah, he definitely got sup'a powas!"

51

"Who?" Victoria snapped. "When we were little, Henry, you used to say stuff like, in code. Now I still have no idea what you're talking about. One day I'm gonna beat you at your own game, so tell me or don't laugh."

"I got orders," Henry said, dumping the box of biscuits in front of the dogs. Their claws screeched as they lapped up the crumbs.

"Well, I got needs," she said seriously. "I have to get a job and my own place, somehow. I am not going back into Kay-Kay's lecherous lair."

Henry let out a deep laugh. The dogs growled. "Girl, you be *sayin'* some words! Now I see why he want you."

Victoria stared hard at her cousin. "*Who* wants me?"

"You ain't heard it from me," Henry said, "but you gon' get offered e'rything you need and much, much more, so chill."

"If it's anybody around here," she said, glancing toward the street where a souped-up Monte Carlo with window-rattling rap music and three barely visible black heads was rolling past, "then the offer probably has far more strings attached than I want to pull."

"You a trip wit' yo' words."

She tapped his shoulder and said, "I need a job, I'm a snob, no urban mob to rob, make someone sob."

Henry grinned. "Yo, lay some beats an' we got Eminem half-black sistah in'a house!"

She smiled, rhyming to her own beat. "I need cash in a flash to live away from Kay-Kay and lay in peace. Eat, sleep and breathe, free to be me."

A white blur made her turn toward the street.

"Do *not* tell me *they're* here for me," Victoria said. Her heart was pounding as two big black guys, the same ones who'd been here before, got out of their Porsche. "They were front row spectators earlier."

Henry leaned close. "Listen, cuz. I know you ain't used ta seein' six-foot-six brothas unless you in yo' daddy suite at the Palace watchin' the Pistons." Henry's voice deepened. "But you in anotha world now. You asked me to help you, so I went straight to the top o' hood hierarchy." He smiled. "That sound like one o' yo' words, don't it?"

As the guys walked toward the porch, the tall, bald one moved so gracefully and powerfully, he reminded her of an animated superhero. Wow, Henry wasn't joking. That guy's expensive-looking leather sandals seemed to barely touch the ground as he approached with a step as soft as a cat's, like a giant black panther—powerful, stealthy, quick, dangerous and elegant.

"Always follow your instincts and make decisions quickly," Daddy would say. She glanced back at the house. Inside, she could suffer with roaches, hunger, smoke and Kay-Kay's debauchery. *If* she got past those wicked little dogs. Or outside, she could step into the urban version of a fairy tale's knight, galloping in on a white horse to rescue a damsel in distress. Ha! Try an enormous black man in white linen with a pearl-colored Porsche, who may or may not be living the glamorous life through legitimate means.

He was probably the neighborhood drug lord. Probably didn't even finish high school. Probably had a gun. Or three. On him. And a criminal record. A whole bunch of out-of-wedlock babies by different teen mothers who were probably part of a whole busload of those flashy, sexy girls who shook their butts in rap videos. Besides, who knew what STDs were dripping into this petri dish of a neighborhood under the lowest rung of the socio-economic ladder? It seemed like a news report about HIV and gonorrhea was always coming out to say Detroit was one of the most infected cities in the country. Yuck.

These were two more reasons Victoria wanted to stay a virgin—to stay healthy and not get pregnant. No, the longer she looked at this guy, the more she thought about all the statistics he could help her become, and none of them were good.

But the same media that had filled her mind with so many stereotypes about young black men had also made her father sound like a psychotic criminal for the past week. And today that same media was after her.

SEX IN THE HOOD

Daddy's deep, comforting voice echoed in her head. "Never prejudge," her father used to say. "Remember, the black farmer in overalls and a straw hat may be holding a sack full of hard-earned cash to buy a new pick-up truck, while the white man in the Brooks Brothers suit driving the Cadillac may be on his way to federal prison for bribery and murder."

Victoria's head ached from hunger. Her stomach cramped. Her pussy was finally quiet and calm.

"Vee," Henry whispered. "Tha's the only cat you got to know 'round here. Let me at least introduce you. Then decide if you wanna go wit' him."

Victoria nodded, taking Henry's hand as he led her down the steps. They stopped on the sidewalk where a golden beam of sunlight was slicing through the trees. The guy in the Pistons jersey was looking around, casting a mean look at those girls on the porch across the street, his hand on the right front pocket of his baggy, saggy jeans.

She would talk with the bald guy first and figure out if he felt safe. Even though his whole image, when viewed through her lens of aristocratic suburbia, was screaming "Drug dealer!" he actually looked just like that new NBA star, Tyrell Jackson. Victoria knew, because her brother was a basketball fanatic. He was always talking about games and players and statistics.

I have no way to reach my own brother. Don't even know where he is . . . or my sister. Melanie is probably going straight to the convent. I'm all alone.

Her jittery insides were making her pussy ache for attention. This fear, on top of the grief of losing her father and her whole life, made her throat burn with dryness. Maybe it was because all the moisture in her body was getting sucked between her legs. She was so hungry and horny and sleepy, she could pass out right now and sleep for three days.

She shivered because this guy was *hot,* so physically gorgeous that he didn't look real. His vibe was so cool, so sexy, so powerful that it stunned her. All she could do was stare.

54

WHITE CHOCOLATE

He was so tall, her eyes were level with his solar plexis, the center of the chest that DaVinci was always diagramming as the central point on human beings. His open-necked shirt made a little frame around that swath of hairless skin. It contrasted with the white linen so vividly, it mesmerized her. She couldn't help imagining what it would look like if their bodies were tangled together—her buttermilk legs, arms and ass wrapped all around his dark chocolate muscles.

She wondered what it would be like to press against his skin. It looked as smooth, shiny and rich in taste and texture as an expensive coffee bean. She always marveled at the beans on display at the coffee house where she used to do spoken word poetry with her friends. Now this guy's luscious skin was that same deep brown, and so velvety-plush looking that she wanted to reach out and touch it. His pec muscles curved up on each side, creating a gentle cradle that looked like it was made for her cheek.

"Vee, this The Duke. Duke Johnson," Henry said. "Duke, Victoria Winston."

Victoria looked up into his eyes.

Oh. My. God. Her pussy creamed. She felt dizzy because his eyes were like giant onyx jewels, just like the ones in her necklace. The way he was looking at her, his eyes were sparkling down with equal intrigue. He was foreign, but—

I feel like if we touch, we'd both melt into a butterscotch puddle right here on the dirt. I let myself trickle into his train of thought and go with his flow to someplace I don't know, but feels oh so . . .

His face was as masculine and sculpted as Michelangelo's David. His skin was taut and flawlessly stretched over a broad jaw, angular cheekbones, a wide forehead, and a thick neck so dark in the creases that it shimmered with iridescence.

His arms, from where his shirt ended just above his elbows, all the way down to his enormous and elegant hands, were just as beautiful. The distance between the base of his thumb and the tip of his index finger—which all the girls at school swore equaled the length of a guy's dick—seemed to stretch from here to eternity.

Victoria's body ached for the comfort of cuddling up and curling up in his length and his strength. What she was feeling was far more than physical. Just standing there, gawking at this god-like statue, she felt like his spirit was wrapping around her like the sheared mink coat she abandoned at her house. Right now it felt like she was connecting with this complete stranger on another level—a soul-deep dimension where she'd known him forever.

Her pussy throbbed. Celeste was going wild with the idea of hopping up on this guy and solving the mystery of what fucking was all about. At the same time, she had the urge to run. Fast and far. But that hot, gushing sensation surged up to her brain, which flashed an image.

She leaps up to embrace him . . . he's holding her up around his waist by cupping her butt with those giant hands . . . and she's kissing him as if the very touch of her lips to his keeps her heart beating . . . and if she pulls away even to breathe, the spark of electricity that makes blood pump through the body would fizzle out and she would dry up and blow away, leaving him with two handfuls of white confetti . . . but she doesn't have to pull away to breathe because his expelled air, the oxygen molecules dancing around his windpipe with carbon dioxide and heat and moisture, that's all she needs to sustain her own life . . . just him, inside her, his big dick inside her hot, hungry pussy.

A boiling sensation sizzled across every inch of her skin. Her cheeks were burning. Lips were scorched. And Celeste was bubbling, as if that geyser inside her turned upside down and was blowing steam and frothy splashes onto the pink velvet shores of her pussy.

She had to run, get away from this overwhelming feeling. No way could she maintain her vow of celibacy if she were around someone who, in a split-second, aroused more potent sensations than she'd ever felt. And even though Celeste told her, during that awesome orgasm inside the house, that she had to share her mix-race woman powers in order to set off their true, phenomenal potential, she didn't believe it. Her physical and emotional state of mind today was so crazy, Celeste was liable to say anything in the heat of the moment.

Your sweet little cherry is about to get plucked, sucked and fucked by this black superhero, Celeste said through the inner voice in Victoria's head. Victoria's mouth watered with a hunger for—

Oh my God, this guy could turn me into a certified nymphomaniac serial killer.

She turned around and ran toward the house.

"Vee!" Henry called.

She stomped up the first two steps.

The pit bulls growled. They got into attack stance. The brown one glared with red-rimmed eyes and leaped at her.

A blur of white teeth . . . brown fur . . . claws dog-paddling mid-air.

Pow!

A red splotch exploded on the side of the dog's round belly.

Chapter 8

Duke couldn't stand the sight of fear in her huge eyes. They were like blue-tinted mirrors, flashing code that only he knew. Good thing he was seeing this message here right now, because he was going to make it his life mission to erase it and never let it flash on her fine-ass face again. Ever.

And so it is written, and so it is done. That was what Ramses would have said, to just know that the power of his vision could make anything happen. Like right now, Duke just knew this chick was going to be putting herself out of her virgin misery in a Motor City minute. Tonight. On his dick. If she thought she was in shock now, she couldn't even imagine the raw dog dick-down that was about to rock her world like a meteor. And make her fly . . . tonight.

She gon' be so ridiculously horny she gon' be throwin' that sweet pussy at me befo' midnight tonight. In my penthouse.

Timbo was burning and tingling just as tough as Duke's right hand from the kick-back. He balled it up, along with his left fist, to stop himself from rushing up on her and sweeping her into his arms. She'd probably pee on herself if he did that. If she hadn't already. She was a suburban, half-white princess one day, and standing in the hood with dog blood on her pretty toes the next. A dead pit bull was staring right up at her. Now she knew never to run from The Duke, but she also knew if she were in trouble, she would be safe.

Damn, fate was a motherfucker, the way stuff was happening at the right time to help The Duke manifest his destiny with The Duchess.

"Oh my God!" she shrieked, spinning around. Her big eyes were trying to figure out who shot the dog, but she'd never know. Henry was walking as cool as he could up to the porch to take the other dogs inside and grab the hose to rinse off her feet.

58

WHITE CHOCOLATE

Beamer was strolling back to the car with the smoking dog defense.

And I'm standin' here cool as Luke. The fastest, slickest ma'fucka on the planet. He wanted to say this to Beamer and Pound: *That quick draw was some Wild, Wild West shit!* But Duke had to play it cool, standing there waiting for her introduction as if he hadn't just popped his top fight dog. The way she was looking at him before the bullet, Duke knew there was no question. She was already struck. On Duke.

Ain't gon' take but a minute to crown her queen o' Babylon. And queen of my bed.

"You coulda shot me!" she screamed. Her right foot stomped the patchy grass. All that long, black hair swayed like a cape from around her back, tickling her ass and swooshing around her right hip. "Who did that?"

"Divine intervention, baby girl," Duke said. "Immaculate ammunition. Don't matta the who, jus' the what. That we gon' protec' you."

"Who's gonna protect me from *you*?" she snapped back. Just as quickly, she stared down at her bloody foot.

"Yo, Vee," Henry said, splashing her feet with water from a green hose. "Iss cold but clean."

She kicked off her shoes. Her toes looked like candy — each little toenail resembled a shiny cinnamon Red Hot — good enough to suck, which he would do soon. Henry handed her a small orange towel to dry her feet as he washed her sandals.

"Now," Henry said, kneeling to slip her feet into the clean shoes. "I know you starvin'. Duke takin' you out to eat." Henry put his hand softly on her back and guided her toward Duke.

"From the frying pan into the fire," she said, striding so elegantly, even though she was mad, on those long giraffe legs.

Funny she should say "the fire," because every inch of him was flaming, and the closer she came, the hotter he got. It was like he was that volcano he'd seen on a TV show he was watching with his kids. First, the rock down in the Earth melted then boiled and finally burst up through the surface. It singed everything in sight. That was exactly how he felt when she aimed her blow-torch eyes at him.

Damn, Duke, be cool, man.

She stopped so close that he could have reached out and squeezed her big, juicy titties, pointing at him in that innocent pink sweater. She was close enough for him to smell that hot, virgin pussy—sweet, salty and served up fresh, just for him. It was probably as wet as his watering tongue right now. She was ripe, ready to get plucked like a big, juicy grape bursting under his tongue, squirting sugar every which way.

Timbo was throbbing like a mug, aching to poke into that tight jar of jelly and stir it, spread it, whip it, dip it, flip it and sip it dry. But if the look in her eye was any indication, this chick was the type who would stay wet because she liked it so much. Duke just knew. He had pussy radar like that. Some bitches had a dry look in their eye. They'd fuck you, but they weren't in it for the pleasure. They were in it for the treasure. This chick, she was hungry as hell for something she hadn't tasted yet. She was scared to take the first sample because she knew she would be addicted. Fiending.

"As we were saying, I'm Victoria Winston." She held out her hand in a business-like way. Her exotic eyes were hard but sexy and soft, too, fringed by thick black lashes. She was the perfect chameleon to snowplow the Moreno Triplets. She looked white enough to make them lose their minds, but once he brought out the sistah in her, she would be fatal.

And Duke would reign.

Duke's mind was a filmstrip of Duchess going into meetings, representing him, putting folks at ease with that creamy skin and drop-dead beauty, using her king's English and brilliant business mind to manifest the Babylon that was his birthright.

The touch of her fingers snapped him out of his visions. She was taking his hand, the one that was still burning from the gun, and shaking it. Her baby-soft fingers disappeared in the hot wrap of his huge hand. She felt so hot, he imagined steam shooting out of his palm like Momma's iron. Sweat prickled up through his skin, from his head to his toes. And Timbo . . . good thing his shirt was long and swaying, or else she'd see the tree trunk with her name written all over it.

I ain't neva felt like this . . . like I'm 'bout to bust.

"I'm Duke. Duke Johnson."

It felt like time stopped when he stared into her eyes. Every time he looked at her, those creamy cheeks turned more pink and those lips became more red. Her chest rose and fell as she breathed hard. He almost couldn't stop himself from bending down to taste that smooth, pretty skin on her chest where her sweater made a U-shaped scoop on top of her pretty titties.

"I'm hungry as ten men," Victoria said. Her voice was deep and smooth, like warm honey in his ears. "Let's go." Still holding his hand, she pulled him toward his own car.

"I'll have you at any restaurant you want in a Motor City minute," Duke said. He nodded toward the car. "That mean zero to sixty in five seconds."

"Thanks, but I don't need a translation. I'm pretty quick. So, let's rock."

Duke's feet would not move. It felt like he was wearing cement boots and his whole body was numb. Except for his pounding heart. His pulse was so strong and loud, it sounded like a hammer inside his ears.

Damn, Duke. Be cool, man. Ain't no woman ev'a sucked yo' powa. She s'pose ta make you stronger.

She turned back. "What are you waiting—"

Duke made his right foot take a step, then his left. He remembered Momma telling him, Knight and Prince at the dinner table, "Be careful what you ask for, 'cause if you get it, you bett' be ready. I loved y'all daddy mo' than life itself. Finally got him, blessed me wit' three babies, but stole my heart, my soul, an' my settlement check. I jus' wasn't ready to take on somebody so slick."

Then Momma would always get that sad look in her brown eyes. Duke never knew if it was for losing his daddy or for the baby that died, or both. Her lawsuit against the hospital won her

61

$200K, but gave the man she loved enough loot to book while she raised three babies in the ghetto. Now, Duchess's sad expression made him realize they had both lost their fathers.

"Where is there to eat around here?" Duchess asked, sliding into his passenger seat. Henry closed the door, leaning over it.

"Vee ain't hip to Grammomma Green ghetto-style cuisine," Henry said with a laugh.

"I'd be as wide as this car if I ate things that are fried and smothered beyond recognition," she said as Duke slid into the driver's seat. "No wonder there's epidemic obesity and diabetes in the black community."

"Baby girl got the socio-economic analysis of our inner-city plight down like a mug," Duke said, speaking in exaggerated proper English. He had learned it by studying the newscasters on TV.

Shocked amusement flashed in her eyes.

"Perhaps, Miss Winston," he added, "we can discuss some statistics to illustrate your point over our evening meal. I want you to dine like a queen."

Henry laughed. "Quit, dog. Soundin' like a white boy."

Her eyes blazed, making him feel like he was about to burst into flames.

"Anywhere you wanna go, baby girl. D-town your oyster tonight."

An' I'm yo' dessert.

Chapter 9

Now that Duke was with Lily White, Beamer had the freedom to meet Milan at a hotel room. As he walked down the hallway, he thought about how to focus on his coup. And what better partner in crime than Milan, who wanted exactly what he wanted: money, power and Babylon. Being a 'round the way girl at heart, Milan was smart and sexy enough to pull it off right under Duke's nose. Plus, he was so caught up with that suburban creampuff who would no doubt crumble after a day in the hood, Duke wasn't good for anything right now. This hostile takeover was going to be a done deal before it even started.

Check it out, world. We the new Duke an' Duchess.

"Damn, you gotta be the finest female in D-town," Beamer said as she opened the door of the Presidential Suite.

"You're early."

"Naw, you said six." He flipped up his watch. Six on the nose. "The Swiss Army don't lie."

The disapproval in her light brown eyes made his blood bang through his veins like rattling pipes. Maybe she was mad because she was standing there in a dark green silk robe. She must have been butt-naked underneath because her titties looked like two of those little dum-dum lollipops poking at him, tempting him to take a lick. How could a bitch so small have such big nipples? And damn, her toenails looked like more candy, all shiny pink and curled into the plush white carpet. "Why Duke ain't on you twenty-fo'/seven, I jus' don' know."

"You would know better than anyone," she said with those intelligent, analytical eyes. They looked like they were moving back and forth with little quick movements from one of Beamer's eyes to the other. Like she was looking in each eye, real close, to see what he was thinking.

No chance. I got this.

63

SEX IN THE HOOD

See, Milan was slick, having them meet at this fancy hotel in the suburbs, far away from all those nosy-ass, jealous niggas in the hood who would love to see them both shot for doing what would look like a triple taboo booty call. But it was all about business right now for the future bosses of Babylon.

Future boss, really. Milan thought it would be a partnership, but Beamer was going to be the new sheriff in D-town. She would take her proper place for a female, at his side, doing what he told her to do. Nothing like what Duke was talking about with Victoria Winston, wanting to share the power with the woman he hoped would someday be his baby momma.

"What's the password?" Milan said, crinkling her little nose that was more pointed than Lily White's. Her big, light brown eyes looked devious and delicious. Her straight, dark hair was bouncing off her shoulders as her bitch-stare dissolved into a smile. "Say it or you can't come in and play."

"Damn, you look sexy," Beamer said playfully, stopping in the threshold. His dick was so hard, it felt like it was going to rocket-launch straight at her, even though Chanel had just given him the supreme dick-suck over at the party on Chicago Boulevard.

Tha's gon' be my every-hour existence when I become the Duke.

"Wrong answer." Milan screwed up her face like he was stupid.

"Bonnie an' Clyde," he said with a more serious tone.

She closed the door. A lock clicked, a bolt slid.

"Milan, if you gon' change it, let me know first."

Silence.

He knocked. "Milan?"

An old white man in a hotel uniform walked past. Then he turned around, came back and asked, "May I help you, sir?"

"No," Beamer said, his heart beating faster. If he were to get kicked out of the hotel, he would not be able to talk with Milan about their plan. And it wasn't like he had a lot of time, either, because if Lily White were telling Duke to kiss his black ass right now, the first thing he would do would be to call Beamer to

64

handle the business that Duke had put on hold to chase some almost-white pussy.

"My fiancée mus' be 'sleep," Beamer told the hotel man. "I'll call her cell phone."

Beamer turned so the man could see the cell phone clipped to his jeans pocket. Otherwise, the man might think he was pulling a gun, then he would call the cops, and the next thing he knew, Duke would be riding up to ask why Beamer was at a hotel with his female. With sweaty palms, Beamer flipped open his red, white and blue Pistons phone. He scrolled down his missed calls—the whole screen said MILAN from top to bottom. Six times. Every time she called him that day, Beamer followed Duke's orders to let it ring. Otherwise, she would just be asking too many questions about who they were with and where they were.

But now *she* was playing let-it-ring.

The white man stepped close, stared down hard, and asked with a snooty tone, "Do you have a room key, sir?" Adding the "sir" on to a sentence that was spit out with so much disrespect was like adding insult to injury because it was so false.

"She'll answer," Beamer said calmly, but his insides were spinning. She did not answer.

The hotel man knocked on the door. "Madame, are you there?"

Dang, why Milan playin' me? Beamer knew better than anybody what kind of tricks Milan had played on Duke. It was crazy shit that nobody but a devious bitch could come up with, like crashing her brand new Benz into a pole, with the kids in the back seat, just so Duke would come home early from the trip to the Superbowl in Jacksonville. If she were that mad thinking he was fucking around with a couple chicks, Milan would lose her mind if she knew the truth. Duke had been down there fucking a whole team of cheerleaders by the hotel pool.

"Let me try one more time." Beamer dialed again. "She must be 'sleep." The man's hostile stare—which Beamer did not look up into—felt like fire on his cheeks. The man had his arms all crossed, breathing in hard, acting like he was going to let his stress make like an army and attack his damn heart, all over a nigga in the hallway who was trying to get with his girl.

"Sir, I'm going to have to escort you to the lobby."

"A'ight."

A few minutes later, the man was on the phone behind the polished wood reception desk. "Ms. Henderson, a young man claiming to be your fiancé is trying to reach you."

A lady next to him, who *wished* she were still as fine as she might have been twenty years ago, turned her skinny ass that looked like a board under her St. John skirt. She pulled her Prada purse up against her half-starved-looking body and looked at Beamer like he was crud in an old, dirty shower. The bad way she was looking at Beamer only made the already angry hotel dude cut his eyes harder.

"Darling," the bitch said to her husband, "aren't there hotels down in Detroit for people like him?"

The hotel guy cleared his throat. Then he coughed, as if he were going to keel over if Milan said no and he had to sweep Beamer's ghetto ass out of this snobby lobby.

"Darling!" the wife-bitch said in a way like she was used to being ignored.

Her husband, a clean-cut white man with brown hair and a dark blue suit, looked up from handing over his credit card to the receptionist who was checking them in. The man turned red. His eyes got big as golf balls. In fact, his eyes were now as big as his own balls, which Beamer had seen slapping against three Sluts' asses Friday night at a Babylon freak party. That one was three times bigger than the one they had attended today on Chicago Boulevard. It was all white men, all in from out of town, trying to get their freak on in the Motor City during some kind of automotive executives' convention.

This guy here, with his snooty-ass wife, was the host. He had requested three flavors of ass: licorice black, chocolate brown, and coffee with cream. That was how he had ordered his pussy, and he personally went to town with all three of them, looking like a yogurt-covered pretzel twisted up with the dark chocolate, milk chocolate and butterscotch candy jar. He had a big dick for a white dude, too, fucking in a frenzy like he knew he was about to die and wanted to fuck himself to death instead.

Beamer smiled. He couldn't help it, because the image in his head of this dude's wife walking in on her husband with his head bobbing between two blue-black thighs would have given her cardiac arrest her damn self.

Ain't this some shit! That dude was the one who had given Beamer the bulging bag of Benjamins when he and Duke stopped by as planned. That scene was some crazy-ass shit, filling up the whole penthouse of one of D-town's most exclusive apartment towers. All white men. All black Sluts. Barriors doing protection, with all the right people on notice so no shit could go down to jack up the operation.

Beamer would bet that freaky automotive man's wife was *not* getting her freak on with three Studs while hubby was out being triple nasty. No, that bitch looked like she hadn't had any dick since Kennedy was president.

Sandpaper pussy bitch. She was all uptight, looking down her powdered nose like she was queen. That kind of bitch, Beamer liked to say, needed to be locked in a room with the biggest, blackest Mandingo Stud that the Squad had to offer. Let somebody like Flame go at her for a while, then see how stiff she would look when he was through. Beamer could just imagine her crying out like she was at a fucking tea party when she first saw the big-ass fire hose in Flame's pants. Then, in her prim an' proper voice, she would beg, "Oh yes, give me all that black cock!" That stuck-up broad would probably be speaking in tongues and fiending for black dick every day for the rest of her life.

Damn, I wonder if Duke hittin' it wit' Lily White. Wonder if she as juicy as she look . . . an' if she gon' stick wit' Duke like he want. Not after me an' Milan get through . . . an' take ova Babylon.

"Yes, Ms. Henderson," the hotel dude looked relieved. "He's—"

SEX IN THE HOOD

"Barb," the woman's freaky-ass automotive executive husband said, trying to nod real cool at Beamer. It wasn't necessary, since the husband already knew Babylon's strict code of confidentiality, which Duke had gone over with him at their first meeting. Normally, Duke did not handle the one-on-one details like that—Milan did all of that—but with monster deals, Duke had his hands all over them, just to make sure all the dollars got delivered to the right place.

Right now, the man was talking to his wife like she was a child. "Barb, you really should keep up on the kids' music. That young man is one of the most famous R&B artists in America."

"Wha'z up!" Beamer pointed real quick.

The hotel dude smiled.

"In fact," the freaky husband said, "we used his latest hit in our ad for the Sports Coupe ZX. It's been airing around the globe for three weeks now."

The woman turned as pink as her lipstick. She pivoted toward the receptionist, talking about the spa. At the same time, her husband nodded, flashing a look that said, *Can't wait to see ya at the next pussy party.* Then he looked at the hotel dude and said, "Your hotel should feel honored to have a man of this stature patronizing your establishment. I feel privileged just to shake your hand. Your talent is phenomenal." His eyes flashed something real sneaky, like he wanted to ask, *Where da party at?* As if he were going to put his wife to bed and come creeping up to a suite full of black pussy.

Beamer cracked up. He patted the auto-freak on the back. "Thanks, man. I 'preciate yo' props."

The hotel dude was all flustered, hurrying around the corner of the counter so fast, he bumped himself in the hip. He took Beamer's arm, leading him to the elevator. "I'm so sorry about the inconvenience, sir. We get all kinds of riff-raff here and make sometimes aggressive efforts to filter out those who don't belong. We have a very particular clientele."

"Iss a'ight."

68

WHITE CHOCOLATE

"May I offer you and Ms. Henderson a bottle of champagne to make up for the misunderstanding?" The elevator stopped and the doors opened.

"We already got the Cristal on ice," Beamer said, knocking on Milan's door. She opened it instantly, flashing a smile and holding out her arms.

"Oh, baby, I'm sorry. I was in the shower," she said all sweet, pressing her hard nipples into Beamer's chest.

"If there's anything you need," the hotel dude said as he walked away, "please don't hesitate to ring me."

Milan pulled him inside, closed and locked the door. The high-ceilinged suite was all white, from the leather couch and matching chairs to the marble fireplace, the chaise facing it and the TV in a glass-and-silver cabinet holding plants and books.

"Oooh, Peanut, you look delicious tonight," Milan said, posing on the chaise. Beamer was sure that if she took that robe off, she'd look just like a centerfold, no joke. Her sexy playmate attitude rattled Beamer inside. It felt like steam was shooting out of his ears.

"I know I'm delicious," Beamer said playfully, "but no joke, Bonnie an' Clyde don't need no romantic distractions."

"Bonnie *and* Clyde," she said in her white girl way of talking.

"Damn, why you gotta say e'ry letter?"

"I know it's a crime to sound intelligent where you come from—"

"We grew up around the block from each other, Michelle Henderson." He sucked his teeth, wishing her big brown eyes and her still-hard nipples were not so distracting. He wanted to talk about their coup, but his dick was trying to talk louder. He needed to tone down her attitude before they got down to business.

"You might could blow them airs up e'rybody else ass, but wit' me, you gotta keep it real. Michelle Henderson always gon' be a hood rat. I don't care if you havin' tea wit' the queen o' England. You from the hood in D-town, so keep it real wit' yo' boy."

SEX IN THE HOOD

She stood, stepping toward him with that fake-sophisticated walk that she'd been perpetrating ever since she went to the fashion shows in New York. Every time she took a step, she would put one foot directly in front of the other, to make her hips sway, sashay, or straight-up switch. It made her look sexy as hell with those titties bouncing, the satin flowing around her, and her lips opening as she came at him.

"I learned to keep it real at my prestigious prep school," she said, poking his chest with a fingernail. "Private school taught me that in the *real world,* you have to know how to —". Her lips got real tight and her hard nipples looked like they were going to cut holes in that robe as she said, "Speak like a white person."

"You trippin', Michelle."

"My name is Milan. Obviously you need training before you're ready to embark on our plan."

"I don't need shit but some cooperation from yo' ass. You might be in charge o' the Squad by day, but when you an' me is workin' this deal, you gon' call me Boss."

She threw her head back, laughing. "As if I would bow down to your dim-witted mumblings."

Damn, how could somebody look so sexy while they were being so mean? Beamer's whole body was shaking as he thought about pulling open that robe, laying her on that lounge chair and fucking her until she started talking like she used to. Something about her made him feel weak as hell, like a nigga could think tough all he wanted, and say it, but when he looked in those eyes, he turned to grits inside.

She clawed her fingernails over his cheek, stopping to tickle his lip. "If you think it's cool to dumb yourself down to the lowest common denominator of every hoodlum you know, then I'm going to smarten you up until you're intelligent enough to partner with me on our Duke Deal of the Day."

All of a sudden, something in her eyes made Beamer remember how when they were eight, she sweet-talked him into going to the corner store and stealing some Blow Pops for her. "I'll kiss you if you get me three green apple ones," she said. But when he came out and delivered the goods, she was sitting on the porch with Duke, so Beamer gave each of them a sucker and kept one for himself. Never did get his kiss.

Right now, the way she was cracking up just looking at him—and he hadn't said squat—it was making him feel retarded. It made hot energy, like steam, blow through him, making him want to punch something.

"You know, Peanut, there are two kinds of people in the world: leaders who make decisions, and imbeciles who wouldn't know how or what to think if it weren't for the leaders thinking for them. Duke and I, we're the leaders. And you, sorry little punk, happen to fall in the second category. Now, here's my plan that you're going to help me execute."

"Aw, hell no!" Beamer shouted, balling his fists. "You nothin' but a trick! Fulla tricks!"

She looked at him with excited eyes. Her lips poked out the way models always look in pictures—like they were about to kiss their own picture.

"What the fuck you doin'?" he asked, sounding much more angry than he had intended. "I coulda got arrested up in this snobby-ass joint. The suburbs ain't no place to play."

"You didn't get the password right, Peanut. And if you're going to do business with me, I need you to pay attention to the details. Now, what is the password?"

"Don't fuck wit' me."

She tossed back her head, making that straight hair bounce all over the place. She leaned on one hip, spreading her fingers out on her thighs to press the fabric down. The robe fell open wider on her chest.

Damn, if I could fuck her jus' once . . .

Beamer's dick was ramming up against his jeans. Benzo wasn't even this hard when Chanel was sucking it this afternoon. Something about Milan's bitchy drill sergeant way of talking make Benzo iron hard.

If he closed his eyes, she would sound white, but looking at the way she jerked her neck when she talked, there was no question she was a sistah when she said, "I'll fuck with you every second of every day, you stupid motherfucker, until you can concentrate on business."

He stomped closer. Their bodies were almost touching. "Don't call me a stupid motherfucker, you bourgie wanna-be, two-timin' bitch."

She craned her neck forward. Her eyes grew bigger as she said, "You don't have the balls to make this happen with me."

Beamer stared hard into her eyes. His right hand yanked open the top button on his jeans, which he pulled hard enough to unzip. He whipped out his big dick in his right hand and cradled his balls in his left hand.

"These some big muthafuckin' balls," he said angrily, "an' a big black dick ta go wit' 'em. So don't tell me—"

"Maybe you have the equipment, but you're scared to use it." Milan shook her head. "Put that little mess away. I been dealin' in dicks way bigger than that all day long."

Beamer could feel something inside snapping, like his rattling veins had just blown a pipe and steam was blowing every which way but out. He was like a pressure cooker, and Milan's haughty expression, her words, her sexiness, were making his gauge tick even more violently.

"I said put the dick away before I jump up on it."

Benzo throbbed harder, like that pressure cooker was about to blow right through the head of his dick. All that steam would shoot straight back into Milan, where it came from. And either pair of her lips would do.

"Peanut, if you think I want that little earthworm of a dick-"

I got this. No joke.

Beamer lunged. He wrapped his arms around her waist, lifted her up and let that robe fall open. He slammed her down on his dick like she was a bubble and he was sticking out a pin to pop it.

"Peanut, stop!" She clawed the collar of his Pistons jersey. Was she trying to hold on or get a grip so she could fuck him back? She didn't exactly wrap her legs around him, but she didn't

72

push off either. Her pussy was hot, wet and gripping him like she'd been wanting it all along.

"Damn, yo' pussy wet." She was so small, all he had to do was hold her in place, lift and lower her real quick, and bang up. He inhaled the smell of her designer perfume and salty pussy. That put Benzo on swole even more.

This some good pussy. No wonder Duke —

Beamer's whole body went cold.

I am one dead mothafucka. No joke.

He looked up into Milan's eyes. She was loving this dick. She was evil, just like Duke said. She'd sell her own momma to get her way, to get paid, to get some dick, just to be a bitch.

Then how could her pussy feel so good?

"You started now, Peanut. Don't you dare get guilty an' pull some *coitus interruptus* unless you're lusting for *rigor mortis* in return. 'Cause the number one way to royally piss off Milan Henderson is to get stingy with the dick."

I'm double-crossin' Duke, now she's gonna double-cross me. Threaten me, too! An' I'm too stupid to have known better. Talk about stuck between a cock and a hard place. Beamer would laugh if he were thinking about some other dumb-ass fool. Duke was right. The reason it was so easy for him to knock down Pinks was because Beamer had been holding him up.

Then why does Duke rely on me so much?

"Fuck me!" Milan ordered. She tossed off the robe, letting it fall to the floor. Her fingernails clawed under the collar of his jersey, scraping over his shoulders. Stripes of pain burned his skin. Her hair was bouncing all over. She pulled the holder off his braids, letting them fly wild.

She was making her ass bounce like she was riding a horse. The sharp little heels of her slippers were stabbing his thighs, and he was galloping right underneath her. Yeah, galloping toward the barrel of a gun if Duke were to find out.

They fucked until they were both dripping, then they each blew a nut so hard, they collapsed on that couch and guzzled champagne straight from the bottle. After she put on her robe, Milan picked up the remote, pointed it at the TV and clicked.

"Where is it?" she asked, pushing buttons.

The screen flashed with images of green fabric sliding to the floor . . . brown hair bouncing . . . redbone braids flying . . . and Duke Johnson's number one baby momma getting fucked by his number one boy. His servant. His back-stabbing right hand with a death wish the size of Michigan.

Beamer's whole body shook so violently, he was afraid he was having a convulsion. He half wanted to tell Michelle to call 911. "Why the fuck—"

She raised her eyebrows, crossed her arms and looked at him like he was stupid.

"Give me the tape," Beamer said with a dead-serious tone.

"Thought you'd like a copy," she said, pushing a button and ejecting a tape.

Beamer threw it on the floor. His gym shoe slammed down on the tape, making the plastic crackle.

"Why you laughin', bitch?"

"My new camera is so handy," she said, aiming the remote at the TV. There they were, still fucking on the screen.

"Erase that shit. Now!" Damn, Beamer's voice sounded just as deep and powerful as Duke's usually did. "'Fore I tear up this room to find yo' hidden camera."

"Cameras," she said, pushing buttons. "See, I have multiple angles. Do you know anything about digital film? It's wonderful. You'll never guess where it's hidden. I can download the images, print them out, copy them to tape, email them around the world if I want to. And the way you came at me—"

Beamer shot up to his feet.

I'm gon' fin' e'ry last one o' them cameras an' break 'em. No joke.

"Of course, if you act up, Peanut, I can ring our friend down at the front desk, who'd be happy to call the police about the unruly nigga up in the Presidential Suite. Then you'd have to call Duke to bail you out of jail. After he and I enjoy our home movies."

74

Beamer stomped back to the couch. He stood over Milan and glared down. "What the fuck you want from me?"

"I want you to make sure that Duke Johnson does not do whatever he's planning to do with that white bitch." Her lips got real tight against her teeth and the words came out like a growl, like she was biting down hard. "Whether he plans to fuck her, hire her, pimp her, I don't know. I don't care. Just make sure she doesn't step one foot into Babylon."

Milan opened her robe again, lay back on the couch, and spread her legs wide open. Her body looked like an evil face: nipples for eyes, an "outie" belly button for a nose, and that gapped-open brown-and-pink pussy was the mouth trying to suck him into hell.

"You're going to do all of that, of course," Milan said with that playmate/drill sergeant voice, "after you eat my pussy."

Beamer's mouth watered because her pussy was beautiful. It was still tight, even after two babies, and it was still good, real good. But that bitch who was attached to it made everything sweet about her body go sour.

"Don't make me have to cum by myself." She pressed her long, gold fingernail onto her inch-long clit, rubbing it in circles. Her nipples pointed at him like poison darts.

Damn, that pussy look good. But she makin' a triple-dead sucka mothafucka outta me.

"Eat my pussy. Now!"

If I'm gon' die, I might as well get as much good pussy as I can first.

He pressed his face into his own sticky nut all over her pussy. He rubbed his face around. He wasn't just going to drink the poison; he was going to savor every sip.

"Ooooh, shit. Think about how you ain't gon' let Duke fuck that white bitch. Think about how if he try, you gon' tell me so I can get a fresh manicure before I kill the bitch with my own pretty little hands."

75

Chapter 10

Even though she was dizzy from hunger, the first thing Victoria did when they arrived at the upscale restaurant on the river was go to the bathroom and make herself cum.

The whole drive there, she had squirmed in her seat, making a soaking wet mess of her panties. Panic was gripping her throat, anxiety about her life turning her insides into a nest of wasps stinging her from the inside out. Something about that guy — that enormous, dark chocolate god who twenty-four hours ago she never would have never even considered talking with much less going to dinner — was turning her into a boiling vat of cum cream. And that rap music, the kind Brian was always playing, was arousing something rebellious and wild within her. She'd almost made herself cum in the car by squeezing her pussy muscles in rhythm to that music that Duke said was Bang Squad.

I can't believe how hard I just came, in the bathroom, thinking about his lips.

Making herself cum mellowed her mind. It cured the sting. Especially when she thought about his dick and how he would feel. Fucking was a totally abstract idea because she had no real-life reference point. All she knew was what her friends told her, and they'd all complained that losing their virginity was painful and disappointing. Even Tiffany complained, though she was like a little rabbit with Jake because, she said, "Once you pop it, you just can't stop it. You crave it constantly."

If that were true with nerdy-looking Jake, then what would happen with sexy, studly Duke? Whatever it was, Victoria wanted it. But she would never, ever get it.

This is so dangerous. I'm already a nympho by myself, but if I let Celeste loose on him, I might never get out of bed! My deathbed. Or his.

So, walking back through the restaurant to Duke Johnson, sitting so cool at a table framed by the bright blue Detroit River and the downtown skyline, Victoria focused on her goal tonight.

WHITE CHOCOLATE

She had to strategize how he could help her find a better place to live. Then she would figure out how to start classes at the University of Michigan without the $250,000 Daddy had set aside for college and graduate school for her master's degree in business. If this guy had so much pull, maybe he could help her get an emergency loan.

Henry said he wants to help me, so –

As she sat down, a gray-haired white man in a business suit glared at her from a nearby table. He said something to his frothy-haired wife, who shook her head with disgust. Had they seen her on TV? Had they known Daddy?

"Why is everyone staring at us?" Victoria asked. "The whole drive here, people in other cars were looking at me like I'm some kinda freak."

The corners of Duke's mouth raised up slightly. His eyes sparkled. "They tryin' to fig'a out what NBA ma'fucka wit' a vanilla shorty."

"Oh, I love those," Victoria said, remembering her favorite coffee drink at the Java Joint, which just days ago was her favorite hangout with Brian and Tiffany. "With cinnamon and whipped cream on top."

"They're just some jealous ma'fuckas," Duke said playfully. "Hatin' on a brotha for ridin' with the finest shorty in D-town."

"I'm *not* short. I'm five-eight." Victoria pointed to her red leather mules. "Make it five-eleven in these heels."

"You short next to six feet six inches o' this Mandingo warrior ma'fucka," Duke said coolly, his eyes roving down the exposed "V"of her cleavage to the round curves of her breasts. His stare made her nipples pop so hard against the pink satin of her bra, they made two points on her sweater. Then he said, with the sexiest deep voice she'd ever heard, "See, you hearin' me loud an' clear."

She squirmed. His bad boy command of cuss words made Celeste throb even hotter and wetter. She turned away, staring out the wall of windows at the glow of blue lights around the white Windsor Casino across the river. Yeah, this guy was

77

definitely a high-risk gamble. Even his jackpot couldn't be anything but trouble. He was a one-armed bandit, all right—his penis. If she pulled it, let him drop it into her slot and let the images spin, she would live a life of lemons, addicted to a game she could never win.

Yet the simple act of looking into his eyes made her feel out of control. She had the same feeling as when she was dieting with perfect discipline—until she walked into Mrs. Fields Cookies. Just a few weeks ago, her friends had said she had the best discipline for sticking to the South Beach Diet, but then Tiffany put a Mrs. Fields frosted brownie in front of her. All her discipline melted under the warmth of that fresh-baked goodie in her hand. The sweet chocolate scent literally turned off the part of her brain that said "no" to all other fattening treats. She devoured every bite, every crumb, loving every second of that brief blast of heaven.

To make up for it, she'd go running for an hour because if she gained an ounce, it would go to her ass. Brian was always harping on her for having a big butt, needing to lose weight, telling her to wear baggy clothes to cover up the shape that was exactly like her mother's beautiful body. And it was as hungry for love as her mother's was.

But if Victoria succumbed to the temptation of this male god sitting in front of her, how could she make up for that? What if she got pregnant? What if she caught something? What if she loved it so much she lost her mind and become a slave to her sex?

"Wherever your mind takin' you right now," Duke said, "let me go too. 'Cause the look on your face be sneaky as hell. Sexy as hell, too."

She glared at him. "My thoughts have a big DO NOT ENTER sign. You'll never know."

"One look in your eyes," Duke said, "and I got a fuckin' all-access pass into your horny-ass mind."

"Don't talk to me like that," she snapped.

"Oh sorry, Miss Daisy," Duke said. "You ain't used to hearin' words like that."

"My dad had a potty mouth too. I hated it."

"Then I'll speak," he said with that playful proper white cadence, "like a perfect gentleman."

Victoria smiled. *But I don't know if I can keep being a lady with you.*

"My pops booked. Never met him. You lucky you had one."

"I can't talk about my dad right now." Victoria squeezed back tears, closed her eyes and inhaled the delicious cologne/skin scent that was wafting from Duke. She kept squeezing her pussy muscles to soothe away the stares, the worries, the sheer terror that was gripping her soul.

The scent of salmon made her open her eyes.

"I ordered fo' ya," Duke said with an adorable smile. It was like his eyes sparkled and tenderness washed over his face, which was all the more dramatic because he was so enormous and tough-looking at first glance.

"Mmmmm, exactly what I had in mind," she said, ogling the big slab of grilled salmon over mixed greens with gorgonzola cheese, walnuts and dried cherries. "Duke, I can't remember the last time I ate. Or slept. It's been, like, half a week. I don't know how I'm staying awake."

"You gon' sleep good tonight," Duke said with a warmth in his eyes that made her shiver. It wasn't just in his eyes; it was radiating from his entire being. Just like it did from Daddy and Mommy. The energy registered in her mind like *I'll take care of you no matter what.* Duke flashed those big, beautiful white teeth and said, "I tol' you I got'cha back, baby girl."

"I'm not sleeping a wink at that hellish house of dogs," Victoria said as the waiter placed a bread basket overflowing with hot whole wheat rolls. "Paradise." She smiled as the waiter set a plate of steak and lobster before him. A platter of giant crab cakes descended between them. "No, I'm in paradise right now, and if this is my last meal in life, I'm gonna savor every bite."

Duke let out a quick, deep laugh. "Oh, baby girl, it ain't the las'. It's jus' a little taste o' what gon' be yo' life e'ry day."

She stared hard into his eyes, looking for answers, but radiating back was pure male domination that told her without words, *Your wish is my command as long as it fits into my mysterious master plan.*

"The house specialty," the waiter said, putting on the table an elaborate arrangement of fresh pineapple, strawberries and blueberries with a dish of fresh whipped cream. "Indulge."

"Thank you," Victoria said between bites that transformed the acid burn of hunger in her gut into a warm, mellow fullness.

"Damn, baby girl," Duke said playfully, his dark eyes sparkling. "You eat like a man."

"Thank you! This is *so* good!" she said, savoring every flavor. She speared a big piece of pineapple, dipped it in cream, stuck out her tongue and chomped in an exaggerated way. "All my friends were always starving themselves. They were so scared to eat in front of guys. Stupid."

"I love a girl wit' a big appetite," Duke said with a mischievous smile. "Cain't stand them salad-eatin' chicks. Always mad 'cause they so hongry."

Victoria laughed. His eyes were mesmerizing. She could not look away from the rich, black depths of his pupils and irises, the super whiteness of his eyes, the beautiful radiance of his flawless, coffee bean brown skin. She had never really looked this hard into a black face. Gramma Green and other relatives, of course, but somehow a man, a young handsome man, was different. Way more intense. And scary.

He represented everything opposite her, and her body was electrified. If she were to put her fingertip to the bottom of a lightbulb right now, it would no doubt glow brightly. She never felt this electric, even after hours of heavy petting with Brian. But now, all of a sudden, she was analyzing the whole race-sex vow that she had made to herself. She ached to talk to Mommy, to hear the adult version of what she had told her in the vanity mirror.

What if the power that Mommy described only worked on white men? What if an inner-city tough guy like this was so used to sex power that he was immune, so nobody would get hurt? If so, then Victoria could satisfy the incredibly distracting craving to indulge her virginal body in sex—especially a hot mouth on her pussy. Celeste would go wild. Oooh, what would it be like for Duke to wrap those full, chocolate brown lips around her clit? And his dick was probably huge. Would it hurt? Or would she love it so much that her pussy sucked him inside her forever?

"You a'ight, boo?"

"Why do you keep calling me that?"

"What?"

"Boo. Like you think I'm scared or something."

"We alike like that," Duke said. "You got a poker face like a mug."

"A what? I've never had a mug shot. Don't plan to."

Duke laughed. "Girl, I gotta school you on the language of the street if you gon' make it."

"That's not a question," she said. "I'm gonna find a job and move out as soon as I can."

"I know," Duke said.

"How do you know?"

"I see it in your eyes. You and me, we just alike. You'll see. We got the same soul, but it was split apart and born in different worlds. But now—"

"I'm trapped since the lawyers took away my car," Victoria said. "What can you recommend that's close to my grandmother's house, where I can work?"

"Work for me."

"Doing what?"

"Represent me. At meetings. Help me run my business. The way you talk and carry yourself, that'll give me a lot more credibility."

"With who?"

"Various business partners."

"Duke, I'm eighteen."

"I'm twenty, and I'm runnin' the shit. I learned it from my brothers startin' when I was twelve. I took ova wit' Knight when Prince—" Duke looked down. "Jus' say we on the fas' track business plan here in'a hood. Life short, so you gotta shoot to the top quick or —"

Victoria's stomach cramped. "Where's your brother?"

"The same place a whole lotta niggas go befo' they see twenty-one. Elmwood Cemetery."

"Was he a drug dealer? I'm not doing anything illegal."

"Hear me now," Duke said, taking her hand. "You help me out, I will make sure your fine ass never takes a fall. I'll confess it right now, you are my new reason for living."

Victoria stood up. "I'm sorry, but you know nothing about me. I'm going to college to start my own business someday, and I don't want anything to do with whatever business you're in."

"Think about it," he said. "Workin' at McDonald's by yo' Grammomma house or workin' for me with your own apartment, a car, and protection."

Tears stung Victoria's eyes.

"Now come on," he said. "I'm takin' you grocery shopping so you can get some white girl food for your grammomma house. Anything you want."

His eyes scanned her body. "And you can come to my crib for a shower if you still want."

Celeste throbbed, but Victoria shook her head and looked at him like he was crazy. "Your crib?"

He laughed. "That's ghetto for 'home.'"

"I feel like I need a Berlitz book when you talk," she said playfully, ticking down a grocery list in her head: green apples, yogurt, tuna, baked chicken, peanut butter.

"A what book?" he asked.

"It's a travel guidebook, for when you visit a foreign country. It has a bilingual dictionary of common words and phrases. You say something, I look it up, get a translation."

"Yeah, write that book," Duke said. "Whitey's Guide to the Hood."

She stopped, turned, glared at him. "I don't like racial jokes."

"Nobody ever called you a nigga bitch, have they?"

"You just did." She stared back without flinching.

WHITE CHOCOLATE

"Nice," he said, those piercing eyes glowing with approval.

As they walked past tables toward the exit, that white man and his wife who had stared at her earlier stood up.

"Victoria Marie Winston," the man said. Her heart pounded. Not that she was scared, just that after being all over the media for a week, she was expecting lunatics and perverts and racists to come crawling out of their gutters to say or do vile things.

Duke wedged himself between her and the man. He was so tall and wide, he entirely hid her like a big, black wall. "Can I help you?"

"No," the man said, stepping around Duke. "Victoria, I worked with your dad."

"She don't want to talk right now," Duke said.

"Wait," Victoria said, allowing the man to approach. Maybe he was looking angry because he was grieving.

"The apple doesn't fall far from the tree," the man said with furious eyes. A bit of spit landed on his lip.

Duke blocked her as gracefully as a giant cat. "Yo, step back."

The man did, but he shouted, "Your dad was a despicable, nigger-loving bandit!"

"A criminal!" the woman shrieked. She shook her over-powdered cheeks, which were dusted with giant ovals of rouge. "You're obviously following in his footsteps!"

Duke swept Victoria away from them so quickly, it felt like she was floating. His big, strong arms curved around the back of her waist so quickly and powerfully that he lifted her up and out, away from those freaks.

Her brain was like an out-of-control radio, spinning past dozens of ear-splitting stations. *People hate Daddy. Now they hate me. Can't go anywhere public with Duke. Arouses racist hatred in strangers. Makes people think I'm bad. But I like him. He protects me. And I've never felt so comfortable with a guy . . . like when I move he moves . . . when I think he feels . . . when he breathes I melt. We're connected on another level.*

83

SEX IN THE HOOD

And the way he was looking down at her right now as they walked past the scowling maitre d', Victoria shivered with a sense of *us against the world*.

And she loved it.

Chapter 11

"There they are!" that crazy-ass white lady from inside the restaurant screamed as Duke and Duchess stepped to the valet stand facing the water.

Hell no. We out two hours an' 5-0 on us like a mug.

That old geezer and his cow were leading the cops straight their way. Duke kept his usual stance, cool as a cat.

"Are you all right, ma'am?" the young black cop asked Duchess.

"We were both fine," Duke said with his TV voice, "until this gentleman confused us with somebody else."

"This is Tyrell Jackson," Duchess said with a strong business voice. She looked up at Duke. "Don't you recognize him from all the media coverage? He's like the talk of the NBA right now. The hottest draft pick since Shaq."

Duke raised his chin a little as four pairs of eyes rolled up and down him, along with a dozen others waiting for their cars at the valet. They were mostly fancy white people, but one bourgie-ass Erkel type was looking down his nose—up, actually, because he was about a foot shorter than Duke. His bitch was doing the same from behind little glasses.

Look like she ain't had no real dick ev'a, 'specially from that soft ma'fucka.

They might've been black, but that couple was just like the older white one and the cops—all their eyes were going from glaring to staring, from mad to glad in a Motor City minute as Duchess worked the magic Duke knew she had in her.

The white cop shook his head, smiling as he said, "Jump shot Jackson! From the University of Texas. Forward."

The other cop, who had a smile as goofy as Beamer's, added, "Congratulations on your contract that could run a small country!"

SEX IN THE HOOD

Duke knew he had seen this dude someplace. Those undercover cops thought they were fooling somebody, but not The Duke.

"Give me your info an' I'll get you into the suite for the celebrity charity game tomorrow," Duke said. "We got everybody from the mayor to Motown stars comin' out to support a good cause."

"It's gonna be hot," Duchess said, smiling. "I work for my school newspaper, and I was interviewing Mr. Jackson over dinner, about the game. It's raising money for kids with cancer because Mr. Jackson's nephew—"

"We've already got tickets!" the angry white man, who was happy now, interrupted. "Our grandson has the same lymphoma. Bless you, sir." The man shook Duke's hand.

The old white witch put her hand on Duchess's shoulder. "I'm sorry, dear. I apologize for both of us. You're the spitting image of a young lady we knew in a very bad situation. We thought—"

"That's okay," Duchess said. "I embarrassed myself just yesterday, speaking French to this girl in the mall. She was like the twin of my roommate when I was an exchange student in Paris. Wrong! She answered me in Arabic! It was hilarious."

Duke knew the sound of his car coming without turning around.

"Becky," Duke said, turning to open her door. "We still gotta run out to the Palace for the pictures."

"Oh, your car," she said with that happy white girl cadence. She waved as she stretched her long giraffe legs onto the seat. "Nice meeting all of you."

"We'll be lookin' for those passes," the white officer said, handing over their business cards.

"I'll hook you up tonight," Duke said as he got in the car.

"Keep up the good work," the angry white man said as Duke drove away to the blasting beat of the Bang Squad.

"Oh my God," Duchess said, laying her head back and looking up at the lights on the Ambassador Bridge. It looked like a sparkling necklace draping over the river between Detroit and Canada. "That was hilarious and horrible all at once."

"You talkin' about life." Duke did a quick U-turn on Atwater, a two-lane street that wound past a police station near Joe Louis Arena. Streams of people in red-and-white Detroit Red Wings jerseys packed the streets on their way to the hockey game.

"Whoah," Duchess said, leaning toward him over the center console. The heat of her body made the hairs on his arm raise up. "That feeling of being wrongly accused," Duchess said in a way like she was about to cry. It made Duke hurt inside. "Is that how my dad felt?" she asked. "Like no matter what you say to explain the truth, it's pointless because your accusers are already so convinced that you're bad."

"Soun' like you describin' a whole lotta brothas I know in the joint right now. But baby girl, you get a Oscar fo' that performance. They ate it up!"

"What a relief," Duchess said as he blew back past the restaurant with the deep blue river flowing to their right. "Love how you just played along. I didn't even have to tell you."

She got quiet, like she was realizing what she was about to say.

We so natural, no words required.

She answered with a fresh windful of pussy perfume. The smell of her sex was so strong, it was like a sweet cloud, like when Grammomma in Alabama used to crack the oven door open to check on her famous sweet potato pies. Everybody in the room would be sniffing and smiling because they knew if it smelled that good cooking, it was going to taste like a big, juicy slice of heaven.

Duchess was quiet as they passed all the abandoned warehouses on the left, the huge silos at a cement company where a tanker docked on the water, and Chene Park, the outdoor theater on the river with pretty grass, a pond and a curvy white tent for a roof. She lay back, closed her eyes, and didn't open them until he pulled up to Astoria Bakery in

Greektown, a crowded, block-long strip of bustling restaurants, bakeries and a casino.

"There's too many people," she said, glaring at the packed sidewalk where street artists were sketching pictures and people were standing around eating ice cream. "I'm not getting out. I don't want anyone to recognize me or bother us like at the restaurant."

"Come wit' me. I know you like ice cream," he said, opening her door and guiding her past a sidewalk musician who was blowing a saxophone. They entered through the glass-and-wood door, past the mouthwatering display of chocolate-covered strawberries, the Greek honey-nut baklava pastry, and ridiculously gooey cookies.

"Oh my God, it smells so good in here," Duchess said, inhaling the heavy-sweet scent of waffle cones cooking.

Duke's fingertips brushed the small of her back. She responded with a fresh breeze of pussy perfume rising up to his nose. Damn, her cunt smelled ten times sweeter than any waffle cone.

He was sure that nobody around them could smell her. No, their senses weren't tuned to pussy scents or sense. They probably just picked up on that lemony-flowery white girl scent coming from her hair—hair that he couldn't wait to twist up in his fingers while fucking her doggie style. It *would* happen. Soon. First he had to strip away the stiff white layers and unleash the wild black beauty within. She was horny as hell, and her animal instincts were trying to claw out anyway.

An' I'm gon' let 'em run free. He felt like God, taking white clay and molding it into the perfect black Eve.

He inhaled. Her heavy-sweet sex smell made Timbo surge with red-hot blood. His dick hit his thigh so hard, he was sure it would cause a bruise.

"Every flavor looks good, but I already know what I want," Duke said as they stood in front of the ice cream counter. She was beside him, ogling the pink Michigan cherry, brown Mackinac Island fudge and his favorite, the blue-yellow-pink swirl of

WHITE CHOCOLATE

Superman. Duke opened his mouth to ask her what she wanted, but no words came out.

Damn. What's her name? In his mind he'd been thinking of her as Duchess so much, he couldn't remember the name her parents gave her.

"Baby girl, tell me yo' flava," he said, licking her up with his eyes. He could feel the girl behind the counter pitching hardball attitude at them with her eyes, her snarled-up lips and her head cocked to one side.

"I don't usually eat ice cream," Duchess said. "I'm like a chocolate addict. One bite and I totally lose control."

Miss Attitude cut her off. "Den you ain't gotta be havin' no chocolate." The girl cut her eyes at Duke then slammed her scooper in the vanilla. "Yeah, honey, you betta leave da chocolate fo' dose o' us who can han'le it." She raked her eyes all up and down Duke.

He stared back hard and said, "My baby girl want a double scoop o' that Godiva dark chocolate fudge decadence." Duke pointed to the label in front of a tub of the flavor that Beamer ate almost every damn day. "Make it extra big. Mandingo size."

The attendant sucked her teeth and mumbled to herself as she dragged the scoop through the glistening dark chocolate ice cream. She filled a waffle cone then handed it to Duchess.

"Now fo' me, a triple scoop o' Superman." Duke didn't look at the chick behind the counter. He locked his gaze on Duchess's tongue, which was coming out slowly, wrapping around that huge tower of black. Her candy-pink tongue licked up the side of the dark chocolate. She closed her eyes like it was the best thing she had ever tasted. So far. She'd have the same look when she slurped up on his dick for the first time, and an even more lustful look after he fucked her good and she truly knew the powers of Timbo.

Duke smiled, imagining how someday he would lay her on the kitchen counter at his crib, fill up her pussy with ice cream then hold his mouth open at her pussy lips and let it melt out. Anything that didn't come creaming back at him, he would suck out. Then he would stick Timbo up in that creamy hot-cold canal and stir up a smoothie with nut, melted chocolate ice cream and her cum cream. She'd want to taste it so bad, she'd beg him to pull it out and let her slurp their love mix off his dick, just like she was licking that cone like there was no tomorrow.

Duke took his cone, tossed a ten at Miss Attitude and led Duchess back to the car. They sat in the convertible, in a no parking zone, watching the crowded sidewalks and flow of cars on Monroe Street. Greek music played from overhead speakers, mixing with rap from niggas on cruise with their females, and white folks walking up and down the street, their bellies full of lamb and that *opa!* cheese they set on fire and let sizzle before they sloshed it up on some bread.

Duke tucked a napkin into his collar so no pink, blue or yellow Superman ice cream could drip and stain his white linen.

Damn, Duchess looked gorgeous, sitting right next to him where she was destined to stay. His pulse was pounding.

"Baby girl, why you look so scared?"

"I think I have a chocolate addiction. It makes me feel totally out of control. I mean the first drop on my tongue, it sets off this crazy, runaway train of thoughts, like I wish I could eat chocolate constantly. I wish I could taste this—" She took a lick, closed her eyes and said, "Mmmm . . . every second of every day."

"My boy Beamer always eatin' chocolate."

"It shows."

Duke laughed. "See, you ain't scared. Half my crew be scared to say a damn thing 'bout Beamer 'cause he my boy."

"He's fat. That shows no control. Disregard for the consequences of your actions. Just like teen pregnancy. Emphysema in smokers. Wrinkles in girls who lay in the sun, like my friend Tiffany. She's only eighteen, but years of frying herself, sunbathing—"

"Don't wanna be black, but tryin' ta look as black as they can," Duke said.

90

"I tan easy and I get dark in a heartbeat. It looks beautiful, but I usually only do it on our boat in the summer." She moaned. "Used to."

"Baby girl, I got a yacht that'll make you feel right at home," he said, licking his Superman scoops like they were the little man in her boat getting swept over by a giant tongue wave.

She stared blankly at the street with a look in her eyes like her mind was far, far away.

"Seriously, baby girl, you got all the right instincts. You know it's death to show fear, 'cause now you know you gon' get eaten alive in'a hood an' in'a fancy white world you used to. You need protection. From me."

"No, I *don't*." Her neck jerked ever so slightly in a way she wasn't even aware of. Her silver-blue eyes flashed with defiance.

He smiled. *The sistah-girl inside tryin'a break outta white girl bondage already.*

"You do need protection. Already proved it tonight, twice. Pit bulls, ghetto hoes, the media, the cops and angry white men. An' the brothas. Walk down Babylon Street an' e'ry thug gon' try an' stick you on they dick an' roas' you like a marshmallow."

"Do you have to say it like that?"

"By the look in yo' eye, you hear ma point loud an' clear." His motor hummed loudly. "Ma brotha Knight always say, 'Show, don't tell.' Now I showed you what I do. Serve an' protect."

She licked fiercely, looking down on the ice cream. The way her thick black eyelashes constrasted against her milky skin looked sexy as hell. She shifted her feet and something made a crinkle noise. It was the four-day-old newspaper Beamer had been reading earlier. About her. She snatched it up.

"Are you like, a stalker? You planned to meet me!" she accused. "I mean, why would Henry call *you* when I—" She turned as gray as the newspaper.

"Listen, baby girl, you got balls. Wit' five-oh no less! Balls as big and black as mine."

"You are so crass." She crossed one arm over her ripe titties. "Can you say, 'Victoria, you speak with such confidence and courage. I'm impressed with how you think on your feet to resolve problems with finesse.'"

"Naw, I can say, 'We the D-town new dream team,'" Duke said. "The Duke an' Duchess dream team."

"I was thinking I'm actually in a nightmare. But if this is a dream team, then what, exactly, is our game?" She took a big lick, like it would sweeten her situation.

"Manifest destiny fo' my company, Babylon. All my turf in Detroit, we call it Babylon, named after the street we on an' the ancient Arabian city known for the wildest shit in history. Crazy gold, the sexiest goddesses . . . " He let his eyes lick all over this chick who had to be finer than any bitch in the real Babylonia. "An' straight-up ridiculous wild abandon."

"And wickedness and sexual obsessiveness," Duchess added in a way that was sassy but innocent. "So, what do you sell at Babylon?"

Duke tossed his head back and let a deep laugh boom up and out. "We sell what e'rybody want, any kinda way. Iss always a fresh supply, e'ry flava, e'ry style, for e'ry taste. Ain't nothin' like Babylon anywhere, an' you gon' love it."

"What do you sell?"

"Pleasure and protection," he said. "We mostly do parties and patrols. Now, we rollin' west an' east. An' Knight, he got two mo' weeks."

"Of what? Two more weeks of school?"

"He in the pen, framed for somethin' he didn't do. He finally comin' home, so we got a tight deadline. I gotta make a whole lotta shit happen, 'cause by time you meet Knight, you an' me gon' be flexin' from Cali to da Bronx. An' we gon' have my boys wit' da Bang Squad at his comin' home party."

"Why do you sound excited about your brother but—" She looked hard into his eyes. "You have a weird look in your eyes. Like he intimidates you."

WHITE CHOCOLATE

Duke bit down hard. Her comment started that game of hot potato in his head. Instead of hands holding a potato, it was his emotions pitching his brother back and forth, shouting "Love!" and "Hate!" so no area of his body or brain would get burned. Sometimes "Love!" won, other times "Hate!" got the last word. Right now, they were both screaming at equal volume.

"I learned e'rythang I know from Knight an' Prince. So naw, I love 'em to death. They blood. We got a vision."

Victoria's face scrunched with confusion. Her eyebrows drew together, the corners of her mouth drew back, her eyes got big, as if all that would help her figure out what he was saying.

"How do you expect me to help you with your 'vision' to sell protection and pleasure? What in the world! That could mean anything from a condom company to porno flicks. And having a brother in prison, that's serious. Did you guys get audited like my dad?"

Duke imitated her white girl way of talking. "Did you guys get audited like my dad?"

She snarled, "Don't mimic me!"

"You so sexy when you mad. Make me wanna instigate somethin' jus' to see how them pretty lips curl up an' yo' eyes flash like lightnin'."

She bit the waffle cone, crunching as if it would shut him up.

"Iss a'ight, 'cause you gon' be bilingual in a minute."

"Je parle français. So, what's the third language? Español?"

"Naw, Black. Ghetto. Street. Ebonics. You gon' converse like Becky when we be steamin' the Moreno Triplets, but you gon' be rappin' like a hardcore bitch when we deal wit' Izz an' any otha orn'ry-ass ma'fucka."

"Duke, translate. What the hell does *we be steamin'* mean?"

He licked his cone. "Cool it, baby girl. This meeting, it's about turf. About me holdin' the Moreno Triplets to their promise. Just before Prince got shot, he made a pact that Babylon would take ova they turf, from Jersey down to the Keys."

"Sounds like mega-bucks. As in, help me pay my college tuition if I agree."

"Millions, baby. It's a win-win situation for everyone."

"Then why do you need me?"

"To soften them. Yo' exotic face—when I get through makin' you ova to fit my vision—gon' distract 'em."

"So it's like *My Fair Lady* in reverse. He took a street urchin and made her into a proper English lady. Now I'm the next contestant on *Extreme Ghetto Makeover*."

Duke laughed. "You sexy as hell, naturally. How you think Cleopatra made Caesar an' Mark Anthony do whateva the fuck she wanted? The power o' pretty pussy, an' knowin' how to use it to whip any ma'fucka into submission."

Her whole face blossomed into the biggest, most blinding-bright smile she had flashed all day.

"See, baby girl, you gon' be dangerous wit' a Big D!" Laughing, he admired his diamond "D" ring. He felt like a snake charmer—he had to bring it out of her without getting stung himself. "So when these dudes see yo' light-bright face, you gon' come off like beige Barbie wit' a business degree from Harvard."

"Then you'll help me to go to college."

Yeah, Inner-City College, where you gon' major in Streetology, get a masters in Babylonology, an' a PhD in Sexology.

"Anything you need, baby girl."

"Then what's the catch? Daddy always said if something sounds too good to be true, then it probably is."

Duke shook his head. "It's a straight-up equal exchange on the table. I help you, an' you help me make sure they cain't get over on a nigga."

"Get over. Get over what?"

"Take advantage 'cause we from the hood and they from a big white dynasty on a hill. They still gangsta as they wanna be."

"I hope I've never seen them before," Victoria said. "I mean my ex-boyfriend's parents are the richest, but they had some mafia-type friends. This one guy, with slicked-back hair and the most gorgeous Asian girlfriend—"

Duke glanced at traffic on the busy street. Five-oh in an undercover squad car crept past, nodding.

WHITE CHOCOLATE

"Keep your voice down low, on the cool gears," Duke said to Miss Daisy, who was eating that ice cream like she was going to cum. "Don't let it ride up. Slow, steady, cool at all times."

"Duke, I haven't agreed to do anything for you."

"Protection, baby. Just like I protected you twice tonight. From that dog—"

"So it was you! How did you draw so fast?"

"Practice," Duke said. "Wit' Warrior Protection. We guard the hood—old ladies to the bus stop, kids walkin' to school. Twennie-fo'/se'em."

"That doesn't make money." Her words shot back like a question mark.

"We got legit contracts for sports events an' political rallies at all the stadiums an' convention centers in Metro Detroit."

"Oh, then that would earn a lot of money," Duchess said, "and you get minority business status. That's why my dad put my name on the company." A glazed look spread on her face as if her brain had just pushed the in-case-of-emergency TOO MUCH INFORMATION button. She licked her ice cream, staring up at the colorful signs outside the row of restaurants and shops.

"What in the world could I possibly do for you, Duke?"

"You work at HQ. My building is that warehouse down from your grammomma house. It's laid like you gotta see to believe—hundreds of employees, 'bout to be thousands—an' it's all legit. You handle my books, keep things runnin' smooth, and work with my clients to arrange what they need. Travel to the wes' coas' an' eas' coas', help me expand."

"What's in it for me?"

"I set you up to live like you wanna live. You'll have time to go to college and study too. Just think on it tonight, especially when Kay-Kay creep into your sheets, smackin' her lips."

Her eyes widened. "Can we stop for a newspaper, please? I need to look at the Want Ads for a job. And an apartment."

"Who gon' hire the chick on the news who, if you listen to Mr. and Mrs. Mad back at the restaurant, people be thinkin' you jus' like yo' daddy?"

"I can't work for you. I have to get my old life back."

"Look like the media blackwashed that all away," Duke said, peeling away from the curb between two sweet-ass red motorcycles and a black Escalade with silver spoke rims. "Your secret out, shorty. You black and everybody know it now. And once you go black, you can't go back. 'Specially when I can see it bubblin' out your blood."

"What?"

"You ain't wearin' no makeup," Duke said, but ev'a since I saw you, your lips been gettin' redder and redder. I see it. A strong, sexy diva bitch that's beatin' you up inside to escape the stiff-ass way you talk and carry yourself."

"Don't talk to me like that. You don't know my life. Just take me home."

Duke let out a sinister chuckle. "Home, right. Miss Daisy gon' wilt up in that mug. And that other bitch inside you gon' come out, come to me, neva look back. You'll see, 'cause I see it. I'm a visionary, and you the vision."

WHITE CHOCOLATE

Chapter 12

The only vision Victoria had right now was her naked body next to his. As he drove with his left fingers draped so cool over the bottom of the steering wheel, she imagined hers clasped with his, like the posters for that Spike Lee movie, *Jungle Fever*—a black and a white hand, fingers intertwined. She'd never seen a black dick, just Brian's, which was like beige and dark pink when it got hard.

"What? What is that enormous black fist in the middle of the street?" she exclaimed. He stopped at a red light on downtown's huge, car-clogged Jefferson Avenue. "Is it supposed to be there?"

Duke's deep laughter boomed through the car and up into the early evening air. "Damn, you ain't neva even been downtown Detroit?"

"I saw *The Nutrcracker* ballet at the Fox Theatre at Christmas. Daddy took me to the opening of the Hard Rock Café and the Auto Show at Cobo. But I've never—" She was mesmerized by the black iron fist and forearm that were parallel with the ground. It was suspended by wires hanging from the center of a long, pyramid-shaped frame of posts or pipes, like that toy on Daddy's desk with about six silver balls. When he was on the phone, he would always pull one silver ball back, let it fall. Tick, tick . . . then it made a sort of domino effect on all the balls, which swung to the first ball's momentum.

Domino effect . . . that's what happened to Daddy, and it killed him. The investigation, the false claims, the foreclosure, the scary phone calls in the middle of the night, the calm on his face when she found him with his brain put out of its misery of worry and anger and fear.

Now my domino effect, driving around with this guy who wants me to work for him in a world where I have nothing and no one.

"You *lost*," Duke said. "You so deep in thought I need a submarine to bring you back up."

97

Victoria pointed at the fist. "From a distance, you could mistake it for a big black middle finger saying 'Fuck off!' to the world."

"Look like a big black dick, too!" He roared. "Baby girl, if you could see yo' eyes right now!"

"So, what is that thing?"

"Coleman Young, when he was the mayor, he put it up to remember Joe Louis. You know, the boxer."

"So, it's his fist." Victoria studied the forearm and fist suspended from a metal triangle. It was on the strip of land dividing the eight or ten lanes of Jefferson Avenue, which ran from Cobo Center, past the riverfront Hart Plaza, where people gathered for the Motown Hoedown, the biggest July fourth fireworks display in North America, the African World Festival and the Montreux Detriot Jazz Festival. Victoria had heard about them, but Daddy never let her attend. "A fist where the two biggest streets in Detroit come together."

"The seat o' powa," Duke said, thrusting his right hand in the air. "Babylon!"

"It does look kind of intimidating," Victoria said.

"Sho' do," Duke said, nodding toward it. "An' e'rybody got mad when he put it up 'cause they say it look violent. An' like when Jesse Owens 'nem raise they fist wit' a black glove during the Olympics."

"Right, I read about it in history class. The Black Power fist."

Duke imitated her. "The Black Pow-werrrr fist."

As he drove, blasting rap music, she closed her eyes, squeezing her pussy muscles. She stuck her butt deeper into the clean, butter-soft leather bucket seat. It embraced her ass, and her full stomach pressed into her waistband.

Now with her stomach satisfied, an overwhelming hunger for Duke Johnson made her want to yank down her jeans, sit on the steering wheel and spread herself wide open in his face. Her pussy was as pink and creamy as that vat of ice cream inside the bakery.

WHITE CHOCOLATE

How's this for a Michigan cherry? she could tease while popping her pussy-fruit into his mouth.

Her crotch felt like a wild animal screaming and squirming and starving to spread open its lips and suck down that big, juicy sausage bulging in his pants. Yeah, his dick would get squeezed, chewed and slurped up and down by Celeste. Then they could sit quietly for a little while, satisfied and full, until the raging and insatiable hunger made them devour each other all over again.

If Duke felt half as good as Dildo Dick . . .

Victoria smiled. Maybe the fact that she'd been using her dildo would make it easier to take all of Duke. Did that mean she was still a virgin? Would she still feel like a virgin? Would he be able to tell?

Victoria couldn't stop thinking about how it would feel to straddle his lap, kiss him like there was no tomorrow, and slide down on his dick while his giant hands cupped her butt cheeks. He would be like the Greek god Atlas with her whole world in his fingertips.

He was so big and strong, he could lift her up and down. She saw that once, in one of the porno movies she found in Daddy's bedroom while he was out of town. Of course she watched — until she realized it was a video of her own parents having sex! Yuck!

But her mother looked so beautiful and happy. And her father, he had an expression that changed his face so much, she didn't recognize him at first. Victoria would watch the movies (she found a half-dozen, including one of them making love on a tropical beach) every once in a while, to see her mother looking so happy and spellbindingly gorgeous.

The familiar ache to sit on Mommy's lap passed through her. And now it was worse. She couldn't even call Daddy for advice or look into his eyes for comfort. Without a cell phone or numbers for her sister and brother, she had no way to call Melanie or Nicholas. Maybe she could find them and they could save enough to move into an apartment together. The lawyers had taken all of their cell phones, and she did not have contact information for the relatives they were staying with. Were they in equally bad situations?

I can't work for this guy, no matter what definition of legitimate he's working with. Her father always said, "Shady comes in every color." As examples, Daddy had pointed out money launderers and mafia families at the yacht club and high-class events. They were people like that man with slicked-back hair who used to come to Brian's family's functions. He had an exotic Asian girlfriend who stood at his side like a decoration, never talking, just looking super sexy in skin-tight leather cat-suits of every color, leopard print dresses and tiger-striped shoes. Victoria always wondered what it would be like to be her for a day. How would it feel to be that sexy and dress so boldly? But she was a gangster's girl. She was part of a mysterious underworld that Victoria wanted no part of. Not in the suburbs, and not in the inner city, because all of them, whether black or white, were gangsters. Their brilliant business minds—which could have been used to help people—were instead put to work to make money in unscrupulous and illegal ways that no doubt hurt people.

"Duchess." That deep, delicious voice rumbled through her chest, snapping her out of her thoughts. "You thinkin' 'bout my proposal?"

"Kinda," she said over a hot lump in her throat. Her eyes stung with tears. She kept them closed.

I'm stuck in hell. She thought of the works by Faust she'd just read in Honors English. *Do I have to make a deal with the devil just to survive? Could I ever escape? And if I deal with him, will I break my race-sex vow to myself, about Celeste? Then where does that leave me the rest of my life?*

Chapter 13

Duke turned off Jefferson onto Iroquois, where giant oak trees shaded huge, fancy houses built by auto barons like the Dodge family. This would make Duchess feel more relaxed, like he wasn't as much of a hood rat as she thought. For now.

"I've been here," Duchess said softly. "Indian Village. My dad's ex-partner lived right—" She pointed. "There. You should see how they restored it to its turn-of-the-century grandeur. It was even in *Architectural Digest*."

Duke pulled up to a brick colonial with white shutters and pink flowers blooming from window boxes and along the brick walk leading to the white wood double doors.

"Pretty," Duchess said.

Duke got out, grabbed a brown leather backpack from the trunk, and opened her door. "C'mon."

"Who lives here?"

"The real boss," he joked.

"Henry said you're the boss. Is this like, an investor in your company or something?" The curious flash of her silver-blue eyes made his heart pound. His dick swelled harder.

His every cell was on fire, but he had to stay cool. He couldn't confess—yet—that with one look, he'd lost his mind through those windows to her soul. No, Duke would never just blurt out some corny-sounding Casanova bullshit lines like that.

In fact, this was the first time they had ever formed in his head. Milan, she was his childhood girlfriend, but fine as she was, he hadn't felt anything this deep about her. Maybe it was because she could be so evil when she didn't get her way. Maybe it was because she could be so sexy when she wanted something, but as soon as she used sex to get it, she would go right back to being evil.

Duchess, on the other hand, who should have been a raving crazy bitch after what she had gone through, was as cool and as calm as he had been when Prince got killed, when Knight went to prison, and when Pinks staged that hostile takeover of Babylon.

Stupid dead ma'fucka.

"This way," Duke said, keys jingling in his hand as he led her up the sidewalk. He walked behind her, resting his fingertips on her back, so he could watch her ass cheeks pop as she took long strides on her giraffe legs. At the same time, he inhaled her wind trail of pussy and lemon-flower shampoo. He almost moaned, sniffing like a dope fiend.

He put in a key, turned, then pushed open the door.

"Do you live here?" Duchess asked with wide eyes. It smelled like furniture polish and hazelnut gourmet coffee. At the center of the foyer, pink tulips sat in a vase on a table. Above it, the crystal chandelier sparkled with sunlight beaming in through little square windows around the door. Duke watched Duchess check it all out, from the white marble floor to the white-carpeted staircase and the polished banister that led upstairs.

"This is beautiful," Duchess said, turning around and looking up. "Where are we?"

"You'll see in a minute. Hold up." Duke walked down the side hallway to the garage door. He opened it, but inside all he saw were a lawn mower and extra patio furniture.

"This way, baby girl," he said, leading her into the kitchen. "There's a guest bedroom wit' a full bath." He pointed down the tiled hallway. "I know you wanted ta take a shower."

"If you think I'm gonna get naked in a big house alone with you—"

I do, but not right now. Duke kept his face serious, but he wanted to laugh because she was fooling her damn self. *She wish I would just take the pussy and put her outta her horny-ass misery right now.*

"Lock the bathroom door." He handed her a phone. "An' dial 911 if you hear me breakin' it down." Duke smiled. "It should be some stuff yo' size on'a vanity table."

'Cause I put it there, knowin' you'd wanna freshen up when you stepped down into the hood.

WHITE CHOCOLATE

Duchess stared up at him like she was trying to figure out what was really going on. She crossed her arms. "I'm *not* putting on your wife or girlfriend's clothes."

"The tags still on e'rythang. Don't belong to nobody but you. Anything else you need, we can go shoppin'."

She glanced down the hall, which looked like an enchanted garden with all the pink pots of English ivy vines hanging over the high white window sills and walls. She looked at the phone in her palm then glanced back up at Duke.

Damn, she beautiful. That little nose, he just wanted to bite it off. And that skin, he wanted to slurp every inch, suck the pretty out of it. But this definitely was neither the time nor the place. Duke's heart was pounding already about how folks would respond to this visit once they got home.

Duchess sharpened her eyes on him and said, "My dad always advised me to listen to that little voice in my head. The instinct in your gut. Mine is always right. And right now it says this is safe."

"You ain't gotta convince me," Duke said with a laugh.

She spun toward the hall, all that hair slapping him in the chest. If he hated her, or if any other bitch flipped her long-ass hair on him like that, he'd hate her even more. But something about this chick was so humble, so unaware of just how fine she was, it would be impossible to hate her. It was like she was so busy thinking from the inside out, she forgot how she looked from the outside in. Most chicks, especially Milan, were always thinking from the outside in, like, "I'm so fine an' sexy, he *betta* buy me a Prada outfit an' take me to dinner at the Ritz."

That was the opposite of what Momma had taught him, Prince and Knight: "Judge men and women by how they is on the inside. Close yo' eyes an' feel 'em. The looks department be the Devil's workshop. He know how to paint a pretty picture over the wors' nightmare, just ta fool you an' get you into the wors' trouble. An' you cain't escape the nightmare once you done paid big bucks for the artwork."

Duchess's silky-sweet voice snapped him out of the memory.

"Duke," Duchess called, standing in the arched white doorway to the bedroom. "Thank you." She flashed the biggest, brightest smile then closed the door.

Click. It sounded like she put a chair up to it too. Duke's heart pounded as he laughed a little. She was trying to protect herself from her own pussy.

He smiled as he walked into the kitchen, but returning Milan's call and hearing her bitchy attitude made him stiffen and scowl.

"What took you so fucking long to call me back, Duke?" Her voice shot through the phone like every word was a nail. He held the phone away from his ear, hating how she was always trying to sound so white and proper.

He stepped to the white-tiled kitchen island, where the brown backpack sat next to a cake plate full of fresh-baked oatmeal raisin cookies. Duke raised the clear glass lid and sniffed his favorite homebaked treat. He took one, bit down and savored its thick, chewy sweetness.

I bet Duchess pussy jus' like this, washed down wit' a steady stream of her own warm milk.

"Duke!" He went to the refrigerator and grabbed the milk, concentrating on the delicious cookie to block out Milan's voice.

"What evil, stiff-ass bitch," he said, "took ova the sweet, natural Michelle I use' ta love?" He remembered riding his bike with her to their secret spot in the tall grass in the empty lot beside her momma's house on Babylon. They were only six years old, kissing as the wind blew the grass all around them, promising each other that one day they'd get married, have some kids, and be happy.

Right now, if she knew he was fantasizing about loving and fucking Miss Daisy, Milan would straight up try to bite his dick off, chew it up and spit it up his ass. But the thought of touching the bag of bones around her evil spirit made him shiver as if he were watching a scary movie. Even the oatmeal cookie suddenly tasted bad as he thought about sex with Milan.

WHITE CHOCOLATE

"I saw you on TV, Duke. I don't know what you have in mind, but you need to delete any vision you might think you might be having about our new neighbor."

"You one crazy bitch." Duke stuffed the cookie into his mouth as if it were medicine to sweeten her bitterness, just like when Momma would give him honey to soothe a bad cough.

"No," Milan said, "I'm afraid you haven't seen crazy. If you even think about letting that girl usurp my position at Babylon, the position I earned by building everything with you, Knight and Prince—"

"Oh, hell naw." Duke swallowed the cookie. "Listen up. Firs', you been so mad since Mahogani an' the baby moved into Babylon, you been miscountin' money an' makin' mistakes wit' the Squad schedules. Yo' evil ass say you lost the appointment book for the Sluts and the Studs."

Right now, Duke couldn't even picture Milan's face that he'd been kissing more than half his life. His brain drew a blank when he tried to remember what he thought was the finest face in the hood, and the world, for a while. Now, all he felt was evil, like the taste of cold, hard metal, making him remember the time Knight shoved a gun in his mouth to scare him. His big brother was trying to toughen him up, saying something about what that philosopher, Nietzche, said: if something didn't kill you, it would make you stronger.

Knight loved that quote so much, he had it tattooed over his left bicep. And it proved true for Duke, because the next week, he got jumped by some thugs from a hood across town. They pulled a gun, but Duke was one fearless ma'fucka. Now he couldn't say "Boo!" to those same punks without them shitting on themselves.

But fearlessness in Milan's case was what made her so dangerous.

"You was mad about e'rything under the sun," Duke said, "but soon as I show you some love, you had a coincidence an' *found* the book and my twennie-five K you had los' wit' it. So play e'rybody else, Milan, but you don't play The Duke, 'less you wanna lose in the wors' way." Duke glanced down the hallway. The shower was still running behind the closed door.

"You don't scare me, Duke. But if you even think about getting with some dejected suburban slut who's whiter than me, I will show you crazy."

Duke scarfed down another cookie and guzzled milk. "I don' know nobody like that. You an' me ain't married, an' you ain't got no claim on who I talk to or work wit'."

"You belong with me, Duke, the lightest, prettiest girl on the block who gave you two babies and believed your promises that we would get married and rule Babylon."

The hiss of the shower stopped. Duchess would be walking in soon, and she never needed to even hear the name Milan, much less meet the bitch.

"Milan, you need to look in the mirror and see how small a speck you is in Duke's big picture. We grew up together, fucked around, had some kids. Now you work for me. Don't act right, and you know I *will* pull the plug on your glamorous life."

"I'll get immunity and you'll get *life*," Milan said.

"Now you really crazy," Duke said. It was time to take care of her for good. "Maybe you forgot what happened to Sunnie."

"I want to know what happened to us," Milan said. "You don't even call me to check on business." She sounded white as snow until she said "business." It came out "bee-yass-niss," like a certified sistah.

"Duke, how do you know I haven't been dealing with a crisis here with the Sex Squad?"

"You woulda tol' Beamer when I was in my meetin'."

"I need to tell you something very important, Duke."

"Tell me."

"In person."

"Milan, if you tryin' ta script anotha soap opera scene, I ain't comin' to the set. So jus' say it."

"I'm not going to play by your bad rules right now. I'll brief you on everything, including the baby, if you can schedule me into your rotation." *Click.*

WHITE CHOCOLATE

Baby? The baby she wished she could have.

Ain't no way her skinny ass could get pregnant again. The way her hip bones were sticking out lately, that womb was nothing but a hostile environment for his sperm. And as little as they been fucking—he was just turned off by how she was wasting away, a sack of bones with no ass to hold on to—no way could she be knocked up.

This jus' anotha o' Milan tricks. Work wit' tricks all day, schemin' wit' her own the rest o' the time. I ain't got time fo' no drama.

Footsteps in the hallway made his heart hammer, and his skin prickled with sweaty excitement to see Duchess. They'd been apart fifteen minutes and it felt like forever.

She walked toward him wearing the baby blue velour warm-up suit with matching satin gym shoes and a white tank top that held her titties up just right. She was drying her hair with a big, pink towel. Her face was clean and shiny. Her cheeks and lips were naturally red.

"A shower never felt so good," she said. "I was so dirty."

"Come in here," he said, guiding her to the family room off the kitchen, where he sat on a plush, pale green couch.

"Duke, who lives here?" she asked, lowering her ass to the cushion beside him. "Would they mind if I spend the night in that guest bedroom? I mean, just one night. Then tomorrow I'll figure out where I'm going."

"We'll see how it go when you meet the owner," he said, keeping his voice low and steady to mask his excitement. "You handle ya bidness just like me. The mo' shit come at'cha, the cooler you get. E'rybody know, when Duke calm and quiet like a lion, I'm thinkin' about how I'ma pounce somebody or something. An' I get my way e'ry time."

"I noticed that," Victoria said, sitting Indian style on the couch cushion, facing him so that her knee was touching the side of his thigh.

Timbo was pounding, but this was the last place he needed to get busted trying to mix ebony and ivory. Yet.

"During dinner," she said, "when you were watching me eat and walk and talk, you get so still you're like a mannequin. I wanted to reach over and take your pulse."

Duke let out a low, sexy laugh. "Oh, my pulse 'bout as strong as it's gon' get." He raised his hips slightly, shifting to let huge, hard Timbo roll to a looser spot under his white cotton briefs. "My pulse poundin'."

Her big blue eyes cut at him in a way that only a sistah could do. She just didn't know it yet. "Please," she said with her white girl business tone, "whatever private detail you were about to share, keep it to yourself."

Damn, her sexy-ass voice, especially with that prim and proper in-the-boardroom talk, put his dick on swole. Her voice was deep, kind of raspy, not slow but not fast, just right, and every word came out like she was in complete control of how she pronounced each letter. If she could suck his dick into her mouth as elegantly as she blew out words and sentences, Duke was in for one helluva treat. One helluva life.

"You walk like a panther, too," Victoria said. "Like every step has this feline grace, like your joints are liquid and you're just flowing along silently. Like the most powerful, most treacherous king of the jungle."

"Make a nigga scared, too." He laughed, remembering how he pounced on Izz this afternoon. It was exactly how she described it, and she didn't even see it. "Callin' me a treacherous panther. Miss Animal Planet. Baby girl, I could listen to you talk all day long." The lust in his voice hung in the warm air. A fresh waft of hot, clean pussy made him dizzy.

Damn, that girl horny as hell. Prob'ly made herself cum in the shower and she still hot an' bothered.

"You a virgin?" he asked.

She got perfectly still. Her thick black eyelashes lowered then that giraffe neck turned with a slight jerk. She pulled all that black hair to the opposite shoulder and fixed her gaze on him.

He stared back. Her unblinking eyes were like blue ice — cold, hard as picks. That would come in handy when she was negotiating for him. Otherwise, all he would have to do was blow on her horny ass and she'd melt in a creamy puddle all over his face. Yeah, someday very soon she was going to squat on his face, take some tongue up that virgin pussy, and blow her nut all over his nose, cheeks, mouth and eyes.

"Baby girl, if you think you can beat the Duke in a stare-down—"

"You have panther eyes," she said in a way that made her lips look extra sexy. They stuck out, pouting and shining like she had just licked them.

"I won!" she laughed. "You looked at my lips!"

His body and eyes were still, facing her as she tossed her head back, laughing.

"Tough guy." She giggled. "But seriously—"

"Seriously my ass." His hard voice cut her off. "Don't trick me."

"Don't lose your own challenge," she said with a slight neck jerk that said *Fool!* "See, look at your eyes right now. They shimmer like a panther's eyes. Like, they're so rich in color and texture. During our stare-down, they were tough and like, aroused. Now they're analyzing the situation."

Timbo was jumping with every word.

Someday I'm gon' fuck her while she talkin' just like that.

"Damn," he exclaimed. If she kept it up, he was going to have to taste that intelligent language. Kiss her. Suck that skill right out of her mouth and try to pull it into himself. That was why she was going to work for him, so she could literally be his mouthpiece, an extension of his brain.

"My dad was like that," Victoria said slowly. "After my mom died, he would just sit and stare at people. Like he was figuring out who was on his side, and studying people. Then, boom. He put everything he'd learned to work and built his business bigger and better."

"That's my plan for Babylon," he said, his lust now turbo-charged by exciting visions of her at his side, building their kingdom bigger and better than any inner-city thug could ever imagine.

"What's that?"

"My company. You'll see, tomorrow, when you agree to work for me."

"I can't work for you," she said, crossing her arms. "Don't say that again."

His heart skipped a beat then pounded harder than ever. The hot surge of blood went straight to his dick. It made Timbo *hurt*.

A nigga could get some lead pointed toward his head, just to scare him, for talking to Duke Johnson like that. Cussed out, beat down, showed out. But this white bitch was talking to him like she was the boss, and that hard glint in her eyes, sharp as a knife blade, as she sliced a look his way—

"Damn, baby girl, you like that movie, *Clueless*, about them valley girl chicks in California. Ain't got no clue. You got balls as big as mine, and ain't scared to swing 'em right in Duke Johnson face!" His voice rose on his last name in a mock shocked tone.

Her cheeks turned almost as red as her lips. She crossed her legs, squirmed her ass deeper into the seat. The idea of that hot pussy cradled inside the baby blue velour, shooting flames against the couch, made Duke want to lift her up and pull her down on the telephone pole that was jolting so hard it felt like it could split his pants.

But footsteps in the hallway made his dick deflate. Instantly.

Chapter 14

Victoria felt more hope than she had in a week when an older woman's cheerful voice echoed into the family room. Maybe it was Duke's mom or his aunt, and she would let Victoria stay there until she figured out where in the world she was going to live. Anywhere but that horrible house of hell on Babylon Street.

"My baby boy," the woman called.

His expression was still cool and calm, but his eyes flashed something different than she'd seen all afternoon and evening: nervousness. He stood, smiling like a kid who wanted his mom to tell him he'd been a good boy.

"Lawd ha'mercy," the woman called. "Ma baby boy come see his momma."

Victoria smiled, letting all the love in the room give her the hug she'd been aching for all week. Not that she expected a hug from Duke's mom, but she was giving off such strong mother love, it was enough for Victoria too.

The woman, who was a good foot shorter than her son, whisked toward them, raising her hands to grasp Duke's cheeks. She was wearing a pink straw hat with big flowers on top and a delicate net covering her full, bronze face. Her pretty pink dress was belted against her trim hourglass. Its chiffon skirt floated behind her as she approached on white pumps and stockings that matched the satin gloves dangling from the pink straw purse over her shoulder. Her face glowed as her dark brown eyes focused only on Duke, as if Victoria were invisible.

"My baby, Knight! You come home early!" The woman's sing-song voice echoed with gratitude so strong it gave Victoria goosebumps.

"Naw, Momma, it's me, Duke," he said as her hands cupped his cheeks and he wrapped his arms around her back for a hug.

"Lawd ha'mercy. I miss that boy so much I be 'lucinatin' my baby boy done turnt into my biggest boy," she exclaimed, stroking the back of his bald head. "Call me bad as e'rybody else, mixin' the two o' you up like you one an' the same."

Duke's jaw muscle flexed and something bad flashed in his eyes. Did he resent that he looked like his older brother?

"That's okay, Momma. Two more weeks you'll have him back." He glanced at that brown leather backpack on the coffee table. "I brought—"

"You brought Ellie Mae wit' a suntan up in ma home, boy." She kept hugging Duke, but her voice turned from sweet and soft to razor-sharp. "You tryin' to follow in yo' big brotha footsteps? How you 'spect me to love somebody who look like the reason Knight in jail? Ain't no half-white girl welcome in ma house."

"Momma, she black."

Victoria's brows drew together. *I am?* If that was what it would take to sweeten this lady's voice, then—

"Cain't nobody who grew up that white be black in they heart," she said. "She might could be mulatta, but hist'ry show you cain't neva trus' somebody wit' that much enemy flowin' through they blood. Knight the locked-up proof o' that."

"Momma—"

"You wanna see twenty-one next week, don't let Knight hear 'bout ya new little friend. An' don't ev'a let 'im see you makin' a mockery o' his sit'ation."

Duke's tall, broad shoulders appeared shorter and more narrow as she spoke, as if his mother's words were hammering him down.

"Momma, she different," he said softly. "This the girl we seen on the news when I brought you Chinese food Tuesday night. You said—"

"Boy, don' tell me what I saw or said. That was in general, not a invitation to come up in here wit' her an' you lookin' all love-struck. Now y'all go 'head."

Victoria's heart was pounding. She was almost as scared as when that pit bull came at her, when the police approached

112

outside the restaurant. What in the world happened between Knight and a white girl that got him sent to prison? And how could this lady in pink who looked at Duke with so much love possibly transfer her hate for Knight's white female friend onto Victoria?

She doesn't even know me. She's letting the bad feelings she has about the whole White race taint her view of me. Just like Brian's parents and Tiffany's parents. They did know me, like a daughter, yet their negative attitudes about the Black race made them hate me too. And all of them, just like Duke's mother, said they couldn't trust me.

The white people who used to love her hated her blackness. Now this black lady wouldn't love her either, because she hated white. And all of them were hating her based on their malice toward the whole race, not her personally. She hadn't done anything but show, and crave, love.

This is so unfair. It had nothing to do with what a sweet, intelligent, polite girl she was. And judging how big, bold Duke had that wimpy expression and even wimpier posture under his mom's disapproving glare, Victoria was going to keep her lips zipped.

Chapter 15

Duke could not believe he exposed himself like that. He never let anybody see the power his mother had over him. Nobody. And the only person who had even more juice over him than Momma? Knight. Momma was wrong comparing Duchess to that bitch whose family went crazy when they found out she was trying to kick it with Knight.

Duchess one o' us. Momma gon' see. Soon.

As for now, the sooner he and Duchess drove away, the better. Maybe when Momma opened the backpack and saw the cash, she would feel better. And in time, she would warm up to Duchess.

She will. It ain't a question.

It was just a matter of Duke bringing out the black in this beauty, and Momma would warm up in a Motor City minute.

Something pink flashed to his right. Duke turned. Momma was in the front doorway, throwing Duchess's sweater, jeans, pink panties and bra and red sandals out on the front walk.

"Oh my God," Duchess gasped with huge eyes.

Momma slammed the door.

Duke walked up to collect her clothes. He folded them and put them in the trunk.

"I'm sorry she actin' like that," Duke said softly as he drove away from the curb. "In time she'll see."

"I guess I should get used to arousing hatred in complete strangers," Duchess said in a way that made his heart hurt. "Now what? I am not going back to that filthy house with dogs and smoke and roaches."

"I know a spot where we can talk and relax for a minute." Duke turned onto five-lane Jefferson Avenue, driving past apartment buildings on the river to the Belle Isle Bridge. He loved how the bridge's white arcs extended across the deep blue

114

WHITE CHOCOLATE

Detroit River to the lush green island park. It was city folks's only place to play on a hot September night like this.

"Did you say relax?" She turned to him, glaring as if he were crazy. "Take me to my grandmother's. They find bodies on Belle Isle. People get shot there!" Her head snapped and a sistah-rhythm rang in her words. "And if black people hate my appearance so much, I am not tryin' to be somebody's target practice."

A laugh from deep in his gut made Duke toss his head back. He cracked up at the deep blue sky.

"This gon' be quick," he said.

"What! Turn around!"

"It's your transition, baby girl. Your fade ta black. Know this at all times: Anyplace you go wit' The Duke, anytime, you safe. I rule D-town. Don't nobody mess wit' The Duke."

He pulled into the first parking lot near the river's edge. The setting sun was a huge orange fireball casting a wide red stripe over the rippling river. The mirrored round towers of the General Motors world headquarters in the Renaissance Center looked like five gold fingers stretching into the pink sky.

"What if people decide to mess with you if they think you're havin' jungle fever?" Victoria glanced around at black folks barbecuing at picnic tables, fishing and rolling past in SUVs with the jams blasting. "If you expect me to sit here chit-chatting—"

"Ghetto survival lesson numba one: Be fearless. If you scary, e'rybody smell it. If you act like you the boss, like cain't nobody touch you, then people respect that."

"My dad told me that too."

"Then do it."

"He meant in business."

"If you ain't scared here, then you won't be scary in a board room facin' some pit bull ma'fucka who wanna rip yo' throat out if he don't get his way." Moreno's sneaky eyes—all three of those dudes were just as sneaky as the next—flashed in Duke's mind. Victoria Winston would disarm those sleazy bastards so tough, none of them would even know their own name.

115

"Duke, when you say I'm scary, that means I scare you."

You do, but I ain't neva gon' confess it. He stared back, silent and still.

"If you say 'I'm scared,' that means 'I feel afraid.' The words 'scary' and 'scared' are not interchangeable."

"Let me go get an apple for the teacher. Ain't that what white kids do? At my school, kids gave teachers a knock upside the head."

She leaned close. His lips parted. Was she doing a 180, about to kiss him?

"See, your eyes." She stared the same way that doctor did in the emergency room when Duke cut his eye as he was trying to save Prince. "Panther eyes."

"So, doc, you ain't scared I'm 'bout to pounce your fine ass?"

"You want something from me. You wanna butter me up."

"Ain't like you got no chips."

"I am my own trump card." She raised her chin, poking her chest out. "And only I choose how and when to play it."

"Damn, girl. Soundin' just like me."

"See," she said, her hot breath tickling his cheek as she stared into his right eye. "When you get excited, your eyes sparkle, like onyxes, these beautiful black jewels. My mom had an onyx choker and earrings, but they didn't sparkle as much as her eyes."

The sadness in her eyes made his heart hurt.

"But what am I thinkin'?" When she looked into his eyes, could she see the fantasy film strip playing his mind, of them fucking on the hood of this car in the orange haze of sunset, right here on Belle Isle? Could she see how he wanted to bend over that round ass and bury Timbo deep up in that virgin timberland, make her cum so hard she wouldn't be staring hard at anything but him when she begged to get fucked senseless all over again?

"Well—" She sounded real scientific. "Since thoughts are electricity popping between the neurons, I mean the cells in our brains—"

WHITE CHOCOLATE

This chick was seriously concentrating on his eyeball. Her face was close enough to kiss. If she didn't move back and stop pushing her left titty up against his arm, making her soft, sweet sex smell make him want to pounce like that panther she was describing—

Duke shivered, not just with lust but with fear, because when he kissed her and she agreed to work for him, when she became his Duchess ruling over Babylon with him, could he handle that? Just like Momma always said: "Be careful what you ask for."

The only successful relationships—partnerships—Duke had seen between a man and a woman in love were on TV. He'd never met his own daddy. Never knew any kids whose daddies were around for a long time, living like the ridiculous-ass Huxtables. What made him think he could succeed at it himself?

Because I'm The Duke, and when I want somethin', I make it happen. According to my vision. Just like Ramses. And so it is written, and so it is done.

"We literally think at the speed of light," Duchess said.

"I'm gon' kiss you at the speed o' light if you don't stop teasin' me."

"Your eyes captivated me," she said with that scientific stare into his eyeball, "when we met at Gramma Green's. The way your irises shift, it's so cool, like I see these fascinating sparkles of bronze and copper and onyx all set in dark brown velvet."

The way her lips were wrapping around all those big words and blowing them out, right in his face, it was just too much. If there were a big CONTROL switch in Duke's brain and he had been holding the lever back as tightly as he could, then something just sucked away all his strength and he let go. Let that ma'fucka slam into the red, alarm-ringin' OUTTA CONTROL zone. It could have been worse, in the black, LOBOTOMIZED BY DUCHESS PUSSY zone. Naw, right now the red zone just meant he had to kiss her.

Duke pressed his mouth to hers. Her words jammed into his lips. She tried to close her mouth, to pull away, to push his chest

117

with her long, elegant fingers, but the scent of her sex coming up like a cloud from her pussy let him know that her mind over matter didn't mean a thing when he took control of her body. She got still. Her lips were open, letting him nibble them like the juiciest barbecued ribs in sweet-spicy sauce that been smoking all day, the smell making his mouth water for hours. Now he was going to slowly savor every bit, knowing he could feast on this for a lifetime.

Chapter 16

Victoria felt dizzy. She hated that Duke's hot mouth on hers was erasing every bit of stress, sadness, anxiety and fear. She loved the physical sensations of his lips, his delicious, expensive cologne mixed with his macho-as-hell guy smell, the huge bulk of his body, his exotic dark skin, and the tenderness in his eyes.

His affection feels so good to my love-starved body, mind and soul. This was the first time she had been touched since all those hugs at the funeral, and her whole body was aching for a warm touch, for assurance that she could somehow get her normal life back — her safe, pampered, privileged life back. She could go to sleep right there because when she closed her burning eyes, the physical sensations of his kiss sucked her mind and body into a luscious lullaby where she was sure he would hold her in his arms and rock her all night long.

"Mmmm." Her heart pumped boiling blood with such ferocity that her ears were ringing. It was threatening to drown out her resolve to keep her mix-race sex power in check. Duke didn't know it and wouldn't believe it, but by kissing her, he was literally flirting with suicide. He would laugh if she tried to tell him, but every second longer that he electrified her soul like this, he was unleashing her danger within. Danger that would be unstoppable if they went to second, third and fourth base.

No way. But never had she been kissed like this. Duke's lips were so soft and full and gentle. His breath was clean and slightly spicy. His nose against hers was more warm satin against her face. He nibbled slowly, and she responded the same way. It was the total opposite of Brian's frenzied oral assault with pursed-hard lips.

I could do this 'til I die.

Just this afternoon, at first glance, Duke Johnson looked like the worst stereotype of an inner-city, drug-dealing gang member

119

thug. But now she was kissing him and loving it. Was this what he meant by her transformation, her fade to black?

One of Duke's giant hands raised up. He ran his fingertips down her hot cheek, as if touching to prove she was real.

She sucked his bottom lip into her mouth, wishing he would do the same to her clit right now, because Celeste was writhing like a wild pink animal trying to claw her way out of these comfy velour pants. Even the blue panties fit perfectly, but now they were so wet, Victoria was sure she'd look like she peed on herself if she stood up. Tonight, she would stroke her pussy again.

I have no idea where I'm going to sleep tonight. I am not going back to Gramma Green's house.

Right now, she would be happy to spend the night right here, kissing him, not thinking about tomorrow or school or her life or her dead parents or her femme fatale mix-race sex power. Nope, if she could stay in this safe, innocent bubble, kissing this gorgeous knight in a shining Porsche at sunset after he rescued Alice from Ghettoland . . .

Can't stand the hand that fate just slammed and rammed me, damned me. Don't understand this man who planned to demand that I hand him my soul that he stole with one look, all it took, and I'm hooked on this god. Yes, this god whose eyes can't disguise love 'til he dies. No lies, just whys. Why is it me that he sees on his dream team? Yes, dream team. I will scream if he touches the seam between my legs. Make me beg —

No, I will never beg.

She begged Brian so many times to kiss her pussy after she'd given him enough oral sex to make his eyes pop. But all he could do was talk about "secretions" and "period blood" and "yeast infections," which she'd never even had. "It's disgusting," he'd say. When he begged her to finally go all the way, she demanded to know why he wanted to stick his penis — without a condom — into a place he'd called disgusting.

Thank God I never had intercourse with that jerk!

A soft moan from Duke — a deep, wonderful sound that vibrated through her chest — drew her from her thoughts. Would

WHITE CHOCOLATE

Duke kiss her there? Would she have to ask? Would his giant dick feel as good as movie stars made it look on the silver screen?

Suddenly, her lips felt cool. Exposed. His mouth was like a thousand feathers dancing over her cheek—soft, slow, airbrush kisses that made Victoria's head swirl. Over her nose, across her forehead, down her eyebrows and onto her eyelids. He was kissing her eyelids with such exquisite softness, she gasped. Moaned. Her eyes burned with tears.

Love. That was love, kissing someone's eyelids like that. For a moment, she had no mental picture of him, couldn't remember what he looked like, couldn't even think of his name. She had never felt this in her brain, her body or her spiritual being. The feeling was similar to the rock-solid sense of comfort and security she had felt with her parents, but this was more delicious. Intoxicating. Exhilirating.

And terrifying.

Oh my God. He sucked both her lips between his then ran his tongue between them. Victoria moaned. She grasped his jaw, her fingertips on his hot, thick, baby-soft neck. She had to suck on it, taste it, smell it. Her lips trailed down his jaw.

The rosy haze of sunset was casting a surreal glow, as if this were a scene in a movie she was watching and it wasn't really happening to her, even though her chest was rising and falling violently. For the first time ever, she was panting with need. Sure, she had breathed heavy with Brian, but he never made her feel dizzy. Never made her tingle down to her fingertips with the desire to do that mysterious act that men and women were supposed to love so much.

That was so good it killed Mommy.

Silvery explosions of fear and panic and resolve snapped her brain to attention for a second, but they were splashed down, melted, drowned by the gush of molten lava that was her body's blood boiling away her brain's ability to reason and control her lips, her limbs, and her pussy.

Her tongue trailing down Duke's neck inspired him to tip his chin up, offering a wide plane of delicious, dark chocolate skin. Victoria inhaled it loudly.

"Oh my God, you smell so good," she whispered. Her mind was spinning. "And you're so soft." Her wide-open mouth took in his flesh, sucking, tickling the sensitive nerves underneath.

"Oh, baby girl," he groaned. "Feel like fireworks in my neck."

She squirmed in the seat, rubbing her clit against the crotch of her pants, squeezing her pussy muscles. She could cum just like this.

No! I can't. This is beyond wrong. I have to stop.

But as she nuzzled his neck and ran her hands over his rock-hard shoulders and pecs, wishing she had the nerve to touch the huge bulge in his pants, he was as irresistible as Mrs. Fields brownies. His lips and his skin were as moist and sweet and rich-tasting as her favorite confection, but if she could exercise and burn off the extra calories from a brownie, how could she make amends with herself for this? For shimmying from the white elite at the top of the socio-economic ladder, all the way down into the black pit of inner-city blight. How could she ever climb back up and out? If she got involved with this guy even for a minute, if he were a true thug, then he would never let her leave. Or maybe she'd get tangled up in his illegal enterprises and get in trouble with the law. Maybe she'd get pregnant.

She stiffened. Pulled away. Leaned her head back on the seat. Languid, she kept her eyes closed, slowly wiped her mouth with the back of her hand.

"Please take me away."

Chapter 17

Duke tapped the stereo to turn on his favorite R. Kelly CD as they crossed back over the Belle Isle Bridge. Beamer better have his ass back at Babylon with a good explanation about why he hadn't answered his phone when Duke called from the restaurant. Twice. It wasn't like Beamer's goofy ass could forget what happened the last time he didn't pick up the fucking phone when Duke called.

As he drove, glancing at the dark blue river under the shadows of sunset, he flexed his jaw muscle to bite down the anger he felt toward Beamer and mixed-up-in-the-head Duchess. They needed to straighten out a few things before they got back to Babylon Street, which was just a few minutes away on the East Side.

"Yo, Miss Daisy." She was still lying back with her eyes closed. "If you tryin' to snooze so you can wake up from this black dream, I got some news you can use as a reality check."

Her nipples poked through her shirt.

Timbo was an iron rod. Damn, he couldn't stay mad at her because she was so damn sexy. But that was what got him in trouble with Milan—being blinded by her sex and not seeing the evil scheming in them eyes.

Naw, Duchess was different. The complete opposite, as a matter of fact, so however he was feeling right now, it was all right. It was all going to work out perfectly, according to his vision.

Part of him wanted to wait until Duchess was ready, which wouldn't be long. If he changed his mind, he had plenty of pussies back at Babylon to take care of it in the meantime. Chanel, yeah, she was looking so fucking sexy at the party today. She'd be the one he'd call. But she was all sex.

I want more. A chick who excite my body an' my brain. Any other bitch who teased him like Duchess just did would never get away with it. He'd have something loud to say. Not that he'd do anything. Duke never took pussy that wasn't offered. Shit, this afternoon he didn't even take the pussy that was offered. But if a chick were a tease, he'd tell her something about herself, to warn her about other brothas who'd say any kiss like that—and on the neck, too?—was an open invitation to some buck-wild fucking. Period.

But Miss Daisy, being in such a clueless state of mind, was so horny she didn't know up from down. No surprise then, that one taste of Duke and she was hooked. She would be back for more, especially after that nasty-ass cousin of hers tried to do a dyke dive on her tonight. If losing her daddy was making her feel anything like Duke had felt when Prince got killed, her mind was as mushy as a bowl of grits right now. He was surprised she hadn't straight-up lost it, at least for a minute.

"I believe I can fly," he sang softly as they wove through traffic. "I believe I can touch the sky."

She slapped the stereo, but rather than turn it off, she switched it to the radio. A male newscaster who sounded excited and sinister was saying, "—new developments in the suicide scandal of millionaire businessman Dan Winston. The IRS is now producing documents that prove the suburban family man was laundering money for a powerful crime cartel that is expected to be named in an indictment."

Victoria sat up, eyes wide open, reaching to poke the dial into silence, but her fingers stopped mid-air.

"Authorities are also re-opening the investigation into the mysterious death of Winston's young black wife, and are now trying to locate the couple's three biracial children for questioning."

"Oh my God," she whispered, turning as white as her teeth.

"One daughter in particular, Victoria, worked in Winston's offices and may have crucial information about his suspicious business dealings."

Duke focused hard on the metallic green Crossfire sport coupe ahead of them. His left hand kept a cool grip on the bottom of the black leather steering wheel, but inside, he was grinning like a mug.

I got her now. She gotta hide.

She would hide in style, though, at Babylon, doing things that would flip a big-ass middle finger at those fed ma'fuckas who killed her daddy and now wanted to rape her fine ass with their wicked ways of the white world.

And what better way to hide than to turn black?

Chapter 18

Victoria slapped the stereo button.

"Oh . . . my . . . God. They say it like I'm some armed and dangerous mafia princess. I'm eighteen!"

She crossed her arms hard. Her bottom lip poked out and trembled. That news report set off a sob that was slicing through her gut, squeezing her chest, threatening to burst out of her sleep-deprived body.

No, I will not have a breakdown in front of Duke. Daddy said never let 'em see you sweat. She maintained her hard, serious tone.

"I'm never gonna talk to those wicked pricks again. After Daddy died, they questioned me with this accusatory tone, as if I'd shredded all the documents then pulled the trigger myself!"

Actually, she had fed box after box of files into the shredder, all late on a Wednesday night while Daddy rummaged through boxes of papers he'd pulled out of the storeroom. Was he trying to hide something wrong that he'd done? Or had he been wrongly accused and wanted to make sure nothing in the office could be used against him?

That sob zig-zagged up her neck, making her throat swell into a hot, aching lump. Her head was light, spinning like a tornado inside. Fatigue fogged her mind.

If she had helped Daddy destroy evidence of wrong-doing, did that make Victoria guilty of a crime? If the feds caught her, could they prosecute her and send her to jail?

"Miss Winston," Duke spoke with a cool, flat tone. "They got you on a BWB."

"No, I am totally innocent." The corners of her mouth curled down. That sob was surging up, ricocheting around her mouth with her words. "I'm the victim! I have no parents, no nothing, now I'm thrown into the ghetto with a perfect stranger . . . driving around aimlessly with no place to sleep tonight."

WHITE CHOCOLATE

Duke swerved to the right. He screeched to a stop in front of a tall apartment building.

"Now I really can't go back to Gramma Green's. The FBI is after me! Right?"

The sob shot out. It was a gut-churning groan that filled her burning eyes with tears. Hot droplets spilled down her cheeks. Her shoulders shook. She gulped air, exhaled hard. She couldn't let Duke see her like this. He might think she was weak. Her open palms met her face as she bent toward her lap. There, in the darkness of her hands, with stinging eyes closed, she sobbed into the baby blue velour of her long legs.

A huge, hot hand stroked circles on her back. It was as if he were smoothing over her jagged emotions. His hand on her back, rubbing in slow, gentle circles, reminded her of the way her mom used to tuck her in bed and tell stories while she rubbed her back.

"Let it out, baby girl." Duke's deep voice was like a cozy blanket over her senses. "I got'cha back. I always got'cha back, baby girl."

Victoria's every cell trembled as she expelled a week's worth of anger and anguish and anxiety. She was breathing violently, loudly sucking down lungfuls of air then heaving forward as her lungs flung it out just as quickly. Was she hyperventilating?

I gotta get a grip on myself before Duke drops me off at the mental ward at Detroit Receiving Hospital. Wouldn't that make a hot news story! Never! I will make it. And I'll be bigger and better than anyone ever imagined. So much so, they won't even know it's me.

How? She was as clueless about the world as Duke said she was. Green. Naïve. Totally unprepared to make her way in what looked like a wicked world. But she knew, deep down, she could do it. Duke would help her. She would figure out a way to make it happen so that she would be untouchable if things came crashing down like they did for Daddy. Whether he was right or wrong.

"Duke," Victoria whispered, rising. Her face felt hot, wet and swollen, just like her pussy. "I have to tell you something."

127

His eyes glowed with tenderness as he said, "My station is tuned to all Duchess, all the time. Ev'a since I firs' seen you on the news last week."

"Well I got a news flash, and I can already hear you saying 'ridiculous.'"

He smiled.

"I have like, a sex curse. It could hurt you."

"A curse," he said playfully. "You mean like a witch? You already put me under a spell."

"Stop laughing!" she shouted to stop another sob from exploding up, out, at him. "You and the whole world think I'm a stupid little girl who—"

He grabbed her wrist. His touch made her gasp. If only she could press up to his chest, let him wrap his arms around her trembling body, and just sleep in the soft, sleek protection of this sexy panther named Duke Johnson.

"Ooooh, them eyes stormin', like lightnin' shootin' at me."

And they'll strike you down if I'm not careful.

A fresh, hard sob made Victoria burst into tears. Her whole body was shaking, hurting with sadness, fear, extreme sleepiness. She was crying like a baby. She couldn't stop. Didn't want to stop. Didn't care what he thought. She bent at the waist, cupping her face in her hands as her knuckles pressed into the soft velour covering her knees.

What if she just gave up? What if she just gave in? She could let her sex-crazed body take over her mind, let her circumstances take over her life, let her curiosity run free into the darker side of her heritage. Her first grade school picture in Gramma Green's living room flashed in her thoughts.

My roots really are here, on the black side. The white side doesn't want me, never has. I could see Daddy's relatives in the next car and wouldn't know they were my own blood.

But the delicious-smelling man leaning over to stroke the back of her head, with the soft, soothing lullaby voice and the warmth she felt without opening her eyes, was all she had right now. It felt like more than she'd ever had outside of her mother's lap and Daddy's hugs and guidance to groom her into an intelligent person in business and in life.

But how can that be? Duke and I are opposites.

Or are we?

Sobs made her whole body tremble under his gentle stroke on her back. The overwhelming grief and anger and unknowing of the moment swirled in her head.

"Iss a'ight, baby girl," Duke whispered into her hair. "I'd be scared, too, if I was fallin' in love with some big black dude from the hood. An' come to find out the feds was after me too? Shoot, you deserve to go *off*! In full effect."

"If you knew the truth, you wouldn't touch me." She sobbed, feeling light-headed. "My curse could hurt both of us. Plus if I work for you, those blood-thirsty investigators—"

"Would never find you."

She raised up, staring at him through tear-blurred eyes. "This is so bizarre I feel dizzy. The job you have in mind would only get me in more trouble, whatever you do at your so-called company. Whoever you are!"

"Yo' stomach full?" he asked softly.

"I could've found something to eat—"

The tenderness in his eyes hardened. He had a scolding tone when he said, "An' I coulda lef' yo' white ass in yo' Grammomma house wit' roaches, pit bulls an' yo' dyke-ass cousin. I coulda let that dog attack yo' pretty face. I coulda let you go hungry. So, go back tonight and think about exactly who I am. Duke Johnson the hand that feed you. So don't bite."

"I already did," she said with a sassy tone. She sat up straight, staring hard-as-nails right back into his beautiful onyx eyes. "I bit you on your neck. And you loved it. Now, what crime did you say they got me on?"

Disbelief flashed in Duke's gaze. Then he said, "A BWB."

"What in the world is that?"

"Breathing While Black."

"I'm not—"

"Ain't no gray area in them white ma'fuckas' eyes. One drop of nigga blood, you black. So now, to them cock-suckin', sell-they-own-momma-up-the-river FBI cats, you black. And they wanna get'cha, 'cause they couldn't get'cha daddy. He gone. Stay wit' me, baby girl, an' they'll neva fin' Victoria Winston. She jus' changed her name to The Duchess."

Duke screeched into traffic. She laid her head back, staring up at the darkening sky. Suddenly, a rhyme spun in her mind. She recited it with spoken word rhythm. "I'm so confused, bein' used as a news scandal muse."

Duke turned. His eyes sparkled with intrigue.

"Don't know where to go, feelin' so sad, so mad, so bad, 'cause the life I had," she looked closer into his eyes, "went up in gun smoke. A cruel joke, like a yoke around my neck. What the heck am I doin', thrown into the hood? Am I no good? Misunderstood?"

"Yeah, baby. Rap that." Duke smiled, touching the stereo. A deep bass beat by Bang Squad played under her poem.

"Now I'm black, catchin' flack, with a lack of money. It's not funny. My life was honey, now it's—" She hit the radio. "That music is distracting."

"You rappin'. Tha's all rap is, rhymes wit' music."

"I suppose you want me to put pasties on my boobs and say vulgar things about sex. I'm a poet, not a rapper chick."

"A flower by another title still a flower," Duke said, trying to remember what he learned in eighth grade English.

"Ugh, get it right or don't say it. 'A rose by any other name would smell as sweet.'"

"You a'ight, baby girl," Duke said with a laugh.

She laid her head back, yawning like she could sleep for three days, but soon as he turned onto Babylon, she turned white as a ghost. Her pretty hands gripped the sides of her seat. She shook her head, fear flashing in her eyes. Her chest was rising up and down quickly like niggas had a tendency to do when Duke pulled them aside and evaluated their performance at Babylon.

Duke ached at the sight of Duchess looking so scared.

WHITE CHOCOLATE

Ain't no way I'm gon' let her back up in Miss Green house. She mine now.

Chapter 19

I'm a dead fool.

Beamer's whole body shook as he sped down the Lodge Freeway after leaving Milan's hotel room. He had to get back to Babylon with a good excuse for why he didn't answer his phone when Duke called twice. Doing that once was enough to get jacked. But twice?

'Cause I was fuckin' his girl?

If Milan still was Duke's girl. She wasn't officially, because Duke was probably on Lily White right now, getting her hooked on his power—and his dick. But with Duke being so super-mack, the unstated rule was "once his lady, always his lady." This made her off limits for anybody else to take a taste. Or a fuck. Or scheme an overthrow.

"What I'ma do?" Beamer cried into the loud beat of Tupac inside the black Hummer. It was Babylon's Hummer, of course. Beamer wouldn't have shit if Duke hadn't given him life two years ago.

Fo' real.

"I mus' have a death wish. Nineteen years old, plottin' my own murder."

By bein' stupid. Clownin' wit' my job, my life.

He'd been writing out the instructions with his own nut. Why hadn't he known Milan couldn't be trusted, that trying to work with her was like trusting Judas? Impossible. He was thinking with his dick, that was why. What could he do now? Would it be smart to play like he wasn't sitting on the fence, waiting to get shot from both sides?

He could tell Milan that he wanted out, but she would bust on him, no joke. If he tried to tell Duke it was a set-up, boss man would ask why he was in a hotel room with her in the first place. Then he'd ask why the fuck Beamer didn't have the sense to keep his dick in his pants when she started scheming and using sex to get what she wanted, like she'd been doing since she was born.

He could confess to Duke what happened. Beamer let that conversation play out in his head, but he felt like he had an audience: all the ghosts of too many other dead motherfuckers who also jacked up their own lives and got themselves killed. They were proof that nobody could play Streetopoly or Ghetto-opoly by making up their own bad-ass rules as they went along, especially when they were playing against The Duke.

"Listen up, Massa Duke," Beamer said out loud. "I was plottin' my coup wit' yo' girl in a hotel room, see, an' she was lookin' so freakin' sexy, I jus' had to tap that ass, see, an' then she showed me she videotaped it all. *Hell* naw."

Beamer accelerated toward the back of a semi-truck. Nobody would miss him. He hadn't seen his parents since Mama went crazy from having eight kids, no food, no money and some kinda VD that ate away at her brain. He never had a daddy to even know what happened to him. Beamer didn't even know his name. Grandmama was dead. His cousins were all in jail. Auntie June, who named him Beamer, was laid up with diabetes and every other health problem. Beamer didn't even have a female to call his own, and Duke had made him cut off all ties with old friends, fearing he would leak information to them.

I cain't get or keep a girlfriend o' my own 'cause I'm so goddamn goofy. Why am I even here? Jus' takin' up space.

It would be best to just put himself out of his misery before Duke found out he fucked Milan. Hearing that would be bad enough, but seeing it on video too?

"Shit!" Beamer looked forward at the back of the eighteen-wheeler. He slammed his foot down full force on the gas pedal.

Chapter 20

No, I can't faint. Victoria focused hard on the garbage heaps, rusting cars and abandoned houses on Babylon Street. The surrealness of it—like the set of one of those futuristic movies about a city destroyed by war—made it harder to hold onto her consciousness.

I'm okay. I'm okay. I'm awake . . .

She felt like she was about to faint, like that time last year when Brian told her she had a fat ass and she didn't eat for nearly a week. Right now, she felt the same as she did back then, when an ear-ringing blackness rumbled into her brain. She closed her eyes and slept until her sister Melanie shook her awake, forced her to drink orange juice and eat a good meal.

"Duke," she said. Her voice sounded like it was at the end of a tunnel, echoing back at her.

Celeste, help me. Give me some strength.

"Baby girl, you white as snow right now. Omma take you in, let you sleep."

She shook her head. Panic was transforming her insides into a live electrical wire, buzzing and sparking and jolting her senses.

"Check this out," he said, pulling up to a ten-story warehouse building with big wooden double doors, sandblasted brick and new paned windows. The sidewalk was clear of the broken glass that glittered everywhere else.

"When I was growin' up right there," Duke pointed to a neat Cape Cod-style house next door, "this buildin' was abandoned. All the windows was broken out." He was talking fast. Somehow Victoria knew he was trying to keep her conscious.

"Crackheads used to smoke up in here, an' a girl got raped while she was walkin' to school. Man, I was 'bout to kill a nigga when that shit happened."

Victoria strained to hear him over the constant scream of sirens, the bass beat of rap music, loud voices and old cars rumbling past. The noise, at least, was helping to push back that dark cloud in her head that was trying to knock her out.

Duke turned toward the building on their right. "So I built my own Trump Tower. Me, Prince an' Knight was visitin' some associates on the East Coast. Soon as we seen that shit on Fifth Ave, took my vision to another level."

The empty lot next door and the boarded-up, graffitti-covered house beside that made Victoria want to ask why he'd build a palace in the ghetto. But she didn't have the energy.

"This home base, baby. I'm a leader. E'rybody 'round here look up to Duke and the Johnson brothers. Right now, though, I'm solo, rulin' like a king."

The deep drone of a military-style chant made Victoria glance to the right. Her mouth dropped open.

Jogging toward the car, up the almost-dark street, was a column of shirtless men in black-white-gray camouflage pants and black combat boots. Their skin glistened with sweat over muscles rippling in a mosaic of colors: jet black, cinnamon, nutmeg, oatmeal, redwood, cocoa, and cream as white as hers. Some were bald, some had huge, wild afros, others had tiny braids, loose and bouncing or curving against their heads.

There were dozens. Yeah, four columns of twelve. As they jogged past the car, each man let out a deep call to Duke that vibrated through Victoria's chest.

"Babylon!"

They accented the last syllable, "Baby*lon!*" with a sort of upward swing on the end, like a call out with the greatest pride. The word was also tattooed in small scroll across each of their right pecs.

Victoria stared with wide eyes. If she had stepped out of her former life and into this spot—without the past week's events—she would faint from fear. She still felt like she could. This was just part of her wild-and-getting-wilder Alice in Ghettoland experience.

Maybe if I live through this I can write a book and use it to pay for college.

135

SEX IN THE HOOD

It looked like an NFL team was coming at her, and it was making Celeste absolutely roar.

Oh my God. Those guys are like letting off a cloud of sex power. If I go anywhere near that —

At the academy, there were two black guys on the football team, and Victoria's pussy would cream as she watched them run in those little tights. That's why she loved watching Lions games at Ford Field from the private suite Daddy's business paid for. All the clients and friends thought it was cute that Dan's daughter had such passion for the game of football. Little did they know that all her staring through the binoculars let her ogle those athletic asses, their curving hamstrings and their super-strong quads as they ran and tackled.

Now, Victoria crossed her arms to hide the fact that she was panting so hard. Her chest was rising and falling as hard as it had when she kissed Duke on Belle Isle.

"Baby girl, you safe. Chill. This my army. My Barriors— Black Warriors. The women, they B'Amazons." Duke was beaming as the men thundered past. As he nodded proudly, his diamond ring sparkled when his hand fell to his lap.

The cloud of testosterone exploding from Duke and all those men made Victoria melt into the bucket seat. All she could think about was sex, but not in a way that she'd ever experienced. The only frame of reference for sex she had were memories of Brian's erections. Movies with love scenes. Suddenly Victoria was overwhelmed with curiosity at what it would be like to do it with Duke—and all these men.

"Huu-uuut!" A deep female voice called.

Victoria turned around. More soldiers were coming.

Women! They were wearing fatigues, boots and tank tops. Their heads were adorned with braids, ponytails, bald heads, afros. Their skin represented every hue from pinky white to black satin, and it glistened with a super-sexy sheen of sweat.

Their faces were so beautiful. One reminded Victoria of the black Barbie dolls her mother bought when she was five. Daddy had taken them away after Mommy died, just like he stopped bringing her to Gramma Green's house for visits with the black side of her family. Not because they were black, he said, but because this part of town was "treacherous and crime-infested" and "a bad influence."

Now Victoria felt a burning pang of resentment that she'd been shielded from this part of her roots. Who, in her past privileged life, would believe this sight? It was surreal even as she stared through her own fatigued eyes.

She felt a jolt of sex energy as the women jogged past. It was impossible not to feel a prickle on her skin or a hardening sensation in her tingling nipples or a hot gush in her pussy, because those women were like Amazon goddesses. They radiated nothing but power, strength, confidence and sex.

As the women—they ranged in age from about thirteen up to a woman with silver hair—jogged past, they charged the air with sex. They looked so powerful, confident and strong. She watched the way their nipples were poking through tight tank tops. Each had BABYLON tattooed on chiseled biceps, triceps and deltoids.

They followed the men through the field, around the back of Duke's building. He drove the other way, down an alley. A huge door opened. A futuristic, neon blue light glowed from the opening as Duke wheeled inside.

The enormous garage could hold a football field. The three-story-high ceiling was a silver network of exposed pipes and whirring fans. Brick walls displayed airbrushed murals of ghetto fabulous city scenes in vivid cobalt blue, magenta, bright yellow. A giant sign, made from neon blue block letters, said BABYLON across the left wall.

It shined on the silver floor, which was made of metal tire-tread. It seemed to stretch forever as Duke drove past rows and rows of black Navigators, Hummers and Escalades. A yellow H2, a cobalt blue Corvette and a baby blue Bentley were also on display. To the right was a set-up worthy of an authentic rock or rap concert hall: a grand, black stage with enormous speakers. The far corner looked like a nightclub with a long bar and sleek silver stools. Behind that, a mirrored wall held endless glass shelves of liquors.

Victoria looked up and back as the garage door closed. Near it, a spiral staircase, also made of that silver tire-tread metal, led up to a balcony furnished with cobalt blue plush couches and silver tables. A glass elevator connected the garage floor to the balcony and upper floors.

All those male and female soldiers were inside now, their chants echoing through the cavernous garage. They were filing up an industrial-looking staircase that led somewhere beyond the elevator. Motors revved, drowning out their chants. Lights glowed on four Navigators. The vehicles filed out.

Victoria felt dizzy. Awed. What the hell kind of operation was this? Was this legal? What were all these people doing here? And what in he world did Duke want *her* to do here?

"Duke," she said, turning to him. "What—"

A blue light flashed through his white linen shirt. Duke stopped the car in the center of the garage. He raised the bottom of his shirt, reaching for one of two phones clipped to his waistband.

Oh my God.

His stomach was exposed for a second—a flat, hairless expanse of skin as smooth, beautiful and soft-looking as his bald head and gorgeous face. His belly button was perfectly round and taut. Without thinking about it, she licked her lips as if she were tracing his "innie" with her tongue.

Victoria shifted, making the fabric of her baby blue velour pants rub her pussy. Celeste and her hungry imagination had already made a puddle in these fresh panties.

"Mass' Duke," a male voice echoed through the garage.

Did he say Master *Duke?* Victoria squinted, as if that would help her hear better.

It was that guy in the Pistons jersey, the chubby one with the little braids and the BMW necklace. The guy who'd been with Duke when she arrived at Gramma Green's, and when he picked her up, the one who helped kill the dog.

WHITE CHOCOLATE

The guy's pudgy fingers wrapped about the edge of Duke's door, but he did not look up from his phones. Instead, Duke pressed a button on the center console. The window raised.

Beamer moved his hands.

"Yo," Duke said deeply into the tiny silver square. "It's 361 down."

He squinted toward the speedometer. She heard a male voice so deep it reminded her of that rapper Tone Loc, one of Brian's favorites. His voice was so bass it felt like it could rumble through her body and alter her heartbeat. It was the same feeling as when she would stand too close to a giant speaker during a concert. The vibration upset the body's rhythm. Now that voice on the phone was so deep, Victoria could not decipher any words.

"Ain't it." Duke flexed his jaw. Over the past few hours, she had noticed that when he seemed irritated or lost in his thoughts, the little muscles under the smooth skin on his jaw rippled, as if he were grinding his teeth. But something was different. Duke's super-cool expression had suddenly transformed into that same look he'd had at his mother's house.

Fear. Subservience. Nervousness.

Who in the world was on the phone? It was a man, for sure. Was Duke in danger? Was it the person or the subject matter of the conversation that was making Duke like that? Or was he just annoyed that Beamer was standing on the other side of the car window, looking even more scared?

"Yeah," Duke groaned. "Straight up." He tossed his head back and let out a hearty laugh that echoed through the garage, and returned Duke's usual machismo to his face and eyes.

"Like beamin' up some shit!" Duke said the last word with a high pitch so playful it made Victoria smile, even though she had no clue what he was saying.

Duke hung up, clipped the phone to his waist, and kept his shirt pulled up longer this time. Victoria's mouth watered. She could not look away from that incredible skin on Duke's bare stomach. If she could just plant her lips there for a few seconds and taste . . . suck . . . lick . . . She leaned forward. Her mind felt foggy with fatigue, curiosity about this place, and raw lust. She imagined her body twisted up with his, their skin hot, their sweat gluing them together, their complexions contrasting in a way that would be breathtakingly sexy—and dangerous in ways Victoria didn't even know. Her pussy was gushing. She kept bending forward, and re-tied her shoes.

"Baby girl," Duke said, "you remember Beamer from earlier. B, this Victoria Winston."

"Hi," Victoria said. "Are you named after a car?"

"Naw, I'm jus' goofy," he said. Why was his voice higher than earlier? Why was he so nervous? The way he kept looking back and forth between her and Duke, it was like he was waiting for someone to scold him and tell him he'd been a bad boy. But he kept talking as if everything were fine.

"As a kid I was always clownin', crackin' jokes an' carryin' on. My auntie said I beam like the sun, so she nickname me Beamer, no joke. Then cats got hype to the luxury ride." He tapped the BMW medallion that dangled at the point where his belly bulged outward. "It's natural, you know?"

"You a crazy ma'fucka," Duke said playfully, but in a split second his tone got deeper and threatening.

"Why the fuck ain't you called me all night?" Duke glared up at Beamer, who quaked so hard his braids shifted on his thick shoulders.

"Dude, I got sick. All that chocolate I ate—"

"I don't care if you laid up in the ma'fuckin' morgue. You betta write a note on yo' toe tag, tellin' somebody to call The Duke an' tell 'im where Beama at."

The hair on the back of Victoria's neck stood up and her nipples got rock-hard. The toughness, the machismo in Duke's voice made Celeste squirm so wildly, Victoria squeezed her pussy muscles to make her favorite milking motion—like the whole length of her vagina squeezed from top to bottom, making the milky cream squirt down onto the swollen, slippery lips as they massaged her clit.

WHITE CHOCOLATE

Duke's deep voice vibrated through her. She wasn't even hearing his words as he scolded Beamer; it was just the macho power potency shooting out of his voicebox that was making her dizzy.

Right now, her pussy reminded her of the pretty little purse she took to the prom. It was velvet, with a satin drawstring, holding her lipstick and cellphone within its folds. Now her pussy felt the same way, holding her nerve endings that were sparkling like diamonds and jewels. It was a wet, sunken treasure waiting for a pirate to dive down and crack open the chest.

Victoria poked her butt deeper into the seat.

Oh my God, I could cum right now.

Except Beamer looked like he was about to pee on himself.

Why aren't I scared? I'm in a garage in the middle of a Detroit ghetto with a big black guy who's talkin' about a toe tag . . . and I'm horny as ever. What is wrong with this picture? Everything. Because Alice is starting to like Ghettoland.

Victoria felt dizzy. This whole scene was so unreal, it couldn't possibly be happening. She was going to simply wake up from a bad dream, look around her pretty aqua blue bedroom overlooking the Winston family's private lake, get dressed in her giant walk-in closet, then go to the University of Michigan to start college. Nightmare over.

The machismo radiating from Duke on her left made her want to climb out of the bucket seat, straddle him and suck on his lips for three days. She wanted to rub her pussy all over his bald head and spear herself on that log he couldn't possibly think he was hiding in those loose linen pants. How could she be in such mental turmoil, and still her body was more on fire than it had ever been?

It spelled only one thing: D-A-N-G-E-R, for herself and everyone around her. She remembered what Daddy used to say, quoting Eleanor Roosevelt: "Anger is only one letter away from danger." Daddy would add, "Never let anyone see your anger. Never let 'em see you sweat or you'll lose, you can bet."

SEX IN THE HOOD

What if she were to start talking black, acting black and taking on the ways of the street? When it was time to go to college and enter the white business world, she would be viewed as black, and therefore inferior. She couldn't believe that in just a few hours here, the cadence of how they talked was already taking hold of her thoughts.

Also, the danger of this new world felt deliciously rebellious against a world that had suddenly scandalized her. The media, the FBI, the white family whom she'd never met, her boyfriend and her best friend, all turned against her when she needed help the most. Yeah, hanging with Duke and immersing into this urban black world felt seductively lawless, as if she were screaming "Fuck you!" to all the people who let her down.

But it was terrifying too. How could Duke's business possibly be legitimate? Even if he did supply bodyguards for sports events, how could that finance this operation? It didn't feel one hundred percent legitimate. Not that army. Not this garage. Not Duke's mysterious phone call, or his domination over Beamer. No, this whole scene, especially this garage inside this nondescript building, was like something straight out of one of those *New Jack City* type movies Brian was obsessed with watching.

If I stay too long, the only way I'll ever get out of here is in a police car or an ambulance. I'll stay just long enough to get what I need and get out.

Yeah, she could survive life as Alice in Ghettoland for as long as she had to. Then she'd pop a reality pill and find the white Wonderland where she belonged.

"I'm sorry, Massa Duke." Beamer dropped to his knees, lacing his hands as if he were praying. "Please forgive me."

All that for not calling? It was just a few hours ago they were together at Henry's. Beamer laid his elbows and forearms on the car, bowed his head and sobbed like a baby. It reminded her of *Roots* when a slave would beg not to get whipped.

WHITE CHOCOLATE

"Sorry ain't gon' erase my worries 'bout Izz jumpin' back on yo' ass. You know what happen to e'rybody who ev'a thought about schemin' on me."

Beamer shook his head. "I serve you, Massa Duke."

Duke reached out with his left hand, grabbed Beamer's jersey and twisted it under his chin. Beamer's eyes bugged as the fabric cut into his neck.

"Act like a punk, you get treated like you one," Duke said. "Now, go take yo' pussy-stank ass an' think about how you s'pose to act an' what gon' happen if you fuck up again." Duke's voice was ice, completely void of sympathy.

"Now, me and the lady got some serious bidness to han'le." Duke glanced at Victoria with the same tender gaze he'd had all evening, but he glared back at Beamer. "Y'all two get used to each other. Vee 'bout to plug her white business mind into the engine that drive Babylon. Fo' real."

Victoria let his words vibrate through her head. *Drive, hmmm.* She might drive this car. She might climb on top of Duke and drive his dick-stick at every gear. But drive this mysterious, inner-city empire?

"Duke," she said with a sultry-serious tone. "We still need to talk. I haven't agreed to anything, so until you give me a tour and tell me exactly what you do here, I am not a Babylon employee. And you are not my boss."

Beamer's mouth dropped open. He stared at her with envy glowing in his eyes.

Duke tossed his head back, flashed those beautiful white teeth, and let his deep, sexy laughter echo through the garage.

Chapter 21

Milan threw the binoculars so hard against the exposed brick wall of her apartment, the glass and plastic shattered all over the hardwood floor. She stood by the window, where she had just seen Duke drive up with that white bitch in his Porsche.

"I told Beamer not to let her onto this property!" She trembled, seething inside, hating him. She'd done everything to please him—got the best education, took care of herself so that she was still the finest of the fine, worked her ass off for his empire.

"And he is not going to just toss me aside like a used piece of trash. Especially for that white bitch."

Milan crossed her arms. Nausea washed through her. She hated this goddamn morning sickness that lasted all fucking day and night!

Milan's mind spun. She had to figure out how to take over. Beamer was too much of an idiot to execute a plan. Who else could she recruit to her side? Knight. He was coming home soon, and nobody scared Duke more than Knight or their momma. Duke was always so worried about Knight coming back and trying to regain the power he and Prince had back in the day, before Prince died and Knight was wrongly convicted.

Yes, Knight was definitely the way to bring Duke down. It would probably happen anyway, but if Milan played her cards right, she could do better than Duchess altogether. She could be Knight's queen. Now all she had to do was figure out how to get in touch with Knight and seduce him into seeing things her way. Then putting Duke in his place would be easy.

"We can take control of Babylon together," Milan said out loud. "Easy." No matter how tough Duke thought he was, he quaked in his damn boots when Knight just looked at him. Knight didn't even have to speak. He was even worse than his mother.

144

"Punk!" Milan screamed.

"Madame Milan." Renée came running from the boys' room. "Sound like you kickin' somebody ass out here."

"Are the babies okay?"

"Sleepin' like little angels," Renée said, her thin lips breaking into a grin. "You shoulda seen how little Zeus was teachin' Hercules how to count on that computer game Duke got 'em for Christmas."

Milan hugged herself, hoping these awful waves of nausea would stop.

"Madame Milan, I tried calling you earlier, but—"

"But what?" Milan snapped. "I told you don't bug me while I'm working unless it's an emergency."

"Well, it wasn't an emergency, but—"

Milan sucked her teeth, rolled her eyes, and wished this nausea would stop getting even worse.

"That rash Zeus has on his leg," Renée said. "Seem like the ointment ain't workin'."

"*Isn't* working. Can you say 'isn't working'? 'Ain't' is not a word you will ever speak around my children. And we put a 'G' at the end of I-N-G words. Say it!"

Renée's eyes grew huge. "Isn't working," she said, bowing her head.

"Unless you want to go back to working in that disgusting nursing home up the street, you'd better take your work as my nanny more seriously. In fact, I'm going to get you a tutor so you can speak properly around my children."

"Yes, ma'am."

"Call the pediatrician about the ointment."

"Do you want to see it?" Renée said every letter clearly and deliberately like she should. "I can show you while Zeus sleeps."

Milan grasped her stomach. If she took one step, she'd throw up. And looking at a nasty rash certainly wouldn't make her feel better, nor would looking at two little faces that were mini mirror images of Duke Johnson.

"I trust that you'll take care of it."

"Yes, ma'am." The nanny returned to the nursery.

Milan talked herself out of heaving up the crackers she tried to eat in the car while driving home from the meeting with that imbecile named Beamer, who didn't know his dick from a donut.

The thought of fucking Peanut and his silly ass made an acid burn surge up her throat. "Ugh."

I will not throw up in the middle of my green velvet couch set or on my glass coffee table or on my leather shag rug or anywhere in this fabulous apartment that I shouldn't even have because me and our babies should be living up on the tenth floor in Duke's penthouse. Our penthouse. As a family.

She should not have been down here with the other baby mommas in their apartments. Those stupid, gold-diggin' hoes! Those two bitches were so far beneath Milan Henderson. She was educated, knew etiquette, had a strong business mind. She had vision, like Duke.

"I'm the whole package—brains, beauty, companionship," she said out loud. They were just a piece of ass for Duke, like so so many he'd had, all under Milan's nose, since they grew up together.

Of course he'd been with countless girls. After all, he was a gorgeous twenty-year-old black Adonis whose business was the hottest sex in Detroit.

We deal in sex. And I've sampled more than a few Studs myself, but Duke is my number one. Always has been, always will be. I will be moving myself and our two little baby boys up to our rightful home, with him—or Knight—when he gets back and helps me take over. Let's see . . .

Milan needed to talk to Knight, now, to set this in motion. She needed to tell him something that would make him all the more eager to wrench power back from his baby brother.

What about the upcoming meeting with Moreno? What if Milan called Knight, let him know that Duke was mishandling Knight's vision to partner with Moreno to expand the Sex Squad into five major cities across America? That upcoming meeting—if it went right—would be worth a fortune, but only if it were done

WHITE CHOCOLATE

with the kind of finesse and sophistication Milan could bring to the table. Yet despite her insistence, for months, Duke had ignored her pleas to let her represent Babylon at the meeting. After all, who knew the Sex Squad arm of Babylon's affairs better than the brilliant business mind who ran it every day?

That would be me. Madame Milan.

Now she just had to enlighten Knight on these points. He'd be so grateful she gave him the heads-up on baby brother's incompetence, Knight would only be too happy to hand over control of all five cities—and the millions they'd make—to Milan. Then she'd be in charge of Sex Squads in six cities.

And I'll be tellin' Duke what to do.

To make up for all the humiliation that would create in him, maybe Milan would be kind enough to let Duke keep his little cream puff . . . No, no, definitely not. Duke deserved nothing but misery. The same misery he'd inflicted on Milan all these years, ignoring her, fucking her so she'd keep sharing her brilliant business mind with Babylon to run the Sex Squad as efficiently and profitably as possible.

Maybe Milan could kidnap the white bitch Duke just brought into Babylon. Maybe she could open up her own business and sell expensive white pussy all day long until Duke's cream puff was as blew out as a five-dollar trick in the Cass Corridor.

That could work.

But first she had to see for herself what Duke was doing with that Victoria Winston who was all over the newspapers, the TV and the radio. She had to see if Duke really had the idiotic idea that it would be all right to bring that suburban rich bitch up in here.

Where I live with our children.

Milan's heels pounded the hardwood floor as she headed to the door of her apartment. She'd start down in the garage. If they weren't there, she'd go up to the penthouse.

She swung open the door.

SEX IN THE HOOD

Two Barriors stood in the hallway, facing her door, arms crossed. She'd seen them around, but didn't know their names. With so many new recruits lately—250 to be exact, on top of the 500 who lived in the area and 500 others on reserve—it was impossible to know all their names.

Besides, Milan's department was the Sex Squad, and Studs and Barriors were two different things. Studs fucked for a living. Barriors did bodyguard work, and if they fucked in the line of duty, that wasn't on Milan's watch.

Her heart pounded. Her gut cramped with nausea. No Duke wouldn't have her on lock-down in her apartment! That would mean either he knew she was scheming as he always accused, or he wanted her kept far away from whatever he was doing.

Milan wanted to scream, but she bit it down, along with the vomit burning her throat. "Excuse me," she said, stepping into the hallway, turning to dash to the elevators.

"Go back inside," the taller Barrior said. And he was tall, like as tall as Duke. Six-six, with huge muscles. Like the Hulk. He looked like he was going to pop right out of his black T-shirt and sweatpants.

Milan said, "I need to go downstairs to my office to do some work."

The other Barrior nodded, making his Afro sway as he said, "You want somebody to pick it up? We can do dat."

The Hulk grunted. "But you gotta stay here, Madame Milan."

She flitted past them.

A huge arm came down like gates at train tracks. His forearm pressed into her chest.

"Don't touch me!" she shouted. Hot, sour vomit burned up her throat. "I'm going downstairs!"

"No, you not," Hulk said. "Go back inside befo' we follow orders to carry yo' skinny ass back into yo' crib."

"Don't talk to me like that, you overgrown barbarian."

They came at her. She spewed stomach acid and chewed-up crackers all over their big, bulging chests.

148

Chapter 22

Duke watched his Duchess's juicy ass pop as she walked in her baby blue velour pants toward the glass elevators. Those two fat, round bubbles of undeniably black booty were the perfect size to squeeze like ripe melons then bounce, bite and bury his face in.

Her ass had personality. The way it rose up with every step on her long giraffe legs then lowered down when she stepped with the other leg, it was like two giant pens handwriting a secret love note that said: *Come get this good pussy, but only if yo' name The Duke.*

Timbo felt like a big, heavy log. One look at Duchess's booty, it was instantly rock-hard, because she had just as much attitude in her ass as she had on her face.

This chick crazy.

She still didn't have a clue who she was talking to, or what she was dealing with. Or what kind of bank just dropped into her sexy-ass lap.

But she would in a minute.

Wit'in twennie-fo' hours, max, she gon' be signing her life away to me. Not wit' ink, not wit' blood, but wit' cum. Hers mixed wit' mine.

It would be the ultimate power potion that would rule, coast to coast. And so it was written, and so it was done.

"Massa Duke," Beamer whispered, "I cain't b'lieve how you lettin' her disrespec' you."

She turned around, looking straight in Beamer's eyes.

"I hate girls who are scared to speak up," Duchess said. "Meek, mild, letting others make decisions for them. My parents taught me to be a very take-charge person."

She started to turn around, but looked back at Beamer. "And what do you know about self-respect when you call another person Master? Emancipation Proclamation. 1864. You should look it up."

SEX IN THE HOOD

Beamer's goofy eyes looked like hardboiled eggs, they were so big right now. He looked at Duke, but Duke was staring at Duchess. He was smiling down into her big, silver-blue eyes. He loved how she handled herself.

"I still have my integrity," she said.

"An' you got The Duke, yo' black knight in shinin' armor," Duke said.

Beamer stared at her like he was so shocked he couldn't see straight, and he said, "You so pretty you hard to look at. Like how a man s'pose to look in them eyes an' think wit' his head?"

Duke smiled. "Maybe you cain't, ma'fucka, but The Duke ain't got a problem."

Duke laughed, leading Duchess into the glass elevator near the staircase. He and Beamer dropped some names of musicians, comedians and athletes that Warrior Protection provided security for, including a highly promoted concert that night.

"If I work for you," Victoria said as the elevator rose, "I want you to agree to pay my college tuition. I'm supposed to be at U of M right now. That's my number one priority. The lawyers said my college fund is gone, so I need to find another source."

Duke stared down with amused eyes. She wouldn't need college after she got her undergrad degree in Dukeology, her masters in Streetology and her PhD in Babylonology.

"And one more thing." She looked up in Duke's eyes with a serious expression. "My dad always stressed, the first thing you do when you enter a deal is establish the out clause."

"The out clause." Duke echoed flatly.

Timbo went soft. He couldn't believe this bitch who had nothing but the brains and beauty he needed, who was on a private tour of Babylon that nobody ever got, who was up for a job that a whole lot of niggas would kill for, was talking about an out clause.

"You bold as hell an' don't even know it," Duke said, staring down at her hard. Her big, silver-blue eyes flashed with defiance but not fear. "A nigga could get jacked for talkin' shit like that to me."

150

WHITE CHOCOLATE

She blinked. "Shit like what?"

Duke bit down, making his jaw muscles flex. He glared hard at her; she stared back without flinching. Beamer was just as still and silent as he was supposed to be. Part of Duke was amused by her innocence and impressed that she wasn't scared to speak her mind to get the business done. Even with him.

"Damn." He shivered with self-satisfaction. Timbo surged again. Even his nipples were hard against his shirt. He could take her right now, let all this ridiculous energy he hadn't ever felt before just go wild on her pretty ass. And she'd love it. She *would* love it. It wasn't a question. Tonight.

"Miss Winston," he said with a playful business tone. "You know how many ma'fuckas cringe when I look at 'em like that? And you just sittin' there, starin' back like *la-dee-dah*. You a triple threat: brains, beauty and balls as big as mine. You gon' be *bad* — "

She drew her brows together. "No, I don't want to be bad. At all."

He smiled. "Bad. That's black for 'good.'" He laughed long and hard. "You and me gon' be so good together, I'll let you do whateva you want — go to college, start yo' own bidness — "

"Let?"

Duke nodded slowly. "However you want to do this, it's done. On one condition."

"What?"

"Yo' name Duchess."

"My parents named me Victoria Marie Winston."

"Ain't that the chick the feds is lookin' fo' right about now? The chick who was on the news tonight, bein' lef' at her Grammomma house? The firs' place they gon' look."

"Well, obviously," she said with a slight neck jerk and very attitudinal tone, "I'm not there. I'm here with you in this urban underworld called Babylon."

The elevator stopped on the second floor, where the doors opened onto the gym. The three of them stepped into the huge expanse of mirrored walls, red mats on the floor, silver-and-black weight machines and rows of cardio equipment. If kissing him at

151

sunset didn't get her ready for the dick-down of the millennium, then this would.

Duchess's eyes were all over the Barriors and B'Amazons, who were pumping iron, jumping rope, doing push-ups and sweating on Stairmasters. Her eyeballs rolled up and down their fine-ass bodies on display in snug shorts and sports bras.

"I love this gym!" Duchess said, swaying to the relentless bass beat booming from the top of the line sound system. "It's huge, and the equipment, it's better than my fitness club. And that was state of the art."

"You ain't seen nothin' yet," Duke said as Lee Lee stepped to the front, by the mirrors, and blew her whistle.

All seventy-two of them—one of four Squads—filed onto the big open space on the red mats. Standing in three rows of twelve, they peeled off their clothes. Noah and his assistants walked between them with baskets. Everybody tossed their clothing, including shoes, into the basket. Then they walked by with a basket of condoms; all the men took one.

Miss Daisy stared like a mug. She didn't know what the fuck was about to happen. When the first dick, then another, then another came swinging out of so many pairs of shorts, her eyes popped.

Duke bit his lip to stop from laughing. He wanted to tell her to close her mouth, but the way she was looking at all those titties flying loose and all the pretty asses, Duke wished he had a video camera.

Milan. Stupid scheming bitch. Did she really think she could take Duke's video camera and get away with trying to blackmail Duke's boy in her plot to do whatever she thought she was going to do? She had never been more ridiculous than today, fucking Beamer's pudgy ass on camera.

Didn't she know Duke knew everything? The Duke had godlike powers. God was in charge, no doubt. But certain men, like Caesar and Alexander the Great and the Egyptian pharoahs and Moses and Ghandi and Martin Luther King, Jr.—they had

WHITE CHOCOLATE

superhuman powers to help them do what they did. Make change. Rule. Improve people's lives.

That's me. I give folk jobs. I provide needed services, whether protection or pleasure. I take care of Momma in grand style. Got her livin' like she ain't neva imagined she would. I'm a role model to the kids in the ghetto who see a young, black man can become somethin' great. A leader. A visionary.

So, if gold-digging Milan Henderson thought she was going to bring him down by tossing some of that skinny ass at his boy who never turned down pussy, and she was going to use some kinda whack videotape scheme to do it, she was beyond crazy.

That was why she was on lock-down right now, the first step toward booting her out of Babylon. It was going to happen while Miss Daisy was getting schooled on the ways of the world here at this "urban underworld," as she called it. Duke was sure she had never dreamed she'd be in what she called a "fitness club," where seventy-two motherfuckers were banging booty like the turbo-charged, robo-dicked warriors that The Duke had made their asses into.

The sight of all of them made Duchess gawk. She was creaming those pants like nobody's business. She was so horny, her mouth was twitching. Her pussy was blowing gusts of pheromones, the natural scent that people and animals gave off when in heat.

He inhaled, loving how the hot, sweet fumes of her pussy rose up and tickled his nose. Timbo was rock hard and ready, just like she would be in a minute.

Chapter 23

The prison guard who was passing Knight Johnson's cell was the meanest one in the joint. When that hillbilly bastard's face appeared between the bars, Knight focused harder on his book, *As a Man Thinketh* by James Allen. He was on the top bunk, lying on his stomach in the arc of soft light glowing from the mini reading lamp Momma had sent him. The small, yellow book was open to pages sixty and sixty-one, propped up on a fold in the dark blue wool blanket on his bed.

Bang! The guard's baton hit the bars. The guard passed to the next cell and hit their bars.

Knight read his favorite sentence in the book, which he had highlighted in orange: "He who cherishes a beautiful vision, a lofty ideal in his heart, will one day realize it." It was only being in prison—though Knight Johnson was wrongly accused and wrongly convicted—that had prepared Knight's mind to believe and appreciate that incarceration had been a blessing in disguise.

Here at Monroe Prison, in its library, through books, audiotapes and volunteer tutors, Knight had learned to read, write and speak the king's English.

An' I can still rap as raw as any otha ma'fucka.

Now he had the ability to speak the white man's language. Moreno's language. Wall Street bankers' language. Business moguls's language. He would be able to communicate with them on level intellectual ground. Actually, he would be on superior intellectual ground, but they didn't need to know that.

In his peripheral view, the guard was standing there, still and silent, just staring into the cell, radiating evil energy as usual. Knight put up his Teflon mental deflectors to stop and push back the literal gusts of hatred that were hurling into the cell, at him and his cellmate, from the guard.

WHITE CHOCOLATE

In the lower bunk, Knight's cellmate, Lonnie, rattled the newspaper he was reading. He spoke in a tone just loud enough for Knight to hear. "Look like somebody wanna play gladiator."

Knight focused harder on the page, refusing to poison his thoughts with stories about that secret sport when guards bet money on which inmate could beat the shit out of another. Gladiator was just like the dog fights back home, but here in lock-up, they used niggas, rednecks, spicks, even a coupla Indian brothas.

The guards never dared mess with Knight, although lately this guard, who either was not aware of Knight's status or didn't care, had been mumbling about "brangin' a proud nigger down a peg er two."

Knight barely let that man's presence register in his mind. Instead, he was envisioning every detail of himself walking out of this place, into the wildest welcome home party Babylon could pull off, and taking his proper place at the helm of an empire begun by Prince, rest his soul. First on his list: giving Moreno an offer he couldn't refuse to surrender—not share or partner as Duke was planning, but straight-up hand over territories a.k.a. Erotic Zones throughout the Midwest, East Coast and South that Moreno had promised Prince.

Two more weeks and I'm free to cash in on a broken promise.

It was a promise buried with one brother and banished by another brother's fear. Not so with Knight. He was ready to go after what was rightfully his—the property and domain of Babylon.

The West Coast operation was basically a done deal, since Priscilla and Larry Marx were leaving the business to start Question Marx, a multimedia company. Just the other day, Knight had read an article in *The Wall Street Journal* about how the couple—already millionaires when they purchased a chain of upscale strip clubs that made them even richer—planned to produce Hollywood movies, documentaries about the sex industry, entertainment websites and a glitzy, mainstream magazine for couples who, they told *The Journal*, "want to keep their love life sizzlin'."

Knight had met the couple years ago, when they were in Detroit and contacted Babylon to arrange a party on a yacht. That was Knight's first deal. Sure, Prince was watching over his shoulder, checking every detail to make sure it was perfect. And it was.

Mr. and Mrs. Marx were phenomenally impressed with the Sex Squad, from the flawless transactions to the extreme discretion to the documented health status of all fifty Studs and Sluts. The Marxes were most pleased with the quality and performance of the fifty Sluts and Studs who fit the exact profiles that were desired, requested and enjoyed by the Marxes and the twenty-four couples who were their guests on the luxury yacht that summer night on the black waters of Lake St. Clair and the Detroit River.

"If you ever want to follow the American tradition of Manifest Destiny," Mrs. Marx told Knight.

"That means moving west and taking what you want," her husband said, handing Knight a champagne flute in their plush master suite on the yacht. "Like when the white man snatched everything west of the Mississippi from the Natives."

"Call us first," Mrs. Marx said. "We've got a vision, a plan for a whole new game in a couple years. Right now we're just recruiting folks who we think are worthy when we pass our golden baton."

With that, Mrs. Marx's left hand, the one with her grape-sized diamond wedding ring, wrapped around the hard-as-lead pipe in Knight's slacks. In a flash, she was on her knees, sucking it all as her husband jacked the biggest dick Knight had ever seen on a white man. She bent over, legs apart, hands grasping her ankles, husband standing in front of her, steadying her suntanned skinny ass. Knight instinctively knew to lay pipe in the foundation of what would become the Taj Mahal of business relationships.

WHITE CHOCOLATE

Now, after frequent communications from the pen, Knight was going to luxuriate in their generous accommodations, in a business sense. That pipe was hot, about to burst right now.

Two weeks can't pass fast enough before I'm free.

Every time Knight talked with Duke, his little brother sounded recklessly power hungry. It made Knight realize that Duke's ambition was about to inspire premature moves and fatal growing pains, like taking over more turf than he could manage, expanding the ranks of the Squad to such huge numbers that quality control would be impossible, or promising protection for notorious celebrities whose parties and concerts were always known to have a gunbattle sideshow.

Bang! That guard slammed his baton on the bars then walked past, doing the same at the next cell.

Knight gripped his book, staring at the pages, feeling so confident in its message that it was only a matter of time until his own dream became reality. He knew it would happen even if his dream clashed with Duke's dream when big brother got free.

Li'l Tut was twenty, going on twenty-one. That wasn't nearly as wise or as capable as twenty-five, like Knight. And in inner-city black man years, a quarter-century was ancient, venerable, respectable. Sage. And highly qualified to take charge of Detroit's most unique underground entrepreneurial venture ever.

As the boss.

Knight's eyes focused back on his book, to a yellow highlighted spot on the next page. "Ask and receive." Below that, he read, "Dream lofty dreams, and as you dream, so shall you become. Your Vision is the promise of what you shall one day be; your Ideal is the prophecy of what you shall at last unveil."

For Knight, that dream, that vision, that ideal was multi-faceted: Freedom. Power. Happiness with *one* woman who loved Knight for Knight, who believed in strong family values, who shared his vision, his passion, his purpose.

And my voracious libido. It had been self-contained and self-satisfied for two years and six months. Nobody had even thought about trying to do unnatural acts with Knight's muscle-pumped six-foot-seven inches of brawn. Even if he were a pee-wee runt, his special status as top Babylon Barrior would be all the protective shield he needed.

Now I need a wife, one woman who'll cherish and celebrate me. I don't want to swing Shane left, right, at every pussy in sight. That reputation is what got me locked up. Now I only want a single female for life who's a spellbinding beauty on the inside, first and foremost. Being beautiful in appearance is appreciated but not mandatory. And if she wants some sexual adventure, she and I can certainly indulge together by bringing extra playmates to our party.

Knight's dream for his life and for Babylon required security—for himself, for Momma, his family. And he wanted fulfillment, by spending money on his community to improve it and make it safer. On that last one, during his two years and six months here, Knight had decided to start a foundation for people in his hood. Feeding hungry children, providing prenatal care to mothers to remedy the high infant mortality rates in the inner city, and building safe playgrounds and community centers; that was what he planned to do with the millions he'd make after Moreno agreed to submit to Babylon in five cities. That would make Knight Johnson's business the biggest of its kind, anywhere. Duke, of course, would help as second in command.

Bang! Bang!

"Mister Knight Johnson," the guard called.

Knight looked up, facing the man without letting his eyes focus on the windows of that evil soul. His mind felt so pure and inspired and focused on his vision of freedom and fulfillment out in the world, there was no point letting anything leap out of the guard's miserable mind and try to ride his evil stare into Knight's brain.

The guard laughed as he unlocked the bars. "Yo' momma named you right, Mister Knight Johnson, 'cause you shore as hell is black as night." He slid the bars back. "Come with me, sir. Some folks up in tha office picked yer name outta somebody's lucky hat. They wanna tell ya the prize."

WHITE CHOCOLATE

Knight sharpened his eyes on the guard's face. Was this just a ploy to take him off to the gladiator pit?

Chapter 24

Victoria wanted to scream. No way could she stay here and not become a sex addict—or a nymphomaniac rabbit, as Tiffany and her friends back at school liked to call themselves.

If I unleash my wild, pussy power in this place, whatever it is, it will kill me or Duke or some of these other people.

"Is this like a sex army?" she asked Duke, who was standing close, to her right. His body heat, his delicious scent, his overall sexiness made her head swirl. Looking at all those naked bodies—beautiful, toned men and women of every hue, their bodies already glistening with sweat from their workout—this was an impossible situation. Even a nun would get horny up in here.

Nobody back home would believe her if she told them she'd been in a gym watching three rows of twelve men, all gorgeous, laying on the floor as thirty-six women fucked them.

And it wasn't anything close to normal, missionary-style sex.

The women were squatting over them, their butts pointing to the men's faces. Just like Victoria learned at the fitness club to do squats, either on the barbell machine or free standing with weights in her hands, the women were doing squats down onto big, swollen, shiny penises!

The girls' knees were all pointing out, and their hands were on their knees. It was as synchronized and graceful as a ballet. Knowing how painful squats were to the quads, Victoria was doubly amazed that they were so in shape they could go and go.

All those dicks were enormous. The music was too loud to hear if they were moaning, but the mellow expressions on their faces left no doubt—they were lovin' it.

"Oh my God," she whispered, her cheeks on fire as Duke glanced down and over at her. He smiled.

Was this a normal, everyday activity in the hood? What in the world were they training for? Was this some kind of porno video shoot? Even the movies Brian watched never had anything like this. They always had orgy scenes in someone's living room, but never this many people in a gym!

"Faster!" shouted the woman with the whistle. She looked like a model — tall, thin but muscular, in skin-tight black leggings and a ballerina tank top. Her skin was deep tan, and the slight slant of her eyes reminded Victoria of a girl in her school whose father was black and whose mother was Vietnamese. The sexercise coach had a wild mane of curly, jet-black hair with maroon streaks framing her dark eyes, button nose and full cheeks. She was very hip, with a sort of *Bride of Frankenstein* look.

"Okay, girls. Slow down," she shouted. Her voice was raspy and commanding. "Faster . . . faster . . ."

The girls were literally slamming their butts down on the guys's six-pack abs. One guy in particular looked like Duke. He was tall, muscular and dark chocolate, and he had gray eyes. The woman fucking him was even darker, like blue-black, and she looked like that popular New York runway model from Africa who was showcased in all the fashion magazines — super tall, thin, with strong facial features and short hair.

Every time she rose up, Victoria stared at the guy's giant dick, which was pointing straight up, covered in a glistening red condom. A few veins zig-zagged on the side.

Did Duke's dick look like that? Was it that big? Bigger? How could all *that* go inside that girl? It looked like she was sitting on a telephone pole!

The scent of sex made her dizzy. It was salty, sweet, intoxicating.

This is sheer torture.

Her hands were trembling with lust, with fear, with excitement. There was no way she could stay here and remain true to her vow to stay a virgin. No way.

But what about her mix-race sex power? Did it only have lethal effects on white men? Did everything that Mommy said apply if she were with a black man? Or woman? These women looked just as delicious as the men. And what if she made love with Duke and wanted more men? Could she control the power? Her mother said she could use it to get whatever she needed or wanted. But how? She had died before she could explain any of that.

Victoria squeezed her pussy. It was so wet that if she stuck her fingers in it, she could pull them out, make a scissor motion with her fingers and form a web of clear pussy juice. One touch to her clit right now and she'd cum.

"I have to leave!" She stood on her tip-toes to shout into Duke's ear over the loud music. Celeste throbbed in the heat of his body, his scent, that mesmerizing onyx sparkle in his eyes that were devouring her like candy. "Duke—"

"Ain't no way in hell I'm gon' let you leave right now," he said with a hard tone. Every word sent a wave of goosebumps over her hot skin. Inside, she felt numb. An icy fist of fear squeezed her breath.

"What, are you gonna kidnap me?"

"Betta me than the FBI. B'sides," he shrugged, "who would know?"

"My grandmother." She crossed her arms.

"What she gon' do? Duke Johnson the police around here. That sick old woman cain't do a damn thing."

"Henry."

"Pound Dog work for me. He ain't gon' bite the hand that feed him. He put you in my hands. Remember, Miss Daisy?"

"Don't call me that. The lawyers would find me."

"Lawyers want one thing—money. And your daddy money gone, so now that massa dead and they shipped yo' pretty black ass off to the ghettolands, they work done. 'Less they gon' take you in themselves, which they ain't. They don't give a damn about a little spoiled half-black bitch wit' no dough."

Victoria glared at him. She did not blink as her brain focused on her mother, her power, Celeste. She had to use that power to escape this situation. Now. She had to use the female wiles Mommy told her about—the mix-breed woman power of many races packed into her brain, body and spirit—to get her way. She had to gain control over her life by figuring out how to tap into that power.

It was the power Duke thought he was exerting over her right now. In a Motor City minute, though, she was about to harness it, hone it and hurl it right back at him. She would do it so fast and sweet that he wouldn't know what hit him. He didn't even realize the monster that he wanted to create would someday dominate him with the same sex that caught his attention.

And so it was done in Victoria's mind.

She wouldn't fight it, for now. She would stay. She would work for him. She would learn any- and everything. She would go inside Duke Johnson's mind, sit down, takes notes and train herself to be the female version of him.

The Duchess.

Then, forever holding onto this feeling of frustration and fear and unfairness at life, she would lash it all back on him, crush him under her submission. And rule—over the Duke *and* his Babylon. Finally, she'd break away, go to college, live her original dream of opening a business, and climb the traditional ladder of success with the stealth and street smarts she was about to learn from Duke.

I'll be his Duchess all right. I'll learn his game and beat him at it in grand style. Celeste style.

"Check mate," she said flatly, staring into his eyes, unflinching. Not sweating. Not breathing hard anymore.

Motherfucker. Let's do this.

"Check mate what?" he asked.

"I'll work for you. Teach me everything I need to know. Now."

Duke's onyx eyes sparkled down on her. They were smiling, probing, questioning.

"Bet," he said, offering a hand. "Let's shake on it."

Victoria shook, squeezing his hand hard so he wouldn't feel that every muscle in her body was trembling. She was lying to herself when she vowed to maintain her virginity and only work for Duke for as long as it would take to move away for college.

But for now, she had to go along to get along as Duke put her on a crash course to learning street life, his vision for Babylon, and the rules of the game.

She would start her education with this bizarre gym class orgy where, for the moment, all her fear and frustration was exploding in the hot throb between her legs. Her palms were so hot, she could hold a piece of bread between them and make toast. She squeezed her pussy lips to get a grip on her lust so it wouldn't take over her mind, but they were so slippery and swollen, it made her shiver.

I am so in trouble.

She leaned closer to Duke. Her right nipple rubbed against his arm. A moan escaped her lips.

"Duke, what is this?" she asked.

He turned slightly, staring down at her with those big, gorgeous dark eyes with the bejeweled irises. His face was as luscious as his bald head, with all that coffee bean brown skin she wanted to slurp and suck and lick and bite.

"Duke, I feel dizzy," she whispered.

"You should," he said playfully. "Anybody would lose they mind, seein' all this pussy an' ass."

"No—"

"Yes," Duke said. "You probably so on fire right now you cain't think straight." He put his arm around her back, resting a hand on her shoulder. She shivered. The hot scent of his cologne, the heat of his body, the hardness and height of him next to her was so intense, her chest was literally rising and falling as if she'd just sprinted at a track meet.

If he touches my bare skin, I'll faint. She couldn't believe how electrified she felt with his hand on the velour fabric of her zip-up jacket. She looked into his eyes; the deep, penetrating tenderness of his voice made her cheeks burn.

"Baby girl, you look like you need some love so bad."

Her gaze trailed down to the spot where his shirt collar met at the top button, where his chest was exposed just enough to show where his smooth, baby-soft-looking pecs rose up to the right and to the left.

That's where I want to press my cheeks and go to sleep for three days. As if he heard her thoughts, he pulled her closer. Her lips felt hot and swollen with lust. She wrapped her arms around his waist.

Oh my God, he is so warm and strong.

Victoria's lips pressed directly into the center of his chest. His hot skin under her mouth was soft and sweet. She inhaled his scent—designer cologne, spicy male musk and sex.

The rise of his pecs touched the sides of her mouth, her cheeks. This was her spot. She rubbed her face in small circles there, not caring that all these people were around them or that Beamer was watching. The men and women who were fucking on the floor were so into their groove they probably couldn't care less.

A whistle blew and a deep male voice boomed through the gym. "Ladies, on your knees!"

Victoria turned to see a man—he was small, with dark, wavy hair and a white warm-up suit—taking over from the Asian-looking chick.

Duke grasped Victoria's shoulders and spun her so that the back of her body pressed into his chest, stomach, thighs. A huge, hard, hot rod pressed into her butt. She arched her back slightly, but stopped herself.

What the hell am I doing? This is a set-up. Henry probably told Duke what he saw me doing in the bathroom at Gramma Green's house. So, Duke would know I'm easy prey. I am.

She imagined Henry saying something like, "Dude, she want it. That horny bitch need some dick bad." So, now Duke felt it was his duty—and part of his premeditated plan to basically abduct her—to take care of her hormonal crisis, which was bad enough for any eighteen-year-old girl.

But I'm different. Celeste has dangerous powers.

"Check this out." Duke's deep voice vibrated through her more potently than ever, since their bodies were touching.

SEX IN THE HOOD

She leaned her head back into his chest. His chin rested on top of her head. He planted a kiss in her hair. Victoria closed her eyes. The warmth of his body, the comfort of it, made her want to stand there forever. It felt so good, nothing mattered at the moment. Not the wild, crazy fuck fest in front of them. Not the fact that she was an orphan in the ghetto with nowhere to go. Not the fact that she wanted to indulge the very urge that terrified her with the threat of deadly consequences. All that mattered right now was the affection and protective embrace of the urban god behind her.

Oh my God, I'm finally getting some love. A hug. A kiss.

Hot tears stung her eyes, blurring the sextravaganza before them. She blinked hard, letting the tears fall down her burning cheeks. With her eyes cleared, her body calm, she watched the action.

In one graceful motion, all the women rose up out of the squat position, aimed their open palms at the red floor mats, and dove forward with the liquid motion of acrobats. They fell to their knees, straddling the men's legs at their shins.

At the same time, the men sat up at the waist, pulled their legs from under the women, and got into a kneeling position. The women leaned forward on their elbows, stuck their butts up. Behind them, the men's giant dicks, rows of them in every color, pointed at all the beautiful, sweat-glistening butts.

"On the right!" The man with the whistle shouted.

The men didn't just fuck them doggie-style. They rose their left legs to a 45-degree angle from their bodies so they were balancing on their right legs only. It was like when a dog would raise its hind leg to pee on a fire hydrant or a tree. Rows and rows of testicles suspended in every color of skin sack from the base of big beige, brown and black dicks.

Then, in perfect unison and rhythm to the deep bass beat, the men drilled forward. Victoria knew how hard it was to do squats on two legs, but the way the men were balancing on one knee required incredible strength and endurace. Not to mention, with that relentless banging action, they had to have a high pain

166

threshold. Were their expressions pain or pleasure? The way some of them were twisting up their faces, it was hard to tell. If this was sexercise, then did the pleasure of one erase the pain of the other, or vice versa?

But it was beautiful. Their bodies were so toned and lean, it was like a lesson in muscle anatomy. Quads, hamstrings and glutes were flexing and glistening under smooth, taut skin.

"Harder!" the man commanded. "Pump it!"

The men fucked furiously.

A few women cried out. Their boobs were bouncing, hard nipples pointing down at the floor. Their faces—

Oh my God, I want to feel that so bad.

They looked like Victoria did in the mirror when she made herself cum. She was sure the giant dick rubbing into her ass right now could only make that sensation a million times more amazing.

"Now, slow and controlled," the man commanded.

The men slowed down, still moving in unison as gracefully as a dance troupe.

A guy who was grimacing cried out, "It fuckin' hurts!"

The commander's legs sliced like white scissors as he strode toward the whiner. "Look like you love this shit or you'll get twenty minutes straight!"

The woman he was fucking half-smiled as the guy pounded harder, his face a mask of false pleasure. He closed his eyes as if he were trying to block out the pain.

The sternness on the commander's face and in his voice made Victoria sober up for a second. This wasn't for fun. This was serious training for something. If Babylon did executive protection, what did fucking have to do with being a bodyguard? Unless these men and women provided a different kind of secret service . . .

Prostitution.

So, right now they were working out to be strong and lean, but also to fuck with Olympic strength and endurance.

SEX IN THE HOOD

Sexercise. Daddy used to always tell her the key to success in business was to do what nobody else thought of, then market, market, market!

The whistle blew. "Switch!" the commander shouted.

The men lowered their left legs to the floor, balanced on their left knees, then raised their right legs.

"Drill!"

They began fucking again, this time using only their left leg muscles—glutes, quads and hamstrings of every shade.

After a few minutes, the man shouted, "Pussy grind!" The men—many of them groaning with relief—knelt so they were sitting on their feet. The women also knelt, directly in front of the men, with their knees straddling the men's knees. The women looked like they were about to sit on the men's laps, but they speared down on their dicks then ground in full, exaggerated circles. The soft, beautiful flesh of their asses was going round and round, grinding against the men's flat, chiseled abs and rock-hard thighs.

It was the same way Victoria was pressing back against Duke. She wanted to run far away from this temptation, but at the same time she wanted to ram him deep inside her hot, slippery pussy. What in the world kind of place was she in?

Her skin was soaked, sweaty and prickly. Her mind was like melted butter, dripping through the rest of her, making a puddle in her panties. She was trembling. Her mind was spinning. What would it be like if she were naked, grinding back on Duke's dick, just like that?

"I can't," she whispered. "I can't."

No, she didn't want to end up like her mother, killing someone—or herself—with her mix-breed woman power that came out in sex.

No! She wanted to scream.

"Don't ever let them see you sweat," she remembered hearing Daddy say so many times—about the backstabbing cheerleaders who teased her when she had trouble doing a double flip; about the chemistry teacher who told her girls never got A's in his class (she did anyway); and about the blood-thirsty reporters who hounded her and her siblings at their school during the scandal just before he killed himself.

Now, Victoria wanted to cry, run, scream and fuck all at once.

I won't. If I have to make myself cum every ten minutes, I will.

She couldn't let Duke win. He planned this whole situation, to get her in here, horny out of her mind, so he could talk her into working for him. For now, since she had nowhere else to go, she would let Duke think he was winning. But she would always be beating him at his own game.

"Market this." She turned, looked up at him and whispered with a cool expression, as if she were seeing this every day. "Call it Sexercise, and you'll be an instant millionaire. All you need is a video camera and a website."

Duke stared down hard at her. "We don't give away our secrets. Not for any price."

The power of his eyes pulled those satin strings on the velvet drawstring purse between her legs. His scent made her dizzy. She turned to face him all the way. His beautiful face made her want to never look away.

That huge rod poking into her stomach made her pussy convulse. She squeezed her pelvic muscles as he pulled her close. Her nipples pressed into him . . . . His lips brushed against her trembling mouth and —

Victoria shivered.

Oh my God, I'm cumming from just a kiss.

Chapter 25

Duke knew she was ready to let him pop that juicy cherry.

I cain't wait no longer or Timbo gon' explode. An' she gon' faint from needin' some dick so bad.

He picked her up like he did his kids when they would fall asleep in the car and he had to carry them up to their mothers' apartments here at Babylon. With Duchess, he was so smooth, he picked her up without unlocking their lips.

Damn, ain't no kiss neva felt like this. Even the air around them was on fire, just like his skin, his dick, his heart, his head. He had his right arm under her knees, his left arm under her back, and she was kissing him while he walked past the sexercise to the elevator.

Ain't no secret. She gon' be e'rybody Duchess in a minute. They gon' bow to her jus' like they bow to The Duke, so might as well come out wit' it now. An' fuck Milan if she get a attitude. Ain't nothin' she can do about it from her apartment.

Duke pulled Beamer a few feet back, so nobody would hear him say, "Yo, B, I ain't available fo' nobody. Anything happen, han'le it."

"I'm on it, Massa Duke."

"I know 'bout e'rythang you be *on.*" Duke stared down hard into Beamer's big eyes, which popped like Buckwheat on them old-fashioned black and white re-runs of *The Little Rascals* he loved watching.

"But I ain't mad," Duke said. "Cain't no normal man keep his dick to hisself when Milan lay on her evil ways. 'Specially yo' stupid ass. An' I don' give a fuck who she screwin', long as they ain't 'round my babies."

Beamer quaked.

Good. "So, B."

"Yes, Massa Duke." His voice was all wavery and high-pitched like a girl.

WHITE CHOCOLATE

"You still ma boy."

Beamer nodded.

"If you wonderin' why I ain't gon' jus' pop yo' dumb ass, let me explain. It's Dominology 101. You gon' kiss ma ass even mo' fierce now, 'cause you know, one wrong move an' you—" Duke raised the last word to a higher octave, "—th'ough." He tossed his head back, laughing, stepping toward Duchess.

In the elevator, she sucked on his neck again, like she did in the car. No girl had ever kissed him like that, making the little muscles under his skin ripple and send sex shocks through his body.

Whatever nonsense she was mumbling about in the car, about a sex curse, that was the craziest shit he had ever heard. The only curse she was going to have was liking it so much she would want it twenty-four/seven. She would be tempted not to get anything done because she would always want to be fucking.

He still had to keep an eye on her, though. Yeah, she agreed to work for him, to stay here, but she didn't have a choice. Those pretty eyes were glowing with scheme, but whatever kind of break-out plan she was thinking, it wouldn't work. Couldn't trick The Duke. Beamer, Milan and his other baby mommas had already tried, along with half the niggas trying to make something happen in Detroit and beyond. So, this white bitch here, his Duchess, the girl he would cherish and protect forever, wouldn't succeed at whatever she tried. But he'd still keep an eye on her pretty ass.

The elevator rose to the tenth floor, opening onto the sharp-ass black marble hallway of his penthouse. It was all black marble, top, sides and bottom, with custom lights that glowed cobalt blue from behind silver BABYLON sconces, three on each side, leading toward the all-cream living room.

Duke carried Duchess through the foyer, past the couches and fireplace and floor-to-ceiling sliding glass doors that opened onto his terrace overlooking the city's skyline and river. Walking with her in his arms was easy. She felt light, like part of his own body.

171

SEX IN THE HOOD

He heard something that made him freeze. It was their song, "Duchess's Theme Song," which the Bang Squad had written, composed and produced for this night right here. Now it was pumping through his top of the line stereo system that played in every room of the penthouse.

"Listen, baby girl." Damn, looking down in those eyes made his heart stop a minute. She glanced up as if it helped her hear better. The tune was as soft as she was, with piano and a soft rumble of drums, just enough bass to make it sound masculine. Jamal was crooning like Marvin Gaye.

"Duchess, be my girl. Help me rule the world. Duchess, be my wife. Share this dream of life." Duke sang along, looking so deep into her teary eyes that he felt like he could dive in and swim around.

"Duchess, be my girl," Duke sang. "Help me rule the world. Duchess, be my wife. Share this dream of life."

She nodded slightly, never looking away from his eyes. He stepped into the bedroom, decorated like an Egyptian pharoah's palace. Custom lights were set behind tall columns along the walls, inlaid with colorful tiles in Egyptian patterns and hieroglyphics. They were already adjusted to cast a sexy peach haze through the huge room, especially on the two eight-foot-tall mummy cases on each side of the black lacquered dresser.

The face part of the cases always gave Duke this look like they were adding their power to his purpose. He loved the black eyeliner around the round, direct eyes, the richness of the gold-covered faces, the sharp contrast of the black stripes on their headdresses. The cases were arranged so they were facing the bed, focusing their power on Duke for when he finally made love with Duchess.

He stepped to the dresser, where he unclipped his phones from his belt, turned them off and set them down. They sat next to candles that were already burning, making the room smell like butterscotch. The burning logs crackled inside the white marble fireplace.

WHITE CHOCOLATE

He had his Duchess in his arms, ripe and ready. She was kissing him like she wouldn't be able to breathe if she unlatched her lips.

She won't. She done breathed Duke vapors, which addictive as hell. But I breathed hers, too, so we both hooked. Fo' life.

"Baby girl," he whispered, carrying her toward the bed. She put her hand behind his head and pulled his mouth back to hers. He stepped up the four white marble steps to the king-sized mahogany playpen surrounded by a canopy of sheer gold panels of shimmery silk.

He angled Duchess's head so she parted the curtains. He laid her on the gold silk bedspread. Her black hair fanned out around her head.

"You look like a angel," he whispered.

Her blue flame blowtorch eyes incinerated him. Timbo flipped harder than ever. Duke was actually trembling from head to toe. He was a little scared because he didn't want to hurt her. The way he felt, it was so overwhelming, he knew he would lose his mind up in that pretty pussy. And he hadn't even seen it.

"Take your shirt off," she whispered, lips and cheeks red as ever.

He unbuttoned his shirt, tossing it to a nearby chair. Her eyes trailed all over his chest, over his shoulders, down his arms and back again. It seemed like forever before she whispered, "Undress me."

He pulled off her gym shoes and her socks. He knelt down, sucked her pretty toes, sliding his tongue between each one.

Duke ran a hand between her legs, fingers outstretched to tickle the insides of her thighs. Then with his middle finger only, he ran it straight up the stretched-tight fabric over her pussy. It was hot, wet and meaty, like a meat flower all bunched up in there that would open up and suck him in like a big-ass stinger on a bee, dripping honey all over the place.

Duchess cried out. It was like agony and ecstasy all rolled into one sound. She was so horny it was hurting her, and it was his duty to relieve her of this suffering. She was his, and he needed to brand her with his tongue, his juice, his love. To burn their souls together into one, forever.

He put his fingertips on each side of the waistband on the pants he bought her. Touching the baby-soft skin of her hips, he pulled slowly.

His fingertips, which caught her panties too, trailed down the outsides of her hips, her thighs, her knees, her calves and her ankles. Then he just stood there, staring at her long-ass legs— smooth, creamy, toned. She had skin the color of the inside of an almond, white with a little bit of yellow-tan, on the prettiest legs he had ever seen. She raised her knees and just stared up at him from between the valley of her legs—like they were framing her face from where he was standing.

Her jacket still covered the tops of her thighs. He unzipped it, peeled it off her shoulders. He lifted each hand, kissed every finger, then pulled the wristband over her hand and laid her arm gently back on the bed.

She shivered when his hands passed over her nipples through the white T-shirt. She let out a little moan. She could start a fire the way she was looking at him.

Duke peeled off her T-shirt and unhooked her bra, letting loose the most beautiful nipples and titties he'd ever seen. Full, round, plump, with cinnamon-color circles that came to a point. And they tasted as sweet and soft as they looked. Duke sucked like a baby, twirling his tongue around that nipple that he would never let go of. Her back arched; her hands grasped the sides of his head. She pushed him up.

"Look at me," she whispered. "All of me."

First he stared into her eyes, which made his skin feel like flames were dancing up and down him from head to toe. Her face was too pretty to believe. His eyes traveled down that elegant, swanlike neck. Some of her straight black hair covered her creamy shoulder and made a fan against the gold silk under her. Her titties pointed straight at him. Her stomach was so pretty it was a sin, the way her waist curved in below her ribs. Her belly button was like a little eye, winking at him as her stomach rose and fell because she was breathing so hard already.

He wanted to take a fork and eat all that smooth, creamy skin over her hips, down to the black hair at the "V"of her pussy and—

"Oh . . . hell . . . yeah," he groaned.

Her clit was big, red and so wet it was shiny. It looked like a red rose pinned to a black mink coat.

She was so hot, her pussy was swole to the size of a blooming flower. She didn't have the man in the boat. Her clit was like a baby rosebud sticking up and out of that silky-soft fur he just wanted to reach out and stroke. All that pussy meat—it was like the petals of a rose all pressed together.

And her clit was moving! It looked like it was trying to jump up and dance around, so shiny it was like a wet watermelon Jolly Rancher that had been sucked enough to round the edges.

Duke's mouth watered so tough, it sprayed tiny dots of saliva over her creamy smooth stomach. He wanted to stare at this forever, but he didn't want her to clamp up and push him away. He had to get it while it was hot, before her mind took back over her body.

Her pussy juice was dripping. A white droplet shined right at the bottom of the slit of her pussy, leading to what was about to be his.

Dewdrops on a virgin rose. That sounded corny as hell, but that was all he could think of right now. Timbo wouldn't last but a Motor City minute up in that.

But naw, I cain't do her like that. Her first time gotta be so good she pass out.

Duchess needed him to saw off some serious timber up in that unexplored territory.

"Baby girl, you got the prettiest pussy on the planet."

"Her name is Celeste," she said matter-of-factly, staring up at him. "And she's been wanting you to kiss her since we first saw you this afternoon."

Day-um! Baby girl had a name for the pussy, talking about "we." All of a sudden he heard Momma's voice saying, *Be careful what you wish for, 'cause if you get it, you betta be ready . . .*

Duke knelt on the bed. He bent down, wanting to kiss her pretty thighs and that stomach . . .

But that pussy—

The sweet scent made Timbo so hard it hurt. He looked straight into her eyes. She was on her elbows, watching him over the smoothness of her stomach.

He almost didn't know where to start. But the tip of his tongue couldn't resist the tip of her clit. The way she was looking at him, her eyes were fiending for him to slurp on it all night.

"Baby girl, you ain't neva had nobody eat yo' pussy?"

"No," she groaned as if the thought hurt.

"I'm the first and the last," Duke whispered into the salty-sweet cloud of pussy vapors making his face feel hot. He had to go there first. It was so soft, so sweet, so clean. He stuck out his tongue as far it would go, then, with a soft, slow, small lick on that hot, wet velvet—

"Oh my God," she cried out. "Oh . . . my . . . God."

Then he wrapped his lips in an "O" shape all the way around that big, red clit. He sucked it into his mouth.

Her whole body heaved.

"Duuuuuke!" she moaned. It sounded so sexy. If he never heard another word, the way she said his name was the most beautiful sound ever to pass into his ears.

And he knew she was *through*. His mouth on her pussy was his magic pass to getting any- and everything he ever wanted from her. Didn't need to string her out on drugs like some thugs did to keep their bitches under control. All he had to do was turn her pussy into his own all-you-can-eat buffet, and she'd serve him every day, every way, forever.

The way she was arching her back, sticking the pussy up into his face harder, grinding her hips up into his mouth, she must have wanted this for a long time. Even if some suburban punk had tried it on her, there was no way he could have done it like The Duke.

Gotta take a big lick, too. So, from the skin between her pussyhole and her asshole—which he couldn't wait to see either, but he'd hold off for now, one thing at a damn time—he extended his tongue to a freakish length like Gene Simmons from that rock band Kiss, and stroked it up past the cream-covered virgin gates to separate the soft folds of pink flesh over the clit, up to the hair.

"Oh my God," she gasped.

He went back down, sucking on each lip, slurping up that sweet cream. It was so sweet it was like the lemon cake batter he used to lick off of Grammomma's bowl when he was little.

This chick pussy tasted like lemon cake batter!

That made Timbo throb even harder. The idea of sliding up into that never-been-entered pussy—

He stuck his tongue in, wrapped his lips around her clit, just to suck it in for a minute, like a scoop of strawberry ice cream melting under his kiss. Now it was time for his sure-fire trick to make her cum hard, so he could make her his forever.

Chapter 26

Tiny dots of light danced behind her eyelids as Duke ate her pussy. So many times she had practically begged Brian to perform oral sex on her, after she'd given him countless blow jobs. Brian always said it was disgusting to put his mouth there, especially when he thought about how period blood and pee came out of the same spot.

That punk motherfucker. A long time ago, when she was crying for her mother, her father told her that life was full of sadness so that people could remember and enjoy the happy times. That never helped much; Victoria still missed her mother. But right now, she knew the disrespect she got from Brian in so many ways was preparing her to take this incredible love from Duke.

Just like the horrible events of the past few weeks were also getting her ready for a new life. Nothing that felt this good—from just looking into Duke's eyes to listening to his voice to feeling him touch her this way—could possibly be wrong.

There has to be a purpose, a reason that I am in this place called Babylon, feeling like I never knew a person could feel. Because Daddy said everything, even the bad stuff, happens for a good reason.

"Duke," she whispered. "Yeah, Duke, do that to me."

His forearms were under her hips, and his giant hands gripped the insides of her thighs. He squeezed her soft flesh then rose up, looking into her eyes.

"Baby girl, you got me. Fo'ev'a. Fo'ev'a."

His head descended back down.

"Love what you do," Victoria moaned. "My pussy, Celeste, loves what you do."

The way his tongue was moving, it was beyond words. The rhythm reminded her of a windshield wiper. The tip of his tongue was like the end of the blade; the thicker part of his tongue was the length of it. He sloshed it back and forth over her clit, first soft, then harder, then soft again, increasing the pressure with every stroke. It went back and forth, back and forth, in a half-circle motion, applying more pressure with every wipe. Then soft again, harder, harder —

That was what it felt like on the outside of her clit. The inside of her clit felt like a starburst, a yellow-orange-and-red ball of fire between her legs. Every time Duke licked her, the fireball got hotter, sending out sparks farther and farther through her body. Pretty soon she knew it was going to explode, making her whole body shimmer with heat and light. But right now, she was loving the psychedelic sensations making her mind, body and spirit look and feel like a Fourth of July fireworks display.

This is unbelievable.

She gripped her fingertips into the soft skin of his head, holding him there as she moaned softly, never wanting this moment to end — except for when he took her all the way to relieve this horrible curiosity and ache. After so long without a hug or any love, after the trauma of losing life as she knew it, she finally felt safe. Loved. Happy.

She felt this, even though she was going against her lifelong vow to never, ever unleash the *femme fatale* between her legs, whose mix-race woman powers named Celeste were so powerful they killed her mother. Fucked to death by the man who just couldn't get enough. Could that be Duke? Or could it go the other way around?

If this is the way I'm gonna die, then so be it, because this is heaven on Earth.

And Celeste, her pussy powers, had answered in Gramma Green's bathroom — the only way to seize the power was to let it free, unleash it with someone she loved.

"Duke, you are a god," she whispered. "You are a *gohhhhhhd.*" She thrust her hips up higher, spread her legs wider.

Never had she even imagined anything so incredible.

Celeste was in seventh heaven. She never would have believed it felt this good. Tiffany had oral sex and said it was great, but she said the prick who did it to her was sloppy and impatient, then ran to the bathroom to gargle for a full five minutes afterwards. And she hadn't even cum.

Not Duke. He acted like he wanted to stay down there all day and would drink a glass of her pussy juice if she gave him a straw.

"Duke," she cried, "what are you doing?"

A finger slid into her pussy. In and out, in and out, all while he did the windshield wiper tongue motion on her clit.

"Aaahhhh," she moaned, her whole body trembling.

The starburst was getting bigger, hotter, radiating through her every cell as if the sun were rising between her legs, as if the black dome of Duke's bald head between her white thighs was the cataclysmic fusing of two worlds. Lightning, meteor showers, tidal waves, volcanic eruptions would surely follow. At least that was what it felt like inside Victoria's body and brain.

She was breathing so hard, her ears were ringing.

And now another finger pressed up into her pussy. He was moving his fingers in her pussy in a way that reminded her of the butterfly stroke that swimmers did: arms spread out, then body rising up and down smoothly, fluidly, making a rippling motion through the water. Through her pussy.

If two of his big fingers fit inside her, and she had no problem with Dildo Dick, then maybe Duke's penis wouldn't hurt as much as she feared.

Brian was always begging her to go all the way, pressuring her by saying if she didn't fuck him, they'd have to break up so he could find someone who would fuck. He would threaten this, even though he was constantly refusing to do exactly what Duke was doing right now.

I'm glad Duke is the first because this has got to be the best, anywhere, ever.

That starburst was sparking, flaming. It was spraying red-hot sparks up her abdomen, through her chest, making the points of her nipples tingle and burn. Her fingertips were tingling. Her toes were twitching. The muscles in her legs were trembling. Her pussy was quivering around his fingers and under his tongue.

WHITE CHOCOLATE

Duke let out a deep moan like this was the most delicious thing he had ever tasted. Like it was his oxygen.

"Oh my God," she whispered. "Oh my God."

The fireball was roaring, rumbling . . . exploding.

Great flames of red, orange and yellow licked out through her limbs, flashed behind her closed eyelids, made her heart glow white-hot.

"Oh, hell yeah," Duke groaned as her pussy pulsated around his finger. Another white-hot flash of fire shot down her legs, up her belly, over her nipples, down her fingertips, into her head, which glimmered in a psychedelic swirl of color and light.

"Yeah, baby girl," he whispered. "You ready for me now."

He kissed her mouth. She licked and sucked off every drop of her own sweet juice. It felt so nasty, so liberating.

And she felt drunk on champagne.

Finally, her pussy powers filled her head with the idea that from now on, she would never go without a man who could make her cum like that. She would settle for nothing less.

Duke ran his hand over her still-throbbing clit, down into the juices, to the satin-soft, soaked skin where Celeste was about to suck him in whole. With his face so close to hers that their noses touched, he stared into her eyes and whispered, "Let Duke make love to his Duchess. I'm gon' anoint you. Make you mine."

Victoria thrust upward, impatient, wanting to shove that big, beautiful dick inside her like the world was going to end tomorrow and they had to fuck right up until they died. She wanted to take every inch of this black god, this Mandingo warrior, this knight in a shining Porsche who rescued her in the middle of Ghettoland. This man she was studying, learning from, so that one day this very act that made him feel like he was dominating her—helpless, homeless, with nowhere to go—would enable her to whip him into submission. So she could dominate.

"Now," she whispered. "Fuck me now, Duke."

Chapter 27

Duke stood at the side of the bed, staring down into two silver-blue moons begging him to make love like he had never done before. Her lips were more red than ever. Her perfect little nipples were pointing at him, calling him. Her pussy hair was a soft black bush at the "V"of her juicy thighs.

Thinking about being with Duchess for the dick-down of the millennium didn't even come close to what it would be like in a minute. If she could cum that hard with his mouth, then she would no doubt damn near kill him when Timbo slid up in the prettiest pussy God ever made.

Duke had seen thousands of pussies. He sold pussies—fat ones, thin ones, long clits, flat clits, plump lips, hanging-down-skinny lips, wet pussies, dry pussies, shaved beavers, bushy beavers, cute cunts.

But Duchess . . . he had never seen a pussy like that in a titty bar, even in Vegas, or in a magazine. And the way she looked right now, laying there waiting on the big, Egyptian king bed he had picked out of rich-ass *Architectural Digest* magazine, this was some shit right out of the movies.

The movie of my life, The Duke, starring Duke Johnson as himself, and introducing The Duchess.

"We 'bout to make magic," he said deeply as he unbuttoned his white linen pants. Timbo bulged like a mug, about to saw right through these pants. His dick had never throbbed like this. He had never wanted a woman so bad, not even the first time. He pulled down his pants and his white cotton briefs at the same time.

Her blue moon eyes grew huge. Her lips opened.

She rose up, crawled over, put her hands up like she was praying—one hand on each side of Timbo, with her fingertips touching. And she stared into his black eye.

182

Chapter 28

Victoria couldn't believe her eyes. She knew it would be huge, but it was breathtakingly beautiful. A giant, shiny head— the way the edge of the head curved around reminded her of Darth Vader's helmet in *Star Wars*. She could almost hear his deep voice saying, "Welcome to the dark side."

I'm already here.

She just wanted to stare at it, let her gaze trace that long vein that ran from the head back to the silky nest of hair. She ran her fingertips along the length of it. The skin was soft as satin and smooth as glass.

She glanced up at Duke, letting her eyes study the perfection of his body, from his slim hips to his tapered waist, his muscular chest, his beautiful delicious neck to his strong-jawed face with those spectacular, sexy eyes and sensuous mouth.

His palms gently stroked the hair on top of her head.

"Duchess," he said softly.

"Yes." She stared into his eyes.

"I want you an' Celeste to meet somebody. Timbo."

She looked at the hole at the end of his penis. The bulging ball of black flesh all around it, the gorgeous head of his dick, almost did look like a face, with the hole as the mouth. It looked like it was making an "O", like when kids would catch another kid saying something bad, they'd say, "Ooooooo, I'm gonna tell!"

Was that her conscience trying to tattle on her, since she was about to break her vow of celibacy?

Victoria puckered. She placed the softest kiss over the "O" that was Timbo's mouth.

"Enchantée." She whispered the French word for "enchanted," which people say when they first meet.

She wanted to suck him down whole, but first—

Victoria leaned close to the soft nest of hair and inhaled deeply.

183

"Ooooh," she moaned. "I *loooove* that smell."

"Damn," Duke whispered.

She leaned down a little, cupped his big, hot balls in the palm of her hand, raised them toward her nose.

Sniiiiiiffff.

"Oh my God," she groaned. "Get me a bottle of this so I can smell it all day. Call it Essence of —"

"Essence of Bo-Bos," Duke said, laughing. "Cain't b'lieve you like smellin' ma balls."

"It's delicious. Like sweet and musky. I knew I'd wanna stick my face right here and stay for a long time."

"Day-um," Duke moaned, gently gripping the top of her head with one hand.

She stuck out her tongue, ran the tip of it against the mauve-black skin of his balls.

He sucked in loudly. "Yeah, do that, baby girl."

Just like she'd done his neck earlier, she sucked in a mouthful of the skin and gently sucked, tickling the flesh beneath.

"Ma'fuck me!" he groaned.

Victoria gave his balls a tongue bath, slurping up, down, all around. Then, cupping his damp balls in her hand, she took his huge dick into her mouth. She slid her wet lips down the length, sucking at the same time, until Timbo hit the back of her throat. Several inches of tree trunk remained between her lips and his nest of silky black hair.

"Yeah, swallow that cock," he groaned.

She sucked for a while longer, never gagging, just savoring the sensation of him inside her as she inhaled his intoxicating male pheromones. Slurping up and down, over and over, with a very wet mouth and slightly open lips, she made super-sexy-nasty, wet-sucking noises that made Duke moan. The slippery hotness of her lips against his iron-hard dick, and the feeling of taking him whole into her hot mouth made her pussy drip.

WHITE CHOCOLATE

The sex smell, all those sweet-musky male scents set off something inside her that made her want to fuck until she couldn't see straight. Victoria pulled back, looked up at him.

"I love the way your dick feels in my mouth. It's like rock-hard dick against my soft tongue and throat. "

"Bite it," Duke said with a harsh tone.

"What?"

"Bite my cock."

He took her right hand, her index finger, and made tiny bites from the tip . . . over the joints . . . down to the knuckles.

"Ow," she said. "Bite that hard?"

"Yeah."

She took a bite at the tip of Timbo's head, just pressing her teeth gently into the firm flesh, which had the same chewy-hardness between her teeth as the escargot she'd eaten in restaurants with her father.

"Harder," Duke ordered. "All the way up and down my dick."

She did it, taking tiny, harder bites, all in a row as if she were chomping a celery stick or a Cheeto or a Twizzler.

"Hell yeah," Duke groaned. "Do that so good, baby girl."

As she bit up and down his dick, suddenly a rhyme came to mind.

This is bizarre . . . Won't I scar this chocolate bar? I'm 'bout to fuck as I suck. What luck, I'm so struck to let him pluck my cherry, my virgin berry that's so very extraordinary . . . 'Cause I need it and he'll feed it. Will he bleed it? No, he freed it . . . from the torture. My sex's a scorcher. Smell his balls and duty calls, my booty calls in mystery halls, this place he calls Babylon. My opinion is Celeste will get caressed by the best, no longer stressed . . . as Duke bangs my ass 'til I pass . . . out!

"Oooh, baby girl, com'ere."

She stood on the bed in front of him. He kissed her stomach then with his hands on her hips, turned her.

"Prettiest ass I ev'a seen in my life!" he exclaimed.

His lips tickled soft kisses all over the round mounds of her butt. His hands traced the curves of her hips, her butt cheeks, her

185

thighs. Then he rubbed his face all over her ass, squeezing it, moaning, raising it up, sticking his tongue down in it, licking it.

"This beautiful ass all for me," he groaned, sucking the curve of her cheek. "Juicylicious. Like a big white chocolate kiss meltin' in my mouth."

Victoria smiled, loving every second of his praise. His appreciation for her size and shape thrilled her after all those cold comments from Brian about how she had a fat butt and needed to lose weight, how she needed to make it flat like all the other x-ray thin girls at school.

That punk. If I ever see him again, I'm gonna kick his ass like I shoulda done a long time ago, especially when he tried to rape me when he found out I'm black.

Yeah, I'm black. My super-round booty is just like the black girls in that gym. It was identical to Mommy's, not flat and tiny like Tiffany's or the other girls at the academy. But it was not that the size and shape of her ass should determine her entire racial identity. After all, Daddy was a big part of her, and he was white. And her skin was practically white.

But I feel different. I feel something changing inside me. Not just Duke's hot tongue slurping between her butt cheeks, and not just the liberation of her lust, but something seriously different.

"Baby girl, let me lay you down."

Chapter 29

Duke wanted to stop because he was about to lose his mind in his own bed. He couldn't build up Babylon and impress Knight when he got out in two weeks if he were stone cold crazy from some pussy. Even if it was sweet, virgin pussy that was spread out on gold silk waiting for him to just take! What made it even more hype was that this was happening on the same day he met this goddess whom he had just *picked* right out of the headlines.

I got what I wished fo'. Now I ain't ready.

Maybe Momma was right, talking about white chicks like she did. They definitely were the reason Knight was in jail, after those hillybilly motherfuckers got mad that their slutty little sister was sniffing around a big black dude who didn't even want her stank ass.

Now maybe Duke needed somebody who wasn't everything all wrapped into one perfect package. Shit, the way Duchess was talking to him earlier tonight, with balls as big as his . . . maybe he didn't need an equal. Maybe he needed somebody less than him, somebody he could control.

"What are you thinking?" she asked, looking up with the kind of eyes that love songs were written about.

"You too much, baby girl. You too much."

An' I'm fuckin' ridiculous, standin' here wit' the biggest, hardest dick of the century, wit' the finest chick on the planet who waitin' to fuck me, an' I'm hesitatin'.

Earlier tonight, when they had pulled into the garage and Knight called, his big brother had said, "Hesitation will get you killed. But a premature move will get you jacked too."

And that was what this was. Now that he was taking a closer look, this chick was too damn pretty. Too bold. Too sexy. She sucked dick too good. She took a tongue job too good. Her body was too bangin' and she was too smart, could talk like a queen.

SEX IN THE HOOD

What if she turned around and tried to beat The Duke at his own game? No, not try, just straight up demolish his ass with all the tricks he was about to teach her. No doubt, he had seen some scheme in her big, pretty eyes all night long. He saw it even though he was playing her, especially in the gym, when he knew she'd get so damn horny she wouldn't care about nothing but sliding down on this tree trunk and trying to break it off for a few days straight.

"Duke, if you're just gonna stand there contemplating life and love, I'm gonna take a nap." She pulled one of the half-dozen gold silk pillows from the head of the bed and rested her cheek on it. "I don't remember the last time I got some sleep."

He stared at the way she turned her body. She was lying on her side and her hip was pointing up, with those long legs across his bed and her candy toes touching his thighs.

I ain't neva had a mo' ridiculous chain o' thoughts than what jus' went through my head. Standin' here wit' Timbo swole, a goddess in my bed, an' I'm playin' fuckin' philospher.

Even his favorite self-help book, *Think and Grow Rich*, said successful men made decisions quickly and changed them very slowly. Meaning, *go wit' yo' firs' gut reaction an' stick wit' it.* And that was what Duke was doing with his Duchess.

'Cause The Duke don't choke.

He smiled, then said deep and raspy, "Naw, baby girl, you so beautiful, I was jus' paralyzed for a minute. Like when I firs' saw you, I couldn't breathe."

A seductive smile beamed up at him. She said with a businesslike tone, "Duke, I want you to wear a condom."

"I'm clean, baby girl."

"So am I."

"We both clean, we don't need—"

"I'm not doin' it without one," Duchess said with a shrug.

He stared into her blue-gray eyes. What if she wasn't a virgin? Her pussy smelled clean, looked clean. No way did she have anything. And if she got pregnant, then good. They'd have the prettiest baby in Babylon and beyond. Plus, that would definitely make her stay forever.

"Baby girl, I get tested all the time."

She pulled her knees to her chest and wrapped her arms around her legs.

"I want you to feel all of me," he whispered. "A condom gon' block the—"

"Exactly," she said. "Pregnancy is not on my agenda right now. And I don't want to have to worry about STDs. Nothing personal. It's just a fact, whether I'm with some rich white guy from the academy or with you. HIV doesn't discriminate."

"You right," Duke said. "I cain't argue when you tryin' to be safe." He went to the nightstand, opened the top drawer and pulled out a condom then rolled it down on Timbo. "There. But after this, you an' me gon' go get tested together an' neva have to worry about it again."

Timbo looked like a black rocketship shooting toward her as he knelt on the bed, crawled over to her, and sucked her pretty mouth between his lips.

Chapter 30

Victoria loved the way Timbo was sliding between her legs. Not penetrating, just sliding down over the wet slick that couldn't wait to suck in that big, black dick.

"I don't want to hurt you," Duke whispered. His hot, damp cheek pressed against hers. The huge head of his cock pressed into the wet lips. He had put a towel under her, in case she bled when he popped her cherry. Tiffany said she made a huge mess when her boyfriend fucked her the first time. It was like her period all over her thighs and the bed.

Ugh, I hope that doesn't happen with me. Seems like Dildo Dick would've already softened the ground.

"I want you to look into my eyes while you come inside me," she whispered. Her legs were spread wide. That totally open, exposed feeling made her pussy dance with anticipation. She studied the sparkles in his eyes in the dim light. He reminded her of a genie . . . his bald head, his bright eyes, and the way his black eyebrows were so perfectly arched, as if they were painted on. It made him look happy, sexy, picture perfect.

She grabbed the round curves of his butt, one cheek in each palm. His glutes were rock-hard. Solid muscle, no fat. The skin was soft, smooth, hairless. Her fingers spread over luscious muscle.

Timbo's head was right inside her cream-covered pussy lips. Victoria pulled his butt toward her. The flesh of her pussy felt so swollen and hot, she imagined his dick slicing into it like a hot knife in already half-melted butter. Easy. Smooth. Painless.

"You sure you ready, baby girl?" he whispered.

She thrust her hips up. He slid deeper. Sharp pain. The voice of her pussy, Celeste, screamed in her mind. *What the fuck are you doin' to me? This torture* can't *be what I've been craving for so long!*

He shoved his dick even deeper.

Victoria cried out.

190

He froze. "My baby okay?"

"It feels like a knife."

"Wanna stop?"

"No. Will it get better?"

"Yeah," he whispered. "If I do if soft and slow."

"Okay." In just a few strokes, it felt like Tinkerbell was waving her magic wand over them and tiny gold stars were lighting up every inch of her body.

Her pussy throbbed, loving the iron-hard rod pounding in and out. The more he pumped, the more her whole body shivered. Her cheeks felt like fire. Her mouth sucked on the beautiful black skin of his shoulder, right where the deltoid muscle formed that little groove that rippled when he moved.

The fucking made tingly waves wash through her, from head to toe, and the more he pounded her pussy, the more intense it got. The waves—big ones, little ones, giant ones—they were hot, rippling through her in a way that made her skin tingle, her nipples harden, her lips quiver, her insides sizzle.

"Oh, baby girl," he groaned. "I ain't never had no pussy this good in my whole life, baby girl. Fo' real."

The sex on his voice, the passion, the adoration, the intoxication made Victoria feel drunk. She reached between her legs, pressing her fingertips onto her clit, rubbing, rubbing.

"Oh my God!" she screamed. Her mind splashed with stars—yeah, she was seeing stars—as her skin, her muscles, her bones, her soul felt as if stars were exploding inside her. Hot, potent, beautiful. She convulsed with orgasm as Duke continued to ram Timbo into her hot, hungry hole.

Her pussy pulsated as she came, squeezing around him, welcoming him into her soul.

This is the power, a sultry voice whispered inside her head. *This is the essence of the power*. It was Celeste.

And then her mother's voice. *Use it here, everywhere, to get what you want.*

"Duke," Victoria moaned. "Duke, I'm yours. All yours."

Chapter 31

Duke savored every stroke. He never wanted to touch or kiss another woman in his life. This queen *would* be his wife.

Ain't no way I'll ev'a let go of this. Let another nigga even think about tryin' to get some o' this sweet stuff. He'll have a sure-fire ticket to join Prince over at Elmwood Cemetery. Nobody. 'Cause this is heaven, and I'm stayin'. Forever.

The way Duchess was responding, even though this was her first time, she would never let go either.

"Duchess, you like my love?"

"No," she moaned. "I loooooove it. Love it."

Duke hoped their heat would melt the condom away, shred it, rip it, so she'd get pregnant right now. Seeing that pretty stomach bulge with his flesh and blood growing up inside this goddess, that would make him Triple Massa Duke. No better present God or the Universe could give him for turning twenty-one on Friday. When he presented his official Duchess to everybody at the party, the shit would be *on*.

"Oh, baby girl, you just don't know."

"Now I do."

"I been smellin' yo' sex all day. 'Bout ta drive me crazy. I ain't neva met a girl horny as you. Damn, I could make love to you for a week straight."

"I'm game." She giggled. "Wear me *out*."

Duke groaned out a little laugh as he fucked her harder. "Soundin' like a sistah already."

Chapter 32

Victoria loved every second of his pumping and pounding.

All I gotta do is lay here and get fucked.

She gripped the round curves of his beautiful shoulders, his deltoids, which were as toned and lean as all those men down in the gym. She pressed her open lips to the soft skin of his shoulder, sucking, kissing, licking. Did Duke work out like that, to that sexercise routine?

I want to. With him as my partner.

Someday she would squat on him like the women in the gym. But right now, she just wanted him to keep on banging relentlessly, with that wild look in his eyes.

A rhyme came to mind. But this time, she spoke it out loud to Duke.

"Oooh, jackhammer," she moaned, gasping for breath. "I stammer, wild pussy rammer . . . Wham! Bam! Slammer!" She glanced up at the beautiful sheer gold fabric around the bed. "Love this glamour. Anybody jealous? Damn her."

"Rap that shit," he groaned, fucking her ferociously.

She rhymed, "Love that sound when you pound the round mound of my ass." She giggled. "Dick me, stick me, lick me, pick me—" She gasped. "With Timbo, I'm in limbo. Ain't no bimbo."

Duke tossed his head back, laughing, flashing those beautiful, big white teeth.

"Girl, you rappin' like nobody business."

"I ain't rappin' while you slappin' an' you tappin'—" She drew her eyebrows together. "Wait, Duke, isn't that an expression, 'tappin' that ass'? Did I say it right?"

Duke bust out laughing. "Don't make me laugh, baby girl, else I cain't fuck you senseless like you need. Matt'a fac', I'ma fuck you 'til you cain't rhyme to save yo' life."

"Oooohh," Victoria gushed. "Bring it on, bring it out, make me shout, leave no doubt."

193

Duke wrapped his giant hands around her legs, just above her knees, then pressed her legs forward. That opened her pussy wider so he could really bang it.

"Fuck me fast, squeeze my ass, make me gasp." The jackhammer action made her voice waver like she was sitting on a washing machine and the load was off balance, making it shake violently.

She loved the union of their bodies. His dark hips over her milky ones. The base of Timbo looking like a log disappearing into a cave covered with black vines. Her thighs raised in a "V" shape as if her body were making the peace sign that hippies made with their index and middle fingers.

"Don't stop," she moaned. He pressed her knees into her boobs then banged harder. "Make my eyes pop out . . . shout . . . your cock . . . knocks me out." She sucked in air. He rammed and rammed and rammed.

"You're bionic . . . supersonic . . ." Orgasmic waves made Victoria go limp. Her arms and hands fell to the bed. Her head turned to one side. Her legs flapped in his grip. "Kronked," she whispered, "out cold."

Yeah, he was bionic. Felt like they'd been fucking forever and a day. Like he could fuck her for eternity and then some.

And I love it. The slap of skin on skin, their bodies gliding on a soft sheen of sweat, the fiery heat between them, their panting—Victoria was just lost in erotic euphoria. She hadn't thought about her situation for a while. No more sadness, no more worry, no more fear. Just pure pleasure, because this was the most mind-numbing indulgence, more than wine, more than eating a brownie, more than watching a good movie.

Sex was pure opium.

The perfect escape from all her worries.

It was something she would take every day, her magic remedy for stress, anxiety. Yeah, Duke could sex her up every day as therapy to the mind, body and soul. She'd never worry again.

"Oh my God, what are you doing?"

WHITE CHOCOLATE

His hands were reaching behind her, beneath her, taking her ass in his palms, squeezing his fingers gently into her flesh, tilting her hips up ever higher, stimulating her even more. He pounded with more ferocity than ever, like he was going to split her in half, pummel her pussy into a banana split full of marmalade.

"Oh, baby girl, we just gettin' started. Before this life is through, I'm gonna flip you every which way you never imagined. Make you cum so tough you won't know which way is up or down. The only word you'll be able to say is 'Duke.'"

She exploded in laughter because that was exactly her plan for him.

"Go for it," she whispered, thrusting her hips up.

Duke wrapped his hands around her ankles, raised them into the air, and thrust from his knees. He pounded and pumped, making her shiver and scream.

"I'm 'bout to cum," he groaned, laying down on her, kissing her forehead, her eyes, her cheeks.

"Cum for Duchess," she whispered. "Cum for me, Duke."

"Oh, baby girl. Baby girl."

He thrust with so much force, her whole body shivered. It was like a heat blast that was mashing their bodies into one delicious mix. Duke and Duchess, cream and coffee, blending into one exotic-erotic fusion of flesh, passion and purpose, power and potency.

"Yeah, baby girl. Oooh yeah." He shuddered, pressed his hot cheek to hers, sucked her lips into his mouth.

She wrapped her arms around his smooth, broad back, tickling the baby-soft mounds and valleys of damp skin, pulling him deeper.

"Oh, baby girl!" he shouted. "Duchess, baby!"

He pulled Timbo out, yanked off the condom, and jacked his dick over her. A fountain of white cream sprayed over her bare, quivering stomach. His face twisted, but he focused hard on her.

"You mine now," he groaned then lay next to her, kissing her face. "I'm yours, Duchess baby. All yours."

SEX IN THE HOOD

Victoria couldn't get close enough to him. She wanted to press her body right through him so their souls could touch. She had no words for this feeling. She couldn't describe the magic he just worked on her body or explain the whole race-sex phenomenon she thought about constantly.

Mommy spoke to me! She said this is the way to get what I want. Now I know . . .

She suddenly felt overwhelmed with gratitude for her mother, her father and Duke, because their words and actions all helped her figure it out. It wouldn't kill her to share her body; it would give her more power.

But right now, all she wanted to do was curl up in the curve of Duke's body and sleep for days. She hadn't slept in half a week, but finally, she was safe in this sexy cocoon of silk and strong man, where a deep sleep in his arms would bring the same mind-numbing euphoria as the lovemaking she just shared with him.

He pulled her into the spoon position. Lying on his side, he drew her back to his chest, her ass into the L-shape of his torso and legs, the backs of her thighs on the tops of his. It felt so good, she closed her eyes.

But her lids raised just as quickly as she thought, *He wants me to work for him. If he makes love to me like this all the time, I'd rob a bank if he asked me to.*

Not really, but what did he possibly want her to do that could be so bad? He was breathing softly in her ear, his cheek nestled in her hair on the fluffy pillows.

No, she couldn't sleep now. This sheltered suburban girl had to figure out how to play this game without losing to his slick street smarts, without letting sex influence her common sense or jeopardize her future.

She lay awake for hours, savoring every sensation of his long body behind hers. Her butt on his hard thighs. Her back against his stomach. His broad chest embracing her shoulders, his long arms wrapped around her, his hot breath on her neck. Their ankles twisted together. His scent all over her.

WHITE CHOCOLATE

She lay awake for another reason: fear. A little voice inside her was laughing. Alice in Ghettoland just danced past the DO NOT ENTER signs on the door marked HOME.

And there was no EXIT sign.

Chapter 33

It was 6:15 p.m. as Knight Johnson rose from the hard brown couch in the rec room. The TV news was blaring, but Knight was too excited to hear it. He had to go call Duke. One step and he felt like he was floating over the beige tile.

I've called Duke every Monday night since I've been in here. But tonight's call is different, more important than ever.

"Yo, Knight," Lonnie shouted. "Eitha tha's yo' baby brotha or yo' papa's rollin' stone jus' turnt up a secret pebble on da news."

Lonnie, sitting on the couch at the edge of a dozen men on couches and chairs, turned his round, acne-scarred face, framed by wild tufts of hair that looked like flames shooting from his head. His face, even after all this time, still made Knight think of when he would sneak a peek into the oven to see Momma's oatmeal-raisin cookies as they baked on the blackened cookie sheet. The shiny, half-baked circles were lumpy, beige and dotted with dark spots.

"Check 'im out." Lonnie pointed at the TV. His legs stretched over the chipped wooden coffee table strewn with sections of today's local newspaper. Knight usually read the paper in the morning, but today his energies had focused on something bigger.

And better.

"An' drivin' a Porsche wit' gold rims!" Lonnie shifted, making the front page of *The Detroit News* crinkle under his leg. "I *know* The Duke ain't that stupid to pose up in the middle o' that mess. The media an' 5-0? He askin' —"

"You right, Lon," Knight said with super-cool nonchalance. "The Duke ain't about to get sprung up in that chick's media storm. An' you should know better. E'ry dark-skinned bald dude don't all look alike."

WHITE CHOCOLATE

"Depend who lookin'," Marvin Dinkins grumbled from the other end of the couch. "Some look-alike the reason I be up in this shithole. An' don't none o' dese cocksuckas in charge wanna hear 'It wasn't me.'" Marvin pointed a long, black finger and deepened his voice, imitating authorities. "'It was *you*, nigga. Fi'teen years! No paro'e!'"

"Who you tellin'?" Lonnie scolded. "If anybody know dat, it's Knight. That was some 1950s Emmitt Till shit they pulled on ma boy." Lonnie focused back on the TV.

"Dey go dat white choc'lit chick who daddy be French kissin' Smith an' Wesson," Marvin said.

Lonnie pointed up to the TV, where the news report showed the young lady walking right past Duke and Beamer in the Porsche. Knight had seen reports about her father's suicide over the past several weeks.

"They talkin' 'bout she look white," Lonnie said. "Ssshhhheeeee-it. One look at that ass oughtta erase e'ry question mark on that page." Lonnie nodded toward the newspaper, which Knight picked up.

Nearly a whole page of articles and pictures surrounded a bold headline: CULTURE SHOCK: MILLIONAIRE'S DAUGHTER FALLS FROM WHITE PRIVILEGE TO BLACK POVERTY. Under that, a smaller headline said: VICTORIA WINSTON'S BIRACIAL LIFE SHOWS HUGE GAP BETWEEN RACES.

In one of the photos was Duke, Beamer and the Porsche, as she was walking past. It also showed kids on bikes, teens in hoopties and Sha'anté and her girls striking intimidating poses on the sidewalk.

Gawkers, the caption said, *greeted Victoria Winston's arrival in the poverty-ravaged neighborhood — which is known for shootings, drug use and an illegal dog fighting ring — with stares, jeers and sinister rap music blasting from cars and houses"*

Knight bit down, making his jaw muscles flex.

Why didn't Li'l Tut know better than to sit in the middle of a media beehive? Didn't matter if it was the Thanksgiving Day parade coming through the neighborhood. Duke did not need his face in the newspaper or on TV, even if he was wearing dark sunglasses. He wanted to run Babylon, but didn't have the common sense to stay out of the spotlight?

He was thinking with the head in his lap.

Was Duke just naively enjoying the spectacle of Victoria being dropped off at Miss Green's house? Was he trying to meet her? Recruit her to work for The Squad? If so, Li'l Tut knew the recruitment of Sluts was always done on the down low, not in front of the media!

The media was making sport out of this poor girl's tragedy. Knight glanced at the newspaper, which even had a satirical sidebar and scoreboard, comparing what her white life was and what her black life could be like.

	Before	*Now*
Home:	$3 million lakeside mansion In suburb	$10,000 Bungalow In Detroit slum
School:	15K tuition @ The Academy	Lost college financing
Guardian:	Father	Ailing grandmother
Car:	New $50K SUV	City buses
Recreation:	Yacht club, shopping, coffeehouse poetry	Illegal dog fights, sex, dodging bullets
Boyfriend:	Son of auto industry heir, Brian Anderson	Local drug dealer
Best friend:	Tiffany Bartlett, Daughter of shopping center mogul	Round the way girls
Income:	$200/wk allowance $5 million trust fund	None

The TV newscaster drew Knight's attention to the screen.

"You may recall," said preppy black anchor Orville Smith, "on Sunday, Victoria Winston was taken from this lakefront mansion in an elite, gated community in the suburbs to this decrepit house in one of Detroit's worst neighborhoods. The business-savvy eighteen-year-old, who worked closely with her father, Daniel Winston, says he is wrongly accused of embezzling ten million dollars from his investors."

Knight was mesmerized and impressed by the young lady's incredible poise as her elegant stride took her past a mob of reporters outside her lakeside mansion. She exuded womanly maturity and intelligence, yet the long, black ponytail bouncing just above her Betty Boop butt maintained her girlishness.

As reporters shouted questions about her dead parents, her race and her life, she stopped and looked straight into the camera. Incredible confidence flashed in her big blue eyes, set in a buttermilk face with very ethnic, come-kiss-me lips whose natural red color had the power to put cosmetics companies out of business.

Knight was awe-struck by how she tilted her chin upward just a little bit. With a voice that was all at once sultry and brilliant, she told reporters, "I refuse to justify or even acknowledge your nonsensical, insulting questions with a response."

That girl has the power. He held the newspaper in front of his khakis. His dick was instantly erect.

One look from me an' she gon' melt into some white chocolate fondue so I can dip my lead pipe in it . . . and my tongue . . . my lips . . . my nose . . . my fingers . . . my toes . . . my soul . . . an' then I'ma let her frost the top o' my bald-ass brown head, let that rich pussy cream drip down and dry like I'm a six-foot-seven-inch bundt cake.

Victoria Winston is mine.

That girl was way too much for Li'l Tut to handle. The potency in her eyes — the raw sexuality burning in that voice and that dewy face that *had* to be virginal — radiated with incredible force from the TV screen. The longer Knight stared, the more bewitching her power became.

I can't breathe. In or out.

It felt like the day, years ago, when he made his first and last mistake relating to Babylon money. Prince slammed him against the exposed brick wall of the penthouse with such force, Knight slumped to the floor, not breathing. He thought he was dead.

Finally, he coughed — and never made that, or any other mistake, again.

"Eh, y'all know what happen to a snowflake when it hit black pavement?" Marvin grunted. "Tttttssssssttttt! It melt." He let out a sinister laugh. "She a snowball in hell right now. Ain't got half a muthafuckin' chance."

Marvin cast a cruel smile up at Knight and said, "Yo, G, if I was you, I'd hate any bitch wit' mo' dan two drops o' honkey blood."

"I don't hate white people," Knight answered.

"You should," said Pete Washington, slouching in a chair with his arms crossed. He reminded Knight of the planet Jupiter: hard core in the center, with an atmosphere of rage and hostility that fumed constantly in great, choking swirls of orange all around him. Knight always kept his distance so that dude's bad gravity didn't suck him in to get poisoned by those hate-vapors.

"Jesus turned the other cheek," Pete said, "an' they beat the shit outta him."

"Condemning a whole race for the act of one gets us nowhere," Knight answered, not so much for hopeless Pete but for the dozens of other men listening. "If a black man hurts a white person, should that victim hate the whole race?"

A chorus erupted. "Hell naw!"

"No, 'cause all black people ain't bad," Lonnie added. "Iss jus' some bad seeds sprinkled in the barrel."

"So we shouldn't think this biracial girl is bad until we know more about her," Knight said.

"Y'all be quiet," Lonnie said. "Now she wanted by the FBI!"

"Federal investigators are still searching for Miss Winston," the news anchor said. "They believe she may have crucial information about her father's controversial business practices. But police say Miss Winston has disappeared."

Knight bit down hard, flexing his jaw muscle. Now there was no doubt Li'l Tut was all stirred up in her creamy mix. Otherwise, Duke would've told Knight all about the media spectacle on Babylon Street. He always told Knight everything that was going on in the hood, whether it was who was having whose baby or how Milan's behavior was composing her own pink slip and eviction notice or who died or whose grandmother died or how the fallen powerline sparked a fire in an alley dumpster last week.

Everything.

Except that every media outlet in the city was there to watch a half-white rich girl find her black roots, and Li'l Tut was front and center.

It ain't right. Bringing someone that high profile and notorious inside the doors of Babylon—no matter what purpose his horny little brother had in mind—would only be trouble. Big, big trouble. It would be bad enough when Duke found out Knight was going to seize control of Babylon. When little Victoria took one look at Big Brother and fell madly in love, that would only make things worse for Duke.

She was made for me. That voice inside Knight's head spoke loud and clear. On the street, Knight used to call it his "gut feeling." Since being in prison, all of the self-help books Knight read said successful men always trust their hunches, their inner voices—the intuition—then Knight decided his sixth sense could only be called Intuition.

Right now, Intuition was expressing himself in his most authoritative voice. *Victoria Winston is The One.*

"This just in to the Channel 3 newsroom," Orville Smith said. "Victoria Winston is now apparently a fugitive of the law. Let's go to reporter Lisa Plateman. She's live on Detroit's east side."

Knight watched intently as live video showed a young black man in a suit on Miss Green's porch, which was surrounded by at least a dozen reporters, TV cameras and still cameras. He was holding up a purse, a suitcase and a hand-written note.

"This is a spokesman for the family," the reporter said, sticking a microphone in his face. "Is it true that Victoria Winston ran away?"

The guy held up the note. "Her grandmother found this this morning on her bed. It's written in Victoria's handwriting. It says she's so grief-stricken by the loss of life as she knew it that she's going to a warm, sunny place to escape the media spotlight."

"Can you be more specific?" the reporter asked. "Where is she?"

"Her grandmother says Victoria left with her passport and just enough cash for a one-way ticket to Miami. She kept talking about her friends there, who were gonna loan her keys to a vacation home in the Caribbean."

"Where in the Caribbean?" the reporter asked.

The young spokesman knit his brows.

"Br'a-man need some schoolin'," Marvin said. "Cain't lie worth a damn."

"He a'ight," Lonnie said. "Just nervous."

The spokesman stared at the note then looked up. "It doesn't say here, but the family thinks she might be either on the island St. John, St. Barts or Antigua."

Knight bit down a smile.

Or perhaps Miss Winston had slipped way below the white man's radar, into the secret chambers of Babylon.

Chapter 34

I fucked her to death.

Duke's big hand shaking her arm did nothing to wake her.

"Victoria!" he shouted. "Duchess! Wake up!"

He slapped her cheek.

Nothing.

He put his ear to her mouth. Couldn't feel breath. He pressed his fingertips to her neck for a pulse. Couldn't find it. Not on her wrist, either.

"Baby girl!" Duke's insides felt like the dude in that movie *The Mummy* when they threw him in a mummy case with a million giant black scarab beetles that ate off his flesh as fast as piranhas. Right now, his whole body stung with fear.

Why didn't I listen to whateva the fuck she was sayin' about a sex curse? 'Bout how her daddy fucked her momma to death? I was so busy tryin' ta get my nut, wasn't listenin' wit' my head.

"Baby girl!" he cried, sitting on the edge of the bed, rocking with her hand in his, raising it up to kiss her fingers. The gold blanket was tucked around her neck; her head rested on one of the gold pillows. One shoulder and arm were exposed, the one connected to the hand he was squeezing.

"You gotta wake up. Omma die if I lose you this fast." Duke hated feeling like somebody else's life had this much power over his. If something really had happened to his Duchess, if she really were dead —

I'm gon' be th'ough.

He squinted in the bright beams of sunshine slicing into the room from the floor-to-ceiling sliding glass doors leading out to the terrace. Even that bright-ass light on her face hadn't awakened her.

Damn, she looked like an angel. Her face was pure — it didn't have one mark or blemish or pimple. But something wasn't the same, like her skin was a little more yellow and her red, pucker-fish lips looked swollen. Her thick eyelashes still looked like black fringe, and her perfectly arched black eyebrows looked the same, as did all that hair fanned around her head like the prettiest peacock at the zoo.

"Massa Duke," Beamer said, rushing in. "Doc Reynolds here."

Duke barely looked back at the purple glasses on her fine-ass face, with her black hair all swirled up into a French roll. She wore all white, with white Nikes and a leather doctor bag. She pulled out a stethoscope and a little bottle with clear liquid inside.

"How long has she been unconscious?" the doctor asked, pulling back the gold sheer fabric. The bottle was the size of her pinky finger. She set it on her lap.

"More than twenty-four hours." He scooted over so Doc Reynolds could sit on the bed. She leaned down, listening for breath. She took Duchess's pulse at her neck. She used a stethoscope to listen to her heart. She felt her cheeks, her forehead. She pulled back the gold blanket to look at her whole body.

"She dead?" Duke asked, hating the high-pitched panic in his voice. "Tell me she ain't dead."

"She's alive," Doc Reynolds said. "But I need to know if she has any health problems that could cause coma."

"Shit!" The last thing he needed was some EMS ambulance crew coming up in here—or him taking her to the hospital. It would be all over the news, and the heat would be all over him.

Stop it, ma'fucka. She gon' be fine. Just sleepin', like she need.

"Master Duke. Tell me exactly what happened."

"I went to sleep. Musta been 4:15 yesterday morning."

"No, before that."

"We kicked it," Duke said. "For a couple hours."

"Was she a virgin?"

"Tight as a vise."

"Did she bleed?"

WHITE CHOCOLATE

Duke pointed to the aqua blue towel heaped on the white marble stairs leading up to the bed. "Not a drop. But ain't no question—"

"Does she have health problems? Is she diabetic?"

Duke shrugged. "At dinner, she ate like it was no tomorrow. Salmon, salad, ice cream. Didn't say nothin' 'bout sugar."

"Asthma?"

"She run track."

"That would account for her slow resting heart rate. Runners who are physically fit often have a nearly undetectable pulse."

"She said she hadn't slept in half a week. Some whack shit had happened in her life."

Doc Reynolds nodded. "Victoria Winston. I saw her on the news. Exactly how long has she been sleeping?"

"She was layin' next to me when I went to sleep, but I don't know if she was 'sleep yet. Then when I woke up at 10:15 yesterday morning, she was still 'sleep. I kept checkin' on her all day. I did my business by phone, right here, so she was never alone."

"She's the millionaire's daughter," Doc Reynolds said. "I just heard on the news the feds are questioning her grandmother. They're aggressively searching for this girl, Master Duke."

"I already took care of it." Duke had Henry's nerdy-ass brother, Mike, who worked at a public relations company downtown, send all those reporters—newspaper, radio and TV— an official press release saying Victoria Winston had run away. Duke had told Mike to hold a press conference yesterday on Miss Green's porch, and hold up her purse and her suitcase. He told Mike to say that even though Victoria Winston had abandoned her purse and her suitcase at her grandmother's house, she had left with her passport and just enough cash for a one-way ticket to Miami, where she had friends who were going to loan her keys to their vacation home on the Caribbean island of either St. John, St. Barts or Antigua. That would keep them investigating motherfuckers scrambling for clues at U.S. Customs down in Miami, not on Babylon Street in Motown.

"Obviously you missed the latest report about her leavin' the country," Duke said, casting a you-know-what-I-mean glare into Doc Reynolds' intelligent brown eyes. She wore no makeup but she was proof that black don't crack because she was almost forty-five and didn't have nary a wrinkle. Even after all those years in the pen for prescription fraud.

"Doc, I didn't bring you up here to play fuckin' Colombo," Duke said. "An' you know, workin' for me, since I hired you when nobody else would, now you livin' large like cain't nobody else pay you. I know you always put Babylon confidentiality first."

"Of course, Master Duke. That goes without saying."

"Within Babylon, too. That mean Milan don't need to know the who, what, when, where, how or why of nothin'. She 'bout to get transferred anyway, an' don't need no info'mation bein' transferred wit' her skinny ass."

"Understood," Doc Reynolds said.

"Now, tell me what Duchess need."

Doc Reynolds's eyes cut to Duchess's pale face like she was trying to figure out that *this* was Duchess.

"This girl needs rest," Doc Reynolds said. "When she wakes up, make sure she gets plenty to eat and drink. She'll be disoriented and dehydrated, so give her orange juice, bananas, healthy food to get her strength back up."

"Her strength was fine night befo' last," Duke said. And she needed to be strong now. He was going to start Hoodology 101 yesterday, so they were already a day behind now that it was Tuesday.

My birthday party Friday night. We got six days to make or break Babylon Monday mornin' wit' them Moreno ma'fuckas. She gotta be on so when Knight come back, he see The Duke be rulin' this shit! By my damn self.

"We gotta wake her up an' get her energy back, pronto," Duke said.

WHITE CHOCOLATE

Doc Reynolds shook her head. "Let me take this moment to let you know about Janelle. She's retired. HIV and genital warts. Milan gave her walking papers."

"Dang," Duke said. "Nasty bitch. Put out an alert to the B'Amazons an' Barriors so she cain't creep up in here."

Doc Reynolds looked serious when she said, "Of course, sir. And Janelle is aware of the penalty for such an offense."

Beamer came jogging back in with a scary look in his eye. "Massa D, newsflash."

"I'll newsflash yo' ass if you think it's more important than—"

"It might be." Beamer never looked that alarmed.

Duke stepped down. "What?"

"A Barrior jus' dropped a dime on Knight. He out. Now. Plottin' a take-over."

Duke bit down hard. His voice was cool and calm as he said, "Yo, B, go tell yo' girl Milan to stop startin' bullshit rumors that could get somebody killed."

Beamer's eyes got almost as big as his BMW medallion. Duke made a *shoo* motion with his hand, making his diamond ring sparkle. "Go. You on evac. Now."

As Beamer huffed away, Duke spun on a heel and dashed back up the steps to Duchess. He shook her arm. "Wake her up!"

"Sometimes after situations of extreme emotional duress," the doctor said, "coupled with extreme sleep deprivation, the body can shut down into an almost comatose state."

"Aw, hell no!" Duke shot up to his feet, pacing the white marble platform around the bed. "Wake her up!"

Doc Reynolds took that clear vial off her lap. She unscrewed the black cap, held the opening of the bottle under Duchess's pretty little nose. Nothing. Duchess slept just as peacefully as she had before.

"Cain't you give her a shot or somethin'?" Duke demanded.

"She doesn't need—"

She held the bottle to her nose and cupped her hand around it so Duchess had to breathe in the bottle vapors.

SEX IN THE HOOD

"Ah!" Duchess cried out. She coughed and tried to sit up.

"Baby girl!" he cheered, punching his fist in the air like he was at a Pistons game.

"Where am I?" Her voice was raspy and sexy as hell, but her blue moon eyes were huge, full of panic.

"You wit' me, Sleepin' Beauty," Duke said, leaning down to stroke her hair. He sat next to her. "This Doc Reynolds."

"Good morning, Duchess," the Doc said.

Duchess held the blanket over her chest, looking back and forth at everybody like she didn't know up from down. The way she looked up at Duke—eyes huge, brows drawn together, shaking her head, scooting back on the bed—

She don't even know who the fuck I am!

"Duchess, baby girl, you been sleepin' for a day an' a half," he said. "Worryin' a ma'fucka half to death."

She focused on Duke. Her eyes were still as intense as blue-flame blow torches. They still set him on fire just as ridiculously hot as the first time he saw her two days ago. Now, his whole body prickled with sweat. And Timbo was on swole!

She froze. The blanket dropped from her chest. Her cinnamon-colored nipples looked so good, they made Cinnabons look like dog biscuits. They were pointing straight out from her round, creamy curves of plump, round titties over her little tapered ribs.

Duke shifted on the bed, letting Timbo roll to a more spacious spot in his jeans.

Her lips curled a little. Something flashed in her eyes as she looked right at him.

"Duke, why the *fuck* you got all these people in our room—" Her voice sounded deeper. And *black*. "—when you *said*—" She delicately cocked her head to one side, making that hair flip over her shoulder. "—you'd make love to me soon as I woke up?"

210

Chapter 35

Milan Henderson threw her cell phone onto the shiny, hardwood floor of the Sex Squad headquarters. It broke into two silver pieces at the base of the reception counter where three Sluts were checking in for their weekly exams.

Milan didn't care that they and the other Sluts and Studs were gawking at her as they sat on the couches, waiting for their exams. They hadn't even turned on the TV. They were too busy watching her flit around, trying not to lose her mind.

I will not become a stark raving lunatic in front of all these people, like they want me to, like I want me to, like Duke wants me to. I will not!

It was no secret that something outrageous and scandalous was going on. After all, nobody could miss the two big, barbaric prison wardens who'd been her constant companions since Sunday night, watching her every move, both yesterday and today. Now everybody was looking at her like she stole something. Whispering when she walked past. Laughing when she left the room. The hundreds of people in this building knew that Duke had been locked upstairs with that white bitch—they were actually calling that girl The Duchess—since he brought her here on Sunday.

Two days! Duke had been fucking that bitch for forty-eight hours straight! She couldn't remember the last time she had Duke to herself for two *hours*. Even when she did, he was constantly answering his phone, making calls, telling her to "hurry up an' cum."

Now he had obviously turned off his phones, because Milan had called dozens of times over the past few days. His voicemail was full. That was why she just pitched the phone.

Not to mention, Beamer hadn't spoken to her since their hotel room tryst. He hadn't returned the phone messages she left, threatening to show Duke the videotape if Beamer didn't call her to talk about their plan. Was he crazy? Peanut obviously had

211

some other kind of plan of his own, but stupid as he was, it wouldn't get anywhere.

But why did Peanut come down here all in a fluster, escorting Dr. Reynolds out when she had important work to do? Duke had better not let somebody up in here get a sexually transmitted infection. If word got out that Babylon's Sluts and Studs weren't as squeaky clean as they were reputed to be, it would be the kiss of death for this multi-million-dollar empire.

Milan smiled. What a shame that would be. She could always call Janelle back for a job or two, or send her up to Duke's bedroom so she could lay some HIV and warts on Duke and his new Duchess. See how long they live happily ever after with *that* shit.

She clapped. Everybody turned, giving her their undivided attention. There, that was better. The way it should be.

"Due to some unforeseen circumstances," she announced, looking at all fifteen Sluts and Studs, "your exams for this week are cancelled."

"Naw," a chick on the couch said. "I got some burnin' an' I don't know if it's just bladder irritation or chlamydia or what kinda shit goin' on. I need to see Dr. Reynolds."

"Ain't no way," said the Stud sitting next to her. "All my years o' workin' here, we ain't neva missed a exam. I'd get my dick checked e'ry damn day o' the week, as many pussies as I be drillin' in a day."

He shook his cornrowed head. "Half these bitches be beggin' me to hit it raw. An' they tip a couple hun'ed extra if I *do*! So I say, well, I'ma see Doc Reynolds to make sure I ain't caught nothin'. So—" He crossed his arms, lifted the heels of his cowboy boots slightly, and banged them back on the floor. "I'ma wait 'til the doc come back."

"I'm here," Dr. Reynolds said.

How had Milan not heard or seen the entry door open?

"And when The Duke hears about this," Dr. Reynolds said, "I guarantee he will not be happy, Madame Milan."

WHITE CHOCOLATE

Milan snapped, "I thought you had abandoned the premises. I was going to call in another doctor for today or reschedule everyone here."

"Naw, that ain't what she said," the Stud in cowboy boots said. "My cock ain't fallin' prey to her hate. She jus' mad The Duke—"

Dr. Reynolds glared at him. "That's enough, Johnny. You can come with me." She led him into the office. "Milan, you'd be wise to resist the urge to sabotage any computer files or employee records." She shut the door.

Milan's cheeks stung. That bitch would be wise not to answer the phone when the IRS called to inquire about how she earned a high six-figure salary at the storefront clinic—which she owned—for indigent patients in the ghetto. She never went there, just let three employees, who may or may not be doctors, operate it. But even all that Medicaid and Medicare reimbursement couldn't pay for her Benz or her big house in the suburbs or her timeshare in Barbados.

What was she talking about anyway?

As if she knows something that I don't know.

Did she just see Duke? Had Duke said something about Milan's status here, or lack thereof? As partner? His children's mother? His top executive?

Milan stomped toward the door.

I am going to see him right now to take care of this! I cannot have people inferring that my status is anything but superior around here.

She grabbed the doorknob, but the barbarians wedged in front of the door before she could pull it open.

And she screamed.

Chapter 36

Duke's body, glistening in the shower, was so beautiful Duchess couldn't stop staring or touching or licking or kissing or sucking every inch—especially that indented line that rippled between his deltoid muscles when he raised his arms to pull her closer under the double shower heads in the huge, iridescent gold-tiled shower.

Everything about him mesmerized her. She watched the way the water streamed over the succulent dark chocolate skin on his bald head, over his ears, those perfectly arched black eyebrows, his thick lashes, down his black Roman warrior nose, his high chiseled cheekbones and wide, clean-shaven jaw, to his thick, smooth neck.

He look fine as hell. An' he mine.

Timbo was poking at her stomach, and Duchess couldn't wait to feel him poke back inside Celeste. How could her pussy feel even more hungry for Duke's delicious dick? How could she feel this wicked craving after hours and hours of fucking this absolute god?

Iss called addiction, baby. You was a freak by yo' damn self. An' you knew once you let Celeste loose, you'd be a worse sex fiend than yo' freaky-ass parents. Good thing you hooked up wit' a Mandingo stud ma'fucka who can han'le it.

"Oh my God!" Victoria cried out into the hiss of the shower. It was like Duke was inside her head, talking through her voice.

"Baby girl, you a'ight?"

She took Timbo into her hands, stroking the shaft, loving the satin-over-rock feel of this giant magic wand she would worship until her last breath. Especially when it made Duke look down at her like she was his reason for living, that his heart couldn't beat without the spark he felt when he looked into her eyes.

WHITE CHOCOLATE

Because that's how I feel. Even though no, I'm not all right. There's a new voice in my head, making me talk black. Ghetto. Ebonics. Like all the people I've been around for the past two days.

Did getting fucked into a coma short-circuit her brain? Even if you were raised white and look white to most people, did the black blood overpower the white blood at some point and make a person talk differently? Or did it just make it easier to immerse into it at will? It was like she could have gone her whole life as Victoria Winston, rich suburban girl, Ivy League college student, CEO of her own company, and never tapped into the black side. But now that she had, did it come more naturally than if she were all white and suddenly tossed by fate into the inner city?

Her mind was spinning a million miles a minute . . . Thank goodness she didn't have to stay at Gramma Green's house of hell . . . and that Duke's penthouse was as luxurious as home was . . . finally got some sleep . . . finally got some dick!

Her heart felt like it skipped a beat.

With terror.

What now? I did what I said I'd never do. I unleashed the mixed-race sex powers. Now I know this is the way to get whatever I want or need in life. But what do I want?

Duke had just told her about the Miami-Caribbean story they'd fed to the media. Victoria Winston didn't exist anymore, unless she wanted to face the feds who would turn around and accuse her of helping Daddy do something wrong. Could she go to the penitentiary for a white collar crime that she unknowingly committed? Would her own father have involved her in something illegal? Or was he truly wrongly accused as he'd claimed?

Right now, after seeing the power of the federal prosecutor who was after Daddy and the power of the press to destroy a man to the point that he took his own life, Victoria had no desire to find out.

I am Duchess, hear me roar!

"Duke," she whispered, wrapping her arms around his firm, tapered waist. She buried her face in that hot, velvety crevice at

215

the center of his chest, where the soft mounds of his pecs came together. "This space was made to cradle my face."

Duke tossed his head back, laughing into the streaming water. "I had a li'l some-some for yo' rhymes the otha night, baby girl. Tol' you I was gonna go raw dog on that ass 'til you couldn't talk!"

"Yeah, lobotomize *me*, baby," she said.

"Timbo musta banged all the way up in yo' brain to flip the black switch," Duke laughed, "'cause you talk black now. Did you see Doc Reynolds and Beama's eyes pop when you woke up?" Duke was cracking up. "Day-um. That was some hilarious shit right there." He kissed the top of her head, ran his hands down the wet black cape that was her hair, tickling the top of her ass.

"It's like the little voice inside my head," she said, "the one that makes thoughts and prepares sentences to shoot out through my lips, that brain voice feels like it's been reprogrammed."

"Yeah, to the Ebonics channel," Duke said, "starring the suburban white chick who got some urban Mandingo dick that woke the sleepin' black diva within."

Victoria pressed her cheek to his chest as she laughed. His voice vibrated in her ear as he said, "The way you talk, that's still gonna be part of yo' Hoodology 101, to get you ready."

"Ready for what?"

"Yo' work for Babylon. As Duchess. This weekend I'm presentin' you to Babylon at my birthday party. Then we got the meetin' of the millennium comin' up nex' Monday. A week from Friday my brotha Knight comin' home, so we gotta make you into the baddest bitch this side o' the moon."

"Duke," she whispered, real sultry, staring up into his beautiful eyes. "Every other minute that you're not hosting my extreme ghetto makeover—" He laughed as she reached down to stroke Timbo. "—can I be the first contestant on *Extreme Pussy Takeover*?"

Duke's deep laugher echoed through the shower.

WHITE CHOCOLATE

"Yo' sex coma already got us a day behind in yo' trainin', so—"

"Kiss me."

As the water streamed over their faces, he pressed his satin-hot lips to hers.

How could one guy's kiss feel so different than another? Brian's lips were hard, puckered in a way that felt uninviting, tense. But Duke's lips were relaxed, soft, moving gently, like little nibbles. Her plump lips against his plump lips equalled one sensuous dance of hungry mouths finally tasting the flavor they'd both been craving.

He kissed her forehead then cupped her jaw in his giant hands, tilted her face up so he could focus those beautiful, black kaleidoscopic eyes down at her.

"Duchess, I ain't neva even thought this befo', but when you was 'sleep and I thought you was dead," his voice cracked, "I realized I cain't, don't wanna live wit'out you."

"You never have to," she whispered. "In my eyes, you're like this masterpiece of manhood and I was made for you," she whispered. "I could stare at you forever. Kiss you forever. Make love with you forever."

He French kissed her so good, she felt dizzy. Then with his hands on her slippery waist, he turned her around.

"Put your hands on the wall," he said, spreading her fingers against the warm, wet stone. He bent her at the waist, grasping her hips like they were hinges he was adjusting to just the right angle. She looked back. Timbo pointed like Cupid's big black arrow at her milky round ass.

"The prettiest sight on the planet," he groaned, dropping to his knees, diving at her butt with an open mouth.

A flash of white teeth . . . his eyes closed . . . his face mellow with passion . . . and he bit her ass. Gently, sensuously, and only for a second before his tongue lapped a circle around the spot where his teeth had touched her skin. Then he grasped both cheeks, pulled them apart.

"Ma'fuck me!" he shouted.

217

SEX IN THE HOOD

What in the world . . .

"How can somebody asshole even be pretty? Day-um!"

Yuck. Why would anybody want to look at my butthole? Her eyes grew wide. Tiffany was always talking about some girl at school who loved to get butt-fucked. Disgusting. Her butt had only one function, something done far and away from any romantic moment.

"Do you see the EXIT ONLY sign there?" Victoria asked.

Duke's smiling eyes appeared over the hills of her ass. Then his eyes disappeared. Only the dark chocolate dome of his bald head was showing, right between the milky mounds of her butt.

Wow, what a picture. The contrast of skin was sexy as hell as he knelt at the temple of her bare behind, an ass whose size and shape—attached to someone most white guys thought was white—had always drawn stares and comments. But now, as Duke celebrated her luscious trophy of femininity, Duchess finally felt accepted for how God made her.

I was in the wrong place with the wrong people who didn't appreciate me for me. She arched her back, sticking her ass further into his face, aching to feel him inside her. As if he heard her yearning, Duke reached between her legs from the back. He cupped his hand over her pussy so that his fingertips were at the top of the hair and the heel of his hand was at her asshole. He pressed his palm down onto her clit.

"Oh yeah," she moaned. "I need that."

He made his hand move in a way that was covering her entire pussy from front to back, and he was stimulating every square millimeter with his hand. In seconds, Victoria convulsed, legs trembling, nipples squeezing, shivers dancing over her skin, mind flashing blue, green, yellow—

Slam!

"Aaaahhh!"

The size and force of Timbo surging up into her pussy was so fucking luscious, Duchess could die right now and be happy. His fingertips pressed into her hips. He banged ferociously. Did sex feel this good to everyone? Was this how her parents felt?

218

WHITE CHOCOLATE

Hell no! That new black voice shouted in Duchess's head.

Her brain was a wild whirl of words, thoughts, pictures, with that new narrator trying to add sassy commentary every which way. Duke's dick ramming her with the relentless force she craved made it hard to focus. She didn't want to make thoughts about anything but the pleasure of the moment, but would it crank up the volume even louder on the black voice?

Yes, she could still think absolutely clearly with the proper grammar and diction her parents insisted she use from the day she spoke her first word at age eighteen months—on the family's video camera.

It happened one evening when Daddy came home from work. She and Mommy were in the beautiful blue-tiled kitchen, making sugar cookies. The video showed Mommy smiling in her frilly white apron as she stirred the dough in a glass bowl. Little Victoria was sitting on the giant kitchen island—it was like an enormous slab of blue granite—and Mommy was letting her press M&Ms into the tops of the cookies laid out on a cookie sheet.

Victoria's chubby little fingers put just as many of the colored candies into her mouth as she did on the cookies. Mommy laughed then smiled even bigger when Daddy came in wearing a business suit. He set his briefcase down, kissed Mommy's forehead and whispered something into the thick, black hair falling straight around her ears.

"Prin-sex!" Victoria exclaimed.

Her parents cracked up.

"No sweetie," her mother said, laughing. "Prin*cess*."

"Prin-sex," little Victoria repeated, because she knew what Daddy said to Mommy every night when he came home and there was no video camera picking up his words. "Prinsex," he would say before they put Victoria in the playpen for a while and disappeared behind the closed doors of their bedroom suite. Mommy's laughter and Daddy's playful sounds meant they were playing, too, and pretty soon they would come out smiling as they all had dinner together.

SEX IN THE HOOD

Now, Victoria opened her eyes. Her thoughts about reality came back slowly. She was in the shower with Duke, making love.

She glimpsed his feet—huge, dark, perfect, with long toes and pedicured nails that shined with polish. They raised up and down slightly, splashing the gold stone floor on each side of her much smaller white feet topped with shiny red toenails. She glanced back, her black hair a cape over her back, tumbling to the left side of her waist. On her right hip, his long, elegant fingers contrasted against the soft, creamy curve leading to a long leg.

Ooooh, the most magnificent sight of all was her ass bouncing against his groin. Round, ivory flesh flattening just a little against the hard, ebony plane of muscle, over and over and over.

Wait, Duke's face. That was the most magnificent. She loved how lust was turning his cheeks red, parting his lips. Tenderness and love glowed in his eyes.

Duchess closed hers. She filed that snapshot away to the most cherished chamber of her heart because this sense of paradise couldn't possibly last in the wicked world.

"If something seems too good to be true," Daddy used to always say, "it probably is."

Chapter 37

It felt like a museum or some wild adventure into Ancient Egypt as Duke stood in front of a floor-to-ceiling King Tut mask—shiny gold-and-black stripes on the headdress, the big eyes with thick black liner, the asp at the forehead. Within the center of the fifteen-foot-wide piece of art: double doors.

"Welcome to Babylon HQ," he said, opening the doors. "I got my vision from Ramses' court on *The Ten Commandments*."

The floor was shiny white marble, just like in the bedroom. A huge glass desk dominated the same kind of platform, which was four marble steps up, just like the bed. Two chairs behind the desk, as well as two satin couches against the walls leading to the desk area, were styled like gold thrones with arms that curved into spirals and gold satin seats. Behind the desk, lighted glass shelves stretched between huge, gold-and-black-striped mummy cases.

From a side door, which was open to a vast office space with desks and cubicles, four gorgeous girls came strutting out, all in costume with Cleopatra-style hair and makeup. They wore little white dresses with gold hip belts and gold spike sandals that laced up their bare calves, gold bands holding their hair back, and serpent-style cuffs in the curves between their sculpted biceps and deltoid muscles.

The girls were a gorgeous spectrum, from almond to caramel to milk chocolate to iridescent blue-black. In the adjacent office, all the women who were answering phones, working at desks and typing on computers were dressed that way.

These girls ooze sex. It was in the way they walked, the expressions on their faces and in their eyes. The four of them stood directly in front of her and Duke, holding their hands up as if they were praying.

They said in unison, "Master Duke, Madame Duchess." They bowed.

Duchess's eyes devoured their shapely bodies, how they radiated sensuality—from their red-painted lips to their hoisted-up breasts to their round butts and long legs. They looked good enough to eat. Where she lived, girls were all super-skinny and horrified by any trace of fat on their bodies. That made Victoria self-conscious about her round butt that was bigger and rounder than anyone else's she knew. Brian's pressure for her to diet and lose weight only made her more self-conscious.

But these girls here had meat on their bones and carried themselves with so much confidence. They looked incredible, solid, not fat at all. Just sensuous and comfortable with themselves. It was another affirmation for Duchess to showcase and celebrate her natural shape—the round, prominent ass that testified to her own mother's beauty and mysterious power. Now she couldn't stop staring at these girls, hoping their secret self confidence would rub off on her even more.

Speaking of rub off, her pussy was going wild at the sight of these women.

I wanna eat their pussies. I wanna see them naked, with their juicy thighs spread wide open so I can see if their pussies are as pretty as mine. I wanna see them press their fingertips to their clits then fuck those crazy-sexy studs down in the gym.

"Master Duke, where you find this sweet sistah?" The girl scorched the length of Duchess's body with a fiery stare. Duchess's lips parted as the girl stepped close. The tops of her glitter-dusted breasts were as mouth-watering as golden-baked dinner rolls glistening with yellow butter.

Celeste was blowing steam into the crotch of Duchess's jeans. Her panties were soaked. Her mind spun with images of herself, Duke and this beautiful girl having a threesome right here in the office. So many girls at school were into that—two guys and one girl or one guy and two girls.

They all thought I was such a prude 'cause I wouldn't even fuck. If they could see me now!

Her reflection in the mirrored wall on the right made Duchess smile. Duke had stocked his closet with clothes for her, even before he met her. It was the hottest in urban wear, including these Fubu faded denims that hugged her ass like no jeans had ever done before. The pink glitter on the thighs and butt were super sexy, and it matched the snug pink tank top and pink stiletto ankle boots she was wearing with it. Her hair swayed just above what Duke called the "ka-pow!" curve of her ass.

These clothes were fine for now, but Duke said they were going shopping as part of her training to get the wardrobe of her choice. Looking at these girls in the little outfits, they reminded her of the women who worked at Caesar's Palace in Las Vegas. Victoria had been there several times with Daddy when he had conventions. He'd always take her, Melanie and Nicholas and let them hang out at the pool or shop in the Forum Shops.

"Duchess," Duke said. Two syllables from his mouth and she broke out in a sweat all over. He was so damn sexy, and the love in his voice when he said her name emphasized her power. It reminded her that she was really the one in control here, that she was learning, planning, pretending to let him be in power until she could wield it entirely herself.

"Yeah, baby," she responded, turning to him with perfect posture that showed him that her nipples were hard because she was thinking about him bending her over that desk and fucking her right here in front of these girls.

"This is your personal assistant," Duke said, turning his palm toward the girl with the glitter-dusted breasts, the one who was standing just a little closer to Duchess than the other three, who were still lined up facing them.

"I'm Honey," she said, pressing a satin-soft hand into Duchess's palm. "Welcome to Babylon. You need *anything*, I am here to serve."

"The pleasure is mine," Duchess said. "You must be named after your eyes."

Honey lowered her thick black eyelashes. Her full lips, glossed with coral-colored lipstick, parted to reveal perfect white squares for teeth. Her cheeks rose like little round apples; her

223

nose was like a mini mushroom. She glanced back up, her honey-brown eyes sparkling, framed by flawless skin as dark as molasses. Her face was round, framed by straight black bangs and hair pulled back in a gold band. Her big, juicy boobs poked toward Duchess.

This is the sexiest girl I have ever seen. Duchess wanted to open up her mouth and take a bite of Honey. Anywhere. Her smooth, hairless arms. Her juicy legs. Her adorable nose. The plump titties. Those lips.

"Anything you need typed," Duke said, "appointments, travel arrangements, phone calls, Honey can han'le e'rything for you. When you got off-site meetings, shopping, pedicure, anything, Honey can go wit' you."

"I'm looking forward to it," Duchess said.

"The other girls," Duke said, "they're back-up. DaLinda, Rochelle an' Tamika." Each girl bowed as he said her name.

"How you doin'," Duchess said, undressing them with her eyes. Whatever work Duke wanted her to do up here, how in the world did he expect her to concentrate with these sex kittens around? Did he think she wouldn't be attracted to girls too?

I didn't think I was attracted to girls until I walked up in this place! And if there was any question, one look at Honey and it's done. I will eat that pussy. She smiled, thinking of how Duke said, *And so it is written, and so it is done.*

Duke watched her closely. He knew. Once he set Celeste free to reign over his dick and Babylon, she'd have to swing both ways to capture the full flavor.

And these four girls definitely represented every flavor. DaLinda was the tall, blue-black African model type who'd been doing sexercise in the gym. Rochelle was short, the plumpest—not fat, just thick. And Tamika, golden tan with freckles and blue eyes.

Duchess wanted to see all of them naked. What did their nipples look like? Their clits? Did Duke fuck them? The way he devoured them with his eyes meant the answer was probably yes. What did that look like? Her insides were electrified with curiosity and a twinge of jealousy that oddly turned her on even more. Did they have orgies right here in his office? If she was responding like this as a girl, she couldn't imagine what a man would be thinking, especially when he was the boss.

Duke clapped. The girls closed their eyes, bowed, then turned and sashayed back into that big office space, where they closed the doors.

Duchess immediately turned to Duke, who was wearing jeans, baby-soft black loafers and a black silk tunic that hugged his muscles and tapered waist. She ran her hands over his black belt and over the log in his pants.

"Celeste needs to talk to Timbo about Honey," Duchess whispered.

Duke kissed her forehead, removing her hands from the bulge of his dick.

"What?" she snapped. Her mind spun. Was he about to say no? Her cheeks burned at the idea of him ever denying her that delicious dick, anytime, anywhere. He couldn't turn her on to the pleasures of the body and not satisfy this constant craving. Girls at school were always talking about how if their boyfriends made them mad, they would "cut him off" from sex. Victoria never understood that. It seemed like she'd do the opposite. If her guy pissed her off, she'd make him fuck her and fuck her and fuck her until *he* collapsed with exhaustion.

Suddenly, looking at Duke as his eyes said yes but his hands said no, she realized she was navigating entirely new relationship terrain. She didn't know the rules, but she did know what she wanted. And the word "no" when she wanted to climb on and ride Timbo was definitely grounds for—

What? Breaking up with the man who was the equivalent of her captor wasn't an option right now. Picking a fight or pouting wouldn't accomplish anything. So, how much leverage did she really have if she were to pitch a fit that he didn't want sex right now? Was he holding out so he could go through those closed doors, into that office, and screw those four gorgeous girls who worked for him? Would he let her watch? Participate?

SEX IN THE HOOD

I can't believe the things I'm worrying about right now. Duchess knew her emotional state was totally off-kilter. The grief of losing her father, her home, her boyfriend, her best friend, her school, her siblings and every other familiar thing in her life was catastrophic enough. Now there was a whole new world to figure out—hiding here, really, as what could be construed as a fugitive.

Since I am fleeing from the FBI.

Celeste's hot creaminess suddenly made her cross her legs and look up at Duke with please-fuck-me eyes. Maybe if he declined, she'd send him away—they could finish the Babylon tour later—then she'd call Honey into this office and ask her for a personal demonstration on the computer system.

"I'll slam you over this desk," Duke said, "and fuck you senseless just like you need, after we talk bidness. Cain't think straight after I lay it on yo' fine ass. Cain't even wake up for a day or two." He laughed, taking long strides to the throne chairs behind the glass desk.

"Come sit at our desk so I can teach you how to rule this mug."

Chapter 38

Ain't no way she can look at me like that an' I don't fuck her!

Timbo got even bigger and harder as Duke looked down at Duchess's long, elegant giraffe legs straddling the gold arms of this throne. The chair was pushed back from the glass desk so her back didn't hit the edge.

"I loooove this position," she whispered, cupping his face in her hot hands as her big, blue metallic eyes glazed and rolled back a little like she was buzzing off too much Cristal. She was riding him so tough right now, he wouldn't be surprised if she shouted, "Giddyup, mothafucka!"

Her right fingertips rubbed her clit, making her pussy drip hot cream all down Timbo. Good thing Duke had pulled his jeans down to his ankles and pulled his shirt up to his chest.

Duchess's titties, which she pulled out of the scoop-neck of her pink T-shirt, were poking over the edge like torpedoes aiming at Duke's mouth. The cinnamon-colored circles with sweet little points made him suck like tomorrow would never come. He loved how those suckers went in soft and got hard against his tongue.

She loved it, too, because her pussy was starting to squeeze like she was about to cum. Seemed impossible that her sugar walls could get any hotter without singeing the skin right off of Timbo, but her pussy was burning up like an inferno up in that mug.

He felt friction so hot it could spark and set his thighs on fire. It could fill the room with the smell of burning hair—both their pubic hair, smoking! Seemed like flames should be shooting out of her, like the bottom of a rocketship at take-off.

Duchess had to have the hottest pussy on Earth. It stayed wet as an ocean, too, at all times, even while she was sleeping for a day and a half and he tried to wake her up by touching her pussy. She stayed 'sleep, but her pussy was a puddle of cream, even though she was semi-comatose!

Her eyes were half-closed now as she moaned, "Oh, Duuuuke." In fact, she looked like she was drunk. He was afraid to see how wild Duchess would be if she got some champagne in her. And blunt? She would *tear* Timbo *up*. Break it off.

No, Duchess would stay intoxicant-free for now. This was all the intoxication she needed, right here. Duke slammed his hips up, up, up. Her long, straight black hair bounced all over the glass desktop, her shoulders, arms, and the tops of her milky white thighs.

She was just wild right now because it was new. This was her first dick, and last dick, so she wanted to try it out every way possible. Then her ass would calm down. Otherwise, if they fucked all day, every day, his work would come to a standstill. They wouldn't get everything ready in two weeks for when Knight was supposed to come home.

Shit, if I wanted to just fuck all damn day long, I coulda did that wit' any one o' these pussies 'round here. He didn't need to play the hood version of executive headhunter, recruiting just the right spokesmodel because she was a creole-looking-caucasian chameleon. Yeah, her face and body were gorgeous, but it was her brain that he needed too. And right now, her brain was thinking about as much as her booty that was bouncing in his lap, making a sweaty slap that reminded him of a clock ticking down seconds, minutes, hours that they weren't working to build up Babylon.

Her sex coma had already put them behind schedule a day and a half. All of Monday was wasted. Half of today, Tuesday, was eaten up by having Doc Reynolds come and give her smelling salts or whatever the fuck that was. Now they could have been halfway through the tour if she hadn't muzzled him with that big red clit she shoved in his mouth as he was describing her job duties up in this Egyptian palace.

"Let me give you a microphone," she whispered as she stood barefoot on the arms of the chair, spreading her knees at his

WHITE CHOCOLATE

shoulders and shoving her juicy pussy between his lips. "Now speak," she said, "so the information will go directly into my body and record on my brain."

Yeah, right. She was joking when she said "Lobotomize *me*, baby!" when they made love before. But that look in her eye right now showed she had no brainwave activity going on up inside that pretty skull.

I wonder how long do it take for Duchess to concentrate after I hit it? If I leave her up here to work, I know she gon' start meessin' around wit' Honey. My girl looked at her new executive assistant like she wanna sop her up wit' a biscuit an' slurp her down whole. Lips, titties, ass, legs, from head to toe! If Duchess was this addicted to dick already, how would she act after she got her first taste of pussy?

She gon' lose her ma'fuckin' mind between Honey legs.

She was losing her heart and soul between his. Duchess was going to cum any second now. Duke could tell by the way her pussy was squeezing around Timbo like a hand milking a cow, just like Mama Johnson had showed him as a kid down on her farm in Alabama. If his dick were an udder and Duchess was the hand that was milking it, then she would suck him dry at this rate.

Naw, I gotta make her cum so we can get back to bidness.

Duke grabbed the sides of her hips. He fucked up, up, up, like an upside-down jackhammer on that pussy. He was beating it up, giving it a black eye. Maybe if she were sore, she wouldn't want to fuck for a while. But damn, she didn't even get sore the first time.

"Yeah, Duke. Pound that pussy! Pound it!"

Her titty fell out of his mouth. She kissed him softly. Her lips were so sensuous and hot, he could suck on them all day long.

Neva tasted anything so good. Just like Adam must have said when Eve gave him a bite of that sweet apple. This kiss was sucking the life out of Duke Johnson. He was breathing hard, heart pounding, ass muscles burning, abs aching.

She gon' kill me. Maybe that sex curse she was rambling about, maybe it was true. Maybe it zig-zagged through

229

generations, so like her daddy fucked her momma to death, now when the daughter found a man, she would fuck *him* to death.

Timbo went soft.

She got still. Her eyes opened real wide. Her cheeks were pink as hell, lips looked like she'd been drinking made-in-Detroit Faygo Redpop. Her pretty black, arched eyebrows drew together. She looked down.

Timbo flopped out with a silvery shine, like a dead fish plopped on a tangle of wet black seaweed. Duke's chest rose and fell as he tried to catch his breath. Beads of sweat on his forehead trickled down, itching all over his face. His shirt was soaked. He didn't sweat this much during their sweet-ass cherry pick-a-thon.

The way she was looking at him felt like her eyes were slicing straight through his heart. Like he failed. Like he tricked her. Like he don't love her.

Hell naw. Timbo surged. His dick rose straight up, like Frankenstein did when the mad scientist flipped the switch and made the lightning bolt jolt life into the creature made of dead body parts.

"Yeah, baby," Duchess purred like a damn cat.

She raised up, speared her pussy down on Timbo, and got that mellow smile back.

"Oh, Duke, I love it. Loooooove it."

Duke loved it too.

Even though I'm creatin' a ma'fuckin' monsta.

Chapter 39

Duchess held back a scream every time Duke said "baby mommas" with so much pride in his voice. As if someone who was not even old enough to buy beer should be proud to have five kids by three different girls! But she was laughing too hard right now as five adorable little kids pinned him to the floor here in the playroom. Carpeted with a plush A-B-C pattern of red, yellow and blue, the huge room had murals of jungle scenes, a giant fake tree whose hollow trunk had cushions for reading, and enormous stuffed animals—lions, giraffes, gorillas, flamingos, tigers. They were all arranged amidst a kid-sized Hummer and Barbie Jeep that really drove, and a movie theatre area with mini recliners, a popcorn machine and a state of the art flat screen monitor. This playroom was a stop on her tour of Babylon's fifth floor, where the three "baby mommas" lived in their own apartments.

"Attack!" shouted one little boy who was a fifty-pound clone of Duke, from the bald head to the genie eyes to the tiny silver hoop earrings.

"Daddy down! Daddy down!" shouted another Duke clone, this one about a year younger than the other.

A chubby girl, about the same size as Victoria's two-year-old cousin, giggled as she climbed up Duke's shoulder.

"Help me!" Duke cried playfully, flailing his arms, which two more toddlers—a twin boy and girl—grabbed. "It's attack of the babies!"

A tooth-sucking sound drew Duchess's attention to the three nannies who were sitting on a nearby plush red couch flanked by book cases.

"Iss gon' be attack o' some baby mommas when they see a snowstorm done blew up in Babylon," said the one with long, brown braids. All of them wore black jeans, crisp white cotton blouses and white leather loafers. No jewelry. No long fingernails. Just snarls on their faces as Duchess glanced their way. Duchess's cheeks stung, slapped by their negative energy.

"I got a cousin who lighter 'n her," said the small, plain nanny. "We cain't hold it against somebody for how God made them look."

"Yes we can!" The other two high-fived each other. They were whispering so Duke couldn't hear them.

"Renée, you always tryin' ta make nice," the girl with braids said. "Even though you work wit' Queen Evil. Milan already half crazy, but she gon' be triple crazy —"

"Not if she remember what happened to Sunnie," one nanny said. "Kicked out on her ass 'cause she didn't act right. Now little Precious think I'm her momma. But I ain't mad at nobody. I love that baby like she mine."

"Plus you got Sunnie's apartment," Renée said with a big smile. "An' clothes. An' maybe even a taste o' The Duke."

The girl made a zipper motion over her lips, but her laughing eyes flashed a big "Yes!"

"Where white girl stay?" one of them whispered.

"Penthouse," another mumbled.

"I escaped!" Duke shouted. He stood. All the kids screamed with delight. They were latching onto his legs like he was a pole they wanted to climb. "Gimme kisses. I need ten. Zeus, do the math. How many kisses each baby gotta give they daddy?"

"Two!" the boy exclaimed. Duke raised him with one arm like a forklift. The boy kissed Duke's beautiful cheeks. Duke did the same for each smiling child.

"Bye-bye, Daddy!" the apple-cheeked girl giggled, waving as he and Duchess stepped into the hallway and closed the door.

"I take care o' mine," Duke said as she walked ahead of him toward the elevator. The hallway had plush black carpet, exposed brick walls and gold Egyptian-style sconces lighting the way past doors stained a rich shade of red.

Duchess's legs felt like pistons being pumped by red-hot sparks of jealousy.

WHITE CHOCOLATE

"You 'take care of mine' what?" Duchess asked. Her insides were vibrating with attitude.

If Duke fucks all these women, then he's gotta fuck me double what he gives them. Duchess privileges.

"My kids. My baby mommas."

"Why are you so proud that you musta been fifteen when you became a father?" Duchess crossed her arms and stared hard at him as they stood at the sleek stainless steel elevator framed by the same exposed beams and sandblasted brick as she'd seen throughout this former warehouse building.

"I'm proud because I'm doin' right. My kids and they mommas got the best o' e'rything. I take care of my own, right here, where I can make sure they fed and not growin' up around the kinda bullshit I saw."

Duke's jaw muscles flexed. "An' all my baby mommas know. Bring anotha nigga up around my kids? That particular female, she out. Evicted. I keep my kids."

"Like Sunnie."

The muscle rippled harder over his jaw. "Sunnie set a good example. Since Knight been in jail, my top boy was Big Moe. But Big Moe an' Sunnie, they storybook romance was turnt into a horror flick. They attraction turned fatal. They liaison turned dangerous."

Duchess wanted to smile at his clever play on movie titles, but the words twisted painfully in her gut, like a sharp gas bubble. Did that mean they were dead?

"Tell me they pulled a Romeo and Juliet and not—"

"Not!"

"Well, who are they, your baby mommas?"

"They gon' hate you," he said. "But long as they get theirs, they straight."

"Their what? Their sex?"

"Money. Apartments. Clothes. Dancin' in videos an' at concerts. Some of 'em doin' a video shoot today, downstairs. An' they practicin' fo' my birthday party. Tha's when I'ma present The Duchess."

233

"Present?"

"Yeah, once they see you a sistah on the inside an' the outside, they gon' respec' you jus' like e'rybody respec' me. All my females dream o' bein' picked as The Duchess. You so clueless, you ain't even hip to how much pull you got."

"All my females?" Duchess busted out laughing, but she got dead-serious just as quickly. "Don't ever lump me into the 'my females' category. Like they're your fleet of sports cars and you just pick which one you want to drive for the moment!"

Duke pulled a phone from his belt. A blue light was flashing on the front until he pushed a silver button on the side then clipped it back to his waist.

All of a sudden, Duchess felt another twinge of jealousy. His phone was constantly ringing. Was it business or booty calls? How could she ever know? Part of her was submitting to this situation as a business deal so she could learn to be just like The Duke. But her emotions were raw, front and center, too, and they were getting in the way when it came to all these women.

"Yeah, girl!" a female voice echoed in the distance, down the hall. She was one of many in a huge crowd of voices that were getting louder. Duchess kept her glare locked on Duke, who was staring into his phone and pushing the button as if to check who had called.

"An' I was like, 'Fo' real?'" one girl said, shooting words out of her mouth with dizzying speed. Duchess turned slightly. A stream of girls—all as flashy and pretty and sexy as if they'd just stepped out of a music video—poured into the small elevator area. Giggles erupted as they approached.

"Hi, Massa Duke," they said, a chorus of sweet voices.

His eyes glowed the same way Victoria's and her friends' eyes used to glaze over with temptation when they walked into Mrs. Fields cookies.

The girls packed the six-foot-by-six-foot space between Duchess, Duke and the exposed brick walls. Duke was like a tower of machismo in a swirl of pretty faces, perfect hair and wild clothes.

WHITE CHOCOLATE

The sultan amidst a tiny fraction of his harem. What if someday I become a sultaness with a harem of equally sexy guys? Then I wouldn't have to worry about whether Duke would give me some dick when I wanted it — like I did today upstairs. I could have my pick of studs all to myself.

"Wha'z up?" Duke's deep voice vibrated through the sex cloud that was rising along with the fruity, floral and spicy scents of the girls' perfumes, lotions, hairspray and gum.

The sultan was surveying it all, especially all the butts packed in tight jeans. One girl's backside was freakishly large, each cheek literally rolling up-down, up-down like two basketballs in a bag that was bumping against someone's leg as they carried it. She stopped near the elevator.

Her side view reminded Duchess of that horrible day, just a few weeks ago, when Brian shoved pictures of the Hottentot tribe in Africa into Victoria's face. The otherwise thin women had enormous buttocks that protruded at a ninety-degree angle from the smalls of their backs. Some of the women were even captured and put on display in carnival-like, traveling freak shows throughout Europe.

Brian, who was apparently doing a paper on it, shouted, "I saw this in the library today and it reminded me of your ass!" Then he busted out laughing.

"If you think I'm so fat, why are you so proud to be with me?" Victoria had shouted back.

"Because you're brilliant. And beautiful. And I'm just teasin' you, sweetie."

Why was I with that jerk? Because his family was so prestigious? Because Daddy said it was important for my future to stay connected to one of the richest and most powerful families in not just Detroit and Michigan but in the country? "Old money speaks louder and deeper than the whisper of the nouveau riche," Daddy used to say.

"I am fo' real," said the girl who first caught Duchess's attention. She kept talking a mile a minute through lips glossed pink. A fountain of maroon-tinted braids danced over her head as

235

she said, "An' he was like, 'Fo' real, doe!' It all jes' happen' so fas'!"

The girl had giant, hot pink letters splashed all over her impossibly tight jeans and denim jacket, which was open to a pink rhinestone camisole in front that was so tight and skimpy, two brown arcs of nipples dotted its top edge.

"Guuuurrrrlllll," her platinum blond friend responded. She had false eyelashes and a see-through white mesh tank top with white jeans. Her nipples pointed through the mesh like brown peanut M&M candies. "You ain't gotta take dat shit, fo' the simple fact that—"

Duchess glanced at Duke, whose eyes were devouring every one of these gorgeous girls. His stare was like an open mouth under a delicious piece of pizza when the cheese dripped, steaming hot. He looked like he wanted to slurp down every drop of the sex that was oozing from these girls, even from the one in the yellow rhinestone bustier. She wore auburn-hued side ponytails that swayed as she talked about testifying in court for some complicated legal matter. The flawless skin on her toned shoulders, and the beautiful curves of her waist above her jeans made it impossible to think straight. If Duchess felt this entranced as a girl, then what in the world was Duke thinking?

His dazed and seduced expression left no doubt.

Those jealousy sparks popped through Duchess's whole body and prickled up through her skin. She was mesmerized, though, by all these girls. Who were they? What were they doing here? Did they always dress like that? Duchess couldn't look away from the girl in white leather daisy dukes and a tiny bolero jacket with knee-high boots.

"Then I seent his rims," the girl said. "Twennie-foes like you ain't neva seen. An' I was like, I'ma get wit' him if it kill me!"

"Guuuurrrlll, you lay some o' yo' sweet shit on dat ma'fucka, he gon' be out cold." She held up her hand like a stop sign. "Guuurrrlll, you know I'd be like, talk to the hand, Negro."

WHITE CHOCOLATE

"You know I did! When he pullt up, he was like," the girl deepened her voice, "'Dang mami, you thick!' An' I was like, 'Is yo' dick thick?'"

Her friend giggled.

"An' my ass," the girl said, slapping her butt, "Sssssttttt. Hot. Gucci, head to toe. Nails, hair, did like a queen. One look an' he was los'!"

Duchess smiled. These girls had so much personality and excitement, but their chick-chatter stabbed Duchess's heart. Though they looked and dressed different, these girls were exactly like she and Tiffany used to be, talking about clothes and boys and music and movies. And this energy, this female camaraderie, was the same that she had enjoyed with the girls in the locker room with the track team, or in the hallway, going to lockers between classes. Just a very different place, a very different race, a very different pace of life, less than twenty-five miles away from where she used to live.

"Duke, we heard 'bout you finally found you a Duchess," said a girl in jeans with rhinestones down the outer seam. The girl raked her fake-lashed eyes up from Duchess's feet to her eyes. Nutmeg-hued eyes smouldered as she stared at Duchess then Duke. "She look soft. Let us show her some moves."

"She'll see all o' y'all dance at my party," Duke said with too much lust in his eyes. The girl turned slightly so that Duke could see how her jeans hugged her ass. It was about the same size and shape as Duchess's, but her jeans were so low-cut, the top third of her pretty butt crack showed. It was creamy brown, plump and luscious.

I bet Duke fucks every one of these chicks.

Duchess's cheeks burned as she imagined all of these girls shimmying their asses around Duke as he stood there with his arms crossed like those rappers did in videos. As if he were the king and all the women in the world were simply born to serve him.

"Y'all goin' to rehearsal?"

237

"Yeah," said another chick who blew him a kiss then glanced at Duchess with hazel eyes aglow with mischief.

Naw, that bitch a ho and she wanna fuck Duke. Period.

Duchess shook her head to stop that black voice in her mind that kept rewording everything she thought. The voice was just echoing the speech cadences she was hearing around her.

"Bang Squad in'a house!" the girls cheered, raising hands over their heads, flashing long acrylic fingernails painted metallic gold. Their voices thundered as they sang, "Babylon rule, wit' D-town cool, urban jewel, win any duel, jack a fool, sexy seductive, serve an' protect. In Babylon, Duke an' Duchess get respect." An equal number of girls were smiling and scowling at Duchess as they sang. Why hadn't Duke introduced her?

He was nodding to the beat as the elevator doors opened. A dozen girls packed in, but a crowd remained. The girls kept singing, but one girl glared at Duchess and sang, "In Babylon, Duke love constant sex." The girl stuck her tongue out at Duchess in a way that was both snotty and seductive.

"C'mon." Duke pulled Duchess's hand toward a door. "Let's take the stairs up."

In the stairwell, their singing was still loud and their sex energy was just as strong. It made words and jealousy and fear shoot up from Duchess's gut so powerfully, her shoulders twitched as she spoke.

"Duke, we haven't finished talking about our agreement for me to work for you." She was racing up two flights of stairs behind him. Were big Moe and Sunnie dead? And if so, was death the penalty for anyone who crossed Duke, even if they were doing what any normal person couldn't help doing in this sex den?

"You need to tell me what exactly you do here besides have sex and get mad when other people do."

"I don't have to tell you shit 'cept what you need to know," Duke said.

WHITE CHOCOLATE

Slam! Duke pushed the silver bar on the stairwell door marked 7. The sound echoed like a sinister exclamation point after his last word.

"Well, don't take it out on me," Duchess snapped, following him into the stairwell. "This place is like all sex, all the time. All those girls! The sex in the gym! How can you blame anybody for wanting to fuck twenty-four/seven under the influence of this place?"

He turned, glaring down. "Bidness always come befo' booty."

"Say business. Bizz! Ih! Ness!"

Duke tossed his head back. Deep laughter echoed up through the stairwell.

"No, you the one who 'bout to get schoo'ed on Ebonics. The Duchess gon' speak the queen's English when she negotiate for Babylon, but here at home, you gon' learn to speak fluent *homegirl.*"

Duchess thought about the swarm of girls they just left. She put a hand on her hip, tilted her head forward with a slight neck-snap, and said with a slow, controlled and very urban cadence, "Den you gon' show me *all* yo' baby mommas."

Duke blinked. "Wait, lemme close my eyes an' hear that. Say it again." She covered his eyes with her hands then repeated it.

"A-plus!" Duke smiled, leading her into the hallway. "But we still gon' have a Ebonics tutorial."

"Answer my question," she said. "Who are all these girls? I mean, do you fuck them? I am not tryin' to catch bumps, blisters, burning or some three-letter death sentence."

The first time they made love, she had insisted on a condom. The time in the shower and the office, she had not, even though Duke ejaculated on her ass or stomach.

Duchess remembered reading news articles about how Detroit was ranked one of the country's "most infected cities" with gonorrhea, syphyllis, genital warts, chlamydia, herpes and HIV. The recent article reported one in four teens in this area had some kind of sexual infection. That meant if there were four

239

dozen girls downstairs at the elevator, then ten of them had one of the above infections!

And if Timbo took a dive in those infected waters, then I'd have that shit. Oh my God.

"Duke, we have to use condoms every time if —"

Duke was walking fast, his jaw muscle flexing.

"Duke, tell me your dick is a hundred percent healthy. All these girls —"

He stopped at an unmarked door, turned. Something wicked glinted in his genie eyes.

"Whatever you're thinking," Duchess said, "that's how the nannies and half those girls looked at me. Like they wanna slap me down a couple shades."

"Ain't nobody gon' touch The Duchess." His words sliced the air like knives.

"Who is Milan?"

"Somebody you ain't neva gon' meet."

Duchess asked more forcefully. "Who is Milan?"

"She my first baby momma. Zeus an' Hercules, the two bigger boys —"

"Is she moving? Because I'm not."

Duke pulled her close for a hug. They'd gone upstairs, showered — where they fucked some more — and changed into fresh clothes. She pressed her ear to the center of his chest as he said, "Damn, girl, I love yo' sassy ass. You come up in here two days ago, an' you rulin'!"

"Well, since I'm staying but I'm never gonna meet Milan, then she must be leaving."

"This a big building."

"I don't like non-answers," she said, pulling back to look straight up into his eyes. "So, Milan may or may not be leaving. Where is she?"

"Workin' here on the seventh floor."

"Is this where you keep baby mommas during the day?"

"There you go," Duke said with an equally sassy tone.

WHITE CHOCOLATE

Duchess rolled her eyes, stepping toward the door as she said, "I guess I have to see for myself since you're so stingy with information."

He swatted her butt as they stepped through the door.

"Miss Hot Booty," he groaned, leading her through yet another hallway.

"So, Duke, tell me this: if all these employees and 'mommas' are your harem and they give you sex, then do I get to fuck those hot guys in the gym?" She shrugged and spoke in a blasé tone. "I mean, I'm hoping that this tour includes an orientation period so you can clue me in on this new game of life. 'Cause so far, I'm playing without a rule book."

"We makin' our own rules, baby girl!" His onyx eyes sparkled down at her, but something else flashed there. Something that twisted wrong in her gut.

She added, "I take that as a Duchess-makes-her-own-rules kinda response."

"There is no 'I' in 'we,'" Duke said, pinching her nipple through the aqua blue tank top, ruffled around the V-neck with tiny pearl buttons down the front. The quick pain punctuated what he said.

"Then let's agree right now. If you get to have sex with all those women, then I get to pick a dick or two and try that out."

Duke laid his hand over his crotch, making his diamond "D" ring sparkle. "My million-dolla dick don't like it when Miss Celeste make him jealous."

"Well, my clean, healthy pussy doesn't want Timbo spearin' bad meat that makes me sick. Or dead!" She cocked her head to one side. "I can't believe I didn't make you wear a condom every time. My head is so fucked up right now. You've probably screwed hundreds of —"

Duke put his hand over her mouth. Her moving lips brushed against his palm. "You got the prettiest pucker-fish lips on the planet, baby girl, but they need to be still right now."

Duchess's eyes got huge. She didn't even try to pry his enormous fingers off.

241

SEX IN THE HOOD

I'm gonna remember this moment, motherfucker, because I have no idea what you've helped me get myself into. I might have AIDS! I might be pregnant! And I was so caught up in the heat of the moment, I didn't even think about it.

She was always thinking about safe sex with Brian, even when they "just" had oral sex. Since at that time she had vowed never to go all the way, birth control and condoms just weren't on her list of concerns.

But now—

She could end up on the fifth floor in a "baby momma" apartment with a wicked nanny and a job for life on the seventh floor of this mysterious place called Babylon.

Why aren't I scared right now?

Because I have no control. None. Whether Duke is telling the truth that I'm about to become the grand dame of this bizarre place, or whether I'm about to become his personal sex slave, I have no idea. But if I make it through this, someday I will have all the power, so now I'm a student at this urban school that's knockin' hard on any sense of security I thought I had in life.

Duke pressed his lips to her forehead. She closed her eyes, loving the warmth and tenderness—and knowing that her emotional state was so out of whack that she was going along with a guy who was literally muzzling her. But it was all an act on her part, getting her toward a mega power play in the grand finale. She still didn't have the details of how that would play out—she had a lot to learn here at Babylon—but someday, she would rule.

Now, she moaned the same way as when they'd made love. Pressed her hips toward his. Spread her knees, squeezing his thigh between hers. He pulled his hand from her mouth, replacing it with his open lips. The hot wetness was like soothing balm on a cold sting. She ground her pussy into the top of his thigh, craving the mind-numbing slide down his tree trunk into timberland, where Alice could climb and swing and bounce for as long as she wanted.

242

WHITE CHOCOLATE

He squeezed her ass upward, thrust Timbo once—he was rock-hard even through their clothes—and whispered into her mouth, "Duchess gon' be queen o' the baby mommas."

She froze from head to toe. Disgust zig-zaggged through her, even though she understood that being a Duke baby momma was a prestigious position. Being anybody's baby momma at age eighteen was just wrong. She had to go to college. Start her career. Get married. Then have a baby. The old-fashioned order of things.

She cast a playful stare into his eyes and let laughter explode through her lust-trembling lips.

"Why you bust out laughin' when I'm dead serious?" His eyes were laughing with her, but his face was stiff.

"Because I am not having a child until I get my M.R.S. degree. If that happens to be Mrs. Duchess Johnson, cool. But I will not be a teen pregnancy statistic."

"You a trip an' a half," Duke said, shaking his head. "And you a whole bunch o' other statistics, now that you fallen way down below the poverty line."

Duchess tilted her chin up. "But then I became Duchess just as fast." She ran her fingertip over his beautiful lips. "Livin' in the lap of luxury with my Duke. Now, what's behind door number three?"

Duke put his hand on the doorknob.

Duchess smiled. "Let me guess. Is this the baby momma work zone?"

"Ding! Ding! Ding!" Duke imitated a game show host. "The triple bonus prize goes to the lady with the scorching pussy and sassy mouth!"

He opened the door onto a lobby-type area with hardwood floors. To the left, sunshine streamed through windows over a TV and plush orange couches. About a dozen men and women—a few who looked familiar from the sexercise on Sunday evening—were lounging on the couches, reading magazines. Everybody sat up straight when they saw Duke. They were downright gawking at Duchess.

Until their jaws dropped.

They turned to the left. A petite woman in a green silk pantsuit sprang at Duchess like those daredevils at the circus who shot out of cannons.

"White bitch!" the woman screamed. Two giant men, one on each side, grabbed her thin arms. She recoiled.

"Duchess, this Milan," Duke said flatly. He nodded to the big men who were holding the woman. They picked her up and carried her through a door to what looked like an office.

Duke knocked on the door marked EXAM ROOM. That woman with purple glasses who'd given Duchess that disgusting smelling stuff to make her wake up this morning, opened the door.

Duke led Duchess inside.

"Doc Reynolds, Duchess need to hear 'bout the strict health code here at Babylon."

The doctor nodded. "You're looking much better, Madame Duchess. Everyone, including The Duke, gets weekly check-ups, on top of using condoms for any sexual contact. Anyone who becomes infected in the line of duty is either treated and given a reprieve until they're cured, or they're retired and tracked to make sure they don't return."

Duchess's stomach flipped. "What do you mean, 'in the line of duty'?"

The doctor cast a probing look at Duke, who sat on the exam table with Timbo in his hand.

"Doc, I need tests right now. Everything. An' show Duchess my HIV results from last week. Test her too."

The doctor stepped to a computer on the counter. She clicked the keyboard for a few seconds, then a printer hummed as she went at Duke with several giant Q-tips. "Any burning, itching, discharge or odors?"

"I'm as perfect as I've always been," Duke said.

"Good," the doctor said. "How should I explain 'in the line of duty,' Master Duke?" she asked while sticking a swab in his mouth.

WHITE CHOCOLATE

He shrugged. "You could say 'While fuckin'. While screwin'. While drillin'. While engaging in sexual relations.'"

"So, sex is their line of duty?" Duchess's brain was spiraling down, down, around a flashing pink neon sign in her imagination that said PROSTITUTION.

Drugs, she would've believed, or illegal gun trafficking, or that bodyguard story. But selling sex? Was that what all those people in the gym were practicing for? And all those men and women in the lobby, were they waiting for their weekly STD check-ups?

The doctor examined Duke's penis. He grimaced as she shoved a Q-tip into the tiny hole at the head.

Duchess asked, "Wait, is the sex for business or pleasure?"

"C'mon, Miss Daisy," Duke said, zipping his jeans. "Don't go clueless on me again. You was really startin' to catch on." He stood up then glanced at the doctor. "Doc Reynolds, you can do the whole deal on her. Blood culture, e'rythang."

"I told you I'm a virgin," Duchess said.

Duke laughed. "Not no more!"

"But I don't need to get tested because—"

"Any type of sexual activity can spread STDs," the doctor said. "Even oral sex."

"Wait," Duchess said. She stepped to Duke, her boobs at the center of his chest. She was taller now in her red sandals. She stared hard into his eyes and accused, "So, you're a pimp? And the work you want me to do for you—"

Duke tossed his head back, his deep laughter ricocheting off the walls of the exam room.

Duchess was not laughing. She was numb. Ice cold. "You came to Gramma Green's house acting like you were rescuing me, just so you could put me on a street corner. As a prostitute! *After* you took me on a test drive for a Motor City minute!"

This was the curse. It was really happening.

I'll be satisfying Celeste's constant craving for orgasm. I'll be following Celeste's order to share my sex. And somehow, I'll be responding to Mommy's whisper that I'm using that power to get what

245

I want. What that is, I have no idea, but it would prove the curse true, because being a prostitute will definitely kill me.

"It's not funny!" Duchess screamed, pounding Duke's chest. Stinging tears dripped from her eyes. She sobbed, hitting him. Hating him.

He grabbed her wrists, pulled her trembling hands to his lips, kissing them.

"Sssshhh, baby girl, baby girl. Sssshhh." He drew her into his chest, where his voice vibrated through her. "You got it so wrong, baby girl. Listen up!"

She closed her eyes.

"Excuse me," the doctor said. "I'll come back when it's time for the test." She opened the door and left the exam room.

Why should Duchess believe anything Duke said?

"Does Streetology include acting classes? Because Duke Johnson, you get an Oscar for most convincing role as a lover." She opened her eyes, glaring at him. "You tricked me in the worst way. And I was so naïve!"

"Duchess," he pleaded, gently cupping his hand around the back of her head.

Yeah, for this time. Next time he'll slap me. Or knock me down. Kick me.

"How stupid was that, believing you really wanted to help me! Your bogus good samaritan act, it was all a trick! The dinner, the ice cream, the sunset kiss, taking me to meet your mother!"

"Baby girl—"

"And making love," she whispered. Her insides felt like they were melting with sadness and disappointment. "I thought that was real."

"It *is* real." Duke's glassy eyes radiated tenderness. His voice was raspy with a sort of desperate plea that she had not heard from him. "It's all real, baby girl."

That needle in her arm was real, too, when the doctor returned a few minutes later to draw blood for the STD tests. She also did a pelvic exam and took a culture from inside her vagina. All that, the doctor said, would test for stuff like gonorrhea, syphyllis, genital warts, herpes, pelvic inflammatory disease and chlamydia. Another swab in her mouth tested for HIV.

"As long as you've had no odors, burning when you urinate, itching or discharge," the doctor said, "you're probably fine. You look perfectly healthy."

Duchess was glad to get tested. What if Brian had fucked around on her, she gave him a blow job, and he gave her some disgusting sex bacteria or virus that had no symptoms? Plus, seeing Duke interact with the doctor and looking directly at his health records wiped away her anxiety about his sexual health. Wow, this was great, actually. She and Tiffany had always said they'd make a guy get tested before they went all the way, but they'd heard of guys who lied and spread genital warts and chlamydia.

"Madame Duchess," the doctor said, "you know sexually transmitted infections can cause major damage to your insides but never give you any symptoms. That's why we're vigilant about testing every week."

Victoria studied the woman in purple glasses. Her vibe was totally trustworthy. "Dr. Reynolds, do you think since Duke gets tested so much, it's safe for me not to use condoms with him?"

The doctor nodded. "Duke deals in sex. He is vigilant about health with himself and everybody here. So yes, I think you're safe. However, if you both have other partners, that creates some risk."

Victoria's father always warned, the number one thing people lied about was sex. She could never know if the man she was fucking—even her husband—was being faithful. Her dad said she couldn't be with somebody around the clock, and it only took a few minutes, really, to sneak a screw.

Victoria wrapped her arms around her waist to hug herself, as if that would help her figure this out.

"You look worried," the doctor said. "I think Duke will protect you." She cast a concerned look down at Victoria. "But let me say, Madame Duchess, unless you're planning to get pregnant, I can prescribe birth control pills."

SEX IN THE HOOD

Victoria nodded. "Definitely."

Chapter 40

The fresh scent of hot pussy rising up from Miss Daisy's flowering pussy made Duke smile as he inserted the security key into the golden door lock. It didn't matter whether Duchess was happy, sad or mad, her pussy always reacted before she did. If she got an attitude, like she had now, her pussy would be on swole. When she smiled, her pussy creamed. When she imagined crazy shit about what he was going to do with her here, her pussy shot flames.

She was jealous of all those hotties downstairs, but her pussy was curious as hell about how every one of them got their freak on. Now that she finally got some dick, she was like an undercover investigator trying to expose the who, what, when, where, why and how of sex.

Right now, she was going to learn the five W's and H of Duke Love, along with her first official Ebonics lesson. They were already way behind schedule, but Duke had to let her know none of what she was saying in the exam room was true. He knew she was clean, but he wanted her to get tested just to show theirs was an equal partnership.

And now he was going to use body language to tell her just how much he loved her.

Timbo 'bout to speak louder, better an' bolder than any words could say. She gon' be a shiverin' lump o' jelly when I lay on this mack daddy powa.

"We gon' talk in here," Duke said as the little green light flashed in the silver box on the gold door. "This the Cleopatra suite."

"I love how the door is just like the Babylon offices upstairs, but this is Cleopatra's mask, right?" she asked, staring up at the enormous gold-and-black mask of the Queen of the Nile. "I've dressed up as Cleopatra every Halloween since third grade when

249

I wrote a paper on her. She was so sexy and confident and powerful."

Duke smiled as he pushed open the door. "Just like you. This where I was gon' have you stay, but now that you made yo'self at home in my penthouse—" He laughed, remembering how she hadn't hesitated saying "our room" this morning. "I'm gon' have Knight stay here when he come."

"No one would believe this is here." Her voice echoed with her footsteps. Her juicy booty bounced as she stepped onto the 3,000 square foot suite. She gawked at the open loft with high, exposed ceilings, brick walls and sunshine shooting down through all the high paned windows. "I love this place."

"Usually the female rappers stay here, five K a night. They into some freaky shit. 'Bout killed twennie Studs las' week. They'll chew up a dick, break it off, swallow it an' hunt fo' the next.

"All them windows new," Duke said. "Three years ago, jus' before Knight took a fall, we sandblasted all the walls, redid all the plumbing. This building a hun'ed years old."

Shiny hardwood floors stretched to a black marble fireplace framed by a mantle that was a huge version of the Egyptian mask on the door. Plush white couches faced it around a zebra-skin rug.

In the corner was the sleek kitchen with stainless steel appliances, black marble countertops, dark cherry cabinets, and an island with black stools with black-and-gold striped satin cushions. Next to that was a dining table with similar seats and a huge gold bowl overflowing with fresh fruit on the glasstop. Nearby, a beautiful desk and computer.

"Oh my God," Duchess said, running her fingers over the frosted glass wall leading to the bedroom. "This etching of Cleopatra, her flowing white gown, her elaborate headdress. Oooh, love that!" She pointed to Cleopatra and the two men in Egyptian-style loin cloths and two ladies in waiting. She traced the design to the edge of the glass door, touched the gold hinges, and went inside.

"Duchess." Duke touched the back of her upper arms.

She jumped.

"Ah! I didn't hear you. Don't do your panther walk up behind me!" Her pucker-fish lips pulled back into the prettiest smile. She glanced at the bed and smiled bigger. "So, you brought me in here so you can explain—" Her voice got hard and loud. "—what the hell you want from me?"

He pressed his fingertip to her pretty lips. "We gotta rap about Duke an' Duchess. That whack shit you was blowin' out them lips a minute ago—"

Duchess's ass sank straight into the big, fluffy white bed. She lay back on all the pillows and looked up at the gold-and-black Cleopatra mask over the bed. He remembered the way the interior designer described how the mask was "attached to the exposed brick wall, gathering an explosion of white tulle that cascades down each side of a mountain of frilly pillows at the head of the bed." It was pretty enough, but Duchess made the vision a complete snapshot from heaven.

"Damn, I wish I had a camera," Duke groaned, running his hand over the tent that Timbo was making of his jeans. He adjusted his gat in his waistband under his black shirt. "The way yo' hair fannin' out all ova them white pillows, an' yo' body all stretched out, you look like the mos' innocent an' sexy playmate ev'a."

"Duke, what do you want from me? Is this like a mini-honeymoon where you fuck my brains out then toss me into the masses of girls you keep here?"

Duke pulled his gat from his jeans. Her eyes got as big as her fist. He laid the gun on the nightstand beside a big vase of white flowers.

I ain't even gon' acknowledge whateva she was jus' thinkin'.

"I know you ain't *that* naïve, baby girl," he said, pulling another gun from his left black gator cowboy boot, which he set beside the other.

"Tell me your daddy didn't have security." Duke lay beside her, his left elbow on the pillows, his chest pressing into her right shoulder. "I know, as high profile as he was, y'all had at least one gun in that big-ass palace in the middle o' the woods. On yo' own lake!"

"And in his office," Duchess said softly. She closed her eyes. Her lashes were so long, thick and black, they looked like fringe against beige china. "Actually, Daddy loved guns. He had a cabinet full in the house, for hunting, target practice. He even went on a safari in Kenya, after Mommy died." Her voice cracked in a way that stabbed Duke's heart.

He kissed her forehead. "I'm sorry, baby girl. Let's talk about somethin' happy."

She opened her bloodshot eyes, looking at him like he was crazy.

"Duchess, I know this sound whack as hell, since we been knowin' each otha forty-eight hours, but I know you my soul mate." Duke's lips felt hot. His eyes felt extra big, and his heart was banging.

Her eyelashes lowered so her eyes were half-closed, staring down at his mouth. She raised her hand to the back of his neck, pulled him down, and kissed him like he had never been kissed. Like his mouth was hot loaf of fresh-baked bread, split down the middle and steaming, and her lips were the sweet cream butter, melting right into him, making the perfect flavor so one wouldn't taste right without the other. She tasted it too, because she was kissing him for what felt like forever.

They were naked in a Motor City minute. Duchess stood over him, one foot on each side of his hips, staring down at Timbo like he was the chrome exhaust pipe on a Harley she was about to straddle and ride into the next millennium.

She took a long step toward his head, putting her right foot beside his ear, then she moved her other foot to his other ear. He was like King Tut in his tomb up under the pyramid, only this boy king was staring up at a pyramid of long, creamy legs, into a peak that looked as good as heaven: the prettiest pussy on the planet. Timbo was going to plunder that temple like a mug in a minute, straight through those black vines and shiny red doors,

WHITE CHOCOLATE

into the chamber of treasures he was claiming as his own, that he could stroke and admire any time he wanted.

Oooohh, looked like the pyramid was caving in. Duchess's knees folded down, lightning quick. She squatted so his face was right at the temple door. He inhaled the scent of sweet-salty incense. The heat was blowing out from inside; some of the holy water dripped on his forehead, like he was being anointed as The One to enter this sacred chamber to pray.

"Talk to the pussy." Duchess's voice was hard, like every word came out dipped in gold. She said it just like the sistahs would hold up their palms and say "talk to the hand."

"Celeste wants to hear it straight from the source," Duchess said, but he couldn't see her face because a big, wet pussy was blocking his view, "what this urban sex lord has to say about The Duke and The Duchess."

Duke's ears were ringing. His body was stiff. Her words cracked on him like a dominatrix whip and he froze, not knowing how to react to the lash he *asked* for.

Ain't no girl ev'a talked to me like that or taken this bold-as-hell stance over my body.

She squatted lower, hands on her knees like strippers did, lowering the pussy just above his eyes . . . over the tip of his nose . . . then hovering over his mouth.

I couldn't talk right now to save my life. Not nary a word is comin' outta my ma'fuckin' mouth.

His eyes got big, like hers did in the hall when he put his hand over her mouth.

"I didn't *think* you'd have anything to say," Duchess said in that same sistah-girl-power way. She made her hips circle so the pussy went 'round and 'round in his face. Not touching, just going 'round and 'round like she was going to hypnotize him with it.

And ain't nobody ev'a been hypnotized by somethin' so pretty. If they did, it'd be a national pastime. 'Cause I got this peep-show-freak-show all to myself. Fo' life.

I gotta tell her. But I cain't —

He could hardly think, much less wrap his lips around some words. It was like her pussy was a big red mute button on his brain, just like the mute function on his phone. If he pushed it, he could make a motherfucker shut up. Then he could say whatever he wanted to say and they couldn't say shit back. He would have all the control, just like Duchess had right now.

Hell naw!

Duke felt like his heart was going to explode. It was pumping so hard and fast with fear, with adrenaline, with excitement—with rage that this lily white girl was mackin' The Duke!

I gotta get up. Get on top. Dominate!

But that pussy, going in circles in his face . . . the scent . . . the hot dampness like a warm washcloth, the thrill that this was where every motherfucker wished he could stay 24/7, face to face with a hot, hungry pussy.

He felt so drunk he could hardly keep his eyes open. Timbo was about to shed his skin like pythons did at the zoo when they grew so big their skin split, then they'd slither out and grow some new, bigger shit.

'Cause Timbo so ma'fuckin' giant!

Duke's lips curled up into a mellow smile.

Cain't look away from that pussy goin' 'round an' 'round. Yeah, this where e'ry cat he know wanna be at, starin' up at prime, premium 100% certified good pussy.

Slam!

A groan like Duke had never heard from his own mouth shot out from between his wet lips because she just slammed down on Timbo like she was a big cube of filet mignon poking herself on a skewer. Ready to sizzle.

The shock of hot, tight pussy that was so wet he just slid in— damn, it made his whole body shiver and convulse like he was cumming, and she just got down on it. Her blue blowtorch eyes shot down at him in a way that was hotter than ever. She took a position like she was leaning forward on a motorcycle, so her ass pooted up.

WHITE CHOCOLATE

Timbo was deep up in the pussy. Damn, Celeste was sucking him in, squeezing him around, steaming right through this thick dick.

"I'm gonna ride you," Duchess moaned, "'til you beg me to pull over an' let you rest."

He hoped she would ride so good and so fast that flames shot out around them. Her hair was all down her back, falling to the sides over her waist and ass.

She pumped her hips at just the right angle so Timbo slid in and out. Faster, faster, faster . . . She bounced now. That ass on his thighs, slapping.

"What'cha wanna tell me, Duke?" she teased. "Thought you wanted to rap."

She fucked him harder, and he still couldn't talk. Didn't want to talk. Or think.

Her whole body glistened with sweat now, from her long, pretty neck to her titties pressed between her fingers, her toned stomach, her thighs. Clumps of hair stuck to her shoulders. Some strands fell and caught between her fingers. He couldn't have scripted a more sensuous scene if he were Hugh Hefner.

"Rap," she whispered, keeping a steady beat of her butt pounding his thighs. "I wanna rap as I slap my ass."

He smacked her butt, one hand on each cheek. It was so loud the slaps startled them both. She laughed but didn't stop fucking.

"Yeah, I'm crass. Jus' ask the mask." She nodded at the Egyptian artwork over the bed "Witness this kiss—" She leaned to suck his mouth. "—as I whiss-per my love like a glove on Timbo. I know he's so fat, so I sat like a cat, with my pussy soft and squooshy—"

Her pussy was pulsating like she was about to cum.

"Oooohhhhh, yaaaaay-yaaaaahhhhh."

Celeste squeezed so hard around Timbo, it was like the head was going to pop off. Duchess was cumming so hard, it felt like an earthquake was shaking up inside that temple, threatening to break off this great black obelisk.

"I love this dick," she moaned. She sounded just like Duke would be thinking while he fucked, whether he was with Duchess or any other of the hundreds, if not thousands of pussies he'd had. Some were just OK, but right now Duchess was saying "I love this dick" the same way he would rate some really good pussy, even pussies that he couldn't remember the name or the face they were attached to. Just good-ass pussy.

"I love this dick."

Yeah, girl. Get yo' groove.

"I looooooove this Duke."

It felt like fire was spreading all over his skin. In a bad way. Like she had just lit a match on The Duke. That *Ttttsssstttt!* sound filled his ears, and he was getting scorched up under this pussy inferno.

She was using "dick" and "Duke" as interchangeable, like they were the same word. And like they meant the same thing.

Like niggas be thinkin' the female an' the pussy be one an' the same. So instead of saying, "I'm takin' my girl to the show tonight," a dude might as well say, "I'm takin' my pussy to the movies," because the goal of taking her to do something she enjoyed was, in the end, to get something back that he liked. Pussy. But now, the sting of feeling like he was just a dick, well, that wasn't going to work for The Duke.

I gotta flip her over an' fuck her senseless, squirt so much nut up in that pretty head it drown out any crazy-ass way o' thinkin' like a dude.

Hell naw. The Duchess got juice, but it ain't ev'a gon' be equal to The Duke juice. Neva.

He grabbed her thighs. He would just raise her up, now that she was weak from cumming, and tackle—

"Seems like the better angle," she whispered, glancing back at his knees. "Yeah."

Before he could grab her thighs, she spun on his dick like a toy top and faced his feet. It looked like two moons were rising over his stomach.

WHITE CHOCOLATE

All I can see is ass. Look almost as good as a face full o' pussy. Day-um.

Duchess tried a stroke, thrusting her hips forward.

"Oh yeah, tha's it," she moaned, sounding all black now.

Stroke, stroke, stroke . . . She leaned down so her nipples brushed over his legs, just above the knee. She wrapped her hands under his knees and —

Rode! Like a jockey bolting out of the gate, hips galloping at full speed, faster and faster and faster.

She made some round motions, like her hips were going in circles. Her ass was just grinding into him like she would never get tired. Then she moved faster, looking like a rabbit up there.

His fingertips danced up her back, tickling her flawless skin. She shivered, moaned. "Ooohhhh, touch me so good."

Duke wanted to ask, *Damn, how can a girl be so erotic she shiver when you just touch her back?* But he still couldn't talk. *I ain't even tryin' to spend a ounce o' energy on anything but gettin' fucked wit'out movin' a single muscle.*

She raised up so her upper body was upright all the way. She moved her feet out at his sides, put her hands on her knees, and raised up in a squat position, just like she had seen the Sluts do in the gym.

Duke smiled. She couldn't wait to try this shit. Without letting Timbo out of the pussy-vise grip, she squatted down, up, down, up.

Dis da bomb! Faster, faster, she was shaking, moaning and crying out like she was cumming, banging down on his dick like she was nailing her soul to his.

"Ah," she sighed like her muscles were sore. She slid down to her knees and bent just a little bit, sucking Timbo up in that creamy pussy tunnel. Her hair was all clumped on her back. Sweat dripped down her ass, onto him, making a pool of hot, salty sweat in his belly button.

Ma'fuck me! Something jolted through him so strong, his head suddenly filled with the image of sticking Timbo in a big electric socket.

257

I'm gettin' electrocuted up in here.

Pussy shock treatments.

That gon' fry my brain an' make me dumb as Frankenstein. He would be a kitten in her lap as she sat at the throne of Babylon with just a shell of The Duke at her side. She could rule and just have him fuck her whenever she wanted.

Slam! She was ruthless, bouncing that booty, taking all of this dick. And all of The Duke.

Hell naw!

"Ddddd . . . " Her name came out through his mouth as a grunt. "Ddddduuuuu—" What was worse, saying nothing or sounding retarded when he tried to talk?

The scent of their sex made him as mellow as when he breathed in second-hand ganja smoke. Except Timbo was about to blow. Duke's whole body was trembling. Her electric jolts made him convulse, making his dick feel like it was about to shoot with the force of a firehose.

She was cumming again, shaking so hard her shoulders were shimmying, her legs twitching, her hands trembling as she held them out at her sides like she was flying while she was fucking. Like R. Kelly's song, "I Believe I Can Fly." Yeah, she was definitely touching the sky right now.

She was pounding the pussy like there was no tomorrow. Timbo was taking it, too.

Oh shit, yeeeaaahhhhh. A ma'fuckin' seizure takin' ova The Duke.

"I *got* this dick!" she moaned. "I got *all this* dick."

He groaned. Deep. Raw. Like he had never heard himself groan before. Like a bubble was rising up from the deepest part of his core. Like that sound that came out of Prince's mouth as he died. It was a sound he never wanted to hear again, especially from his own mouth. Like a part of him was dying.

Duchess glanced back. Her eyes looked supernatural, all glazed with lust, chunks of hair stuck to her wet cheeks, lips red, open, like a lion that just took the juiciest bite out of the panther it killed.

WHITE CHOCOLATE

She was still fucking. Her pussy squeezed as she came. His dick throbbed as he blew his nut, and their sex power juice mixed into some toxic chemical that was going to make both of them crazy.

Duchess banged down more, more, more, until Timbo got tingly like his elbow when he hit the funny bone. He wanted to scream "Stop!" but pussy shock treatments stole his voice. He wanted to grab her, push her off, but his arms felt like lead. He wanted to buck up and toss her off, but the stallion was tame.

So all I can do is lay here like a pussy an' get fucked.

Duchess shot up, letting Timbo slip out and collapse like a dead seal on his groin, which looked like a black sand beach frothing with their salty sex juice.

Duke trembled, every muscle in his body. And he couldn't stop, not even when she stepped off the bed and walked toward the bathroom. Her body was wet, like a newborn colt that stood up in the first minute of its life and ran beside its momma — sleek, shiny, graceful. Her pucker-fish lips were ruby red now after sucking the king of the sea down whole and makin' chum out of his ass.

My ass. Duchess glanced back at him with so much power in her eyes, Duke felt sick. *Look like my body language spoke loud an' clear all right . . . that I'm the punk ma'fucka who layin' here like some limp-ass jelly. Hell naw!*

Chapter 41

Duke is crazy if he expects me to concentrate on super fly girl clothes, Ebonics and ghetto psychology while Honey is prancin' around in that little white dress.

Duchess strutted across the white marble floor in blood-red patent leather stiletto boots and a sleeveless black cat-suit. She stepped up the four stairs to the raised area where Duke was sitting on a gold throne behind the huge, thick glass desk.

"So, you're making me into a thugstress, right?" she said playfully, strutting the way runway models did it on TV reports of fashion shows in New York. "That's a cross between a temptress and a thug, with a sort of Cleopatra feline look."

"You my chameleon who can switch between ghetto fabulous, Wall Street white girl, an' sexy diva," Duke said. "Damn, baby girl, yo' booty be poppin' in nat. Bend over an' shake that ass." His hand was over a huge bulge in his lap.

"Oooohhh, I've never looked so sexy," she said as the designer, Gregor, rolled that giant mirror in front of her. In it, she could also see the rack of equally seductive jeans, dresses, skirts and jackets she had already tried on.

"Especially with this tan," Duchess said, loving her darker skin thanks to the tanning booth Duke had installed in the penthouse for her. "I feel like one o' those sexy comic book women with superhuman powers. Duke—"

He looked pale.

A soft cloud of Honey's perfume—musky with a hint of floral—enchanted Duchess's nose moments before she turned to see the girl's titties come to halt just inches under Duchess's mouth.

I'm gonna drip pussy juice all over these clothes.

Honey's fingertips on Duchess's arms brought to mind that lightning ball at the science center. The girl's touch made purple bolts shoot through Duchess's skin, through her body, lodging in a hot, sizzling glow between her legs.

She attached two gold armbands in the inward curves just above her biceps.

"Just like Cleopatra wore," Honey said with a husky voice that flowed like slow molasses over her lips. Her honey-brown eyes mirrored the lust that was making Duchess feel like she could touch her finger to the bottom of a lightbulb and make it glow.

"I love it," Duchess said, glancing down at the gold cuffs on her arms and Honey's fingers on her skin.

"That cuff is superb," the designer, Gregor, called across the white marble floor here in the Babylon HQ offices. The slender, cocoa-brown guy pushed his silver glasses up into a mop of black ringlet curls. Wearing a blue suede pantsuit, he made "OK" signs with each hand.

"Duchess," he said, turning toward the rack of clothes that Victoria Winston wouldn't have taken a million dollars to wear in public. "The whole Cleopatra look is just spectacular with your long hair. I've got one more thing. Honey, get her some eyeliner."

Duke laughed. "The finishin' touches on the sex monsta we creatin'. You still so horny, you turnin' yo'self on jus' lookin' at yo' own damn thighs in the mirror. You finally free to love how yo' round ass curve up like two big buttered buns, makin' yo' pussy drip."

She threw a satin glove at him. "Stop!"

"Gregor, you see Duchess musta hid yo' iron between her juicy thighs. Honey, don't y'all see steam shootin' outta her pussy? *Whoosh!* Hot steam burnin' e'rythang in sight. Come burn me, baby!"

Honey giggled as she strutted over to one of the mummy cases flanking the desk. Duke's eyes were on Duchess — she could see him in her peripheral view — while she watched Honey's round, plump ass move under the flowy white chiffon of her little dress. Her thighs caused automatic mouth opening and watering.

When Duchess looked at them, all she could do was imagine her open mouth sucking on that soft, flawless skin.

As the designer jingled something behind Duchess, Honey opened the mummy case, which contained shelves. She bent over at the waist. The dress rode up, and wet, molasses-brown pussy lips smiled at Duchess. Honey's pussy was fat and bare; shaved hairless, nestling a sweet brownberry treat with a side of fresh cream, displayed right under perfect curves of a plump ass.

Duchess wanted to crawl up behind her and just eat. Her knees weakened; her whole body felt like she just fell into a hot bathtub. Celeste shot hot gusts of steam into the crotch of this sleeveless black bodysuit.

"Here we go," the designer snarled over that jingle sound. "You all can have a little sexcapade on your own time. I have three more clients."

"We'll take e'rything." Duke's voice boomed across the office. He did not stop staring at Duchess as she watched Honey strut back to her. "Leave the rack."

Duke pitched a hand-sized black-and-gold King Tut mummy case. Gregor caught it. The suction sound of a tin being opened then closed inspired the designer to whisper, "Every day is Christmas at Babylon. I'm most grateful, Master Duke." There was the sound of the clothes rack wheeling out, doors opening and closing, and Gregor was gone.

"Yeah, all them clothes make me wanna have a sexcapade," Duke said, "wit' my chameleon. Hope you know how lucky you is. My baby mommas would suck dick for days to get all this loot for free."

Honey giggled, sending gusts of hot breath against Duchess's neck. Honey's mouth stayed slightly open as she leaned up with a black cosmetic pencil. Duchess closed her eyes as the soft tip lined her lashes, with one outward stroke at the corners of her eyes.

The heat of Honey's body drew Duchess's nipples to hard points in the black cat-suit. Her chest rose and fell.

WHITE CHOCOLATE

"See, yo' body heavin' 'cause that homegirl within tryin' to bust free," Duke said, his hand on his dick. "Now you got a ghetto space ranger to the rescue."

"Here, let me adjust this," Honey whispered, unfastening the halter top at the back of Duchess's neck. It fell open.

Gregor dashed back in, jingling. "Wait, one more—" He stopped in his tracks. "Thing." He was holding a gold chain with coins attached.

Duke nodded.

"Here," Gregor said, attaching the belt around Duchess's waist. "Hell, who needs clothes anyway?" Then he dashed out.

"You gotta stay a chameleon," Duke said. "I seent it on my kids' videos, a lizard that change colors to match the background."

"Our colors match nice," Honey whispered, curling her fingertips into the belt, gently scratching Duchess's waist. She stuck out her tongue, and while staring into Duchess's eyes, Honey tickled her tongue across those exposed nipples.

"Mmmmm," Duchess moaned and twisted, making the necklace jingle. "My pussy could boil an egg right now."

"I bet it would come out gold," Honey whispered.

Duke's tone was all lust as he talked. "Wit' Moreno, you gon' be lily white in a pinstripe suit, an' the baddest black bitch crossed wit' yo' daddy business brains on the inside."

Honey's face was like a doll. Her lips were so perfect, Duchess had to taste them.

"You smell like sugar," Duchess whispered.

"My lotion and lip gloss," Honey said. "It's called Brown Sugar. Taste." She leaned close.

Duchess's head spun. She closed her eyes. She had kissed Tiffany so many times, but she'd never been so excited.

Oh my God. Honey's lips were soft fire. They parted when they met Duchess's trembling mouth, and Honey just placed them there for a long moment, like she knew this was all new to Victoria, so she was taking it slow.

Deliciously slow. Dizzying. Satin soft, hot, loving . . .

263

SEX IN THE HOOD

I could suck on these lips all day long.

Victoria's pussy convulsed. One touch and she could cum. Her entire being felt so electric, she felt like she could look up at the sky and make lightning shoot from her eyes. Touch her pussy right now, or let her just see Honey's sweet playmate for Celeste, and thunder would pound the sky.

Honey pulled back just a few inches. She was pouting. Her beautiful eyes glowed with lust, mirroring Victoria's emotions exactly. Her back arched, rising and falling with heavy breathing.

"Right now, we fadin' to black," Duke said. "An' seein' how you can become one wit' female beauty."

Duchess was drunk, as if Honey's lips were a champagne fountain. Honey pulled back then purred, "Aren't we s'posed to be teaching you how to talk like a sistah? As your executive assistant, it's my responsibility. So," she whispered, "if you ev'a meet up wit' one o' dem fed pinpricks, what'cha gonna say?"

"Ahm gon' say," Duchess jerked her neck a little, tightened her lips, "hell naw, I ain't neva heard o' no white bitch name Victoria Win—what?"

Honey's deep, raspy laughter was infectious. Duchess and Duke cracked up.

"She don't need coachin'," Honey told Duke.

"Yeah, she do," he answered. "Let me sprinkle some wisdom on Miss Daisy. In the hood, rule numba one: Anything you say or do and anything anybody make up about you can and *will* be used against you, so don't tell nobody nothin'."

Duchess could stare all day at Honey's plump, dark brown breasts. They were all hoisted up in her face, mounds that invited her to rub her face all in the crack, on the soft parts, suck on those nipples forever.

"I always had a 'no information' policy," Duchess said. "Most things are nobody's business, for sure."

Honey pulled both sides of her dress so that her nipples popped out. With her mouth open, Duchess moaned as she dove toward them.

WHITE CHOCOLATE

Oh my God, the sensation of stiff nipple against the soft, wet inside of my mouth —

"For sure, Miss Daisy," Duke mocked. "Now say, 'Fo' sho'. Where you come from, Miss Daisy say 'fer shewer.' Now The Duchess say 'fo' sho.'"

"Maybe you didn't notice the big, pretty tittie that *was* in my mouth," Duchess said, playing mad. She pressed her lips together, drew the corners of her mouth back, tilted her head slightly and said, "Quit pissin' me awf, ma'fucka!"

"Day-um," Duke exclaimed with sparkling eyes. "You quick. Com'ere, bof y'all."

As they went up the steps, Duchess watched Honey's ass, her juicy legs and the hump of her plump ass in that little Cleopatra dress. The hot, wet swell between Duchess's legs created torturous friction.

"Duchess," Duke said, patting her throne. "Come sit next to me. Honey, show her what you got."

Duchess sat on Duke's thigh, facing the desk. Honey sat on the desk. She leaned back, stuck her legs in the air, and with a flash of those gold lace-up sandals, she spread her legs.

The round curves of her ass cheeks against the glass desktop formed a sort of platter for Honey's sweet meat. All those shiny folds of pink-brown flesh, it was like those party trays with ham and roast beef sliced so thin it looked like a crumpled piece of satin.

That was what this girl's big, brown clit and shaved pussy lips looked like. All Duchess could do was bend down to indulge in this most feminine delicacy. First, she ran her tongue up one lip, down the other. All the while she was grinding her pussy against Duke's leg.

Honey cupped her big, juicy breasts, sticking her tongue out to lick her own nipples. Duchess wrapped her lips around the plump brownberry, and delicious shivers wracked Duchess's body.

I'm cumming at first bite.

Duke felt it, so he raised her a little, yanked down the bottom half of the cat-suit, and shoved his huge, rock-hard dick inside her. She gasped into Honey's pussy. Then she did the windshield wiper motion. Honey quivered immediately.

"Ooooh, Duchess, you do that good." Honey frantically sucked her own nipples, staring with hungry eyes down at Duchess, who was peering over a bald brown hill, the dress crumpled around her waist and under her boobs. "You eat pussy like a pro."

As Duke thrust up into Celeste, he reached around and stuck his index finger inside Honey's pussy. His knuckles bumped Duchess's wet chin. Duchess pulled back to watch, loving Honey's round, juicy ass pressed down on the glass desk, two circles forming a base for that fat, plump, bald pussy dripping honey as sweet as the name implied.

Duke's fingers pumped in and out of her pussy. His dick slammed up into Duchess's pussy. She shivered faster, more intense. Her nipples were hard as rocks between her fingertips. She loved the sight of his beautiful brown hand contrasting with Honey's meaty folds.

Honey's pussy was wide open in her mouth; it was a dream. So was Timbo inside her right now, giving Celeste what she needed.

The fireball between Duchess's legs was about to explode. Honey was quaking, moaning, shrieking, clawing, pulsating around Duke's finger.

Duchess screamed as orgasm melted her core. But she was terrified, because her veins were pumping red-hot opium. It just melted her mind into a raw, fiendish mass that would make her do anything to get more of the sweet stuff she just sampled with Duke and Honey.

Chapter 42

Duchess was now Alice in Pleasureland, and behind every door lay something even sexier. But these stripper dance lessons were going too far. No way in the world would she ever dance like those girls in videos, or worse.

"Madame Duchess," Honey said, guiding her into the gym, "you'll be doin' these dance moves like a pro. I can tell by the way you flow when you walk."

"I don't know why Duke wants me to—"

Duchess's mouth watered at the sight of dozens of beautiful, bare derrières lined up at the ballet bar in the mirror and across the red floor mats. Thongs in every color rose up and out of each luscious crack and double bubbles of black velvet, caramel suede and creamed coffee.

Duchess's breath caught in her throat. At the end of the bar, stretching her thin arms over her head, was Milan.

The main baby momma who got hysterical at the sight of me today. But those two bodyguards were still with her. Maybe that was why she was making that snarling expression instead of charging at Duchess like she'd done earlier today.

Now I'm definitely not gonna do this in front of her.

"Welcome, Madame Duchess," said Lee Lee, the tall Asian-black woman who was leading Victoria's sexercise session. Her long, cinnamon-brown legs stretched forever from her bare feet on the red mats up to the black thong arching over her hips. A black tank top with a center zipper held her hand-sized boobs in place.

"Can I just watch?" Duchess asked.

Something red flashed to her right.

"Put this on," Lee Lee said.

A red thong formed a silky cloud in Victoria's outstretched hands.

SEX IN THE HOOD

"I ain't givin' nasty dance lesson number one with you lookin' like a nun all covered up," Lee Lee said playfully. "Didn't Duke tell you? When you come to Hood School, we got a certain dress code."

Duchess felt dizzy. The kinds of moves she was learning to make with Duke, and now with Honey, were not something she wanted to do in front of anyone else, especially while she was wearing a thong in a room full of girls.

"An' hurry up," said India, the tall, blue-black girl from the office who handled the fleets. Her stare was seductive as she said, "We all wanna see how much black showed up on that ass. Once you start to bounce it, we'll know."

Laughter echoed through the gym.

"That white girl probably can't dance her way out of a paper bag," Milan snickered. "'Probably doesn't have an ounce of rhythm anywhere."

A few girls laughed, including one who looked like Honey with short, straight black hair. She was already doing really sexy exercises, raising her leg all the way up so her foot pointed up beside her face like a ballerina, except she was wearing a thong.

Lee Lee glared at them; they got quiet. If it weren't for that, they'd be cracking up. Duchess wanted to disappear. Why had she felt so comfortable with her newly blossoming sex—until now? Because Milan was here. She was radiating so much hate, Duchess didn't want to be in the same room with her, much less feel sexy or dance or do anything scandalous in front of such a hostile witness.

I'd feel safer if Duke were here. He said he had to go handle some details about his birthday party coming up in a few days.

India bent to touch her toes. The bulge of baby blue thong stretched over her pussy, making it look like a sling full of plump meat. That little strip of fabric could barely cover the fat lips and big clit within.

Victoria had read once that women in some African tribes had a daily ritual of masturbation that caused their clits to grow inches long. It would just hang there and get full and fat like ripe,

268

bursting fruit between their legs when they were aroused. Like all you'd have to do was kneel in front of them and slurp that nectar, chew on the pulp until your jaw joint couldn't take another lick.

Duchess squeezed her pussy lips again, but rather than calm Celeste, they only stimulated a hot, cream-colored throb. A gust of steam heated her jeans.

Why was she suddenly finding women so beautiful? So delicious-looking? Why did she keep staring at and thinking about Honey's boobs, how one look made Duchess want to bury her face in all that soft, round, creamy flesh? Rub her cheeks in it, lick them all around, suck on the pretty tips pointing through that paper-thin black cotton.

Right now, Honey's toned arms looked just as creamy and shapely as they had in her Egyptian maiden mini-dress in the office. Her legs were toned, bare and holding up that super-round, firm butt. That sexy bubble looked just as smooth and pretty as Duchess had imagined as she stared at the white chiffon of her dress whooshing back and forth, from the gold belt cinching her waist to the tops of her thighs.

Duchess balled her fists to keep from reaching out and cupping her hands around Honey's ass in front of all these girls — especially Milan, whose stare was so angry she could start a fire with one glance.

Suddenly, Duchess wondered if what she did in Babylon would stay in Babylon. She wasn't going to stay here forever, so what if one day, when she had become a successful business woman, her pussy-slurping activities with Honey came back to haunt her? If former presidents could confess that they had experimented with weed, then certainly she could say she had fully explored her sexuality. But she'd twist it around if she were ever called on it, saying her critics *wished* they could have watched — her or anything else that went on at Babylon.

Right now she had no choice but to stay in this place of wild, sexy abandon, but when the time was right for her to go back out into the world as Victoria Winston, go to college, start her own business . . . she would make sure her activities inside this nondescript building in the hood never caught up with her. Duke would teach her how to cover her tracks.

Daddy used to always say, "Never do anything you don't want to see in the newspaper, on TV or over the Internet." She'd have to be extra careful, not let her lust overrule her mind. Who knew? Maybe Milan had a camera phone that could download a picture of Duchess and shoot it all over the world — and to the FBI — saying, "Here's Victoria Winston! I found her, butt-ass naked, dancin' like a stripper! Eating pussy too!"

But if Duke had so much power and Milan was involved in the still-mysterious work he did here, she wouldn't want to cross him. Plus, she'd be busting on herself. Still, that didn't mean Duchess wanted to give that hater any ammunition, especially while she wrestled with the meaning of her life over the past forty-eight hours.

Am I in love with Duke? Is it love or lust or both? How do I feel different? Black, white, both? Am I a dyke? Do other girls feel like this when they look at other females? Touch them? Kiss them?

Dance lessons, she could do without. If Duke thought she was going to shake what her momma gave her like those video chicks, he was the one who was clueless. Why was he so adamant about her getting this tutorial from the B'Amazons?

"Don't just stand there droolin'," Lee Lee snapped. "Let's work."

Victoria clutched the thong and headed into the locker room.

"Where you goin'?" India teased. "We gon' see it all anyway."

A minute later, Victoria's cheeks burned with embarrassment as she watched herself strut across the gym in a red thong. Her super-long legs looked toned and lean, as did her stomach and butt in the mirror. Her nipples were like two copper pennies showing through her tight white jog bra.

"I see why they call it a ponytail," Honey said, running her hands over Duchess's hair. Honey's body heat made Duchess relax, but Milan's angry stare in the mirror made her step out of

WHITE CHOCOLATE

Honey's reach. If Honey was her assistant and Milan saw their relationship was both business and pleasure, then she could poison that.

"Honey, I really don't feel like dancing."

"Do it for Duke. He'll love it, sweetie."

Lee Lee blasted the music, a hard-driving bass beat with girls singing nasty lyrics about "a muff-drivin' bitch, quick as lipstick, switch! Gotta get a girlie fix!"

The rhythm made Duchess want to dance and have fun, but the way Milan's eyes were boring a hole through her backside chilled any notion of enjoyment. If those big men weren't standing on each side of Milan, what would she be doing?

"Line up, hold the bar," Lee Lee commanded. "Madame Duchess, just do what we do."

The girls gripped the bar. With legs straight, they tip-toed a little, bent at the waist, and bounced their butts.

Victoria was frozen, standing up straight.

No way.

Next to her, Honey's butt was going up and down beautifully. When she bent, her butt cheeks parted, revealing the black thong that arched up over her cheeks and around her hips.

"Just try it, sweetie," Honey whispered as she grasped Duchess's waist and bent her over. She put a hand on each hip and lifted them, helping them roll. Like fucking air.

"Puuurrrrrrfect." Honey smiled, resuming her own sensuous movement.

Lee Lee shouted, "Now roll it!"

Honey bent down a little, stuck her butt way out, then rolled it up. Duchess was sure her own wet pussy would soak right through the thong as she watched Honey. Lust was melting her inhibitions, and the movements felt fun and natural.

Forget Milan. I'm gonna dance to my heart's content.

Duchess felt sorry for her. Milan looked so unhappy. Had Duke made her crazy or had she started off that way? Would Duke someday put Duchess down for the next horny new toy and leave her bitter and sad-looking, just like Milan?

SEX IN THE HOOD

I can't worry about all this right now. Because this new freedom and excitement were delicious. People in her town would be appalled to see girls dancing like this, but it felt so good, especially when she suddenly felt hands on her ass. Her eyes bulged. "What—"

"Stick your ass way out," Lee Lee ordered. She was cupping her ass, pulling it up. Her fingertips were dangerously close to Duchess's wet, throbbing pussy. "Rrrrroooolll it, girl. Think of your hips as havin' wheels inside. Smooth, rolling motion."

Duchess did it.

"There you go. Beautiful, girl. Make my cunt drip."

Duchess couldn't wait until this was over so she could go up to the penthouse with Duke and make love again. Just one touch, she was sure she'd be having a damn sexual seizure all over the place. Away from any mean stares or curious eyes.

"You got it, sweetie!" Honey exclaimed, staring back to watch her own cheeks rise and roll. "Work that pretty ass."

A couple more demonstrations and Duchess was actually joining them to do a group dance. They formed a circle facing each other, sticking their butts out, shimmying from shoulders to hips, and swinging their hair. Never had she felt such wild, wonderful abandon. The loud, pulsating music, her body totally exposed in a thong, and the incredible beauty of these women—

"Simulate!" Lee Lee shouted.

"Simulate what?" Duchess asked Honey.

"I wanna show, not tell," Honey whispered. She took Duchess's shoulders, danced with her, pressed her forehead to hers, then eased her to the floor.

Oh, hell no. This is about to become way too much of a public display of nasty-girl freak show.

Duchess stood up. "I gotta go," she said, glancing toward the door.

I am not having sex with a girl in front of all these people. Especially that most hostile witness, Milan.

"Relax," Honey said. "I know what you thinkin', but Duke is not about to let that connivin' bitch touch you." Honey ran her hands down her own body. "Plus you know I'll take good care of you."

Duchess's pussy throbbed. The way Honey's crotch was filling out that thong, her nipples were poking through her top, and her lips were all shiny and parted, Duchess couldn't wait to get another taste of her.

Duchess balanced back on her elbows, her palms on the floor beside her body stretched out flat. Honey hovered over her, kneeling with each leg straddling Duchess's hips. Her thong was wet, throbbing with plump female filling that made Celeste drip.

The soft, round flesh of Honey's boobs, with that flawless creamy skin, was all pressed up and together by her black sports bra. Her nipples were two hard points just inches from Duchess's face. She was panting, her head spinning at the sensory shock and excitement of this experience. She was even more excited this time.

"Mmmm," she moaned, letting the opium of lust melt away all worry. She felt absolutely euphoric right now. All her fears and anxieties were gone.

Honey bent down, rubbing her nose over Duchess's nipple. Then she bit it, gently. Duchess tossed back her head, feeling her hair dance over the backs of her hands. Honey licked her neck; rubbed their boobs together. Tingles shot through her.

Then Honey rose up, cupped her boobs, and pulled down the tank top, revealing those succulent brown cones. She stuck out her tongue, raised them up to her mouth, and licked both at once.

"Wanna taste some more?" she whispered.

Duchess nodded seconds before a soft, sweet nipple that smelled like sugar and tasted even more so poked through her lips. She sucked softly, sure that she was melting so entirely that she'd soon be only a puddle of milk and black hair all over the floor.

Honey pulled her nipples out, tracing the outer edge of Victoria's mouth with it. Then Honey rubbed her face in Duchess's chest. She wanted to scream. This was the first woman who had ever touched her nipples. It felt so soft, so beautiful. Her face was all over Duchess's stomach, and, pushing her back, she rubbed her face in her crotch.

Honey's nose rubbed against Duchess's clit.

"Aaahhh," she moaned. "I looooove this."

Honey spread her legs, yanked the thong up so that it went between her butt cheeks and was tight against her swollen pussy. She thrust it up into Duchess's face several times. The sweet-salty scent made Duchess pant. She wanted to bite at that pussy.

"Wanna see it again?" Honey purred. "I know you like it. You wanna suck on it."

Duchess nodded with eyes at half mast. Honey pulled the thin strip of fabric away from her pussy.

"Yes, just as pretty as before." Beautiful. Clean shaven. Not a single hair on the smooth, perfect flesh. It was time to snack again on those rows and rows of thin-sliced ham arranged in pink-brown ripples.

Honey raised it to Duchess's face then pulled away. Every cell in her body was on fire. All she wanted to do was put her mouth on that pussy. What did this mean for the mix-race woman power? Did it come out doubly strong when pressed with another woman-power source?

"Kiss my pussy," Honey whispered as she raised it up to her face. Duchess's parted lips pressed into the fat flesh. It tasted sweet, like orange juice. She opened her jaws wide, slurped all over it.

Honey moaned but then pulled away, aiming her swollen clit straight toward Duchess's wet pussy.

Chapter 43

Near the door, about twenty feet from Victoria and Honey, Milan was lying on her back, on a floor mat. She had a mouth full of Lee Lee's pussy meat. The head female B'Amazon soldier was straddling Milan's face, grinding her pussy around her mouth.

"That bitch is getting *turned out*," Milan said as she drilled her fingers up into Lee Lee's hole and licked at the silver ball piercing her clit. "But now we know she's got a big weakness. She likes honey."

Lee Lee moaned. "We all love honey."

"I love money more," Milan said, reaching down to rub her own hungry, aching stuff. Finally, the nausea had subsided, but her horniness had not. "I love Duke, too, and that white bitch is not about to take what's mine. This whole supervision thing—" the bodyguards were still at her side "—is only temporary, until Duke sees the error of his ways and puts me in my proper place."

"Shut up and eat my pussy," Lee Lee ordered.

"You know better 'n anybody," Milan said. "Duke and I have been together since we were in diapers. He and Babylon are mine."

"You a crazy bitch."

"A damn good crazy bitch. And I am going to do whatever I have to do to keep what's already mine—Duke and Babylon."

Lee Lee pressed her knees into Milan's ears. "I'll squeeze if you don't shut up and lick, bitch."

Milan laughed. Lee Lee loosened her knees.

"That's right. Suck it like that. The secret walls o' my pussy are the only place you need to talk like that. If Duke hears that shit, you're gonna have a boot in that pretty ass o' yours before it lands on the street. Without your kids."

"Beamer and I have a plan, but Duke can't know," Milan said, using her fingers to rub her own clit. "You'll be addressing me as Duchess in a minute."

"Zip it, girl. I do not want to be an accessory to the suicidal shit you rattlin' off into my pussy. Then again, you wouldn't be under supervision if you was actin' right. You already in trouble."

Lee Lee muzzled Milan with her pussy by grinding hard. Trembling, the sexercise coach tossed her head back, moaned, and opened her eyes.

"Duke!"

Milan's teeth clamped around Lee Lee's clit.

Lee Lee shot up. "Stupid bitch! Don't bite my meat like you a pit bull!"

Milan went numb. She just signed her death warrant in pussy juice. A rigor mortis stiffness froze her every cell.

Duke would understand, pregnancy makes my imagination go wild. He'll remember the crazy stuff I did during my last two pregnancies, and he'll laugh this off too. Besides, how could he have heard me talking over that loud music?

"Duke, baby," Milan called up, her lips wet with hoochie cream. "Finally we get to talk."

He stared down with a stiff face—the same way he stared down a gangsta or 5-0 or anybody he didn't trust. But now, his eyes were laughing. At her. She could almost hear him thinking, *You stupid-ass skank ho, too ill in the head to keep a scheme quiet.*

"Duke, you caught me under the influence of pussy. You know I lose my mind when I put my face up in it. I'm jus' dreamin'."

Not a flicker of response showed in his eyes. She pressed a hand to her stomach to squeeze down a sudden heave.

No, I will not vomit here at Duke's feet.

"Duke," she said with a nervous laugh. Her voice sounded high-pitched and weak.

He raised his eyes as if she suddenly turned invisible. He stroked his dick through his jeans and looked across the room at Honey and that girl.

WHITE CHOCOLATE

Chapter 44

Duke stepped away from Milan then stood over Duchess and her new favorite playmate. Chanel and India were playing Twister right beside them.

He stroked Timbo with lightning speed. His long fingers met the tip of his thumb to form a tube that moved up and down, up and down his legendary dick that he couldn't wait to slide up under the creamy ass of his Duchess.

He blew hot air through his almost-smiling lips. *Look at my baby girl! Gettin' to know her inner freak!*

That thong up her crack was spreading each round cheek. He couldn't wait to take one in each hand and squeeze while he plunged this tree trunk up into that gushing canal. Right now, though, it looked like Honey was getting it in shape and keeping it warm. Hot!

Since she loved his dick, she was obviously becoming a fiend for pussy too.

My baby girl will lose her pretty little mind up in that pussy with dick at the same time.

He jacked his dick, watching Honey and Duchess intertwine their pretty legs. Chanel sashayed toward him in a black thong and bare titties. She pressed her back to him, rubbed the tip of his dick against her juicy ass then bent over.

This some o' the sexiest shit I ev'a seen in my life.

It was just a preview of a lifetime of new freaky-ass stuff every day.

Duchess gon' be through when she learn all the ways o' this world.

She would be through in a good way, unlike the bitch across the room, laying there like the corpse that she already was in her heart. Empty. Cold.

Milan was an evil back-stabber. Just like Brutus did Julius Caesar. He could put her out right now. But no, it wasn't like he trusted her before. She was always scheming. Now he just caught her in the act, so he had a plan to make her work even harder for him. She'd be so scary, she'd bend over and eat her own pussy if he told her to.

Right now, her punishment would be the whack thoughts she was having, worried about what Duke was going to do or not do. He could put her out like Sunnie, or keep her here, or transfer her to another place to work. Send her ass off to work for Moreno.

Damn, look how Honey an' Duchess kissin'. Her ponytail was down her back, her legs were spread, and that ass was grinding into the red mat. In a minute they would press a half-white, rich girl pussy together with a brown, ghetto-fabulous pussy, rubbing together—

India and Chanel were grinding against him. They were both bent over in front of him, offering some double Dutch muffs. He shoved Timbo straight into two hot pussies he had been neglecting ever since he first saw Duchess on TV. He blasted two strokes up under India's beautiful blue-black booty then he plowed two strokes up under Chanel's gorgeous honey-colored ass.

"Ohhhhh, shit!" Chanel rolled her booty back, 'round and 'round to the beat of that nasty-ass music.

"Nothin' like Duke dick," India moaned.

Duke put his hands on his hips, like he was bucking on a bull in a rodeo, loving his ride and loving the view of the other one on the floor. Honey was showing his Duchess the many dimensions of life at Babylon.

"Oh, fuck!" Duke groaned. Delicious waves of hot shivers washed through him. He felt like he could fuck all night.

Duchess mine. All this pussy mine. Babylon mine.

He pulled out, spraying his nut like a fountain all over Duchess and Honey, like raindrops on the sexy seeds he was planting to grow the juiciest fruit ever.

Chapter 45

Duchess hardly noticed Duke standing there, dripping his nut juice all over their sweat-glistening bodies, because her spirit was dancing around the tangle of limbs that was herself and Honey. This was woman-power at its best. Somehow she felt she was learning a secret that she would have no way of comprehending until she experienced it. The intoxicating pleasure of the female body, the woman's soul.

The ultimate power source.

If Celeste already had the power, then pressing her into another hot, hungry hooch—especially one as beautiful and clean as Honey's—could only make her stronger. If there were a fountain of youth, this was the fountain of woman-power. Add the extra mix-race potency that her grandmother spoke of, and Duchess would get anything she ever desired.

Right now, cumming with this beautiful nymph was all she wanted. She tilted her head back and cast a mellow smile up at Duke. He probably knew this would happen, and he no doubt would want to watch. It seemed like everything Duke did was strategized then orchestrated exactly to his vision.

"Make our bodies like an X," Honey whispered, weaving one thigh under Duchess's and the other thigh over hers.

If a mouth on her pussy was pleasure paradise, then this was hedonistic heaven. Nothing could compare to that sizzling wet velvet sensation, slippery flesh, with one clit stimulating another clit. The only thing better was Duke's big, black dick pounding up into her hot, wet pussy. And she would get that as the grand finale.

"How can this be real?" Duchess moaned. "Oooohhhh, Honey, what are you doing to me?"

"Shhh." Honey smiled, grinding so that every circular motion of her hips sent a shiver through Duchess. "It's a secret."

SEX IN THE HOOD

Duchess tossed back her head, looked up at Duke. He smiled back down on her with love and lust. But he was turned slightly, and his whole body was moving, like he was—

Fucking!

He's giving my dick to that girl who looks like Honey. And India. At the same time!

The melody to that nursery rhyme, "Old McDonald," filled her head. *With a thrust-thrust here, and a thrust-thrust there, here a thrust, there a thrust, everywhere a thrust-thrust!*

Duchess couldn't believe her eyes. Duke was fucking two girls right in front of her! Was he serious? Delicious sensations were still radiating between her legs, but her body froze.

"Hey, sweetie," Honey whispered. "It's okay. She's my sister. And India's cool."

Duchess's eyes felt big as baseballs as she stared up at Duke pounding those chicks with great pleasure on his face.

If he's fuckin' two right in front of me, what does he do when I'm not looking?

And Honey thought this was okay since it was a family affair? For a split-second, Duke looked so sexy, she actually felt a burst of pride. And lust. It made her pussy even wetter.

That fine-ass man who can fuck two like a pro is all mine, as much as I want, anytime, in our beautiful Egyptian palace bed upstairs.

But the fact that they didn't talk about this first, or any effort she made to talk about sex with other people was dissed with non-answers, made Duchess sting with betrayal.

If this is an open relationship, let's make that verbal agreement. If it's not, and you think I'm all yours but you can do as you please, wrong!

She remembered when Brian revealed his racist attitudes with cruel jokes and comments. She was glad he showed his true self then, as opposed to after she'd believed in their dream of "married happily ever after." Because in her heart, she knew it wouldn't last. She could never stay with someone who acted like that.

Duke disappeared behind her closed eyelids.

WHITE CHOCOLATE

"Oh, Honey, you do that so good," Duchess whispered, mimicking Honey's motions to intensify the pleasure.

"X marks the spot," Honey said playfully.

The feeling was unbelievable, like a hot mash of velvet-soft girl stuff. Wet pussy against lips, clit, juice. Steaming. Building the starburst into what would be the most psychedelic, ridiculously intense orgasm.

For now, she would let Duke go on with his wild cowboy on the range self, acting like he could hop on and ride any female in his herd of hotties. He said they were partners, so this cowgirl was definitely going to sample a wide range of black angus of her own, after she savored this sweet, honey-covered appetizer.

Honey's lips were pouting as she stared seductively at Duchess and stuck out her tongue to lick the tips of her beautiful nipples.

Duchess was loving the visual image of that big, juicy pussy that was just in her face, now pressing against Celeste, making her feel like she had never felt before. After all, masturbating was dry, thin, warm fingers, not hot, wet flesh that was a perfect match. And the friction—the humps of their clits, the softer press of the lips—every circular grind of the hips was absolute euphoria.

"Oh yeaaaahhh," Duchess cried as violent shivers wracked her body. Honey did the same. Together they trembled and moaned and gasped.

Duchess shivered once again, but this time with fear. Celeste was screaming. She would never be the same. Now she would be cursed to constantly crave dick and pussy. All day, all night. Always.

I'm about to become a sex addict, nymphomaniac. I just bit into the Mrs. Fields brownie on the diet of life. I cannot, and will not, resist.

Chapter 46

Knight had no trouble slipping into Babylon unnoticed, thanks to all the keys he kept stashed at Momma's house, and the secret tunnels and staircases that he and Prince had built into the basement and upper walls of Babylon.

Knight's shoulders brushed the smooth cement walls of the tunnel. Their huge flashlights illuminated Big Moe's pear-shaped nose and small eyes set in a ruddy brown face framed by a black skullcap.

"I'm cool from here," Knight whispered as he unlocked the gate leading up to the building. "I'll be back here to get you at midnight."

"Ya mon," Big Moe said with his gentle Jamaican lilt. His enormous hand extended another flashlight. "Take dis in case de udda one go out."

Knight took it. The turning motion on his full stomach made him smile. "I feel some *black man-itis* settin' in. Full stomach, fresh air, and I'm ready for a nap. All I need is some pussy."

Moe flashed bright white teeth that were as jagged as a picket fence on ground so soft it made a few posts sink deeper and unevenly against the others.

"Ya mon, get some pussy an' you'll be out like a light." Knight turned off his flashlight. The little silver coil inside burned red for a moment then went entirely dark. The light came back on. "Den, you wake stronga dan ev'a!"

"That's how I view my whole time away," Knight said, stepping up into the narrow stone staircase. His flashlight sliced golden beams through the thick blackness. Despite the adrenaline pumping through him, he yawned. All that food at Momma's was hardly making him light on his feet to stealthily navigate the bowels of Babylon.

As he ascended, he burped, loving the sensation of his stomach full of Momma's roast beef, macaroni and cheese and greens. His mouth still tasted sweet from that big bowl of peach cobbler he had devoured. It was the best food he'd had in two and a half years. And she, fuming over Duke's new half-white, high profile girlfriend, promised to let him surprise Duke in a way that would, as Momma said, "Knock some big brotha sense into that boy's head."

The stairwell went on and on, up and up. Even Duke didn't know about the maze of narrow staircases throughout this massive, ten-story building, or the underground tunnels that connected to a house Knight owned around the block.

He and Prince had built these secret tunnels and stairwells for two reasons: to protect in case of outside turbulence, and to safeguard control of Babylon in case of internal mismanagement and out-of-control power trips, as evidenced, lately, by Li'l Tut. First, he had evicted Sunnie and Big Moe. Then there was all that drama with Milan and Beamer. Now he was making Babylon sanctuary for a fine-as-she-can-be fugitive from the feds.

Both Prince and Knight knew that one day, if they had to go away for a while, they'd eventually come back and pull in the reins on Li'l Tut's buck wild ruling style. Li'l Tut sure tried to do it right, but his way simply lacked the maturity to run the empire that was the brainchild of his big brothers, and their domain.

And since Prince is only here in spirit, it's on me, Knight. Stepping back into my penthouse in the dark of night. Friday night, just in time to make my appearance at Li'l Tut's birthday party an' let him start his twenty-first year as assistant to The Knight.

The stairwell led to another, which traversed the center of the building. Ten floors up to the penthouse. *But I'm not going anyplace other than where I belong, inside what's mine.* Before Knight left the penthouse for jail, Duke had his own suite on the ninth floor, just like Knight did until Prince died.

Finally, Knight reached the waist-high door marked 10. It led into one of the enormous mummy cases flanking the dresser inside the penthouse master suite. Little did Duke know, the cases each had a false back that worked like a trap door. Knight would be able to press a latch and release the panel so he could step right into his bedroom.

But here in the stairwell, he heard voices. Male and female. Arguing. As he calmed his heavy breathing from climbing eleven flights of winding stairs, he listened.

"Oh please, Duke, please," said the female voice that sounded as rich and soft as butter melting in his ears. The sound of her words was so sensuous to Knight's woman-starved senses, his pipe turned to lead instantly. His dick hadn't been this hard in years. So, whoever was talking—

Talk to me like that and the world is yours, sweetheart.

Was that the girl from the news? Victoria Winston? Milan tried to talk white but didn't sound that authentic. This girl was the opposite; white trying to sound black, and succeeding.

"I haven't seen you all day, Duke. And it's your birthday!" Fabric rustled. Either somebody was getting undressed or lying across the sheets. "We didn't even make love this morning, you blew outta here so early."

"Baby girl, I'm savin' it for the party." A jostling lock noise preceded a deep hum. It sounded like the lowering of built-in, bulletproof shields that descended over the floor-to-ceiling windows to the terrace.

"Expecting ghetto ninjas to come droppin' in?" the girl asked with an attitudinal tone. "A helicopter drive-by? Duke, who could possibly get up on the tenth floor terrace?"

"A nigga or a bitch on a mission."

"And who might that be?"

"Always got extra security during a party. These niggas get wild an' e'rybody lookin' for a place to get they superfreak on."

Something thudded softly.

"If you need me," Duke said, "or the two Barriors I got out by the elevator—"

"Duke, baby, I really don't like this *Scarface*-type atmosphere."

"You'd like the shit better than the morgue. Just push one number. Six."

WHITE CHOCOLATE

More rustling fabric. A loud kiss.

"Stop, baby girl. I got serious bidness to han'le. That man-eater between yo' pretty thighs can wait a hour or two."

Why did Li'l Tut have to ruin her romantic moment with his thug-talk? Couldn't he see or hear this girl was scared? She needed some real love. Love and lust. That didn't mean she should have the status Duke thought he was giving her, but why would he bring that beautiful girl here and not take advantage of every moment to make love to her?

"I'm scared," she said. "At least hold me for a minute."

The stereo came on playing that damn song that had been all over the radio about Babylon. It was another of Duke's bad decisions, drawing too much attention to what they did. She said louder, "Duke, please just hold me."

"Naw, baby girl." Heavy footsteps echoed. "I got too much shit to han'le befo' I can enjoy my own damn party."

"Duke, I know you're not about to leave me here naked, scared an' creamin' all over my damn thighs!"

"Ain't a safer place in the world than my bed," Duke said, "for all o' dat."

His footsteps echoed across the floor, followed by the sound of a closing door.

Knight eased into the mummy case. He moved the latch so he could step into the front and peer out through tiny holes in the ornate yoke around King Tut. That gave him a perfect view of the sheer gold panels around the bed. They were opened slightly, with a long, light caramel leg hanging to the floor, where a pretty foot with red toenails contrasted with the white marble. On the bed . . .

A goddess. She was sitting so that she faced the end of the bed, her left foot curled up under her thigh as she rested back on her hands, staring up at the ceiling. A cascade of straight black hair fell to the golden bedspread, making a wild swirl behind the round curve of her bare ass.

Tears streamed down a face that was too young and innocent to have been talking like she just did. Her straight black

285

bangs and her black eyeliner extended from the corners of her eyes. Gold cuffs hugged her upper arms. A gold belt with coins adorned her waist and soft, creamy belly. She was like a vision of—

Cleopatra.

Li'l Tut done gone all the way wild!

This was the ghetto version of the witness protection program: Take a rich, suburban, half-white girl who was hiding from the feds and turn her into a clone of Ancient Egypt's most beautiful queen—the sexiest, most beguiling and most powerful. She was a woman who always got what she wanted from powerful men, especially when she got that look in her eye, like the one that girl had right now, staring at the flames crackling under the white marble mantle.

Li'l Tut is playin' with fire.

"Motherfucker!" She sobbed with a voice that was sultry but hard. "I *hate it* when he's stingy!" She snatched up a silver remote and aimed it toward the ceiling. The music cut off.

Silence. Except Knight could hear his own heavy breathing and the blood surging toward the hot pipe between his legs. Damn, the sound of her voice only made his dick even harder. If there were any justice in two and a half years without any pussy, this would certainly be the reward; jamming this giant cock up between those pretty, creamy thighs, satisfying that girl's ache for love, and his own, all at once. For life.

She belongs to me now, just like this penthouse and all of Babylon. Knight's pipe was about to blow steam. He knew he was perfectly healthy, thanks to a battery of tests—including all sexually transmitted infections and HIV—and a full check-up a week ago. Now his dick was hot, healthy and horny as hell. It hadn't been laid inside a woman or anywhere else for eternity, which he would make up for with that Cleopatra goddess right there. She could handle it.

There's a love-starved Cleopatra look-alike on my bed! I know I must've taken a tunnel straight to my Paradise Found. Elysium. Yeah, we need to rename this place The Elysium Suite.

WHITE CHOCOLATE

She slid her other foot to the floor and stood, stretching her long, elegant arms over her head. Those copper penny nipples were hard and pointing straight at Knight. Her body was long and curvy, toned in horizontal lines along her abs, a perfect belly button, a little black puff of hair above juicy thighs, not too thick, not too thin.

"I'll show him!" she announced.

In a flash, she grabbed the pole at the end of the bed so that her ass was facing Knight, who was silent and concealed. He was worried that his dick would get so hard it would shoot through his khaki pants and bang on the inner wall of this mummy case.

He struggled to breathe slowly.

I'm gon' pass out. Every drop of blood in his body was in his dick. Cleopatra's ass was so picture-perfect, Knight felt like he was watching one of those new animated movies where everybody's skin looked airbrushed and flawless.

That was her booty. Two round bubbles of light caramel at the base of a strong back that was exposed, for a second, when her hair swayed to one side. She grabbed the pole with both hands then raised her hips up to it.

She started to grind, ass popping in slow, sensuous circles against the bedpost. That gold coin belt around her waist jingled and shone with her perfect movement. Maybe her pussy was touching the post to stimulate her, maybe not. But from this angle, Knight imagined that pole was his face, smeared and steamed with pussy.

He was breathing harder, sweating inside this mummy case. Claustrophobia . . . No, he was not going hyperventilate.

I'm gonna hornyventilate. Gotta get out.

A deep groan escaped his lips.

Cleopatra froze. She turned around with huge blue eyes glowing with fear. "If that motherfucker has someone watching me *in here* too—" She stomped toward the mummy case, titties bouncing, belt jangling, red lips set to a natural pucker like she was hungry, horny and mad all at once.

She grabbed the side of the case. Rattled the latch.

287

"Doesn't Duke know this creepy shit is for dead people? I'm telling him we need to take the *coffins* out of the bedroom. Don't care how pretty they are."

She rattled harder, but it wouldn't budge because Knight locked it from the inside. She was close enough to smell. Her natural perfume was lemony-flowery with a salty-sweet bouquet of fresh-picked, ripe, juicy pussy.

That made Knight's steampipe vibrate. Damn, he could fuck her for years on end and never want to sleep a wink.

Can a nigga cum from jus' smellin' good pussy after this long?

If his appetite for sex was anything like his hunger for food an hour ago at Momma's table, he was going to gorge on pussy until he passed out.

Knight remembered once when he was little, Momma took him to the hospital. He and Duke and Prince had been playing for hours, building snow tunnels in the vacant lot next door until his hands went numb. Frost bite, the doctor said. All Knight wanted to do was to plunge them into hot water for an hour, but the doctor said that would cause damage. He'd have to warm them gradually.

Would the same happen with his dick? *Naw.*

Cleopatra huffed away, her beautiful ass glowing like two full moons in the peachy bedroom light. She strode with that elegant walk into the bathroom. The shower hissed against the stone floor then sounded softer as the hot water streamed against her body.

Knight reached into his pocket for the tiny key that would unlock the mummy case door.

So I can step back into what's mine and take it.

Chapter 47

If this run-away train of thoughts went any faster, it would crash and burn with Duke in the furnace. That was what it felt like right now in HQ, as every motherfucker in the house came at him with a crisis. All while his twenty-first birthday party was rockin' Babylon like never before.

Sitting behind the desk, he wanted to wave a magic wand and make all the problems disappear. Make all these fifteen ma'fuckas in his office walk out, problem stamped SOLVED. Then he'd wave the wand again and make Milan and Knight appear from wherever they were hiding inside this fortress. Were they trying to double-team The Duke?

He didn't want to believe that Knight was there with an overthrow scheme. With Beamer acting crazy with Milan, and dudes who was tight under Prince and Knight showing signs of trickery—especially that vibe Duke had felt at the pussy party when he confronted Izz—he didn't trust anybody. Dudes who had more juice under his older brothers probably wanted Knight back in charge so they could rise from the lower spots where Duke had put them.

Now Duke had an APB out amongst his trusted Barriors. Any sign of trouble, the battle would be on. Brother or not, he shouldn't be trying to stage a coup during Duke's birthday party at the Babylon that he ruled.

I ain't got time for all this shit. I gotta go back upstairs an' give my baby girl what she need. Cain't stand the look in her eye when I blew outta there.

But he had to take care of everything now, or else there wouldn't be a Babylon for The Duke to have a Duchess in. His mind was so whack, Timbo went limp, comatose for a minute.

An' that definitely ain't right. I don't need all this shit happenin' right now, 'specially if Knight really out early.

289

Duke's heart banged in his chest. His whole body was shaking. It couldn't be a good sign if Knight were free and trying to creep back into Babylon.

Ain't no beef.

Or was there? Deep down, Duke already knew. He already knew what would be going down tonight. His birthday, his party, his girl, his people, and his big brother trying to usurp the power.

Hell naw. I'm runnin' this empire smoov as hell. An' I'll keep running it, starting right now, by replacing all these knucklehead ma'fuckas who let these problems pop in the wrong place at the wrong time.

One of the Hulk-ass bodyguards who was watching Milan said, "It don't make no sense, see what I'm sayin', dat she could jus' be gone. We was like, dang, how she get out?" Scheme shined in this stupid-ass ma'fucka's eyes.

Duke rose from his golden throne. He stepped from behind the big glass desk. His black cowboy boots pounded the white marble as he approached Tweedle Dee and Tweedle Dum.

"I told both you ma'fuckas. Do not let Milan suck yo' dick. Weak-ass punks." He pointed to the door. "Go find her! Inside, outside, just find the bitch an' bring her to me."

"Yes, Massa Duke," they said then ran out.

No way could she hide for long in this high-tech temple and not show up on the security cameras.

Next, a Barrior lieutenant, wearing brown from head to toe, approached. "We checked all the security camera video. Nothing shows that Milan has left the building, but we don't have any video so far of where she is. But we did catch this."

The Barrior held up a wireless video monitor the size of a shoebox. It showed two men, one dark and bald, the other in a black skullcap, holding flashlights.

"It's dark," the Barrior said, "but that looks like Big Moe and Knight down in the tunnels. You recall the hidden security cameras were put in last year. Knight wouldn't know."

"Knight know e'rythang."

WHITE CHOCOLATE

And I'm supposed to know more.

A lot of punks were about to get jacked for letting this happen. Duke's mind ticked down a list of all the locked-up motherfuckers on his payroll who were about to get cut off. Nobody took his money without providing a service in return. Even if it was about blood. Family blood.

The Barrior said, "You know this main tunnel leads to the garage, and we have video of Knight up to the door. But he vanishes after that. Nothing."

Duke asked, "You seen him anyplace else? The garage, the ninth floor apartments, the penthouse?"

"No, Massa Duke."

"No my ass! E'ry hall, e'ry staircase, e'ry elevator got a camera!" Duke shouted. His enraged voice echoed through the marble-floored office. He felt like steam was shooting from his ears. A high-pitched panic was distorting his voice so tough, it sounded like train wheels screeching against a metal track.

"What the fuck?" Duke shouted. "How you gon' miss a six-foot-se'em ma'fucka wit' a big, black bald head an' shoulders as wide as fuckin' Mr. Universe?"

Everybody in the office froze, turned pale and made their eyes big.

"Go find Knight Johnson if it kill e'ry one o' y'all ma'fuckas!"

The doors at the front of the office opened. Beamer ran in, all of his redbone braids loose and bouncing over the shoulders of his white Detroit Lions jersey. He pulled up his sagging jeans.

"Massa Duke, two things," he said, out of breath. "First, Barriors got these two black dudes. FBI tryin' to crash yo' party."

"Hell naw."

"They got bogus VIP passes from the band. No warrant, no ID, but they fed, fo' sho'."

Duke's heart pounded so hard, it sounded like flames were hissing inside his ears.

"Tell the lawyer to stop havin' his dick sucked up in the VIP suite. Send him down to talk to the young men. Tell 'em we'll

291

prosecute they asses for trespassing if they don't get the fuck up outta my buildin' in a Motor City minute."

Beamer nodded. At least his thinking cap was on snug too.

"What's the second thing?" Duke asked.

"A TV crew," Beamer said. "Downstairs. Talkin' about somebody in the hood said Victoria Winston livin' here. No joke."

"Hell naw. That shit got Milan name all over it." Milan would kill Duchess with her bare hands if she had the chance.

Probably kill me too.

Duke glanced at the phone on his belt that he told Duchess to dial if she needed anything. "Hold up." He dialed. It rang. And rang. And rang.

He tried again.

"Hello?" Attitude shot through the phone.

"Baby girl, just checkin' on ya."

"I'm taking a shower."

"Pick up quicker when I call."

"And call you Massa Duke?" The sass in her voice made him almost smile, but he didn't because all these leery-eyed motherfuckers were watching him, waiting for directions to solve their respective bullshit.

"Holla." Duke hung up then turned to Beamer. "Where the media at now?"

"It's a black chick reporter an' a camera dude." Beamer talked fast. "The Barriors caught 'em tryin' to sneak in wit' all the niggas goin' to the party. So now the Channel 6 jokers is on the sidewalk out front."

Duke paced the white marble floor. "Where they gon' be videotapin' all the limos an' cars. They can hear the music. An' they gon' be sniffin' around. Fuck!" If Knight were in the house and he saw media here, he'd have a fit!

Don't no neighbors complain about the traffic an' loud noise, 'cause they know Barriors be patrollin' the streets, the schools, the stores, makin' e'rybody feel safe. So, no matter what else go on, don't nobody snitch on Babylon.

WHITE CHOCOLATE

"That's a lie," Duke said. "If you talkin' to Milan, which I know you ain't, tell the bitch that if she called the media on my ass, then she will be dog meat for Pound to come collect for the midnight feedin'."

Beamer's eyes got as big as those chocolate truffles he was always eating.

"But first," Duke said, "call Pound Dog cousin, Mike, the spokesman. Tell him to talk to the media, say Miss Green got a postcard from Victoria in Barbados."

Beamer scrunched his face. "They talkin' about Customs ain't got no record of her leavin' Miami."

"Then Mike gon' tell 'em she got a lotta connections wit' folk in Florida who got yachts, wit' lotsa places to hide a pretty young girl."

Knight. Milan. The feds. The media.

I am one under siege ma'fucka. But I'm gon' beat 'em all down, 'cause I'm han'lin' it like a mug. The Duke rule.

Chapter 48

Duchess stared into space as the hot water beat down on her bare back. It was so relaxing after a week of intensive transformation—and almost constant sex—she was ready to sleep another two days straight.

Her mind, body and spirit were aching with fatigue. Learning a new way of talking, dressing, dancing. Fucking Duke. Tasting Honey. Beating back a barrage of question marks about life, love, race. She yawned, but Celeste was roarin' to go.

Am I addicted? It seems the more I get, the more I want. And why is Duke trying to ration his dick? Didn't he know he'd have to finish what he started? I warned him.

His attitude did not make her want to celebrate his birthday party tonight. Was he out getting so much birthday booty and blow jobs from all his females that he didn't have the time or energy for Duchess?

"That is totally unacceptable," she snapped into the steam. And what about Milan? What in the world did he have to do with her right now?

Duchess turned off the water. She hadn't even washed or shampooed her wet hair. She was too tired.

I'm gonna get in bed, make myself cum, and take a nap until Duke gets back to dress for the party. Their matching black leather jeans and cream tops were already hanging on clothes trees out in the bedroom.

I have to cum by myself for the first time since Sunday at the restaurant. Wow, she'd never gone five days without doing it herself. She dried off quickly then walked back to the bedroom.

"Duke," she said. The sight of him and the surprise of his return made her heart pound with excitement. And it made her pussy hot and wet, instantly.

"He is so beautiful," she whispered.

WHITE CHOCOLATE

Through the gold sheer around the bed, he reminded her of an enormous Greek god, lying so that the luscious back of his bald head and all the rippling muscles down his back were facing her. The gold blanket was folded under his huge, muscular right arm and hand, which rested on the bulge that was his right leg, bent slightly at the knee on top of his other leg.

Duchess stuck her fingertips between the gold panels. The back of her hand parted the wispy fabric. She put one knee on the bed.

In the dim light, he looked darker. And bigger. He must've had a mega workout down in the gym today. She stared in awe at the little indentions of muscle around his deltoids, his triceps and biceps and forearms, and those big, beautiful hands. The valley of muscle up his spine was deep and marked by muscle around the vertebrae. His back muscles rose up in graceful curves that made her mouth water. Ripples of strength marked his shoulder blades.

He was nothing short of a masterpiece. His smooth head was so big and round and shiny, flanked by perfect ears; he must've taken his earrings out. And that thick neck, so smooth—

I never noticed that scar before. It was like a shiny black inchworm, healed but kind of puffy so it was raised about a quarter of an inch. It was a few inches to the right of the protruding vertebra at the back of his neck. As many times as she'd sucked on Duke's neck and touched him there and slept holding onto him from the back, why hadn't she noticed that?

Because I was delirious from dick.

She smiled because she was about to get some more right now. Celeste was screaming for all that Timbo had to offer, and more.

Maybe since he didn't want to fuck me anyway, he'll stay asleep. I can climb on, ride to my heart's content then take a nap, and he'll never even know.

Duchess walked quietly to the other side of the bed. She slipped through the gold panels. How could a man be so breathtaking? His face looked like a statue of a black god. The angular cheekbones and jaw, the strong nose that really did look

295

like the nose on King Tut's mask. Duchess thought Duke was tripping when he first pointed that out in the bathroom mirror, but it was true. Those lips, just like all his females said, they really were "sucka lips."

He must have spent time in the sun today, because he looked darker—and luscious. Duchess pressed her lips to his forehead, loving the sensation of his smooth, hot skin under the fleshy spread of her lips. He showed no reaction except slow and steady breathing, hard breathing, like he was in a deep sleep.

Slowly, Duchess slid head-first under the gold blankets. It was dark, and that intoxicating aroma of *man* was strong as hell. She inhaled deeply, holding it in.

"Mmmmmm," she moaned.

I need to bottle this stuff so I can smell it all day long. Essence of Bo-Bos.

Then, like a fish trying to swim toward a juicy worm, she pressed forward in the darkness with her mouth open. She hit her lip on the giant head of his dick. It felt like she got head-butted, like she had during track practice at the academy, when another runner lost her balance and came shooting head-first into Victoria's face. Her lip had throbbed and swelled for days.

Now Duke's dick felt like the knob on the post of a big brass bed. Enormous. She kissed it, loving it for the pleasure she knew she was about to take from it. She wrapped her lips around it. He didn't move. She opened wide, sucked the whole thing in until it banged the back of her throat.

He flinched a little, let out a slow groan. Nothing else.

I just wanna suck. Not all that bizarre biting that Duke likes. That's exhausting. How 'bout an old-fashioned blow job?

This sensation—a hot marble dicksicle with that delicious aroma—made her pussy drip. Her nipples were rock-hard, rubbing against the tops of his legs. She wrapped her left hand over his right thigh of steel, squeezing down on pure, lean muscle. It was bionic muscle made to help him fuck her, thrusting into her like The Six Million Dollar Man for hours on end.

WHITE CHOCOLATE

I am so wet right now. The tops of Duchess's thighs felt steamy and sticky. All she had to do was push his leg with her left hand. He'd roll onto his back, she could climb on, and—

In a flash, he rose. He was an enormous shadow of man, quick as lightning, with the grace and stealth of Duke's best panther walk. Giant hands clamped her waist. Lifting her up, he rolled onto his back. His arms raised her like they were the front scooping part of a bulldozer—effortlessly, higher and higher. He hoisted her above him, like a playful dad would lay down on the floor and hold up a giggling baby.

She gazed down, half-smiling at the enchanted genie eyes staring back up at her with the hungriest, sexiest, most powerful look she had ever seen in Duke's eyes. Suddenly his eyes radiated a new maturity, a new intelligence.

Maybe he really was working today and accomplished something important.

I shouldn't have been so hard on him.

He was still staring up at her like she was the most precious creature on the planet that he would always love and cherish. He held her up for a long time, as if examining her for the first time. His arms were like robotic machine parts, gripping her, turning her slightly to the left, to the right. His grip on her waist seemed tireless. She held out her arms, stiffened her legs and raised her chin. Her hair fell off her back, down his arm to his smooth, hairless chest.

"Tinkerbell in the hood!" She giggled, shaking her head so that the ends of her hair tickled his right nipple. It pointed up hard at her. She stared into his eyes. Her voice got deep and sultry. "An' I'm gonna sprinkle my pixie dust, my pussy dust, all . . . ova . . . you!"

Like a laser-quick robotic arm on a machine that attached parts, he pulled her forward.

"I'm flying," she cooed.

He held her in that soaring-bird position, with her hips an arm's length above his face. Those robotic arms yanked her down. She spread her legs, which made a "V" extending out from his head. Her heels landed softly on the fluffy gold pillows.

And he breathed fire-air onto her pussy.

"Oooohhh," she moaned.

He inhaled loudly, even louder than she breathed him under the blankets. The tip of his tongue made an "X" across her pussy. From the top corner of one lip, ooohhh, over the throbbing clit in the center, to the bottom corner of the other. Then the other way.

Was he marking a bull's eye?

"Yay-yaaaahhh," she moaned as his sucka lips did their thing in an "O" around her clit.

"Mine," he groaned in a way that was so potent, so deep, it literally vibrated up through the fleshy canal of her pussy, behind her belly button and into her chest, where it ricocheted against her ribcage, her heart and her lungs then lodged in her throat. Hot, throbbing. In a lump.

The depth of passion and protection in his voice felt so strong and overwhelming, it sparked tears in her eyes. Her vision blurred, her mind spun, and her body was flying up, down the length of him, suspended in his firm but gentle grip with those bionic arms and hands on her waist. Her hair blew on both sides of her as if she were running.

He held her up so that they were face-to-face, just inches apart. She squeezed the tears to see him more clearly.

Whoosh!

Those robotic arms lowered her at turbo-speed.

Duchess screamed. She shivered violently.

I'm cumming at first stroke.

Explosions of fire, like video she'd seen of the surface of the sun, licked red-yellow-orange flames behind her eyes.

Nipples pinching. Skin quivering. Muscles trembling. And her pussy was one big convulsion. Celeste was pulsating at triple-speed, as if her insides were spastic ripples of wet velvet, erotic muscle spasms set off by superhuman sex.

This is the best . . .

WHITE CHOCOLATE

Some people wished for world peace or an end to hunger. Duchess did too. But she wished everybody could experience, if only for a moment, the superb, beyond-words sensations that were making her entire being shoot golden sparks inside and out.

Because his dick was so big and so hard . . .

Feels like the big Black Power Joe Louis fist on Jefferson Avenue just punched up into my pussy.

She wanted to scream that she'd bow at his feet forever if he gave her this, this—what was it? It was not normal. Definitely not just sex. Or making love. This was some abnormal, freaky-ass, supernatural love. Maybe all that Ancient Egyptian stuff they had around here was giving them extra sex powers.

Duchess froze. She opened her eyes without focusing.

This the power. My power. My mix-race woman power.

When blended with true Mandingo warrior sex-power of equal magnitude, it created cataclysmic forces that could move the world.

"With talent comes great responsibility to use it in a way that helps people," Daddy used to say.

"But how?" Victoria used to ask all the time. "What's my talent and what should I do with it?"

"When you find your calling," he said, "you'll just know."

Now, Duchess smiled.

Now I know. I want everybody to let go of their puritanical inhibitions about sex and enjoy the most spectacular gift we can share with another person: an orgasm.

Yeah, that's my responsibility to help people. And I'm in just the right place to share my passion and my purpose with the world.

Chapter 49

Duchess felt wobbly as she and Duke stepped into the elevator to go down to the party. The music in the garage was so loud, even from here on the tenth floor the relentless bass beat was actually vibrating the elevator. It was making it even harder to walk on legs still tremoring from the meteor that had just shot up into her pussy and sprayed intergalactic stardust so thick she couldn't see straight.

"You obviously don't know your power," she snapped at Duke, whose eyes were as tense as his face. "You should be smilin' not stressin'. It's your birthday."

They were both facing the mirrored wall inside the elevator. Dressed alike in snug, black leather jeans, black leather boots and cream tops, Duke towered beside her. His beautiful, dark chocolate face, neck and bald head were clean-shaven and radiant. He had put his little silver hoop earrings back into his ears.

"I gotta look gangsta cool at the party." His tone was flat. His eyes focused on the piece of lint he was plucking from his chest.

"I loooove the way we look together," Duchess said, extending her left hand to his crotch to squeeze. Her fingers were trembling, just like every other muscle in her body. Even her lips felt like she was shivering in the cold, but her soul was smouldering in heat.

So, why wasn't his? There was no way in hell he could be nonchalant about the cosmic sextravaganza that just exploded in their bed. She pulled her hand from his nonresponsive crotch.

"Duke, why you stressin' on your day? I'm the one who should be scared, the way you were battenin' down the hatches, calling to check on me, putting bodyguards—" She crossed her arms.

WHITE CHOCOLATE

Her eyelids felt heavy. She let them fall as a fresh quiver shot through her body. It happened every time she thought of that first dick-stroke. Why was this time different? Did he take some kind of dick-growing endurance drug? He didn't need it, but—

"Duke, tell me you don't use drugs."

"You the one who look drunk," he shot back, turning to face her. "An' we ain't even at the party yet."

"I'm tipsy on Timbo," she whispered, giggling.

"Baby girl, you trippin'." His jaw muscles flexed as he stared down hard at her. He was looking at an entirely different person than the scared girl he had plucked out of urban hell and delivered into this 24-hour-a-day temptation.

"Duke, you need to chill an' enjoy."

"My gangsta chill for my public, an' the private Romeo chill I show you, they two different looks."

She cut her eyes back at him. "Duke, you got more than a look goin' on. It's a vibe. An' it ain't pretty, baby."

He glanced down at the phones on his belt, flashing red, flashing blue.

And she looked past him at her reflection because that black-sounding voice that just came out of her mouth sounded like someone else.

Is this me? Who is me?

Staring at herself, she saw the same eyes she arrived with, but they were now painted with thick black liner like Cleopatra. She saw the same face, but bronze now, thanks to the tanning booth. Same hair, but with straight bangs on her forehead. Same necklace, but with gold serpent bracelets around the upper arms. Same voice with a new cadence. Same body, same lust, but now addicted to ghetto-licious black dick and pussy.

Same mind?

Celeste was laughing, cackling, roaring with laughter. *That big black dick got so high up in your brain, it made it as mushy, as wet and as insatiable as your pussy. You just wanna get fucked!*

"Hell no!" Duchess said aloud.

SEX IN THE HOOD

Duke, who was on the phone speaking in code as usual, looking wide-eyed with stress, made a "ssshhh!" gesture with his index fingertip to his sucka lips.

She turned around, pressed her ass into Duke's hard thighs, her back into his chest. Her stiletto-heeled boots stood between his black cowboy boots. She pressed his open palm to the front of her leg. She nuzzled the back of her head into the body-fitting long-sleeved shirt over his chest, inhaled the sexy cloud of his Black Cashmere cologne mixed with her Cashmere Mist perfume.

He raised the bottom of the phone and said, "Yo' inna freak comin' out in full effect." His free hand rose up to grip her tits, which were raised in a chiffon camisole with flowy fabric that danced over the top of her pants. Like a reflex, she arched her ass harder into him, loving the hard outline of that big, hot tree trunk in his pants.

"When my tongue hit that pussy, you knew it ain't no turnin' back. That sayin', 'once you go black, you never go back,' got a whole new meanin' fo' yo' sexy ass."

"Yeah," he said into the phone then flipped it down, clipped it back to his belt. "Baby girl, it's gon' be a couple Barriors watchin' you at all times. Cain't risk nothin'."

Duchess spun to face him. "What risk? I know you don't let undercover FBI or the media or anybody else into your party!"

"Milan got out." His words hit the air like darts.

"And?"

"We gotta watch yo' back in the crowd. She crazy."

Duchess crossed her arms, tilted her head. "I been meanin' to ask you, Massa Duke, which came first, the chicken or the egg?" Her Ebonics accent was just right. "I mean, was Milan crazy when you met her, or did you *make* her crazy?"

Duke smiled. "There you go! Baby girl, sistah-certified."

She stuck her head forward slightly. "Answer my question."

"Baby girl, when I introduce you tonight, talk like that. Don't be talkin' like Victoria. You The Duchess now. Say a few words, but you gotta sound cool."

WHITE CHOCOLATE

"Look at my forehead." She lifted her bangs. "The word 'clueless' got erased in Streetology 101 class. So—" She tiptoed, wrapped her arms around his neck, kissed his lips soft and slow.

"Happy birthday, baby," she purred. "I'm so glad you came back so I could give you some Celeste-cake."

That kaleidoscope of color and texture in his eyes shifted in a strange way. The rich, dark chocolate hue of his cheeks turned gray.

"That shit was supernatural," Duchess said, smiling as she hugged him and pressed her cheek into his chest. "The best *ever*. I swear we been fuckin' so much it pumped up your dick muscles. 'Cause Timbo felt like he grew an inch wider and an inch longer. I'm still shakin'."

Chapter 50

Knight fucked my Duchess. He snuck up to the penthouse while I was gone an' he fucked the girl I picked right outta the headlines. For myself!

Wait, hold up. That shit cain't be true. Ain't no way in hell any nigga, even one as cool as Knight, could pull that off.

He couldn't sneak past all the security cameras in the building, including the terrace, the elevator entryway and the bedroom.

But what about that drunk look on Duchess's face when he came back to the penthouse and she was just getting outta the shower? She took two showers, or one long one? It was at least ninety minutes between when he called and when he came back.

And she was walking funny across the room to get her leather pants, like she did after he had banged her booty for an hour straight. When he asked her about it, she just giggled in a way like, *You know the answer, silly rabbit!*

Duke closed his eyes. He couldn't turn into some Othello motherfucker, overanalyzing every little detail, letting his imagination slip down into a stinking slop jar of suspicion and jealousy. Maybe Duchess was so tired and so overwhelmed by the past week of fucking, eating pussy, seeing Milan, and everything else, she just dreamed that he was fucking her bigger and better than ever. Maybe now she liked fucking so much, she was hallucinating about it. She was the kind of girl who kept liking it more and more. Some girls would fuck once and say, 'Oh, I had enough dick for the week.' But Duchess, it seemed like every bang just cranked her appetite up to a higher notch. And she had a wild way of thinking, so maybe she wanted it so bad tonight, she imagined she got it.

"Baby girl," he whispered, grasping her upper arms and pulling her back so he could look at her face. But MANDINGO DICK AFTERGLOW was stamped all over everywhere. Her cheeks were extra pink, lips were blood-red, ready to smile when nothing was funny. Eyelids were heavy, but her eyeballs were dancing in the wet memory of that dreamy dick-down.

Naw, my girl would know if it wasn't me. Duchess would know if some other dick had been in Celeste, and she wouldn't want it.

Unless she liked it better.

Duke ground his teeth so hard it hurt.

Hell naw. I ain't believin' Knight could be that bad of a ma'fucka. Until I see him, Duchess be innocent until proven guilty.

The elevator doors opened.

"C'mon, baby girl, this party is on!"

She was in freeze-frame, staring out with spooky big eyes that were even bluer in the glow of the neon light tubing around the elevator. It cast a hip, blue tint over the tangle of male and female bodies—titties, legs, asses, dicks, every kind of hair and a lot of bare skin—on the couches, bar stools and pool tables up here on the VIP balcony looking out over the garage.

Here, there, everywhere, the garage was crammed with dozens of guys and girls—fucking, sucking, dancing, bouncing, licking, drinking, and giving off a cloud of vapors of cigarette and marijuana smoke, expensive perfume and cologne, booze and the salty-sweet smell of sex.

Duchess coughed. He wouldn't have heard her if he hadn't been staring right at her, because the Bang Squad was stupid-loud down on stage. They were doing their hit, "Dick Chicks," and Jamal was shouting, "Gimme a dick chick, love to lick my big bang stick. When I hit that shit, it's legit. I'm just a trick, she gon' get wit' Rick an' Mick an' Nick . . . 'cause she love it. She a dick chick."

Duke looked down at Duchess as she stepped in front of him to walk on legs that might still be trembling from taking Knight's giant dick. Now she was shaking her whole body with the beat, making her ass say "kapow!" in her tight black leather pants. Duke's mind flipped to a filmstrip of her riding Knight like she did Duke in the Cleopatra Suite. What if she saw Knight at this party? Could she smell or feel that it was him who gave her that extra big dick upstairs?

Now she probably thought she was a dick chick, specializing in Johnson dicks. She was looking straight ahead at a chick taking three dicks—one in her mouth, one in her ass and one in her pussy. Two other girls watched the action and stuck out their booties like *Gimme some too!*

Duchess wasn't wasting any time trying to leave this elevator.

Chapter 51

Yeah, come right at me, bitch.

Milan hid behind Flame's huge body as he fucked some girl on the table.

It was so dark over here in the corner of the VIP balcony, none of the Barriors had noticed Milan. Nor did those two buffoons Duke had watching her every move from the toilet to the bed. Too bad for him they were just as stupid as every other man. Just say "dick suck" or "pussy" and it automatically shut off their brains and put their balls in charge—balls which of course had the same conscience and reasoning ability as balls on a dog or a horse or a cow. None. They had one function: to squirt their contents in any direction the head on their dick pointed them.

And that would be me, using my brain to get free from those imbeciles and from Duke's imprisonment.

Not one person had recognized her behind these big gold glasses and this wig. She shook her shoulder to free her elbow from a tangle of brown ringlets, which caught on the studded belt securing her green leather Daisy Dukes. The long hair covered her bare titties so Duke and Beamer and anybody else who'd seen the unique slope of her breasts and the points of her nipples couldn't identify her. They could not see through the blue haze up here anyway.

This air is gonna kill me and the baby. But if I don't bring the bitch down, Janelle will do the job for me.

She coughed, which wrenched up a heave. The thick fumes of smoke, sex and booze wrapped around her neck like a deadly python. A coughing fit made her double over, holding one hand to her gagging mouth, the other hand to her nauseated gut.

Duke has me working in conditions that are hazardous to my physical and emotional health. Anything that happens, it's on him.

But so what if she was on a suicide mission? Losing Duke to some light-skinned bourgeousie bitch that he picked off the six o'clock news would kill her anyway. Inside.

He won't even talk to me long enough to find out that I'm pregnant.

She smiled. *I'm a high-class dick chick my damn self. So?* A girl was entitled to get hers, too, especially in a place like this where her man was so lost in the newest recruits of the harem, he didn't have any nasty left for his one and only.

Me. Always have been. Always will be.

Since I'm slick when I creep, though, he'll have no reason to accuse the baby of being someone else's. Even though it might come from those two big balls slapping right in front of her. Flame's black sack of baby seeds bounced off that girl's bony behind.

It didn't matter. What mattered was Duke walking so tall and proud as the tangle of bodies parted like the fucking Red Sea for him to lead that tacky-ass Cleopatra wanna-be up to the silver throne. The throne where Milan Henderson should have been sitting.

I'm the one who deserves to be treated like royalty. I know how to handle it. How to keep it. These people need a leader like me, who ain't scared to let her true bitch reign. They'll see.

Soon as Duke and his cream puff sat back and enjoyed this circus, all those freaks down in the garage would see a surprise trapeze act starring the death-defying Duchess—with no trapeze.

Chapter 52

Duchess felt like she was stepping into a giant, X-rated rap video called "Urban Babylon." The music was so loud, it vibrated her body. The beat was so hot, she couldn't help but snap her fingers and rock her body to the beat as Duke led her past Barriors three deep on each side of the elevator.

"We stayin' here in VIP," he shouted in her ear as two Barriors guided them through the crowd. "We got the bomb balcony spot."

Familiar faces dotted the mass of bodies: Lee Lee, India, Beamer, and Honey, who blew a kiss.

Duchess stopped. "Duke, I'm not ready for an orgy."

His seductive eyes smoldered down at her. He looked like he was about to kiss her—his eyes were lusty, lips parted, head coming down, but his left hand rose up to the top of her camisole. He yanked it down. Her titties popped out.

He sucked both of them, hard, and squeezed her crotch. Then with a hot, open mouth, he breathed intoxicating fire into her pussy and her soul. His kiss sucked the strength from her knees. She gripped his rock-hard arm to keep steady on her spike heels. He pulled back.

She moaned, loving that melting butter sensation from her head to her toes, making her pussy a throbbing, soaked mess.

"Now you ready," he said with bad-ass Duke style.

They walked past boobs, butts, big dicks of every size, shape and shade. He led her to the silver-railed edge of the balcony, where two silver thrones sat on a raised platform overlooking the party below.

"This the shit!" Duke exclaimed into her ear, the last word rising to a pitch that was a good two octaves higher than his usual deep voice. "An' I'm rulin' all of it! The Duke!"

Why was his whole body trembling behind her? What was he scared of? And why did he sound like he was trying to convince himself that he was in charge?

"Baby girl, let's toast."

He turned back to take gold goblets from trays held by their attendants, two girls and two guys who stood on each side of the thrones. The guys were both in that first sexercise class that drove Duchess to carnal indulgence just five days ago. Now they were wearing gold sandals and wrist cuffs, and short, white loin cloths with gold belts around their six-pack abs. Their thighs bulged under the flowy skirt fabric, which was open about two inches in front, like white curtains around a window display of cocks for sale. They were semi-hard, but both dicks stood at attention as Duchess stared. She squeezed her throbbing pussy that only got hotter and wetter as she checked out the females.

They were styled with Egyptian jewelry—no clothes—just turquoise and gold yokes that came down to their naked nipples. A similar style adorned their waists and hips. They wore about a dozen gold necklaces, connected at the sides of the waist and draped in C-shaped arcs across their abdomens, from their belly buttons down to the spot where pubic hair would be—if they weren't shaved bare. They wore gold sandals that laced up their juicy calves.

Peacock feathers sprayed up from the girls' short, straight black hair and bangs. They batted thick, black fake eyelashes and extended gold-braceleted arms, offering gold goblets to Duchess and Duke.

"After I present you to the masses," Duke said, handing Duchess a cold goblet, "we gon' sit an' watch niggas an' hoes fuck like it ain't no tomorrow."

Duchess let him clink his goblet to hers as he said, "You always gon' be mine, baby girl." Something hard glinted in his usually tender stare. The possessiveness in his tone, like she was his property, made the cold gush of bubbly taste bitter against her tongue.

WHITE CHOCOLATE

She steadied herself by grasping the rail and pressing her right shoulder into his left tricep as they surveyed the see-it-and-still-don't-believe-it orgy below. A wild sexcapade filled every inch of the huge garage, from the stage with the live rap band to a wide-open space for dancing to the rows of Hummers and sports cars to the plush couch seating area to the bar, stools and pool tables in the far left corner.

Neon blue tube lights across the length of the ceiling cast a smoky blue haze that illuminated bare asses, bouncing boobs and big, hard dicks glistening with cum and saliva. On the hood of a gold Corvette, three girls' heads bobbed between corresponding sets of bare brown knees and folds of denim as baggy jeans sagged around ankles. A glittering front license plate between the bent-over girls' bare asses said GANGSTA. The Barriors held the girls' heads like basketballs, bouncing up and down to the rhythm of their bobbing, clamping fingers through bouncing black braids, afro puffs and a waist-length weave. One guy tossed his head back. His red baseball cap tumbled off as his curvaceous lips contorted in what looked like a convulsive exclamation of "Fuck!"

Three B'Amazons on top of an Escalade created a writhing pile of arms, legs, heads and asses. On the dance floor, dozens of women stood taller than the crowd—they were fucking Pogo-stick style, going up and down on guys who stood, gripping their thighs and asses. A few girls were even taller; they sat on guys' shoulders, legs wrapped around their guy's head, pussies pressed into their faces.

Dancing on the bar, strippers popped big, bare butts against silver poles. A guy stood spraying bottle after bottle of champagne, making their nipples, butts and bare skin glisten in the blue light. To the right, about twenty girls were hip-to-hip and bent over so that their bare butts formed the inside of a circle, where twenty guys fucked them from behind. When the music changed beats or went to the hook, each guy pulled out then moved to the chick to his right, his condom-covered dick glistening in the light. So, each guy was basically fucking twenty girls!

On stage, members of the superstar rap group Bang Squad, whom Duchess knew from the videos Brian was constantly watching and mimicking, strutted back and forth across the stage. Some of them fucked girls on pink, round beds inside giant acrylic champagne glasses. The lead singer was screwing a girl who was standing and touching her toes. He pulled out, yanked off his condom and squirted cum toward the crowd. It dotted the stage. A girl near the stage—she had white-looking skin and short, straight black hair—stuck out her tongue as if to catch a white glob with as eager a smile as if it were a snowflake falling from the sky.

That girl made Duchess imagine herself acting like that, losing all decorum, self-respect, dignity, becoming a certified hood ho, fiending for any scrap of sex spewed her way. Disgust cramped her stomach, even though her pussy was gushing. How could it not amidst this flesh-pounding, mind-numbing sexual chaos?

She could not look away from the woman on stage who was facing one of the rappers. It was Honey's sister.

The one Duke was fucking in front of me.

Duchess almost laughed because that thought came just as naturally as if she and Tiffany were at the mall and her friend said, "Oh, there's Julie from our science class."

Like a ballerina, Chanel had one leg up, her ankle resting on the rapper's shoulder. Her other leg was holding her up as he fucked her. Her ass was like two tan basketballs, perfectly round and smooth, bouncing every time he slammed it.

Duchess imagined the woman's pussy stretched open by the standing-up splits, getting rammed. The lips would look extra long. Another woman, dancing up to them, bent down to attach her open mouth like a leech to the woman's ass.

Duchess's pussy was so hot, wet and swollen, she could cum with just a couple of squeezes of her pelvic muscles. She wanted to make love with Duke like they did a little while ago. But not in front of all these people.

"Duke! I wanna leave!" she shouted over the deafening music. "Duke!" He did not look up from an electronic pager. He was frantically pressing buttons. She grabbed his arm.

The music stopped.

Everybody in the garage turned toward them, up here on the balcony, as if she and Duke were the stars of a concert. Except most of them were either naked or had glistening dicks sticking out of peeled-back jeans or had big nipples pointing up from open jeans jackets.

Beamer came out of the mass of bodies behind them and handed Duke a cordless microphone. Beamer stood beside Duke.

"Yo, y'all!" Duke shouted into the mic. "Ha y'all doin'?"

Wild screams pierced the air.

"E'rybody know Duke da boss. And when Knight come back, he gon' be right back beside me, buildin' Babylon to conquer the world."

The crowd roared.

"Iss gon' be three of us." He raised Duchess's hand. "The Duke foun' his Duchess. Y'all got to bow to her jess like you bow to me."

The hundreds of faces below were solemn and silent, some nodding slightly. A guy shouted, "You need a real sistah!"

"She black as you, baby!" Duke bellowed. "The rest o' y'all, just know she ain't white. So zip dat shit now. Duchess a sistah jess like y'all'."

"Y'all be nice, now!" the lead singer of the band shouted into his microphone on stage. "Don't judge a book by the cover you cain't even see through yo' own hate."

Cheers and boos shot up from the crowd.

"So, all y'all plantation mentality ma'fuckas," the singer, Jamal, shouted, "thinkin' about you stuck in the cottonfield of life while that long-hair, light-skin bitch livin' large up in the big house wit' Massa Duke —"

"Yeah!" too many people shouted.

Jamal laughed. "You right! An' ain't shit y'all can do about it 'cept love this sistah like she one o' us. 'Cause she is."

The band played a deep chord. Smiles and smirks rose up from the crowd.

"Preach that shit!" Duke shouted. "Yeah!"

Duchess shivered. Had she been taken from a normal day in her past life and transplanted to this spot, she would faint. So would everyone else she knew back then. Even Brian. This would scare the shit out of his punk ass. He thought he was so tough, knowing all the latest rap, blasting it in his Porsche and Land Rover. But his hip hop clothes and backward baseball caps were fake. He was such a punk deep down that once when a black guy walked up and asked directions to the nearby bookstore, Brian was trembling afterwards, saying, "Man, I thought he was gonna whip out a gat and carjack me."

That's how too many girls were still glaring up at Duchess now. Ripping her to shreds with their stares.

Those bitches have so much nerve, cuttin' their eyes at me while they're standin' there naked with nut drippin' down their chins and thighs.

And Duke wanted her to say something? The last time she addressed a crowd—besides all those wicked reporters—was to introduce the debate team at the awards ceremony at the yacht club. But this here wasn't the time for the traditional "Good evening, ladies and gentlemen." Victoria Marie Winston's white girl cadence would spark an uproar of laughter—or worse.

No, this was the official unveiling of The Duchess. Even though half the people down there were staring at her like she was Marie Antoinette and they were the citizens of France who wanted to haul her off to the guillotine out back.

This is where I belong. This is how I can help people. This is the stage to share my purpose and passion that I just discovered in bed with my soul mate.

But how to connect through the hostility?

"Find common ground," Daddy used to always say. "Disarm your enemies by finding common ground. Then, don't

314

just extend the olive branch, hand 'em a fondue fork with the juiciest chocolate-dipped strawberry you can find. You'll have 'em in the palm of your hand forever."

Duke was already on the subject, with his deep voice booming through the huge, silent space. "Think of her as the male version of me," he told the crowd. "Anybody thinkin' about tossin' up some hate gon' face the same brute as if you messed wit' me. Duchess in charge, so e'rybody make her feel welcome at Babylon."

Duke handed her the mic. She wrapped her hot, damp palm around the metal. He stood beside her, sexy as hell in his black leather pants on legs that rose up forever into a tapered waist, a big V-shaped chest, broad shoulders and muscle-rippling arms. She stared at the beautiful skin on his shiny bald head, his genie eyes that sparkled like onyxes at her, his sucka lips that were gonna kiss her after this.

Yeah, I have the power. Celeste's mix-race woman power. Black power. Duke power. Love power.

She took a deep breath and looked out at the sea of faces.

"A sistah inside," she said, deep and sultry, "who been tryin' to hide . . . won't be denied." She stepped in front of Duke, raised a knee to one side, and ground her hips into the side of his rock-hard thigh. "My sexy ride."

The crowd exploded. Duke's beautiful, white teeth sparkled down at her as brightly as his eyes. She spun back toward the rail.

"Look in my eye, a butterfly, broke out a white coccoon, flutter to black so soon . . . singing a new tune." Her tone and cadence were perfect spoken word sistah-girl.

"From suburban to urban, virgin to vixen, caucasian to mixin' the black—" She turned so that her side was toward the audience then pressed her titties into Duke's arm. "—to the top o' my stack. Step back before I attack—" She strutted in front of him, grinding her ass into the tree trunk in the crotch of his leather jeans. "—and jack, your dick."

SEX IN THE HOOD

The guys and girls in the audience shouted "Yeah!" as they thrust fists up.

"My slick candle wick, you stick in my swirl of melted mix-race girl . . . vanilla-chocolate squaw in us all . . . "

She strutted back and forth along the rail, holding the mic and cutting a flat hand through the air to emphasize her words, just like Jamal did while he rapped. Duke crossed his arms, with a quick point down to Jamal, then nodded to her beat.

"In life's game, we're all the same by any name," she said as a bass beat boomed up from the band. The crowd started dancing, rubbing, kissing.

Suddenly, with the sexy music and the cool vibe from the crowd and the potency of Duke's eyes and the power of her pussy that was wild and free now, she was having a mind-gasm, loving this! She shivered with the thrill of it as she rapped her rhymes.

"I can't blame those lame ma'fuckas who wanna tame my fame and shame . . . me." She stopped, turned to Duke, let her eyes slowly devour him from his boots to the top of his sexy bald head.

"You see," she teased toward the audience, where some guys and girls were back to fucking, "I be—" She ground her hip into Duke's thigh.

"Do dat!" a guy shouted amongst cheers.

"Sexy and free." She turned her butt to the crowd, smacked the round of her ass and said, "A certified Double D."

The crowd whooped.

"So let me shout, this sistah comin' out! Beside your Duke, it's no fluke . . . up in this juke . . . joint. Make a point to anoint yo'self with Babylon juice. Get wild and loose . . . let yo' poos-sees—"

The sea of people roared. The music got louder. Jamal punctuated her rhymes with a deep "Fuck, yeah!"

" —get hot," she said. "Do not waste a drop of that sweet treat . . . from yo' meat. You gotta beat in this heat 'til yo' feet . . . curl, girl, make yo' mind swirl, 'round the world."

316

WHITE CHOCOLATE

Several girls extended their arms into the air and clapped to Duchess's beat.

"Get yo' sex on, chick. Flex on that dick, yo' slick joy stick." She pressed her ass back into Timbo, who was pointing straight out of the open zipper of Duke's pants. The black satin flesh against the leather and brass zipper made Duchess's pussy shoot steam. She would be *on that* in a minute.

"You can lick and do your trick. Get yours, give 'im his and don't miss —" she almost whispered, " — a single kiss."

She turned around, kissed Duke's sucka lips. The noise of the crowd could blow off the ceiling, screaming, cheering, clapping, fucking.

Duke took the mic, raised Duchess's fist in the air and shouted, "Duchess, baby! Babylon, rock on!"

The band cranked the bass. Bodies twisted back together.

And something, someone, knocked Duchess to the floor.

Chapter 53

Knight's pipe was steaming again, about to bust after watching Tinkerbell rap the house with her clever spoken word rhymes. It took a minute, but now the masses were screaming for The Duchess like she was the hottest superstar around. And she would be, on many fronts.

My goddess aced both tests, in my bed and in front of Babylon. Now all Knight had to do was make his chivalrous rescue of the damsel in Duke-stress, and let her sprinkle that pixie dust all over this urban empire and every territory that Knight wanted.

All night, he'd been watching her and Duke from this plush couch near the rail, shielded just enough by a circle of two dozen strong Barriors and B'Amazons. He had a clear view of her ass in those tight leather pants, now and when she rapped. And she took that knock-down by Milan like a champ. She shot back up onto the heels of those sexy-ass boots then body-slammed Milan into submission. The B'Amazons hauled away that poor, emaciated victim of her own manipulative evil and Duke's neglect. All while the Barriors carted Beamer's stupid ass away with her.

If Tinkerbell scared on the inside, she don't look or act like it. At all. Her soft, innocent appearance—but sexy, strong behavior— were making Knight want her so bad, he could taste her again. He didn't brush his teeth on purpose so when he talked to Li'l Tut, he'd have Duchess pussy on his lips and on his breath.

Once she goes black as Knight, ain't no way she goin' back . . . anywhere. And she already gone.

She was physically standing next to Duke right now, but the chemical and spiritual reaction going on inside her was like an internal branding by the fire that started during that intergalactic star show as their bodies and souls united. His sperm was still up there, hitting her insides like God's fingers of fire struck Moses's stone tablets to write the Ten Commandments. Now her uterus, her ovaries, her heart, her soul were branded in words of fire spewed by Knight's big, black pipe: PROPERTY OF KNIGHT JOHNSON.

And ain't no doubt my turbo-sperm is makin' itself at home—at least for nine months—up inside the luxury accommodations of the most exquisite pussy I'll ever need.

"Let's move," Knight said, his deep, sex-powered voice cutting through the ear-splitting cheers and bass rumble of the band.

Big Moe's hand grasped his arm. "Naw, man, we got this easy. But let him get all the way vulnerable for full effect."

Easy was right. With all of Li'l Tut's mismanagement and failure to take action on plans laid years ago by Prince and Knight, the Barriors and B'Amazons couldn't wait for Knight to come back and make things right.

They operated entirely under Duke's stealth radar, giving Knight detailed reports about Milan—keeping her on the job despite blatant violations of trust. Izz's thievery. Duke's hot-head flash and dash all over TV and the newspapers, drawing fed heat and reporters to Babylon. It was all because he brought that media magnet/federal fugitive, despised rich-mix girl up in the heart of the hood.

Knight was sure, when he first heard about it, that she'd have to go out with yesterday's trash along with Milan and Beamer. But Victoria Winston was gone. This chick was someone else entirely. She looked different, sounded different, felt different on the inside. Tonight wasn't a litmus test, where you drop a substance on chemical-treated paper to see if it sizzles or smokes or turns colors.

"Tonight is her blackmus test," Knight said.

Big Moe held up his hand, pressed his fingertips together at the top of his thumb then flicked his hand open like a magician tossing sparkle dust. "Black magic, mon. Ttttsssst! She sizzlin' an' smokin' an' sexin' like dis where she belong."

SEX IN THE HOOD

To have and to hold, from this day forward. Knight ran his hand over the hot lead eternal promises in his snug brown leather pants — a lifetime for her, and a Lager for Li'l Tut.

Chapter 54

Beamer shook just as hard as Milan as they knelt on the basement floor. She had already thrown up some green shit on his shirt. She was a mess with that long, curly-haired wig hanging on one side of her head, her real hair sticking out in a rat's nest that was so close it was scratching his cheek. She stared him down with eyes so wild and crazy, she looked like she would snap at him and bite down on the dick that got him into this trouble in the first place.

"I now declare you man and wife," the two-dollar preacher from the corner church said over them with all seriousness in his voice. But who could take him seriously, standing there with no shirt and just black leather chaps that let his still-wet dick hang loose at Beamer's eye level?

"Mr. Beamer, you get to kiss the bride now."

I'd rather tell her to kiss my stupid ass.

His childhood dream to kiss Michelle Henderson was now finally coming true in the worst fucking nightmare he could have imagined. Driving his Hummer into that semi-truck the other night would have been a better future than locking down with this bitch and chain.

An' I ain't got no choice.

Duke stood by him with arms crossed over his chest, looking down at him like he wasn't shit.

'Cause I ain't. Finally proved it to myself and e'rybody else by tryin' to cross The Duke.

"Y'all can take 'em to they honeymoon suite now," Duke said, "so I can get back to my birthday party."

The Barrior who grabbed Beamer's handcuffed wrists said to the other, "Bet, dude. Which one gon' kill tha otha one first?"

The other Barrior laughed. "I think they gon' get locked up in that room and make—"

SEX IN THE HOOD

Make like Romeo and Juliet and end the drama right there with a double suicide.

Beamer already knew the only way outta this was to stop breathing, because no way was Milan going to be in the mood for love when she was growling at Duke like that.

"Yeah, they gon' make war, not love." The Barrior laughed. He turned to Beamer. "Yo, dude, a word of advice on yo' wedding night. I'd keep my dick on lock-down if I was you."

Chapter 55

Duchess sat on her throne, holding Duke's hand as they watched a writhing tangle of male and female strippers perform up close and personal. Beyond the dancers, a wall of Barriors and B'Amazons in head-to-toe ninja black formed a half-circle around them.

Duchess was still quaking with fear. The sinister, pounding rhythm of the music echoed her racing heart.

"Duke, baby," she shouted so close to his head that her lip brushed his silver hoop earring. "I cain't get our freak on when some other crazy bitch might come flyin' outta the crowd at me!"

He shook his head. "You don't ev'a have to worry about Milan again."

"What about someone else?" she shot back. "The way you keep lookin' around, it's like you know some other whack shit is 'bout to break."

"It won't." He turned toward those boy-girl-boy-girl bodies in black, caramel and brown. They were making a long sandwich of bodies pressed together, all facing forward so their sides snaked in a slow-sexy groove for Duke and Duchess.

The whole line of bodies shook their asses at superhuman speed. It made Duchess's pussy throb and cream all the more, but the terror of being attacked by Duke's baby momma . . . the memory of rage in Milan's eyes made Duchess shiver again.

If I'da been standing any closer to the rail, she coulda knocked me over it. And who knows if she has an accomplice lurking amidst all these orgasmic bodies.

Duke's soft knuckles on her cheek pulled her back to the sex fantasy that was now her reality.

"Duchess," he said with a delicious gust of his Black Cashmere cologne and natural musk. "All these pussies and dicks in here for me an' you. An' you love they stuff just as much I do. They all clean, so do yo' thang."

He nodded at another girl who wore a tiny, light blue crocheted bikini and a silver belly chain that said BABY BLUE. With the help of a gorgeous brown hunk behind her, she put her foot on the arm of the throne, yanked back her bikini crotch and opened her pussy in Duchess's face. The guy ran his big hand over it as if he were in a jewelry store waving a hand over the pearl counter for customers to pick one.

"Lick that pussy," Duke ordered.

She stared at the Brazilian bikini-waxed flesh. Flawless. Thick folds of lips around a plump Raisinette clit and a glistening pink pussy slit. She inhaled the fresh, clean, slight scent of expensive perfume.

The woman gathered her cantaloupe-shaped boobs in her palms and pressed them together. With blue fingernails that matched her bikini, she clawed back the strips of fabric over her nipples. Two more jumbo Raisinettes with pepperoni-sized circles around them pointed straight at Duchess. The woman ran a fingertip over her pussy then sucked it loudly. Celeste was twitching, screaming.

"Lick the pussy," Duke said.

Duchess touched the tip of her nose to the clit. Rolled her head so that her nose stimulated the chick just right.

"Damn girl, do dat."

Duchess made a peace sign with her fingers, licked them then ran them down the pussy lips. Suddenly, another stripper was at her feet, another at her waist. They were taking her pants off.

Duchess ran the tip of her tongue from the bottom of the pussy up to the clit. Then, with her lips making a perfect "O", she wrapped them around —

The stripper sucked air and spit through her teeth. "Oooh, shit!"

At the same time, other girls helped Duchess ease out of her pants and thong. Duke, at her side, stroked Timbo. Another chick with a bruised calf and toe rings tried to put her leg on the arm of the chair and nudge Baby Blue out of the way. The new leg flew back as quickly as it came.

Duchess looked up to see two B'Amazons yanking a hysterical girl away. Her platinum blond braids flew all over like Medusa's snakes. Her tiny red thong showed a red heart tattoo over a plump ass, as a Barrior picked her up and carried her away.

Duke's eyes radiated super macho potency on that girl, then the Barrior's wide back. Duke's glare—a mix of rage and retaliation—made fear prickle through Duchess. That girl must have been here to hurt Duchess somehow. Was she some armed and dangerous renegade sent by Milan? Was she infected with something disgusting and/or deadly?

Duke leaned over, stared into Duchess's eyes and said, "That chick been writin' me letters about how much she love you an' wanna get wit' you. She ain't right." He pointed to his head. "Like a fatal attraction. It's han'led, so don't let the pussy get cold."

He stuck his tongue out and they—tongue by tongue—both chewed on Baby Blue's filet mignon. After awhile, Duke slurped on Duchess's tongue then sat back to watch.

One stripper raised Duchess's right leg up to the arm of the throne, the opposite side as Baby Blue. On her knees, the stripper dove into Duchess's pussy, mouth open.

"Oh yaaaay-yaaaaaah," she moaned. The double pleasure was incredible, a mouth on her pussy while she sucked on a clit.

Her head spun. She was fueling her woman-power with double intensity, and Celeste was loving it. From suburban virgin to Detroit dick-lovin' dyke.

Just keep it comin'.

Duchess peered over Baby Blue's thigh. Her eyes locked with Duke's. Who knew you could have such intimacy with a group? But the look in Duke's eyes screamed, *I am yours. Forever. This is all for you, baby girl.*

The fear from just a few minutes ago was drowning in a torrent of pussy juice. Except when Duke glanced up to the Barriors, around the crowd, then back at the strippers.

Duchess was lapping it up like a kitten. Baby Blue groaned like it was her first time, or her best time. Nina licked Duchess's pussy with perfect precision. She hit that fire spot at the tip of her clit that Duchess could never hit herself. Brian always found it and made her cum quickly. Duke and Honey did too. Now Nina was there, on it. Damn, her clit felt like the center of the universe as Nina worked her tongue all over it.

From the sound of Baby Blue, Duchess was doing just as well. She imitated the way Duke made that windshield wiper motion, from light to harder pressure, all while finger-fucking her.

Baby Blue's thigh quivered. "Oooohhh shit, girl!" Her nipples stiffened. Her whole body trembled, and her pussy walls pulsated around Duchess's fingers. Another stripper sucked Baby Blue's nipples as she came.

"Damn, girl, I ain't neva cum so fas'." Her leg was still up. Her pussy was a beautiful swell of soft, glistening folds of brown satin, like a flower.

Duchess's open lips pressed onto that perfect clit.

"Oooohhh!" Baby Blue shivered. "You my new girlfriend."

"Stay right there," Duchess ordered. "While I cum."

Nina was giving her butterfly fingers in her pussy while she made tiny licks, still on the tip of her clit. Every lick rubbed away the pain of Duchess's recent past and the terror of tonight. Now her mind was a mellow flow of lust clogged by a head full of question marks.

If Alice loved Ghettoland, would she ever want to go back to where she came from? Duchess moaned. The inner dialogue from Celeste made the corners of her mouth rise up.

Why'd you make me wait this long to get some tongue? You know you've been wantin' it for so long. Why didn't you and Tiffany experiment? They'd talked about it, but they had both chickened out.

WHITE CHOCOLATE

"Puuurrrrfect." Duchess lay back on her throne, staring up into the beautiful pussy spread wide open between Baby Blue's legs. She loved that Duke was watching every second, and that they would finish this interlude off with each other, upstairs, in the privacy of the penthouse.

But now, the pussy in her face—those fat folds, the single drop of cream at the pink "V" at the bottom of her slit, the still-pulsating inner lips . . . plus the electrifying bolts shooting up through her clit under the delicate dance of Nina's tongue . . .

Her pussy exploded, spasming under Nina's hot mouth and around her fingers. It felt like fire sprayed from her clit through every cell in her body. Her mind was a spray of bubbling, intoxicating Cristal.

Seize this power, a soft voice in her head whispered.

It was Celeste, her sex power. *Seize this power right now. Store it. Summon it whenever you need it. You will always win. This power right here is magic. It's yours.*

The words . . . the pussy in her face . . . Duke's attention . . . and Nina's licking . . . "Oooohhh. Oooohhh." The orgasm seemed to go on forever.

"My turn," a deep voice said. The girls moved.

Duke stepped between her legs, his dick huge and hard, pointing at her like Cupid's most potent black arrow. The dark chocolate skin on his stomach was smooth, hairless and beautiful. A puff of silk framed his dick, whose swollen, shiny head resembled Darth Vader's helmet, ready for battle. The voice from the movie echoed in her mind with new words.

You all the way on the dark side now, baby girl.

She closed her eyes to focus on a repeat of the supernatural euphoria when her soul mate's light saber penetrated her soul, like it did a few hours ago, upstairs in their bed. Now Timbo poised to make her cum again with just one stroke then make love to her again . . . better than ever.

Wham!

Duchess stiffened. Opened her eyes wide.

No, Timbo ain't it. But . . . who the fuck made love to me like that?

Chapter 56

Duke pounded up into that pussy, even though the look in Duchess's eyes right now might as well have been graffiti across her ass saying: I LIKE KNIGHT'S BIG, BLACK DICK BETTER THAN YOURS, YOU PUNK MA'FUCKA.

She don't even know she fucked Knight. She just know somethin' ain't right.

Love still glowed in her blue-flame blow torch eyes that first cast her spell over him. But now, that knowing look was about to kill him.

If Knight bum-rush me up in front of e'ry eye in Babylon then steal the Duchess that I picked! I made! I love! Then my heart gon' stop right here, right now, on my twenty-first birthday.

He made it to old age for the average inner-city nigga, but love hurt worse than bullets. That sounded corny as hell, but the fact that he was thinking it and couldn't control it, that showed he was a true punk.

But what is, is what is. A pussy-whipped punk by any other name would still curl up and die if his girl left for the bigger, better, badder, blacker warrior.

There was no way she could know who fucked her, but just the fact that she knew somebody did it better than Duke was blowing her mind. As soon as she took a look at Knight, she'd know all too well who tried to impersonate Timbo and gave her the ultimate fuck.

Penis impersonation. That ma'fucka just committed the ultimate felony in my book.

Duke radiated his most mack look down at his Duchess. She was his, and she was innocent. She was the victim here, taken advantage of in her horny state, tricked by a dude in the dark who looked just like her man, even to their own mother in the bright light of day.

328

WHITE CHOCOLATE

I'm gon' fuck her so good right now, my nut gon' brainwash — no, bootywash away any idea that it wasn't Timbo who gave her "the best ever."

"I love you," he mouthed down to her. Bang Squad started playing the song he had made for her, "Duchess," slow and sexy.

He lifted her up, making her legs higher around his waist so he could bang his way back up into first place. He stood in front of the thrones, watching the fuck frenzy in the crowd below as he bounced Duchess on Timbo.

Yeah, he was clearing her mind with the brute force she loved right now. Smashing every question mark to bits with this most mack motion. Her hands gripped his shoulders, her eyes stared down with a new message: YOU THE MAN . . . YOU MY MAN . . . MY ONLY MAN.

All those strippers, males and females, now circled around them like flower petals, swaying in a sexy motion with their arms up in the air and their bodies rolling as gracefully as underwater plants on a coral reef.

Duchess leaned close with those pucker-fish lips open, ready to kiss —

She looked up, over his shoulder. She sucked in air and turned white as a ghost.

'Cause now she sittin' on the wrong dick, lookin' at the bigger, better, blacker one she want.

Chapter 57

I have to see his neck, that scar, then I'll know if he's the supernatural god who made me cum at first stroke. The one who connected with my spirit in a way that's still got me breathless.

The shock of this moment—as Duchess sat speared through the pussy by Duke and speared through the soul by his brother— knocked her brain into an Alice in Double Pleasureland tailspin.

Knight and a whole crew of Barriors and B'Amazons were marching this way. Knight and his boys could pull a Scarface- style gun battle right here in the middle of an orgy. He could blast his brother to bits, and all the bullets would have to make swiss cheese of Duchess's booty, back and brains first.

Or Duke could figure out that I fucked his brother, and he'll just shoot me.

Or, if Knight was going to be more chivalrous with his plan of attack—because there was no doubt in his eyes that this was a siege—then he'd use words and wisdom to wield his power over Duke.

And I'll use words to wield my power over both of these sex gods.

As Knight got closer, Duchess almost smiled as her vision came to mind. Since both brothers would be on serious ego and power trips, she'd send both Knight and Duke on decadent detours.

Then I'll be queen of Babylon. Of course they wouldn't know that. She'd let them think they were both in charge, or keep them in an endless race where they each jockeyed for top position. That would be their distraction while she reigned supreme.

Yeah, Cleopatra down, with Duke and Knight at her sides as she walked into the Moreno meeting or the West Coast negotiations, working it just like Duke envisioned.

As the woman-power sex goddess that I am, on a mission to let everybody share the gift of orgasm. So all men and women could have a Secret Santa like that breathtaking man coming toward the

330

man who saved her life and whisked her into this decadent game of Candyland. Man candy.

As the music continued to blast, and as she sat frozen-stiff on Duke's dick, the air was suddenly so thick with hostility and suspicion, she could slice it up and make sandwiches—delicious sandwiches, with her as the female meat between two slabs of the most succulent rye.

Knight stood right behind them now. His voice was deep as he said, "Victoria, I need you to excuse yourself so me and Li'l Tut can talk business."

He said "business," not "bidness." And that was the first time anyone had called her Victoria in nearly a week.

She stared wide-eyed into his coffee bean brown face, a richer roast than Duke. His eyes were more serious, more mature, and so potent, her vision blurred with the red-orange-yellow sunbursts that flashed when he made her cum at first stroke. Her pussy got hot and wet. It squeezed from the inside out, pushing Duke's limp dick out like a squishy little wet fish.

"Aw, hell naw!" Duke shouted into the still-blasting music.

Suddenly Duchess was spinning. Duke was still holding her, but he pivoted so she could look at both beautiful, dangerous men.

"Pick one!" Duke shouted. The veins on the sides of his neck bulged. His eyes were glassy.

She smiled. *I know he's not serious . . .'cause if he is, he'll kill me before he lets me get wit' Knight.*

"Pick which Mandingo stud ma'fucka named Johnson you want for Duchess."

"Oh baby, you're no fun," she said playfully. "What if I want both?"

Duke's voice went down another octave. "Whoever you pick, he get to run Babylon."

"You so silly!" Duchess tightened her legs around his waist.

"Don't just sit on my dick here lookin' dazed!" Duke shouted. Craziness glowed in his eyes. "I said pick one!"

331

SEX IN THE HOOD

Knight's laughter boomed over the loud bass beat. He put an enormous hand on Duke's bare shoulder.

"Listen up, Li'l Tut. My name is not eenie, meenie, miney or moe. And nobody's gonna catch this nigga by the toe. So, Victoria, if you'll please leave us to talk . . ."

"She about to say somethin'," Duke said. "Now."

"I'll run Babylon myself." Duchess tilted her chin up to hide the earthquake of fear inside her. "You two," she said with a strong, serious voice, "can be my board of directors. We'll actually all make decisions together. But e'rybody know," she said with all the charm, sensuality and power of Cleopatra, "Duchess da boss!"

Chapter 58

Duke felt like a million big, black scarab beetles were eating him alive. He gripped Duchess's thighs hard to keep her juicy booty as a cover over his naked ass.

So big brotha Knight don't see what a limp-dicked ma'fucka I am, standin' in this hornet's nest of problems I brought down on the empire that he and Prince built. The nosy-ass media outside . . . some FBI punk ma'fuckas down in the office talkin' about a warrant . . . my first baby momma losin' her mind an' sabotagin' me in ways I'll still be hearin' about ten years from now . . . a skank-ass ex-Slut tryin' to spread sex warts an' HIV. . . an' my pretty fugitive gettin' her freak on . . . two an' a half years later an' I still ain't conquered Moreno.

The look in Knight's eyes said all that and too much more. He was just standing there like the new fuckin' sheriff in D-town. All six-foot-seven inches of his ass were covered in weatherbeaten brown leather. He had to be burning up in this sex sauna.

But Knight brown leather-down like a mug. From his cowboy hat to his snug beige silk T-shirt, from his pants to that double-breasted coat that hung all the way to the heels of his pointed boots. One look into that bigger, better mirror image of himself set Duke's brain off on a game of hot potato. Instead of hands with a potato, it was his emotions tossing his brother around, shouting "Love!" and "Hate!" so no part of his brain or body would get scorched.

Right now, the "Hate!" was screaming so loud, "Love!" had almost left the game.

What if I was wrong about him plunderin' my female treasure? What if Knight just wants to surprise me on my birthday? Don't nobody here know nothin' about Knight plottin' a coup. Is that just my crazy-ass imagination?

Duke wanted to find out right away by going with Knight to a quiet spot to talk. But he couldn't just put down Duchess, who

333

was shaking like she was naked in the snow. He wasn't about to flash the smaller, weaker mirror image of whatever the fuck Knight had between his legs and—

I'm gon' kill that ma'fucka!

The music stopped. The sounds of sex continued—moaning, groaning, nasty talk, skin slapping skin. Then that stopped too.

"Happy birthday, Li'l Tut." Sheriff Knight's voice boomed like a cannonball through Duchess's backside then through Duke's chest. Babylon felt like the dusty street in an Old West movie, where everybody froze in place to watch the showdown.

Two cowboys.

One turf.

A girl in the mix.

Only here, it was the two baddest urban cowboys this side of the Mississippi. And they were full-blood brothers—one naked, one decked in leather. Would it be a happy reunion? Would they hug and rule together like they were supposed to? Or did Big Brotha come back to D-town for a hostile take-over from Li'l Tut?

And how could Duke draw a gun if all he was wearing was a butt-naked Duchess?

"I said happy birthday, Li'l Tut."

"Happy birthday to you!" Jamal shouted up from the stage. Then the band played the funkiest birthday song ever, and everybody in Babylon screamed along at the tops of their lungs. Duchess, she stayed curled up around his waist, pressing that hot pussy into his stomach, hiding Timbo with her plump ass.

While the song rocked the house and Knight's deep voice sang along, Duchess pressed her pretty lips to Duke's cheek. "I love you, Duke, baby."

The song ended. Silence.

Jamal's amped voice boomed through the garage. "We all know the birthday boy one o' the baddest cats in D-town, but now big br'a in'a *how—ooose!*"

The bigger, badder, blacker version of himself stared hard into Duke's eyes. They were still at the edge of the balcony, so the masses of people were watching them.

WHITE CHOCOLATE

"Welcome to the new Babylon!" Knight's voice blasted through speakers. A cordless mic was clipped to his lapel! No doubt, this siege was orchestrated in advance, in secret—with the band, the Barriors and B'Amazons. Maybe Duchess was even in on the plan of attack.

E'rybody knew but me.

His brother announced, "The Duke's been han'lin' things, but it's time for The Knight to rule again!"

The crowd exploded. The band played the Babylon theme song. Knight unclipped the mic, handing it to Big Moe. Then the huge brown leather tubes that were Knight's arms came down with long fingers spread on giant hands. He almost looked like a robot the way his arms both moved down at the same angle toward the back of Duchess's waist.

Knight clamped down on her baby-soft flesh like he was about to pull her off and leave Duke standing at his own party with his wet, limp dick in his hand.

Hell naw.

Knight pulled, making Duchess's legs unwrap from around Duke's hips. He lifted her up and off, causing a cold wind to hit Duke's dick.

And Knight said, cool as a ma'fuckin' cowboy, "I got Babylon *and* yo' bitch."